maybe someday

By Colleen Hoover

Slammed
Point of Retreat
This Girl
Hopeless
Losing Hope
Finding Cinderella
Ugly Love
Maybe Not
Confess
November 9
It Ends with Us
Without Merit
All Your Perfects

maybe someday

a novel

Colleen Hoover

ATRIA PAPERBACK

NEW YORK   LONDON   TORONTO   SYDNEY   NEW DELHI

A Division of Simon & Schuster, Inc.
1230 Avenue of the Americas
New York, NY 10020

First Atria Paperback edition March 2014

ATRIA PAPERBACK and colophon are trademarks of Simon & Schuster, Inc.

For information about special discounts for bulk purchases, please contact Simon & Schuster Special Sales at 1-866-506-1949 or business@simonandschuster.com.

The Simon & Schuster Speakers Bureau can bring authors to your live event. For more information or to book an event, contact the Simon & Schuster Speakers Bureau at 1-866-248-3049 or visit our website at www.simonspeakers.com.

Manufactured in the United States of America

33 35 37 39 40 38 36 34

ISBN 978-1-4767-5316-4
ISBN 978-1-4767-5317-1 (ebook)

For Carol Keith McWilliams

Special Content

Dear Reader,

Maybe Someday is more than just a story. It's more than just a book. It's an experience, and one that we are excited and grateful to share with you.

I had the pleasure of collaborating with musician Griffin Peterson in order to provide an original sound track to accompany this novel. Griffin and I worked closely together to bring these characters and their lyrics to life so that you will be provided with the ultimate reading experience.

It is recommended these songs be heard in the order they appear throughout the novel. Please scan the QR code below to experience the *Maybe Someday* sound track. This gives you access to the songs and also to bonus material, should you wish to learn more behind the collaboration and implementation of this project.

Thank you for being a part of our project. It has been incredible for us to create, and we hope it will be just as incredible for you to enjoy.

Colleen Hoover and Griffin Peterson

To listen to the songs, please scan the QR code above. To do so, download the free Microsoft Tag app. Then hold your phone's camera a few inches away from the tag, and enjoy what comes next.

You may also visit the website at www.maybesomeday soundtrack.com to access this content.

maybe someday

prologue

Sydney

I just punched a girl in the face. Not just *any* girl. My best friend. My roommate.

Well, as of five minutes ago, I guess I should call her my *ex*-roommate.

Her nose began bleeding almost immediately, and for a second, I felt bad for hitting her. But then I remembered what a lying, betraying whore she is, and it made me want to punch her again. I would have if Hunter hadn't prevented it by stepping between us.

So instead, I punched *him*. I didn't do any damage to him, unfortunately. Not like the damage I'd done to my hand.

Punching someone hurts a lot worse than I imagined it would. Not that I spend an excessive amount of time imagining how it would feel to punch people. Although I am having that urge again as I stare down at my phone at the incoming text from Ridge. He's another one I'd like to get even with. I know he technically has nothing to do with my current predicament, but he could have given me a heads-up a little sooner. Therefore, I'd like to punch him, too.

Ridge: Are you OK? Do u want to come up until the rain stops?

Of course, I don't want to come up. My fist hurts enough as it is, and if I went up to Ridge's apartment, it would hurt a whole lot worse after I finished with him.

1

I turn around and look up at his balcony. He's leaning against his sliding-glass door; phone in hand, watching me. It's almost dark, but the lights from the courtyard illuminate his face. His dark eyes lock with mine and the way his mouth curls up into a soft, regretful smile makes it hard to remember why I'm even upset with him in the first place. He runs a free hand through the hair hanging loosely over his forehead, revealing even more of the worry in his expression. Or maybe that's a look of regret. As it should be.

I decide not to reply and flip him off instead. He shakes his head and shrugs his shoulders, as if to say, *I tried*, and then he goes back inside his apartment and slides his door shut.

I put the phone back in my pocket before it gets wet, and I look around at the courtyard of the apartment complex where I've lived for two whole months. When we first moved in, the hot Texas summer was swallowing up the last traces of spring, but this courtyard seemed to somehow still cling to life. Vibrant blue and purple hydrangeas lined the walkways leading up to the staircases and the fountain affixed in the center of the courtyard.

Now that summer has reached its most unattractive peak, the water in the fountain has long since evaporated. The hydrangeas are a sad, wilted reminder of the excitement I felt when Tori and I first moved in here. Looking at the courtyard now, defeated by the season, is an eerie parallel to how I feel at the moment. Defeated and sad.

I'm sitting on the edge of the now empty cement fountain, my elbows propped up on the two suitcases that contain most of my belongings, waiting for a cab to pick me up. I have no idea where it's going to take me, but I know I'd rather be anywhere except where I am right now. Which is, well, homeless.

I could call my parents, but that would give them ammunition to start firing all the *We told you so's* at me.

We told you not to move so far away, Sydney.

We told you not to get serious with that guy.

We told you if you had chosen prelaw over music, we would have paid for it.

We told you to punch with your thumb on the outside *of your fist.*

Okay, maybe they never taught me the proper punching techniques, but if they're so right all the damn time, they *should* have.

I clench my fist, then spread out my fingers, then clench it again. My hand is surprisingly sore, and I'm pretty sure I should put ice on it. I feel sorry for guys. Punching sucks.

Know what else sucks? Rain. It always finds the most inappropriate time to fall, like right now, while I'm homeless.

The cab finally pulls up, and I stand and grab my suitcases. I roll them behind me as the cab driver gets out and pops open the trunk. Before I even hand him the first suitcase, my heart sinks as I suddenly realize that I don't even have my purse on me.

Shit.

I look around, back to where I was sitting on the suitcases, then feel around my body as if my purse will magically appear across my shoulder. But I know exactly where my purse is. I pulled it off my shoulder and dropped it to the floor right before I punched Tori in her overpriced, Cameron Diaz nose.

I sigh. And I laugh. Of course, I left my purse. My first day of being homeless would have been way too easy if I'd had a purse with me.

"I'm sorry," I say to the cab driver, who is now loading my second piece of luggage. "I changed my mind. I don't need a cab right now."

I know there's a hotel about a half-mile from here. If I can just work up the courage to go back inside and get my purse, I'll walk there and get a room until I figure out what to do. It's not as if I can get any wetter.

The driver takes the suitcases back out of the cab, sets them on the curb in front of me, and walks back to the driver's side without ever making eye contact. He just gets into his car and drives away, as if my canceling is a relief.

Do I look that pathetic?

I take my suitcases and walk back to where I was seated before I realized I was purseless. I glance up to my apartment and wonder what would happen if I went back there to get my wallet. I sort of left things in a mess when I walked out the door. I guess I'd rather be homeless in the rain than go back up there.

I take a seat on my luggage again and contemplate my situation. I could pay someone to go upstairs for me. But who? No one's outside, and who's to say Hunter or Tori would even give the person my purse?

This really sucks. I know I'm going to have to end up calling one of my friends, but right now, I'm too embarrassed to tell anyone how clueless I've been for the last two years. I've been completely blindsided.

I already hate being twenty-two, and I still have 364 more days to go.

It sucks so bad that I'm . . . *crying*?

Great. I'm crying now. I'm a purseless, crying, violent, homeless girl. And as much as I don't want to admit it, I think I might also be heartbroken.

Yep. Sobbing now. Pretty sure this must be what it feels like to have your heart broken.

"It's raining. Hurry up."

I glance up to see a girl hovering over me. She's holding an umbrella over her head and looking down at me with agitation while she hops from one foot to the other, waiting for me to do something. "I'm getting soaked. *Hurry*."

Her voice is a little demanding, as if she's doing me some sort of favor and I'm being ungrateful. I arch an eyebrow as I look up at her, shielding the rain from my eyes with my hand.

I don't know why she's complaining about getting wet, when there isn't much clothing to *get* wet. She's wearing next to nothing. I glance at her shirt, which is missing its entire bottom half, and realize she's in a Hooters outfit.

Could this day get any weirder? I'm sitting on almost everything I own in a torrential downpour, being bossed around by a bitchy Hooters waitress.

I'm still staring at her shirt when she grabs my hand and pulls me up in a huff. "Ridge said you would do this. I've got to get to work. Follow me, and I'll show you where the apartment is." She grabs one of my suitcases, pops the handle out, and shoves it at me. She takes the other and walks swiftly out of the courtyard. I follow her, for no other reason than the fact that she's taken one of my suitcases with her and I want it back.

She yells over her shoulder as she begins to ascend the stairwell. "I don't know how long you plan on staying, but I've only got one rule. Stay the hell out of my room."

She reaches an apartment and opens the door, never even looking back to see if I'm following her. Once I reach the top of the stairs, I pause outside the apartment and look down at the fern sitting unaffected by the heat in a planter outside the door. Its leaves are lush and green as if they're giving summer the middle finger with their refusal to succumb to the heat. I smile at the plant, somewhat proud of it. Then I frown with the realization that I'm envious of the resilience of a plant.

I shake my head, look away, then take a hesitant step inside the unfamiliar apartment. The layout is similar to my own apartment, only this one is a double split bedroom with four total bedrooms. My and Tori's apartment only had two bedrooms, but the living rooms are the same size.

The only other noticeable difference is that I don't see any lying, backstabbing, bloody-nosed whores standing in this one. Nor do I see any of Tori's dirty dishes or laundry lying around.

The girl sets my suitcase down beside the door, then steps

aside and waits for me to . . . well, I don't know what she's waiting for me to do.

She rolls her eyes and grabs my arm, pulling me out of the doorway and further into the apartment. "What the hell is wrong with you? Do you even speak?" She begins to close the door behind her but pauses and turns around, wide-eyed. She holds her finger up in the air. "Wait," she says. "You're not . . ." She rolls her eyes and smacks herself in the forehead. "Oh, my God, you're deaf."

Huh? What the hell is wrong with this girl? I shake my head and start to answer her, but she interrupts me.

"God, Bridgette," she mumbles to herself. She rubs her hands down her face and groans, completely ignoring the fact that I'm shaking my head. "You're such an insensitive bitch sometimes."

Wow. This girl has some serious issues in the people-skills department. She's sort of a bitch, even though she's making an effort not to be one. Now that she thinks I'm deaf. I don't even know how to respond. She shakes her head as if she's disappointed in herself, then looks straight at me.

"I . . . HAVE . . . TO . . . GO . . . TO . . . WORK . . . NOW!" she yells very loudly and painfully slowly. I grimace and step back, which should be a huge clue that I can hear her practically yelling, but she doesn't notice. She points to a door at the end of the hallway. "RIDGE . . . IS . . . IN . . . HIS . . . ROOM!"

Before I have a chance to tell her she can stop yelling, she leaves the apartment and closes the door behind her.

I have no idea what to think. Or what to do now. I'm standing, soaking wet, in the middle of an unfamiliar apartment, and the only person besides Hunter and Tori whom I feel like punching is now just a few feet away in another room. And speaking of Ridge, why the hell did he send his psycho Hooters girlfriend to get me? I take out my phone and have begun to text him when his bedroom door opens.

He walks out into the hallway with an armful of blankets and a pillow. As soon as he makes eye contact with me, I gasp. I hope it's not a noticeable gasp. It's just that I've never actually seen him up close before, and he's even better-looking from just a few feet away than he is from across an apartment courtyard.

I don't think I've ever seen eyes that can actually speak. I'm not sure what I mean by that. It just seems as if he could shoot me the tiniest glance with those dark eyes of his, and I'd know exactly what they needed me to do. They're piercing and intense and—oh, my God, I'm staring.

The corner of his mouth tilts up in a knowing smile as he passes me and heads straight for the couch.

Despite his appealing and slightly innocent-looking face, I want to yell at him for being so deceitful. He shouldn't have waited more than two weeks to tell me. I would have had a chance to plan all this out a little better. I don't understand how we could have had two weeks' worth of conversations without his feeling the need to tell me that my boyfriend and my best friend were screwing.

Ridge throws the blankets and the pillow onto the couch.

"I'm not staying here, Ridge," I say, attempting to stop him from wasting time with his hospitality. I know he feels bad for me, but I hardly know him, and I'd feel a lot more comfortable in a hotel room than sleeping on a strange couch.

Then again, hotel rooms require money.

Something I don't have on me at the moment.

Something that's inside my purse, across the courtyard, in an apartment with the only two people in the world I don't want to see right now.

Maybe a couch isn't such a bad idea after all.

He gets the couch made up and turns around, dropping his eyes to my soaking-wet clothes. I look down at the puddle of water I'm creating in the middle of his floor.

"Oh, sorry," I mutter. My hair is matted to my face; my

shirt is now a see-through pathetic excuse for a barrier between the outside world and my very pink, very noticeable bra. "Where's your bathroom?"

He nods his head toward the bathroom door.

I turn around, unzip a suitcase, and begin to rummage through it while Ridge walks back into his bedroom. I'm glad he doesn't ask me questions about what happened after our conversation earlier. I'm not in the mood to talk about it.

I select a pair of yoga pants and a tank top, then grab my bag of toiletries and head to the bathroom. It disturbs me that everything about this apartment reminds me of my own, with just a few subtle differences. This is the same bathroom with the Jack-and-Jill doors on the left and right, leading to the two bedrooms that adjoin it. One is Ridge's, obviously. I'm curious about who the other bedroom belongs to but not curious enough to open it. The Hooters girl's one rule was to stay the hell out of her room, and she doesn't seem like the type to kid around.

I shut the door that leads to the living room and lock it, then check the locks on both doors to the bedrooms to make sure no one can walk in. I have no idea if anyone lives in this apartment other than Ridge and the Hooters girl, but I don't want to chance it.

I pull off my sopping clothes and throw them into the sink to avoid soaking the floor. I turn on the shower and wait until the water gets warm, then step in. I stand under the stream of water and close my eyes, thankful that I'm not still sitting outside in the rain. At the same time, I'm not really happy to be where I am, either.

I never expected my twenty-second birthday to end with me showering in a strange apartment and sleeping on a couch that belongs to a guy I've barely known for two weeks, all at the hands of the two people I cared about and trusted the most.

1.

Sydney

I slide open my balcony door and step outside, thankful that the sun has already dipped behind the building next door, cooling the air to what could pass as a perfect fall temperature. Almost on cue, the sound of his guitar floats across the courtyard as I take a seat and lean back into the patio lounger. I tell Tori I come out here to get homework done, because I don't want to admit that the guitar is the only reason I'm outside every night at eight, like clockwork.

For weeks now, the guy in the apartment across the courtyard has sat on his balcony and played for at least an hour. Every night, I sit outside and listen.

I've noticed a few other neighbors come out to their balconies when he's playing, but no one is as loyal as I am. I don't understand how someone could hear these songs and not crave them day after day. Then again, music has always been a passion of mine, so maybe I'm just a little more infatuated with his sound than other people are. I've played the piano for as long as I can remember, and although I've never shared it with anyone, I love writing music. I even switched my major to music education two years ago. My plan is to be an elementary music teacher, although if my father had his way, I'd still be prelaw.

"A life of mediocrity is a waste of a life," he said when I informed him that I was changing my major.

A life of mediocrity. I find that more amusing than insulting, since he seems to be the most dissatisfied person I've ever known. And he's a lawyer. Go figure.

One of the familiar songs ends and the guy with the guitar begins to play something he's never played before. I've grown accustomed to his unofficial playlist since he seems to practice the same songs in the same order night after night. However, I've never heard him play this particular song before. The way he's repeating the same chords makes me think he's creating the song right here on the spot. I like that I'm witnessing this, especially since after only a few chords, it's already my new favorite. All his songs sound like originals. I wonder if he performs them locally or if he just writes them for fun.

I lean forward in the chair, rest my arms on the edge of the balcony, and watch him. His balcony is directly across the courtyard, far enough away that I don't feel weird when I watch him but close enough that I make sure I'm never watching him when Hunter's around. I don't think Hunter would like the fact that I've developed a tiny crush on this guy's talent.

I can't deny it, though. Anyone who watches how passionately this guy plays would crush on his talent. The way he keeps his eyes closed the entire time, focusing intently on every stroke against every guitar string. I like it best when he sits cross-legged with the guitar upright between his legs. He pulls it against his chest and plays it like a stand-up bass, keeping his eyes closed the whole time. It's so mesmerizing to watch him that sometimes I catch myself holding my breath, and I don't even realize I'm doing it until I'm gasping for air.

It also doesn't help that he's cute. At least, he seems cute from here. His light brown hair is unruly and moves with him, falling across his forehead every time he looks down at his guitar. He's too far away to distinguish eye color or distinct features, but the details don't matter when coupled with the passion he has for his music. There's a confidence to him that

I find compelling. I've always admired musicians who are able to tune out everyone and everything around them and pour all of their focus into their music. To be able to shut the world off and allow yourself to be completely swept away is something I've always wanted the confidence to do, but I just don't have it.

This guy has it. He's confident and talented. I've always been a sucker for musicians, but more in a fantasy way. They're a different breed. A breed that rarely makes for good boyfriends.

He glances at me as if he can hear my thoughts, and then a slow grin appears across his face. He never once pauses the song while he continues to watch me. The eye contact makes me blush, so I drop my arms and pull my notebook back onto my lap and look down at it. I hate that he just caught me staring so hard. Not that I was doing anything wrong; it just feels odd for him to know I was watching him. I glance up again, and he's still watching me, but he's not smiling anymore. The way he's staring causes my heart to speed up, so I look away and focus on my notebook.

Way to be a creeper, Sydney.

"There's my girl," a comforting voice says from behind me. I lean my head back and tilt my eyes upward to watch Hunter as he makes his way onto the balcony. I try to hide the fact that I'm shocked to see him, because I'm pretty sure I was supposed to remember he was coming.

On the off chance that Guitar Boy is still watching, I make it a point to seem really into Hunter's hello kiss so that maybe I'll seem less like a creepy stalker and more like someone just casually relaxing on her balcony. I run my hand up Hunter's neck as he leans over the back of my chair and kisses me upside down.

"Scoot up," Hunter says, pushing on my shoulders. I do what he asks and slide forward in the seat as he lifts his leg over the chair and slips in behind me. He pulls my back against his chest and wraps his arms around me.

My eyes betray me when the sound of the guitar stops

abruptly, and I glance across the courtyard once more. Guitar Boy is eyeing us hard as he stands, then goes back inside his apartment. His expression is odd. Almost angry.

"How was school?" Hunter asks.

"Too boring to talk about. What about you? How was work?"

"Interesting," he says, brushing my hair away from my neck with his hand. He presses his lips to my neck and kisses his way down my collarbone.

"What was so interesting?"

He tightens his hold on me, then rests his chin on my shoulder and pulls me back in the chair with him. "The oddest thing happened at lunch," he says. "I was with one of the guys at this Italian restaurant. We were eating out on the patio, and I had just asked the waiter what he recommended for dessert, when a police car rounded the corner. They stopped right in front of the restaurant, and two officers jumped out with their guns drawn. They began barking orders toward us when our waiter mumbled, 'Shit.' He slowly raised his hands, and the police jumped the barrier to the patio, rushed toward him, threw him to the ground, and cuffed him right at our feet. After they read him his rights, they pulled him to his feet and escorted him toward the cop car. The waiter glanced back at me and yelled, 'The tiramisu is really good!' Then they put him in the car and drove away."

I tilt my head back and look up at him. "Seriously? That really happened?"

He nods, laughing. "I swear, Syd. It was crazy."

"Well? Did you try the tiramisu?"

"Hell, yeah, we did. It was the best tiramisu I've ever had." He kisses me on the cheek and pushes me forward. "Speaking of food, I'm starving." He stands up and holds out his hand to me. "Did you cook tonight?"

I take his hand and let him pull me up. "We just had salad, but I can make you one."

Once we're inside, Hunter takes a seat on the couch next

to Tori. She's got a textbook spread open across her lap as she halfheartedly focuses on both homework and TV at the same time. I take out the containers from the fridge and make his salad. I feel a little guilty that I forgot tonight was one of the nights he said he was coming. I usually have something cooked when I know he'll be here.

We've been dating for almost two years now. I met him during my sophomore year in college, when he was a senior. He and Tori had been friends for years. After she moved into my dorm and we became friends, she insisted I meet him. She said we'd hit it off, and she was right. We made it official after only two dates, and things have been wonderful since.

Of course, we have our ups and downs, especially since he moved more than an hour away. When he landed the job in the accounting firm last semester, he suggested I move with him. I told him no, that I really wanted to finish my undergrad before taking such a huge step. In all honesty, I'm just scared.

The thought of moving in with him seems so final, as if I would be sealing my fate. I know that once we take that step, the next step is marriage, and then I'd be looking at never having the chance to live alone. I've always had a roommate, and until I can afford my own place, I'll be sharing an apartment with Tori. I haven't told Hunter yet, but I really want to live alone for a year. It's something I promised myself I would do before I got married. I don't even turn twenty-two for a couple of weeks, so it's not as if I'm in any hurry.

I take Hunter's food to him in the living room.

"Why do you watch this?" he says to Tori. "All these women do is talk shit about each other and flip tables."

"That's exactly why I watch it," Tori says, without taking her eyes off the TV.

Hunter winks at me and takes his food, then props his feet up on the coffee table. "Thanks, babe." He turns toward the TV and begins eating. "Can you grab me a beer?"

I nod and walk back into the kitchen. I open the refrigerator door and look on the shelf where he always keeps his extra beer. I realize as I'm staring at "his" shelf that this is probably how it begins. First, he has a shelf in the refrigerator. Then he'll have a toothbrush in the bathroom, a drawer in my dresser, and eventually, his stuff will infiltrate mine in so many ways it'll be impossible for me ever to be on my own.

I run my hands up my arms, rubbing away the sudden onset of discomfort washing over me. I feel as if I'm watching my future play out in front of me. I'm not so sure I like what I'm imagining.

Am I ready for this?

Am I ready for this guy to be the guy I bring dinner to every night when he gets home from work?

Am I ready to fall into this comfortable life with him? One where I teach all day and he does people's taxes, and then we come home and I cook dinner and I "grab him beers" while he props his feet up and calls me *babe*, and then we go to our bed and make love at approximately nine P.M. so we won't be tired the next day, in order to wake up and get dressed and go to work and do it all over again?

"Earth to Sydney," Hunter says. I hear him snap his fingers twice. "Beer? Please, babe?"

I quickly grab his beer, give it to him, then head straight to my bathroom. I turn the water on in the shower, but I don't get in. Instead, I lock the door and sink to the floor.

We have a good relationship. He's good to me, and I know he loves me. I just don't understand why every time I think about a future with him, it's not an exciting thought.

Ridge

Maggie leans forward and kisses my forehead. "I need to go."

I'm on my back with my head and shoulders partially propped against my headboard. She's straddling my lap and looking down at me regretfully. I hate that we live so far apart now, but it makes the time we do spend together a lot more meaningful. I take her hands so she'll shut up, and I pull her to me, hoping to persuade her not to leave just yet.

She laughs and shakes her head. She kisses me, but only briefly, and then she pulls away again. She slides off my lap, but I don't let her make it very far before I lunge forward and pin her to the mattress. I point to her chest.

"You"—I lean in and kiss the tip of her nose—"need to stay one more night."

"I can't. I have class."

I grab her wrists and pin her arms above her head, then press my lips to hers. I know she won't stay another night. She's never missed a day of class in her life, unless she was too sick to move. I sort of wish she was feeling a little sick right now, so I could make her stay in bed with me.

I slide my hands from her wrists, delicately up her arms until I'm cupping her face. Then I give her one final kiss before I reluctantly pull away from her. "Go. And be careful. Let me know when you make it home."

She nods and pushes herself off the bed. She reaches across me and grabs her shirt, then pulls it on over her head. I watch her as she walks around the room and gathers the clothes I pulled off her in a hurry.

After five years of dating, most couples would have moved

in together by now. However, most peoples' other halves aren't Maggie. She's so fiercely independent it's almost intimidating. But it's understandable, considering how her life has gone. She's been caring for her grandfather since I met her. Before that, she spent the majority of her teenage years helping him care for her grandmother, who died when Maggie was sixteen. Now that her grandfather is in a nursing home, she finally has a chance to live alone while finishing school, and as much as I want her here with me, I also know how important this internship is for her. So for the next year, I'll suck it up while she's in San Antonio and I'm here in Austin. I'll be damned if I ever move out of Austin, especially for San Antonio.

Unless she asked, of course.

"Tell your brother I said good luck." She's standing in my bedroom doorway, poised to leave. "And you need to quit beating yourself up, Ridge. Musicians have blocks, just like writers do. You'll find your muse again. I love you."

"I love you, too."

She smiles and backs out of my bedroom. I groan, knowing she's trying to be positive with the whole writer's block thing, but I can't stop stressing about it. I don't know if it's because Brennan has so much riding on these songs now or if it's because I'm completely tapped out, but the words just aren't coming. Without lyrics I'm confident in, it's hard to feel good about the actual musical aspect of writing.

My phone vibrates. It's a text from Brennan, which only makes me feel worse about the fact that I'm stuck.

Brennan: It's been weeks. Please tell me you have something.

Me: Working on it. How's the tour?

Brennan: Good, but remind me not to allow Warren to schedule this many gigs on the next leg.

Me: Gigs are what gets your name out there.

Brennan: OUR name. I'm not telling you again to stop acting like you aren't half of this.

Me: I won't be half if I can't work through this damn block.

Brennan: Maybe you should get out more. Cause some unnecessary drama in your life. Break up with Maggie for the sake of art. She'll understand. Heartache helps with lyrical inspiration. Don't you ever listen to country?

Me: Good idea. I'll tell Maggie you suggested that.

Brennan: Nothing I say or do could ever make Maggie hate me. Give her a kiss for me, and get to writing. Our careers are resting squarely on your shoulders.

Me: Asshole.

Brennan: Ah! Is that anger I detect in your text? Use it. Go write an angry song about how much you hate your little brother, then send it to me. ;)

Me: Yeah. I'll give it to you after you finally get your shit out of your old bedroom. Bridgette's sister might move in next month.

Brennan: Have you ever met Brandi?

Me: No. Do I want to?

Brennan: Only if you want to live with two Bridgettes.

Me: Oh, shit.

Brennan: Exactly. TTYL.

I close out the text to Brennan and open up a text to Warren.

Me: We're good to go on the roommate search. Brennan says
hell no to Brandi. I'll let you break the news to Bridgette, since
you two get along so well.

Warren: Well, motherfucker.

I laugh and hop off the bed, then head to the patio with my
guitar. It's almost eight, and I know she'll be on her balcony. I
don't know how weird my actions are about to seem to her, but
all I can do is try. I've got nothing to lose.

2.

Sydney

I'm mindlessly tapping my feet and singing along to his music with my made-up lyrics when he stops playing mid-song. He never stops mid-song, so naturally, I glance in his direction. He's leaning forward, staring right at me. He holds up his index finger, as if to say, *Hold on*, and he sets his guitar beside him and runs into his apartment.

What the hell is he doing?

And oh, my God, why does the fact that he's acknowledging me make me so nervous?

He comes back outside with paper and a marker in his hands.

He's writing. What the hell is he writing?

He holds up two sheets of paper, and I squint to get a good look at what he's written.

A phone number.

Shit. His phone number?

When I don't move for several seconds, he shakes the papers and points at them, then points back to me.

He's insane. I'm not calling him. I can't call him. I can't do that to Hunter.

The guy shakes his head, then grabs a fresh sheet of paper and writes something else on it, then holds it up.

Text me.

When I still don't move, he flips the paper over and writes again.

I have a ?

A question. A text. Seems harmless enough. When he holds up the papers with his phone number again, I pull out my phone and enter his phone number. I stare at the screen for a few seconds, not really knowing what to say in the text, so I go with:

Me: What's your question?

He looks down at his phone, and I can see him smile when he receives my text. He drops the paper and leans back in his chair, typing. When my phone vibrates, I hesitate a second before looking down at it.

Him: Do you sing in the shower?

I shake my head, confirming my initial suspicion. He's a flirt. Of course he is, he's a musician.

Me: I don't know what kind of question that is, but if this is your attempt at flirting, I've got a boyfriend. Don't waste your time.

I hit send and watch him read the text. He laughs, and this irritates me. Mostly because his smile is so . . . *smiley*. Is that even a word? I don't know how else to describe it. It's as if his whole face smiles right along with his mouth. I wonder what that smile looks like up close.

Him: Believe me, I know you have a boyfriend, and this is definitely not how I flirt. I just want to know if you sing in the shower. I happen to think highly of people who sing in the shower and need to know the answer to that question in order to decide if I want to ask you my next question.

I read the lengthy text, admiring his fast typing. Guys aren't normally as skilled as girls when it comes to speed-texting, but his replies are almost instantaneous.

Me: Yes, I sing in the shower. Do you sing in the shower?

Him: No, I don't.

Me: How can you think highly of people who sing in the shower if you don't sing in the shower?

Him: Maybe the fact that I don't sing in the shower is why I think highly of people who do sing in the shower.

This conversation isn't going anywhere.

Me: Why did you need this vital piece of information from me?

He stretches his legs out and props his feet up on the edge of the patio, then stares at me for a few seconds before returning his attention to his phone.

Him: I want to know how you're singing lyrics to my songs when I haven't even added lyrics to them yet.

My cheeks instantly heat from embarrassment. Busted.

I stare at his text, then glance up at him. He's watching me, expressionless.

Why the hell didn't I think that he could see me sitting out here? I never thought he would notice me singing along to his music. Hell, until last night, I never thought he even noticed me. I inhale, wishing I'd never made eye contact with him to begin with. I don't know why I find this embarrassing, but I do. It seems as if I've invaded his privacy in some way, and I hate that.

> Me: I tend to favor songs with lyrics, and I was tired of wondering what the lyrics to your songs were, so I guess I made up a few of my own.

He reads the text, then glances up at me without a hint of his infectious smile. I don't like his serious glances. I don't like what they do to my stomach. I also don't like what his smiley smile does to my stomach. I wish he would stick to a simple, unattractive, emotionless expression, but I'm not sure he's capable of that.

> Him: Will you send them to me?

Oh, God. Hell, no.

> Me: Hell, no.

> Him: Please?

> Me: No.

> Him: Pretty please?

> Me: No, thank you.

> Him: What's your name?

> Me: Sydney. Yours?

> Him: Ridge.

Ridge. That fits him. Musical-artisty-moody type.

Me: Well, Ridge, I'm sorry, but I don't write lyrics that anyone would want to hear. Do you not write lyrics to your own songs?

He begins to text, and it's a really long text. His fingers move swiftly over his phone while he types. I'm afraid I'm about to receive an entire novel from him. He looks up at me just as my phone vibrates.

Ridge: I guess you could say I'm having a bad case of writer's block. Which is why I really, really wish you would just send me the lyrics you sing while I'm playing. Even if you think they're stupid, I want to read them. You somehow know every single song I play, even though I've never played them for anyone except when I practice out here.

How does he know I know all his songs? I bring a hand up to my cheek when I feel it flush, knowing he's been watching me a lot longer than I initially thought. I swear, I have to be the most unintuitive person in this entire world. I glance up at him and he's continuing with another text, so I look back to my phone and wait for it.

Ridge: I can see it in the way your whole body responds to the guitar. You tap your feet, you move your head. And I've even tried to test you by slowing down the song every once in a while to see if you would notice, and you always do. Your body stops responding when I change something up. So just by watching you, I can tell you have an ear for music. And since you sing in the shower, it probably means you're an okay singer. Which also means that maybe there's a chance you have a talent for writing lyrics. So, Sydney, I want to know what your lyrics are.

I'm still reading when another text comes through.

Ridge: Please. I'm desperate.

I inhale a deep breath, wishing more than anything that this conversation had never started. I don't know how in the hell he can come to all these conclusions without my ever having noticed him watching me. In a way, it eases my embarrassment over the fact that he saw me watching *him*. But now that he wants to know what lyrics I made up, I'm embarrassed for an entirely different reason. I do sing, but not well enough to do anything with it professionally. My passion is mostly for music itself, not at all for performing it. And as much as I do love writing lyrics, I've never shared anything I've written. It seems too intimate. I'd almost rather he had sent me a vulgar, flirtatious come-on.

I jump when my phone vibrates again.

Ridge: Okay, we'll make a deal. Pick one song of mine, and send me the lyrics to just that one song. Then I'll leave you alone. Especially if they're stupid.

I laugh. And cringe. He's not going to let up. I'm going to have to change my number.

Ridge: I know your phone number now, Sydney. I'm not giving up until you send me lyrics to at least one song.

Jesus. He's not going away.

Ridge: And I also know where you live. I'm not above begging on my knees at your front door.

Ugh!

Me: Fine. Stop with the creepy threats. One song. But I'll have to write the lyrics down while you play it first, because I've never written them out before.

Ridge: Deal. Which song? I'll play it right now.

Me: How would I tell you which song, Ridge? I don't know the names of any of them.

Ridge: Yeah, me, neither. Hold up your hand when I get to the one you want me to play.

He puts down his phone and picks up his guitar, then begins playing one of the songs. It's not the one I want him to play, though, so I shake my head. He switches to another song, and I continue to shake my head until the familiar chords to one of my favorites meets my ears. I hold up my hand, and he grins, then starts the song over from the beginning. I pull my notebook in front of me and pick up my pen, then begin to write down the lyrics I've put to it.

He has to play the song three times before I finally get them all out. It's almost dark now, and it's hard to see, so I pick up my phone.

Me: It's too dark to read. I'll go inside and text them to you, but you have to promise you'll never ask me to do this again.

The light from his phone illuminates his smile, and he nods at me, then picks up his guitar and walks back inside his apartment.

I go to my room and sit on the bed, wondering if it's too late to change my mind. I feel as if this whole conversation just ruined my eight o'clock patio time. I can't go back outside and listen to him ever again. I liked it better when I thought he didn't know I was there. It was like my own personal space with my own personal concert. Now I'll be way too aware of him to actually enjoy listening, and I curse him for ruining that.

I regretfully text him my lyrics, then turn my phone on silent and leave it on my bed as I go into the living room and try to forget this ever happened.

Ridge

Holy shit. She's good. Really good. Brennan is going to love this. I know if he agrees to use them, we'll need her to sign a release, and we'll have to pay her something. But it's worth it, especially if the rest of her lyrics are as good as these.

But the question is, will she be willing to help out? She obviously doesn't have much confidence in her talent, but that's the least of my worries. The biggest worry is how I'll persuade her to send me more lyrics. Or how to get her to write *with* me. I doubt her boyfriend would go for that. He has to be the biggest jerk I've ever laid eyes on. I can't believe the balls of that guy, especially after watching him last night. He comes outside on the patio and kisses Sydney, cuddling up to her in the chair like the most attentive boyfriend in the world. Then, the second she turns her back, he's out on the patio with the other chick. Sydney must have been in the shower, because the two of them rushed outside as if they were on a timer, and the chick had her legs wrapped around his waist and her mouth on his faster than I could even blink. And it wasn't a first-time occurrence. I've seen it happen so many times I've lost count.

It's really not my place to inform Sydney that the guy she's dating is screwing her roommate. I especially can't tell her through a text. But if Maggie were cheating on me, I'd sure as hell want to know about it. I just don't know Sydney well enough to tell her something like that. Usually, the person to break the news is the one to catch all the blame, anyway. Especially if the person being cheated on doesn't want to believe it. I could send her an anonymous note, but the douchebag boyfriend would more than likely be able to talk his way out of it.

I won't do anything for now. It's not my place, and until I get to know her better, I'm not in a position for her to trust me. My phone vibrates in my pocket, and I pull it out, hoping Sydney decided to send me more lyrics, but the text is from Maggie.

Maggie: Almost home. See you in two weeks.

Me: I didn't say text me when you're almost home. I said text me when you're home. Now, stop texting and driving.

Maggie: Okay.

Me: Stop!

Maggie: Okay!

I toss the phone onto the bed and refuse to text her back. I'm not giving her a reason to text me again until she makes it home. I walk to the kitchen for a beer, then take a seat next to a passed-out Warren on the couch. I grab the remote and hit info to see what he's watching.

Porn.

Figures. The guy can't watch anything without nudity. I start to change the channel, but he snatches the remote out of my hands. "It's my night."

I don't know if it was Warren or Bridgette who decided we should divvy up the TV, but it was the worst idea ever. Especially since I'm still not sure which night is actually mine, even though, technically, this is my apartment. I'm lucky if either of them pays rent on a quarterly basis. I put up with it because Warren has been my best friend since high school, and Bridgette is . . . well, she's too mean for me to even want to strike up a conversation with her. I've avoided that since Brennan let her move in six months ago. I really don't have to worry about money right now, thanks to my job and the cut Brennan gives me, so I just leave it alone. I still don't know how Brennan met Bridgette or how they're involved, but even though their relationship isn't sexual, he obviously cares about her. I have no idea how or why, since she doesn't have any noticeable redeeming qualities other than how she looks in her Hooters uniform.

And of course, the second that thought passes through my head, so do the words Maggie said when she found out Bridgette was moving in with us.

"I don't care if she moves in. The worst thing that could happen would be for you to cheat on me. Then I'd have to break up with you, then your heart would shatter, and we'd both be miserable for life, and you would be so depressed you'd never be able to get it up again. So make sure if you do cheat, it's the best sex you ever have, because it'll also be the last sex you ever have."

She doesn't have to worry about my cheating on her, but the scenario she painted was enough to ensure that I don't even look at Bridgette in her uniform.

How in the hell did my thoughts wander this far?

This is why I'm having writer's block; I can't seem to focus on anything important lately. I go back to my room to transfer the lyrics Sydney sent onto paper, and I begin to work out how to add them to the music. I want to text Sydney to tell her what I think about them, but I don't. I should leave her hanging a little while longer. I know how nerve-racking it is to send someone a piece of yourself and then have to sit back and wait for it to be judged. If I make her wait long enough, maybe once I tell her how brilliant she is, she'll have developed a craving to send me more.

It might be a little cruel, but she has no idea how much I need her. Now that I'm pretty sure I've found my muse, I have to work it just right so she doesn't slip away.

3.

Sydney

If he hated them, the least he could have done was send a thank you. I know it shouldn't bother me, but it does. Especially because I never wanted to send them to him in the first place. I wasn't expecting him to praise me, but the fact that he begged so hard for them and then just ignored them sort of irritates me.

And he hasn't been outside at his usual time in almost a week. I've wanted to text him about it so many times, but if I do, then it'll seem as if I care what he thinks of the lyrics. I don't want to care. But I can tell by how disappointed I feel that I do care. I hate that I want him to like my lyrics. But the thought of actually having a hand in a song is a little bit exciting.

"Food should be here in a little while. I'm going to get the clothes out of the dryer," Tori says. She opens the front door, and I perk up on the couch when I hear the familiar sound of the guitar from outside. She closes the door behind her, and as much as I want to ignore it, I rush to my room and quietly slide out onto the balcony, books in hand. If I sink far enough into my chair, he might not notice I'm out here.

But he's looking straight at my balcony when I step outside. He doesn't acknowledge me with a smile or even a nod of his head when I take my seat. He just continues playing, and it makes me curious to see if he's just going to pretend our conversation last week never happened. I sort of hope so, because *I'd* like to pretend it never happened.

He plays the familiar songs, and it doesn't take me long to let go of my embarrassment over the fact that he thought my lyrics were stupid. I tried to warn him.

I finish up my homework while he's still playing, close my books and lean back, and close my eyes. It's quiet for a minute, and then he begins playing the song I sent him lyrics for. In the middle of the song, the guitar pauses for several seconds, but I refuse to open my eyes. He continues playing just as my phone vibrates with an incoming text.

Ridge: You're not singing.

I glance at him, and he's staring at me with a grin. He looks back down at his guitar and watches his hands as he finishes the song. Then he picks up his phone and sends another text.

Ridge: Do you want to know what I thought of the lyrics?

Me: No, I'm pretty positive I know what you thought. It's been a week since I sent them to you. No worries. I told you they were stupid.

Ridge: Yeah, sorry about the silence. I had to leave town for a few days. Family emergency.

I don't know if he's telling the truth, but the fact that he claims he's been out of town eases my fear that he hasn't been out on his balcony because of me.

Me: Everything okay?

Ridge: Yep.

Me: Good.

Ridge: I'm only going to say this once, Sydney. Are you ready?

Me: Oh, God. No. I'm turning off my phone.

Ridge: I know where you live.

Me: Fine.

Ridge: You're incredible. Those lyrics. I can't even describe to you how perfect they are for the song. How in the hell does that come out of you? And why can't you see that you need to LET it come out of you? Don't hold it in. You're doing the world a huge disservice with your modesty. I know I agreed not to ask you for more, but that was because I really didn't expect to get what I got from you. I need more. Give me, give me, give me.

I let out a huge breath. Until this moment, I didn't realize exactly how much his opinion mattered. I can't look up at him yet. I continue to stare at my phone for much longer than it takes me to read the text. I don't even text him back, because I'm still relishing the compliment. If he said he loved it, I would have accepted his opinion with relief, and I would have moved on. But the words he just texted were like stairs stacked one on top of the other, and each compliment was like me running up each step until I reached the top of the damn world.

Holy crap. I think this one text just gave me enough confidence to send him another song. I never would have predicted this. I never imagined I would be excited.

"Food's here," Tori says. "You want to eat out here?"

I tear my gaze away from the phone and look at her. "Uh. Yeah. Sure."

Tori brings the food out to the balcony. "I've never really looked at that guy before, but *damn*," she says, staring hard at

Ridge while he plays his guitar. "He's really hot, and I don't even *like* blonds."

"His hair isn't blond. It's brown."

"No, that's blond," she says. "But it's dark blond, so that's okay, I guess. Almost brown, maybe. I like the messy shag, and that body makes up for the fact that his hair isn't black." Tori takes a drink and leans back in her chair, still staring at him. "Maybe I'm being too picky. What do I care what color his hair is? It'll be dark when I have my hands in it, anyway."

I shake my head. "He's really talented," I say. I still haven't responded to his text, but he doesn't seem to be waiting around. He's watching his hands as he plays, not paying a bit of attention to us.

"I wonder if he's single," Tori says. "I'd like to see what other talents he has."

I have no idea if he's single, but the way Tori is thinking about him makes my stomach turn. Tori is incredibly cute, and I know she could find out if he had other talents if she really wanted to. She tends to get whomever she wants in the guy department. I've never really minded until now.

"You don't want to be involved with a musician," I say, as if I have any experience that would qualify me to give her advice. "Besides, I'm pretty sure Ridge does have a girlfriend. I saw a girl on his patio with him a few weeks ago." That's technically not a lie. I did see one once.

Tori glances at me. "You know his name? How do you know his name?"

I shrug as if it's no big deal. Because, honestly, it *is* no big deal. "He needed help with lyrics last week, so I texted him some."

She sits up in her chair. "You know his *phone* number?"

I suddenly become defensive, not liking the accusatory tone in her voice. "Calm down, Tori. I don't even know him. All I did was text him a few lyrics."

She laughs. "I'm not judging, Syd," she says, holding up her hands in defense. "I don't care how much you love Hunter, if you have an opening with *that*"—she flicks her hand in Ridge's direction—"I'd be livid if you *didn't* take advantage of it."

I roll my eyes. "You know I'd never do that to Hunter."

She sighs and leans back in her chair. "Yeah. I know."

We're both looking at Ridge when he finishes the song. He picks up his phone and types something, then picks up his guitar just as my phone vibrates and he begins to play another song.

Tori reaches for my phone, but I grab it first and hold it out of her reach. "That's from him, isn't it?" she says. I read the text.

Ridge: When Barbie goes away, I want more.

I cringe, because there's no way I'm letting Tori read this text. For one thing, he insulted her. Also, the second part of his text would have an entirely different meaning if she read it. I hit delete and press the power button down to lock my phone in case she snatches it away from me.

"You're flirting," she says teasingly. She picks up her empty plate and stands up. "Have fun with your sexting."

Ugh. I hate that she thinks I'd ever do that to Hunter. I'll worry about setting her straight later, though. In the meantime, I take out my notebook and find the page with the lyrics I wrote to the song he's currently playing. I transfer them to a text, hit send, and hurry back inside.

"That was so good," I say as I place my plate in the sink. "That's probably my favorite Italian restaurant in all of Austin." I walk to the couch and fall down next to Tori, trying to appear casual about the fact that she thinks I'm cheating on Hunter. The more defensive I get about it, the less likely she'll be to believe me when I try to deny it.

"Oh, my God, that reminds me," she says. "The funniest thing happened a couple of weeks ago at this Italian restaurant. I was eating lunch with . . . my mom, and we were out on the patio. Our waiter was telling us about dessert, when all of a sudden, this cop car comes screeching around the corner, sirens blaring . . ."

I'm holding my breath, scared to hear the rest of her story.

What the hell? Hunter said he was with a coworker. The odds of them both being at the same restaurant, without being there together, is way more than coincidental.

But why would they lie about being together?

My heart is folding in on itself. I think I'm gonna be sick.

How could they . . .

"Syd? Are you okay?" Tori is looking at me with genuine concern. "You look like you're about to be sick."

I put my hand over my mouth, because I'm afraid she might be right. I can't answer her right away. I can't even work up the strength to look at her. I try to still my hand, but I can feel it trembling against my mouth.

Why would they be together and not tell me? They're never together without me. They'd have no reason to be together unless they were planning something.

Planning something.

Oh.

Wait a second.

I press my palm against my forehead and shake my head back and forth. I feel as if I'm in the midst of the stupidest moment in all of my nearly twenty-two years of existence. Of *course* they were together. Of *course* they're hiding something. It's my birthday next Saturday.

Not only do I feel incredibly stupid for having believed they would do something like that to me, but I feel unforgivably guilty.

"You okay?" Tori says.

I nod. "Yeah." I decide not to mention the fact that I know she was with Hunter. I would feel even worse if I ruined their surprise. "I think the Italian food is just making me a little nauseated. I'll be right back." I stand and walk to my bedroom, then sit on the edge of my bed in order to regain my bearings. I'm filled with a mixture of doubt and guilt. Doubt, because I know neither of them would do what I briefly thought they had done. Guilt, because for a brief moment, I actually believed they were capable of it.

—

Ridge

I was hoping the first set of lyrics wasn't a fluke, but after seeing the second set she sent me and adding them to the music, I text Brennan. I can't not tell him about her any longer.

Me: I'm about to send you two songs. I don't even need you to tell me what you think of them, because I know you'll love them. So let's move past that, because I need you to solve a dilemma for me.

Brennan: Oh, shit. I was just kidding about the Maggie thing. You didn't really dump her for inspiration did you?

Me: I'm being serious. I found a girl who I'm positive was brought to this earth specifically for us.

Brennan: Sorry, man. I'm not into that shit. I mean, maybe if you weren't my brother, but still.

Me: Stop with the horseshit, Brennan. Her lyrics. They're perfect. And they come so effortlessly to her. I think we need her. I haven't been able to write songs like these since . . . well, ever. Her lyrics are perfect, and you need to take a look at them, because I sort of need you to love them and agree to buy them from her.

Brennan: What the hell, Ridge? We can't hire someone to write lyrics for us. She'll want a percentage of the royalties, and between the two of us and the guys in the band, it won't be worth it.

Me: I'm going to ignore that until you check the e-mail I just sent you.

I put my phone down and pace the room, giving him time to take a look at what I just sent him. My heart is pounding, and I'm sweating, even though it's not at all hot in this room. I just can't take his telling me no, because I'm scared that if we can't use her, I'll be facing another six months of a concrete wall.

After several minutes, my phone vibrates. I drop to my bed and pick it up.

Brennan: Okay. See what she's willing to take, and let me know.

I smile and toss the phone into the air and feel like yelling. After I calm down enough to text her, I pick up my phone and think. I don't want to freak her out, because I know she's completely new to this kind of thing.

Me: I was wondering if we could talk sometime soon? I have a proposition for you. And get your mind out of the gutter, it's completely music-related.

Sydney: Okay. I can't say I'm looking forward to it, because it makes me nervous. You want me to call you when I get off work?

Me: You work?

Sydney: Yes. Campus library. Morning shift mostly, except for this weekend.

Me: Oh. I guess that's why I never noticed. I don't usually get out of bed until after lunch.

Sydney: So do you want me to call you after I get home?

Me: Just text me. You think we can meet up sometime this weekend?

Sydney: Probably, but I'd have to talk to my boyfriend. Don't want him to find out and think you're using me for more than my lyrics.

Me: K. Sounds good.

Sydney: If you want, you could come to my birthday party tomorrow night. Might be easier, because he'll be here.

Me: It's your birthday tomorrow? Happy early birthday. And that sounds good. What time?

Sydney: Not sure. I'm not supposed to know about it. I'll just text you tomorrow night once I find out more.

Me: K.

Honestly, I don't like the fact that her boyfriend might be there. I want to talk to her about it alone, because I still haven't decided what to do about what I know is going on between that asshole and her roommate. But I need her to agree to help me before her heart gets shattered, so maybe my silence has been a little selfish. I do admire the fact that she wants to be honest with him, even though he doesn't deserve it. Which makes me think maybe this is something I should bring up to Maggie, even though it never occurred to me before that it might even remotely be an issue.

Me: Hey. How's my girl?

Maggie: Busy. This thesis is kicking my ass. How's my guy?

Me: Good. Really good. I think Brennan and I found someone who's willing to write lyrics with us. She's really good, and I've already finished almost two songs since you left last weekend.

Maggie: Ridge, that's great! I can't wait to read them. Maybe next weekend?

Me: You coming here, or am I going to you?

Maggie: I'll come there. I need to spend some time at the nursing home. Love you.

Me: Love you. Don't forget our video chat tonight.

Maggie: You know I won't. Already have my outfit picked out.

Me: That better be a cruel joke. You know I don't care to see clothes.

Maggie: ;)

Eight more hours.

I'm hungry.

I toss the phone aside. I pull open my bedroom door and take a step back when the shit that's been piled up on the other side begins to fall in on me. First it's the lamp, then the end table it was resting on, then the end table the lamp and the other end table were piled on top of.

Dammit, Warren.

These pranks are starting to get out of hand. I press my arm into the couch that's been shoved up against my bedroom door. I push it back out into the living room and jump over it, then head toward the kitchen.

•   •   •

I carefully spoon toothpaste onto an Oreo, then replace the top of the cookie and gently squeeze it. I put it back into the package with the rest of Warren's Oreos and seal the package shut, just as my phone vibrates.

Sydney: Can you do me a favor?

She has no idea how many favors I'd do for her right now. I'm pretty much at her mercy.

Me: What's up?

Sydney: Can you look out your balcony door and tell me if you see anything suspicious going on at my apartment?

Shit. Does she know? What does she want me to tell her? I know it's selfish, but I really don't want to tell her about her boyfriend until after I have the chance to talk to her about the lyrics.

Me: Okay. Hold on.

I walk to my balcony and glance across the courtyard. I don't see anything out of the ordinary. It's almost dark, though, so I can't see much. I'm not sure what she wants me to find, so I choose not to be too descriptive when I respond.

Me: Looks quiet.

Sydney: Really? Are the blinds open? You don't see people?

I look again. The blinds are open, but the only thing I can see from here is the glare from the TV.

Me: Doesn't look like anyone's home. Aren't you having a birthday party later tonight?

Sydney: I thought so. I'm really confused.

There's movement in one of the windows, and I see her roommate going into the living room. Sydney's boyfriend follows closely behind her, and they both sit on the couch, but all I can see is their feet.

Me: Wait. Your boyfriend and your roommate just sat on the couch.

Sydney: Okay. Sorry to bother you.

Me: Wait. What about tonight? Are you still having a birthday party?

Sydney: I don't know. Hunter says he's taking me out to eat as soon as I get home from work, but I sort of thought it was a lie. I know he and Tori had lunch together a couple of weeks ago, but they don't know I know. They were obviously planning something, and I assumed it was a surprise party, but tonight's the only night that could happen.

I wince. She actually caught them in a lie, and she thought they were together because they were planning something nice for her. Christ. I don't even know the guy, and I have a huge urge to walk over there and beat the shit out of him.

It's her birthday. I can't tell her on her birthday. I take a deep breath, then decide to text Maggie for advice.

Me: Question. You busy?

Maggie: Nope. Shoot.

Me: If it was your birthday and someone you knew found out I was cheating on you, would you want to know right then? Or would you hope that person would wait to tell you until it was no longer your birthday?

Maggie: If this is a hypothetical question, I'm going to kill you for this heart attack. If it's not hypothetical, I'm going to kill you for this heart attack.

Me: You know it's not me. It's not your birthday. ;)

Maggie: Who's cheating on whom?

Me: It's Sydney's birthday today. The girl I was telling you about who writes the lyrics. I happen to know her boyfriend is cheating on her, and I'm kind of in a position where I should tell her because she's becoming suspicious.

Maggie: Jesus. I'd hate to be you right now. But if she's suspicious and you know for a fact that he's cheating, you need to tell her, Ridge. If you don't say anything, you're inadvertently lying.

Me: Ugh! That's what I thought you'd say.

Maggie: Good luck. I'm still going to kill you for the heart attack next weekend.

I sit on the bed, then start a text to Sydney.

Me: I'm not sure how to say this, Sydney. You're not driving right now, are you?

Sydney: Oh, jeez. There are people there, aren't there? Lots of them?

Me: No, there isn't anyone there but the two of them. First, I need to apologize for not telling you this sooner. I didn't know how, because we don't know each other that well. Second, I'm sorry for doing it on your birthday, of all days, but I feel like an ass for even waiting this long. And third, I'm sorry you have to find out via text, but I don't want you to have to walk back into your apartment without knowing the truth first.

Sydney: You're scaring me, Ridge.

Me: I'm just going to rip the Band-Aid off, okay? Something has been going on between your roommate and your boyfriend for a while.

I hit send and close my eyes, knowing I'm completely ruining her birthday. If not pretty much every day after today, too.

Sydney: Ridge, they've been friends for longer than I've even known Hunter. I think you've misinterpreted everything.

Me: If sticking your tongue down someone's throat while straddling him is friendship, then I'm sorry. But I'm positive I'm not misinterpreting anything. It's been going on for weeks. I'm assuming they come out to the patio while you're in the shower, because they're never out there long. But it happens a lot.

Sydney: If you're being honest, why didn't you tell me when we first started talking?

Me: How does one comfortably say this to another person, Sydney? When is there ever an appropriate time? I'm telling you now because you're becoming suspicious, and it's as appropriate a time as it can be.

Sydney: Please tell me you have a warped sense of humor, because you have no idea what you're doing to my heart right now.

Me: I'm sorry, Sydney. Really.

I wait patiently for a response. She doesn't text me back. I contemplate texting her, but I know she needs time to absorb this.

Dammit, I'm such an asshole. Now she'll probably be pissed at me, but I can't blame her. I guess I can kiss the lyrics good-bye.

My door swings open, and Warren barges in, then hurls a cookie straight at me. I duck, and it hits the headboard behind me.

"Asshole!" Warren yells. He turns and marches back out of the bedroom and slams the door.

4.

Sydney

I must be in shock. How the hell did the day turn out like this? How does one girl go from having a best friend, a boyfriend, a purse, and a roof over her head to being heartbroken and naked, standing frozen in a strange shower, staring at the wall for half an hour straight? I swear to God, if this is some huge elaborate birthday hoax at my expense, I'm never speaking to anyone. Ever again. Ever.

However, I know it's not a hoax. A hoax is just wishful thinking. I knew the second I walked through the front door and headed straight for Hunter that everything Ridge had said was true. I flat-out asked Hunter if he was sleeping with Tori, and the looks on both of their faces would have been comical if they didn't completely crush my heart and deplete my trust in one fell swoop. I wanted to sink to the floor and cry when he couldn't deny it. Instead, I walked calmly to my bedroom and began packing my things.

Tori came into the room, crying. She tried to tell me it meant nothing, that sex had always been a casual thing between them, even before they met me. Hearing her say it meant nothing to them hurt worse than anything. If it meant something to either of them, at least I could vaguely understand their betrayal. But the fact that she was claiming it meant nothing, yet it still happened, hurt me more than anything else she could have possibly said at that moment. I'm pretty sure that's when I punched her.

It doesn't help matters that I lost my job just minutes after Ridge told me about Hunter and Tori. I think it's frowned upon in most libraries when student workers begin crying and throwing books at the wall in the middle of their shift. But I can't help the fact that I happened to be stocking the romance section the second I found out my boyfriend of two years was sleeping with my roommate. The sappy, romantic covers on the cart in front of me just really pissed me off.

I turn the water off in Ridge's shower and step out, then get dressed.

I feel better physically after finally getting into dry clothes, but my heart is growing heavier and heavier with each passing minute. The more time that passes by, the more my reality begins to sink in. In the course of just two hours, I've lost the entire last two years of my life.

That's a lot of time to invest in two people who were supposed to be the most trusted people in my life. I'm not sure if I would have ended up marrying Hunter or if he would have been the father of any future children of mine, but it hurts to know that I trusted him enough to possibly fill those roles, and he ended up being the opposite of who I thought he was.

I think the fact that I misjudged him pisses me off more than the fact that he cheated on me. If I can't even accurately judge the people closest to me, then I can't trust *anyone*. Ever. I hate them for taking that away from me. Now, no matter who comes into my life after this, I'll always be skeptical.

I walk back into the living room, and all the lights are out except for a lamp beside the couch. I look at my phone, and it's barely after nine. Several texts came through while I was in the shower, so I take a seat on the couch and scroll through them.

Hunter: Please call me. We need to talk.

Tori: I'm not mad at you for hitting me. Please call me.

Hunter: I'm worried about you. Where are you?

Ridge: I'm sorry I didn't tell you sooner. Are you okay?

Hunter: I'll bring your purse to you. Just tell me where you are.

I drop the phone onto the coffee table and sink back onto the couch. I have no idea what I'm going to do. Of course, I never want to speak to either of them again, but where does that put me? I can't afford my own apartment right now, since financial aid doesn't come in for another month. I don't have enough money in savings to put down a deposit plus get all the utilities turned on until then. The majority of the friends I've made since I've been going to school here still live in dorms, so staying with them is out of the question. I'm basically left with two options: Call my parents, or enter into some odd plural relationship with Hunter and Tori in order to save money.

Neither option is one I'm willing to entertain tonight. I'm just thankful that Ridge allowed me to stay at his place. At least I'm saving money on a hotel room. I have no idea where I'll go when I wake up in the morning, but that's still a good twelve hours away. Until then, I'll just continue to hate the entire universe while I feel sorry for myself.

And what better way to feel sorry for myself than while getting drunk?

I need alcohol. Bad.

I walk to the kitchen and begin to scan the cabinets. I hear the door to Ridge's bedroom open. I glance over my shoulder at him as he comes out of his room.

His hair is definitely light brown. Take that, Tori.

He's in a faded T-shirt and jeans, and he's barefoot, eyeing me inquisitively as he makes his way into the kitchen. I feel a little embarrassed for being caught rummaging through his cabinets, so I turn away from him before he sees me blush.

"I need a drink," I say. "You got any alcohol?"

He's staring down at his phone, texting again. He either can't do two things at once, or he's upset because I had an attitude with him today.

"I'm sorry if I was a bitch to you, Ridge, but you have to admit, my response was a little justified considering the day I've had."

He casually slips his phone into his pocket and looks at me from across the bar, but he chooses not to respond to my half-assed apology. He purses his lips and cocks an eyebrow.

I'd like to smack that cocky eyebrow back down where it belongs. What the hell is his problem? The worst thing I did to him was flip him off.

I roll my eyes and shut the last cabinet, then walk back to the couch. He's really being a jerk, considering my situation. From the little time I've known him, I was under the impression that he was actually a nice guy, but I'd almost rather go back to my own apartment with Tori and Hunter.

I pick up my phone, expecting another text from Hunter, but it's from Ridge.

Ridge: If you aren't going to look at me when you speak, you might want to stick to texting.

I read the text several times, trying to make sense of it, but no matter how many times I read it, I don't understand it. I grow concerned that maybe he's a little weird and I need to leave. I look at him, and he's watching me. He can see the confusion on my face, but he still doesn't explain himself. Instead, he resumes texting. When my phone receives another message, I look at the screen.

Ridge: I'm deaf, Sydney.

Deaf?

Oh.

Wait. *Deaf?*

But how? We've had so many conversations.

The last few weeks of knowing him and talking to him flash through my memory, and I can't recall a single time I've actually heard him speak.

Is that why Bridgette thought *I* was deaf?

I stare at my phone, sinking into a heap of embarrassment. I'm not sure how to feel about this. I'm sure that feeling betrayed isn't a fair response, but I can't help it. I feel I need to tack this onto the "Ways the world can betray Sydney on her birthday" list. Not only did he not tell me he knew my boyfriend was screwing around on me, but he also failed to mention that he's deaf?

Not that being deaf is something he should feel obliged to tell me. I just . . . I don't know. I feel a little hurt that he didn't share that fact with me.

Me: Why didn't you tell me you were deaf?

Ridge: Why didn't you tell me you could hear?

I tilt my head as I read his text and flood with even more humiliation. He makes a very good point.

Oh, well. At least he won't hear me cry myself to sleep tonight.

Me: Do you have any alcohol?

Ridge reads my text and laughs, then nods. He walks to the cabinet below the sink and pulls out a container of Pine-Sol. He takes two glasses out of the cabinet, then proceeds to fill them with . . . cleaning liquid?

"What the hell are you doing?" I ask.

When he doesn't turn around, I slap myself in the forehead, remembering he can't hear me. This will take some getting used to. I walk to where he's standing. When he sets the Pine-Sol down on the counter and picks up both glasses, I grab the bottle of cleaning solution and read it, then arch an eyebrow. He laughs and hands me a glass. He sniffs his drink, then motions for me to do the same. I hesitantly bring it to my nose and am met with the burning scent of whiskey. He holds the glass out, clinks it to mine, and we both down our shots. I'm still recovering from the awful taste when he picks up his phone and texts me again.

> Ridge: Our other roommate has an issue with alcohol, so we have to hide it from him.

> Me: Is his issue that he hates it?

> Ridge: His issue is that he doesn't like to pay for it himself and he drinks everyone else's.

I nod, set my phone back down, grab the container, and pour us each another shot. We repeat the motions, downing the second one. I grimace as the burn spreads its way down my throat and through my chest. I shake my head, then open my eyes.

"Can you read lips?" I ask.

He shrugs, then grabs a piece of paper and a pen conveniently placed on the counter next to him. *Depends on the lips.*

I guess that makes sense. "Can you read mine?"

He nods and takes the pen again. *Mostly. I've learned to anticipate what people are going to say more than anything. I take most of my cues from body language and the situations I'm in.*

"What do you mean?" I ask, pushing on the counter with my palms and hopping up onto the bar. I've never met anyone who couldn't hear before. I didn't realize I was full of so many questions. It could be that I'm already feeling a buzz or I just don't want him to go back to his room yet. I don't want to be left alone to think about Hunter and Tori.

Ridge sets the notepad down and picks up my phone, then tosses it to me. He pulls one of the bar stools out and sits on it next to where I'm seated on the counter.

Ridge: If I'm at the store and a cashier speaks to me, I can mostly guess what they're asking. Same thing with a waitress at a restaurant. It's pretty simple to gather what people are saying when it's a routine conversation.

Me: But what about right now? This isn't routine. I doubt you have many homeless girls spend the night on your couch, so how do you know what I'm saying?

Ridge: Because you're basically asking me the same questions as anyone else who initially finds out I can't hear. It's the same conversation, just different people.

This comment bothers me, because I don't want to seem like those kinds of people at all. It has to get old, having to field the same questions over and over.

Me: Well, I don't really want to know about it, then. Let's change the subject.

Ridge looks up at me and smiles.

Damn. I don't know if it's the whiskey or the fact that I've been single for two hours, but that smile does some serious flirting with my stomach.

Ridge: Let's talk about music.

"Okay," I say with a nod.

Ridge: I wanted to talk to you about this tonight. You know, before I ruined your life and all that. I want you to write lyrics for my band. For the songs I have written and maybe some future songs if you're up for it.

I pause before responding to him. My initial response is to ask him about his band, because I've been dying to see this guy perform. My second response is to ask him how the hell he can play a guitar if he can't hear, but again, I don't want to be one of "those people." My third response is to automatically say no, because agreeing to give someone lyrics is a lot of pressure. Pressure I don't really want right now, since my life has pretty much taken a nosedive today.

I shake my head. "No. I don't think I want to do that."

Ridge: We would pay you.

That gets my attention. I suddenly feel an option three making its way into the picture.

Me: What kind of pay are we talking about? I still think you're insane for wanting me to help you write lyrics, but you may have caught me at a very desperate and destitute moment, being as though I'm homeless and could use some extra money.

Ridge: Why do you keep referring to yourself as homeless? Do you not have a place to stay?

Me: Well, I could stay with my parents, but that would mean I'd have to transfer schools my senior year, and it would put me about two semesters behind. I could also stay with my roommate, but I don't know how much I'd like to hear her screwing my boyfriend of two years at night while I try to sleep.

Ridge: You're a smartass.

Me: Yeah, I guess I've got that going for me.

Ridge: You can stay here. We're kind of in search of a fourth roommate. If it means you'll help us with the songs, you can stay for free until you get back on your feet.

I read the text twice, slowly. I shake my head.

Ridge: Just until you can get your own place.

Me: No. I don't even know you. Besides, your Hooters girlfriend already hates me.

Ridge laughs at that comment.

Ridge: Bridgette is not my girlfriend. And she's hardly ever here, so you don't have to worry about her.

Me: This is too weird.

Ridge: What other option do you have? I saw you didn't even have cab fare earlier. You're pretty much at my mercy.

Me: I have cab fare. I left my purse in my apartment, and I didn't want to go back up to get it, so I didn't have a way to pay the driver.

Ridge frowns when he reads my text.

Ridge: I'll go with you to get it if you need it.

I look up at him. "Are you sure?" I ask.
He smiles and walks toward the front door, so I follow him.

Ridge

It's still raining out, and I know she just put on dry clothes after her shower, so once we reach the bottom of the stairwell, I pull my phone out and text her.

Me: Wait here so you don't get wet again. I'll go get it myself.

She reads the text and shakes her head, then looks back up at me. "No. I'm going with you."

I can't help but appreciate the fact that she doesn't respond to my being deaf the way I expect her to. Most people become uneasy once they aren't sure how to communicate with me. The majority of them raise their voices and talk slowly, sort of like Bridgette. I guess they think being louder will somehow miraculously make me hear again. However, it does nothing but force me to contain my laughter while they talk to me as if I'm an idiot. Granted, I know people don't do it to be disrespectful. It's just simple ignorance, and that's fine. I'm so used to it I don't even notice anymore.

However, I did notice Sydney's reaction . . . because there really wasn't one. As soon as she found out, she just propped herself up on the counter and continued talking to me, even though she moved from speaking to texting. And it helps that she's a fast texter.

We run across the courtyard until we reach the base of the stairs that lead up to her apartment. I begin walking up and notice that she's frozen at the bottom of the stairs. The look in her eyes is nervous, and I instantly feel bad for not realizing how hard this must be for her. I know she's probably hurting a lot more than she's letting on. Learning that your best friend and your boyfriend have betrayed you has to be difficult, and it hasn't even been a day since she found out. I walk back down the stairs and grab her hand, then smile at her reassuringly. I tug on her hand; she takes a deep breath and walks with me up the stairs. She taps me on the shoulder before we reach her door, and I turn around.

"Can I wait here?" she says. "I don't want to see them."

I nod, relieved that her lips are easy to read.

"But cow well you ass therefore my bird?" she says.

Or I *think* that's what she said. I laugh, knowing I more than likely completely misread her lips. She says it again when she sees the confusion on my face, but I still don't understand her. I hold up my phone so she can text me.

Sydney: But how will you ask them for my purse?

Yeah. I was a little off on that one.

Me: I'll get your purse, Sydney. Wait here.

She nods. I type out a text as I walk to the front door and knock. A minute passes, and no one comes to the door, so I knock again, with more force, thinking maybe my first knock was too soft to be heard. The doorknob turns, and Sydney's friend appears in the doorway. She eyes me curiously for a second, then glances behind her. The door opens wider, and Hunter appears, eyeing me suspiciously. He says something that looks like "Can I help you?" I hold up the text that says I'm here for Sydney's purse, and he looks down and reads it, then shakes his head.

"Who the hell are you?" he says, apparently not liking the fact that I'm here on Sydney's behalf. The girl disappears from the doorway, and he opens the door even farther, then folds his arms over his chest and glares at me. I motion to my ear and shake my head, letting him know that I can't hear what he's saying.

He pauses, then throws his head back and laughs and disappears from the doorway. I glance to Sydney, who is standing nervously at the top of the stairs, watching me. Her face is pale, and I give her a wink, letting her know everything is okay. Hunter comes back, slaps a piece of paper against the door, and writes on it. He holds the paper up for me to read.

Are you fucking her?

Jesus, what a prick. I motion for the pen and paper, and he hands them to me. I write my response and hand it back to him. He looks down at the paper, and his jaw tightens. He crumples up the paper, drops it to the floor, and then, before I can react, his fist is coming at me.

I accept the hit, knowing I should have been prepared for it. The girl reappears, and I can tell she's screaming, although I have no idea whom she's screaming at or what she's saying. As soon as I take a step back from the doorway, Sydney is in front of me, rushing into the apartment. My eyes follow her as she runs down the hallway, disappears into a room, and comes back out clutching a purse. The girl steps in front of her and places her hands on Sydney's shoulders, but Sydney pulls her arm back, makes a fist, and punches the girl in the face.

Hunter tries to step in front of Sydney to block her from leaving, so I tap him on the shoulder. When he turns around, I punch him square in the nose, and he stumbles back. Sydney's eyes go wide, and she looks back at me. I grab her hand and pull her out of the apartment, toward the stairs.

Luckily, the rain has finally stopped, so we both break into a run back toward my apartment. I glance behind me a couple of times to make sure neither of them is following us. Once we make it back across the courtyard and up my stairs, I swing open the door and step aside so she can run in. I shut the door behind us and bend over, clasping my knees with my hands to catch my breath.

What an asshole. I'm not sure what Sydney saw in him, but the fact that she dated him makes me question her judgment a little bit.

I glance up at her, expecting to see her in tears, but instead, she's laughing. She's sitting on the floor, attempting to catch her breath, laughing hysterically. I can't help but smile, seeing her reaction. And the fact that she punched that girl right in the face without a moment's hesitation? I've got to hand it to her, she's tougher than I first thought.

She looks up at me and inhales a calming breath, then mouths the words *thank you*, while holding up her purse. She stands up and brushes the wet hair out of her face, then walks to the kitchen and opens a few drawers until she finds a dishtowel and pulls it out. She wets it under the faucet, turns around, and motions me over. When I reach her, I lean against the counter while she takes my chin and angles my face to the left. She presses the towel to my lip, and I wince. I didn't even realize it was hurting until she touched it. She pulls the rag back, and there's blood on it, so she rinses it under the faucet and puts it back up to my mouth. I notice that her own hand is red. I take it and inspect it. It's already swelling.

I pull the rag from her hand and wipe the rest of the blood off my face, then grab a ziplock bag out of the cabinet, go to the freezer, and fill it with ice. I take her hand and press the ice onto it, letting her know she needs to keep it there. I lean against the counter next to her and pull my phone out.

Me: You hit her good. Your hand is already swelling.

She texts me with one hand, keeping the ice on top of the other as she rests it on the counter.

Sydney: It could be because that wasn't the first time I've punched her today. Or it could also be swollen because you aren't the first one to punch Hunter today.

Me: Wow. I'm impressed. Or terrified. Is three punches your daily average?

Sydney: Three punches is now my lifetime average.

I laugh.

She shrugs and sets her phone down, then pulls the ice off her hand and brings it back up to my mouth. "Your lip is swelling," she says.

My hands are clenching the countertop behind me. I become increasingly uneasy with how comfortable she is with all this. Thoughts of Maggie flash through my head, and I can't help but wonder if she'd be okay with this scenario if she were to walk through the front door right now.

I need a distraction.

Me: You want birthday cake?

She smiles and nods.

Me: I probably shouldn't drive, since you've turned me into a raging alcoholic tonight, but if you feel like walking, Park's Diner makes a damn good dessert, and it's less than a mile from here. Pretty sure the rain is over.

"Let me change," she says, motioning to her clothes. She pulls clothes from her suitcase, then heads to the bathroom. I put the top on the Pine-Sol and hide it back under the cabinet.

5.

Sydney

We don't interact much while we eat. We're both sitting in the booth with our backs to the wall and our legs stretched out in front of us on the seats. We're quietly watching the restaurant crowd, and I can't stop wondering what it's like for him, not being able to hear anything going on around us. I'm probably too blunt for my own good, but I have to ask him what's on my mind.

> Me: What's being deaf like? Do you feel like you're in on a secret that no one else knows about? Like you have a leg up on everyone because the fact that you can't hear has magnified all your other senses and you've got superhuman powers and no one can tell just by looking at you?

He almost spits out his drink while reading my text. He laughs, and it occurs to me that his laugh is the only sound I've heard him make. I know that some people who can't hear can still talk, but I haven't heard him say a single word all night. Not even to the waitress. He either points to what he wants on the menu or writes it down.

> Ridge: I can honestly say I've never thought about it like that before. I kind of like it that you think of it that way, though. To be honest, I don't think about it at all. It's normal to me. I have nothing to compare it to, because it's all I've ever known.

Me: I'm sorry. I'm being one of those people again, aren't I? I guess me asking you to compare being deaf to not being deaf is like you asking me to compare being a girl to being a boy.

Ridge: Don't apologize. I like that you're interested enough to ask me about it. Most people are a little weirded out by it, so they don't say anything at all. I've noticed it's kind of hard to make friends, but that's also a good thing. The few friends I do have are genuine, so I look at it as an easy way of weeding out all the shallow, ignorant assholes.

Me: Good to know I'm not a shallow, ignorant asshole.

Ridge: Wish I could say the same about your ex.

I sigh. Ridge is right, but damn if it doesn't sting to know I couldn't see through Hunter's bullshit.

I put my phone down and eat the last of my cake. "Thank you," I say as I put my fork down. I honestly forgot for a while that today was my birthday until he offered to take me out for cake.

He shrugs as if it isn't a big deal, but it *is* a big deal. I can't believe after the day I've had that I'm actually in a semidecent mood. Ridge can take credit for that, because if it weren't for him, I don't know where I'd be tonight or what kind of emotional state I'd be in.

He takes a drink of his soda, then sits upright in the booth. He nods his head to the door, and I agree that I'm ready to go.

The buzz from the alcohol has worn off, and as we make our way out of the restaurant and back into the dark, I can feel myself beginning to succumb to the heartache again. I guess Ridge sees the look on my face, because he puts his arm around me and briefly squeezes my shoulders. He drops his arm and pulls his phone out.

Ridge: For what it's worth, he doesn't deserve you.

Me: I know. But it still hurts that I ever thought he deserved me. And honestly, I'm more hurt about Tori than I am about what happened with Hunter. I'm mostly just pissed at Hunter.

Ridge: Yeah, I don't even know the guy, and I've been pretty pissed at him. I can't imagine how you must feel. I'm surprised you haven't retaliated with some evil revenge plot yet.

Me: I'm not that clever. I wish I were, because I'd be all about revenge right now.

Ridge stops walking and turns to face me. He cocks an eyebrow, and a slightly wicked grin appears. It makes me laugh, because I can tell by his smile that he's mapping out a plan.

"Okay," I say, nodding my head without even knowing what he's about to propose. "As long as it doesn't land us in jail."

Ridge: Do you know if he leaves his car unlocked?

•   •   •

"Fish?" I ask, crinkling my nose in disgust. We've made a pit stop at a local grocery store next to the apartment complex, and he's buying a huge, scaly whole fish. I'm assuming this has to be part of his elaborate revenge scheme, but he could just be hungry.

Ridge: We need duct tape.

I follow him to the hardware aisle, where he grabs a roll of heavy-duty duct tape.

Fresh fish and duct tape.

I'm still not sure what he has planned, but I sort of like where this is headed.

. . .

When we're back at the apartment, I point out Hunter's car. I run up to the apartment to grab his spare car key out of my purse, where I still have it, while Ridge wraps the fish with duct tape. I come back downstairs and hand him the key.

Me: So what exactly are we about to do with this fish?

Ridge: Watch and learn, Sydney.

We walk to Hunter's car, and Ridge unlocks the passenger door. He has me tear off several pieces of duct tape while he reaches under the passenger seat. I'm watching closely—in case I need to seek revenge against anyone in the future—and he presses it against the underside of the seat. I hand him several more pieces of duct tape, trying to contain my laughter while he secures the raw fish with it. After he's sure it won't come loose, he slides out of the car and closes the door, looking around innocently. My hand is over my mouth, stifling my laughter, and he's as cool and composed as can be.

We casually walk away from the car, and once we're on the stairs to the apartment, we begin laughing.

Ridge: His car is going to smell like death in a matter of twenty-four hours. He'll never find it.

Me: You're kind of evil. If I didn't know better, I'd think you've done this before.

He laughs as we make our way back inside. We kick off our shoes at the door, and he tosses the duct tape onto the counter. I use the bathroom and make sure to unlock the door to his bedroom before I walk back out. In the living room, all the lights are out, except for the lamp by the couch. I lie down and check my phone one last time before turning it on silent.

Ridge: Good night. Sorry your birthday sucked.

Me: Thanks to you, it was better than it could have been.

I place the phone under my pillow and cover up. I close my eyes, and my smile immediately fades when the silence takes over. I can feel the tears coming, so I cover my head with the blanket and brace myself for a long night of heartache. The respite with Ridge was nice, but I have nothing to distract me now from the fact that I'm having the worst day of my life. I can't understand how Tori could do something like this to me. We've been best friends for almost three years. I told her everything. I trusted her with everything. I told her things I would never dream of telling Hunter.

Why would she risk our friendship for sex?

I've never felt this hurt. I pull the blanket over my eyes and begin to sob.

Happy birthday to me.

• • •

I have the pillow pulled tightly over my head, but it doesn't drown out the sound of gravel crunching beneath shoes. Why is someone walking on a driveway so noisily? And why can I even hear it?

Wait. Where am I?

Did yesterday really happen?

I reluctantly open my eyes, and I'm met with sunlight, so I pull the pillow tighter over my face and give myself a minute to adjust. The sound seems to get louder, so I lift the pillow from my face and peer out with one eye open. The first thing I see is a kitchen that isn't mine.

Oh, yeah. That's right. I'm on Ridge's couch, and twenty-two is the worst age ever.

I lift the pillow all the way off my head and groan as I squeeze my eyes shut again.

"Who are you and why are you sleeping on my couch?"

My body jumps, and my eyes flick open at the deep voice that can't be more than a foot away. Two eyes peer down at me. I pull my head back against the couch to put more space between me and the curious eyes to get a better look at who they're attached to.

It's a guy. A guy I've never seen before. He's sitting on the floor directly in front of the couch, and he's holding a bowl. He dips a spoon into the bowl and shoves it into his mouth, then begins the loud crunching again. I'm guessing that's not gravel he's eating.

"Are you the new roommate?" he says with his mouth full.

I shake my head. "No," I mutter. "I'm a friend of Ridge's."

He cocks his head and looks at me suspiciously. "Ridge only has one friend," the guy says. "Me." He shoves another spoonful of cereal into his mouth and fails to back out of my personal space.

I push my palms into the couch and sit up so that he's not right in my face. "Jealous?" I ask.

The guy continues to stare at me. "What's his last name?"

"Whose last name?"

"Your very good friend, Ridge," he says cockily.

I roll my eyes and drop my head against the back of the couch. I don't know who the hell this guy is, but I really don't care to compete over our levels of friendship with Ridge. "I don't know Ridge's last name. I don't know his middle name. The only thing I know about him is that he's got a mean right hook. And I'm only sleeping on your couch because my boyfriend of two years decided it would be fun to screw my roommate and I really didn't want to stick around to watch."

He nods, then swallows. "It's Lawson. And he doesn't have a middle name."

As if the morning could get any worse, Bridgette appears from the hallway and walks into the kitchen.

The guy on the floor takes another spoonful of cereal and looks at Bridgette, finally breaking his uncomfortable lock on me. "Good morning, Bridgette," he says with an odd, sarcastic tone to his voice. "Sleep well?"

She looks at him briefly and rolls her eyes. "Screw you, Warren," she snaps.

He turns his gaze back to mine with a mischievous grin. "That's Bridgette," he whispers. "She pretends to hate me during the day, but at night, she *loves* me."

I laugh, not really trusting that Bridgette is capable of loving anyone.

"Shit!" she yells, catching herself on the bar before she trips. "Jesus Christ!" She kicks one of my suitcases, still on the floor next to the bar. "Tell your little friend if she's staying here, she needs to take her shit to her room!"

Warren makes a face as if he's scared for me, then turns his head toward Bridgette. "What am I, your bitch? Tell her yourself."

Bridgette points to the suitcase she almost tripped over. "GET . . . YOUR . . . SHIT . . . OUT . . . OF . . . THE . . . KITCHEN!" she says, before marching back to her bedroom.

Warren slowly turns his head back to face me and laughs. "Why does she think you're deaf?"

I shrug. "I have no idea. She came to that conclusion last night, and I failed to correct her."

He laughs again, much louder. "Oh, this is classic," he says. "Do you have any pets?"

I shake my head.

"Are you opposed to porn?"

I don't know how we just began playing Twenty Questions,

but I answer him anyway. "Not opposed to the principle of porn but opposed to being featured in one."

He nods, contemplating my answer for a beat too long. "Do you have annoying friends?"

I shake my head. "My best friend is a backstabbing whore, and I'm no longer speaking to her."

"What are your showering habits?"

I laugh. "Once a day, with a skipped day every now and then. No more than fifteen minutes."

"Do you cook?"

"Only when I'm hungry."

"Do you clean up after yourself?"

"Probably better than you," I say, taking in the fact that he's used his shirt for a napkin no fewer than three times during this conversation.

"Do you listen to disco?"

"I'd rather eat barbed wire."

"All right, then," he says. "I guess you can stay."

I pull my feet up and sit cross-legged. "I didn't realize I was being interviewed."

He glances at my suitcases, then back to me. "It's obvious you need a place to stay, and we've got an empty room. If you don't take it, Bridgette wants to move her sister in next month, and that's the last thing Ridge and I need."

"I can't stay here," I say.

"Why not? From the sound of it, you're about to spend the day searching for an apartment anyway. What's wrong with this one? You won't even have to walk very far to get here."

I want to say that Ridge is the problem. He's been nice, but I think that might be the issue. I've been single for less than twenty-four hours, and I don't like the fact that although I should have been consumed with nightmares about Hunter and Tori all night, instead, I had a slightly disturbing dream involving an extremely accommodating Ridge.

I don't tell Warren that Ridge is why I can't stay here, though. Partly because that would give Warren more ammunition for questions and partly because Ridge just walked into the kitchen and is looking at us.

Warren winks at me, then stands up and walks with his bowl to the sink. He looks at Ridge. "Have you met our new roommate?" Warren asks.

Ridge signs something to him. Warren shakes his head and signs back. I sit on the couch and watch their silent conversation, slightly in awe that Warren knows sign language. I wonder if he's learned it for Ridge's benefit. Maybe they're brothers? Warren laughs, and Ridge glances in my direction before walking back to his bedroom.

"What did he say?" I ask, suddenly worried that Ridge no longer wants me here.

Warren shrugs and begins walking back toward his bedroom. "Exactly what I thought he'd say." He walks into his room, then comes back out with a cap on and keys in his hand. "He said you two already worked out a deal." Warren slips a pair of shoes on by the front door. "Heading to work now. That's your room if you want to put your stuff in it. You might have to throw all of Brennan's shit in the corner, though." He opens the door and steps outside, then turns back around. "Oh. What's your name?"

"Sydney."

"Well, Sydney. Welcome to the weirdest place you'll ever live." He shuts the door behind him.

I'm not sure I'm comfortable with this, but what other choice do I have? I pull my phone out from under my pillow. I start to text Ridge, because I don't recall closing a deal last night regarding my living arrangements. Before I finish the text, he sends me one first.

Ridge: Are you okay with this?

Me: Are you?

Ridge: I asked you first.

Me: I guess. But only if you are.

Ridge: Well, then, I guess that means we're roommates.

Me: If we're roommates, can you do me a favor?

Ridge: What's that?

Me: If I ever start dating again, don't be like Tori and sleep with my boyfriend, okay?

Ridge: I can't make any promises.

A few seconds later, he walks out of his bedroom and goes straight to my suitcases. He picks them up and carries them through the other bedroom door. He opens it and nods his head toward the room, indicating that I should come with him. I stand up and follow him into the bedroom. He lays the suitcases on the bed, then pulls his phone out again.

Ridge: Brennan still has a lot of stuff in here. I'll box it up and put it in the corner until he can get it all. Other than that, you might want to change the sheets.

He shoots me a wary look regarding the condition of the sheets, and I laugh. He points to the bathroom.

Ridge: We share the bathroom. Just lock the main door to the hallway and both doors to the bedrooms when you're in there. I obviously won't know when you're in the shower, so unless you want me barging in on you, make sure to lock up.

He walks to the bathroom and flips a light switch on the outside of the door, which turns the lights on and off inside the bathroom, then turns his attention back to the phone.

Ridge: I added switches on the outside because it's an easy way for someone to get my attention, since I can't hear a knock. Just flip the switch if you need to come into the bathroom so I'll know. The whole apartment is set up this way. There's a switch outside my bedroom door that turns my lights on and off if you need me. But I usually have my phone on me, so there's always texting.

He shows me where clean sheets are and then cleans out what's left in the dresser while I put the new sheets on the bed.
"Do I need furniture?"
Ridge shakes his head.

Ridge: He's leaving it. You can use what's here.

I nod, taking in the bedroom that has unexpectedly just become my new home. I smile at Ridge to let him know I appreciate his help. "Thank you."
He smiles back.

Ridge: I'll be in my room working for the next few hours if you need anything. I have to go to the store this afternoon. You can go with me and get what you need for the apartment.

He backs out of the bedroom and gives me a salute. I sit down on the edge of the bed and salute him back as he shuts the door. I fall back onto the bed and let out a huge sigh of relief.

Now that I have a place to live, all I need is a job. And maybe a car, since Tori and I mostly shared hers. Then maybe I'll call my parents and tell them I moved.

Or maybe not. I'll give this place a couple of weeks in order to see how things turn out.

Ridge: Oh, and btw, I didn't write that on your forehead.

What?

I run to the dresser and look in the mirror for the first time today. Written across my forehead in black ink, it says: *Someone wrote on your forehead.*

Ridge

Me: Morning. How's the thesis coming along?

Maggie: Do you want me to sugarcoat it, or are you honestly giving me an opening to vent?

Me: Wide open. Vent away.

Maggie: I'm miserable, Ridge. I hate it. I work on it for hours every day, and I just want to take a bat to my computer and go all *Office Space* on it. If this thesis were a child, I'd put it up for adoption and not even think twice about it. If this thesis were a cute, fuzzy puppy, I'd drop it off in the middle of a busy intersection and speed away.

Me: And then you would do a U-turn and go back and pick it up and play with it all night.

Maggie: I'm serious, Ridge. I think I'm losing my mind.

Me: Well, you already know what I think.

Maggie: Yes, I know what you think. Let's not get into that right now.

Me: You're the one who wanted to vent. You don't need this kind of stress.

Maggie: Stop.

Me: I can't, Maggie. You know how I feel, and I'm not keeping my opinion to myself when we both know I'm right.

Maggie: This is exactly why I never whine to you about it, because it always comes back to this same thing. I asked you to stop. Please, Ridge. Stop.

Me: Okay.

Me: I'm sorry.

Me: Now is when you return a text that says, "It's okay, Ridge. I love you."

Me: Hello?

Me: Don't do this, Maggie.

Maggie: Give a girl a minute to pee! Dang. I'm not mad. I just don't want to talk about it anymore. How are you?

Me: Phew. Good. We got a new roommate.

Maggie: I thought she wasn't moving in until next month.

Me: No, it's not Bridgette's sister. It's Sydney. The one I was telling you about a few days ago? After I decided to break the news to her about her boyfriend, it left her with nowhere to go. Warren and I are letting her stay here until she finds her own place. You'll like her.

Maggie: So I guess she believed you about her boyfriend?

Me: Yeah. She was pretty pissed at first that I didn't tell her sooner, but she's had a few days to let it sink in, so I think she gets it. So what time will you be here Friday?

Maggie: Not sure. I would say it depends on whether I get enough work done on my thesis, but I'm not mentioning my thesis to you ever again. I guess I'll get there when I get there.

Me: Well, then, I guess I'll see you when I see you. Love you. Let me know when you're on your way.

Maggie: Love you, too. And I know you're just concerned. I don't expect you to agree with my decisions, but I do want you to understand them.

Me: I do understand, babe. I do. I love you.

Maggie: Love you, too.

I drop my head forcefully against the headboard and rub my palms up and down my face out of sheer frustration. Of course, I understand her decision, but I'll never feel good about it. She's so frustratingly determined I seriously don't see how I'll ever get through to her.

I stand up and put my phone into my back pocket, then walk to my bedroom door. When I swing it open, I'm met with a smell that I'm positive is exactly what heaven will smell like.

Bacon.

Warren looks up at me from the dining-room table and grins, pointing to his plate full of food. "She's a keeper," he signs. "The eggs suck, though. I'm only eating them because I don't want to complain, or she might never cook for us again. Everything else is great." He signs everything he's saying without verbalizing it. Warren usually verbalizes all of his signed communication, out of respect for others around us. When he doesn't verbalize, I know he wants our conversation to remain between the two of us.

Like the silent one we're having right now while Sydney's in the kitchen.

"And she even asked how we liked our coffee," he signs.

I glance into the kitchen. Sydney smiles, so I smile back. I'm shocked to see her in a good mood today. After we got back from our trip to the store a few days ago, she's been spending most of the time in her room. At one point yesterday, Warren went in to ask her if she wanted any dinner, and he said she was on her bed crying, so he backed out and left her alone. I've wanted to check on her, but there isn't really anything I can do to make her feel better. All she can do is give it time, so I'm glad she's at least out of bed today.

"And don't look right now, Ridge. But did you see what she's wearing? Did you see that dress?" He bites the knuckles on his fist and winces, as if simply looking at her is causing him actual physical pain.

I shake my head and take a seat across from him. "I'll look later."

He grins. "I'm so glad her boyfriend cheated on her. Otherwise, I'd be eating leftover toothpaste-filled Oreos for breakfast."

I laugh. "At least you wouldn't have to brush your teeth."

"This was the best decision we've ever made," he says. "Maybe later we can talk her into vacuuming in that dress while we sit on the couch and watch."

Warren laughs at his own comment, but I don't crack a smile. I don't think he realizes he signed *and* spoke that last sentence. Before I can tell him, a biscuit comes hurtling past my head and smacks him in the face. He jumps back in shock and looks at Sydney. She's walking to the table with a *Don't mess with me* look on her face. She hands me a plate of food, then sets her own plate down in front of her and takes a seat.

"I said that out loud, didn't I?" Warren asks. I nod. He looks at Sydney, and she's still glaring at him. "At least I was complimenting you," he says with a shrug.

She laughs and nods once, as if he just made a good point. She picks up her phone and begins to text. She glances at me briefly, giving her head a slight shake when my phone vibrates in my pocket. She texted me something but apparently doesn't want me to make it obvious. I casually slide my hand into my pocket and pull my phone out, then read her text under the table.

Sydney: Don't eat the eggs.

I look at her and arch an eyebrow, wondering what the hell is wrong with the eggs. She casually sends another text while she holds a conversation with Warren.

Sydney: I poured dish soap and baby powder in them. It'll teach him not to write on my forehead again.

Me: WTH? When are you going to tell him?

Sydney: I'm not.

Warren: What are you and Sydney texting about?

I look up to see Warren holding his phone, staring at me. He picks up his fork and takes another bite of the eggs, and the sight makes me laugh. He lunges across the table and grabs my phone out of my hands, then begins scrolling through the texts. I try to grab it back from him, but he pulls his arm out of my reach. He pauses for a few seconds as he reads, then immediately spits his mouthful back onto his plate. He tosses me back my phone and reaches for his glass. He calmly takes a drink, sets it back down on the table, then pushes his chair back and stands up.

He points to Sydney. "You just messed up, little girl," he says. "This means war."

Sydney is smirking at him with a challenging gleam in her eye. Once Warren walks back to his bedroom and shuts his door, she loses the confident smirk and turns to me, wide-eyed.

Sydney: Help me! I need ideas. I suck at pranks!

Me: Yeah, you do. Dish soap and baby powder? You need serious help. Good thing you have the master on your side.

She grins, then begins eating her breakfast.

I don't even get my first bite down before Bridgette walks out of her room, sans smile. She walks straight to the kitchen and proceeds to make herself a plate of food. Warren returns from his room and sits back down at the table.

"I walked away for dramatic effect," he says. "I wasn't finished eating yet."

Bridgette sits, takes a bite of bacon, then looks over at Sydney. "DID . . . YOU . . . MAKE . . . THIS?" she says, pointing at the food dramatically. I cock my head, because she's talking to Sydney the same way she talks to me. As if she's deaf.

I look over at Sydney, who nods a response to Bridgette. I look back at Bridgette, and she says, "THANK . . . YOU!" She takes a bite of the eggs.

And she spits them right back out onto her plate.

She coughs and rushes to take a drink, then pushes away from the table. She looks back at Sydney. "I . . . CAN'T . . . EAT . . . THIS . . . SHIT!" She walks back to the kitchen, drops her food in the trash, and heads back to her bedroom.

The three of us break out into laughter after her door closes. When the laughter subsides, I turn to Warren.

"Why does Bridgette think Sydney is deaf?"

Warren laughs. "We don't know," he says. "But we don't feel like correcting her just yet."

I laugh on the outside, but inside I'm a little confused. I don't know when Warren began referring to himself and Sydney as *we*, but I'm not sure I like it.

• • •

My bedroom light flicks on and off, so I close my laptop and walk to the door. I open it, and Sydney is standing in the hallway, holding her laptop. She hands me a piece of paper.

I already finished my homework for the rest of the week. I even cleaned the entire apartment, excluding Bridgette's room, of course. Warren won't let me watch TV because it's not my night, whatever that means. So I was hoping I could hang out with you for a little while? I have to keep my mind busy, or I'll start thinking about Hunter again, and then I'll start feeling sorry for myself, and then I'll want Pine-Sol, and I really don't want to have any Pine-Sol, because I don't want to become a raging alcoholic like you.

I smile, step aside, and motion her into my bedroom. She looks around. The only place to sit is my bed, so I point to it, then take a seat and pull my laptop onto my lap. She sits on the other side of the bed and does the same.

"Thanks," she says with a smile. She opens her laptop and drops her eyes to the screen.

I tried not to take Warren's advice this morning about admiring the dress she had on today, but it was hard not to look, especially when he so blatantly pointed it out. I'm not sure what kind of weird thing he and Bridgette have going on, but it rubs me the wrong way that he and Sydney seem to have hit it off so well.

And it really rubs me the wrong way that it rubs me the wrong way. I don't look at her like that, so I don't understand why I'm sitting here thinking about it. And if she were standing next to Maggie, there wouldn't be a doubt in my mind that Maggie is more physically my type. Maggie is petite, with dark eyes and straight black hair. Sydney is the complete opposite. She's taller than Maggie—pretty average height—but her body is a lot more defined and curvy than Maggie's. Sydney definitely fills out the dress well, which is why Warren liked it. At least she changed into shorts before showing up at my bedroom door. That helps a little. The tops she wears are usually way too big for her, and they hang off her shoulders, which makes me think she took a lot of Hunter's T-shirts with her when she packed her bags.

Maggie's hair is always straight, whereas Sydney's is hard to figure out. It seems to change with the weather, but that's not necessarily a bad thing. The first time I saw her sitting on her balcony, I thought she had brown hair, but it turns out her hair was just wet. After playing guitar for about an hour that night, I looked at her as she was walking back inside her apartment, and her hair had dried completely and was in piles of blond waves that fell past her shoulders. Today it's curly and pulled up into a messy knot on top of her head.

Sydney: Stop staring at me.

Shit.

I laugh and attempt to brush away whatever the hell that internal detour was I just took.

Me: You look sad.

The first night she showed up here, she seemed happier than she does right now. Maybe it just took time for reality to sink in.

Sydney: Is there a way we can chat on the computer? It's a lot easier for me than texting.

Me: Sure. What's your last name? I'll friend you on Facebook.

Sydney: Blake.

I open my laptop and search her name. When I find her profile, I send her a friend request. She accepts it almost instantly, then shoots me a message.

Sydney: Hello, Ridge Lawson.

Me: Hello, Sydney Blake. Better?

She nods.

Sydney: You're a computer programmer?

Me: Already stalking my profile? And yes. I work from home. Graduated two years ago with a degree in computer engineering.

Sydney: How old are you?

Me: 24.

Sydney: Please tell me 24 is a lot better than 22.

Me: 22 will be good for you. Maybe not this week or next week, but it'll get better.

She sighs and puts one of her hands up to the back of her neck and rubs it, then begins typing again.

Sydney: I miss him. Is that crazy? I miss Tori, too. I still hate them and want to see them suffer, but I miss what I had with him. It's really starting to hurt. When it first happened, I thought maybe I was better off without him, but now I just feel lost.

I don't want to be harsh in my response, but at the same time, I'm not a girl, so I'm not about to tell her that what she's feeling is normal. Because to me, it's *not* normal.

Me: You only miss the idea of him. You weren't happy with him even before you found out he was cheating. You were only with him because it was comfortable. You just miss the relationship, but you don't miss Hunter.

She looks up at me and cocks her head, narrowing her eyes in my direction for a few seconds before dropping them back to the computer.

Sydney: How can you say I wasn't happy with him? I was. Until I found out what he was doing, I honestly thought he was the one.

Me: No. You didn't. You wanted him to be, but that's not how you really felt.

Sydney: You're kind of being a jerk right now, you know that?

I set my laptop beside me and walk to my desk. I pick up my notebook and a pen and go back to the bed and take a seat next to her. I flip open my notebook to the first set of lyrics she sent me.

Read these, I write at the top of the page. I set the notebook in her lap.

She looks down at the lyrics, then takes the pen. *I don't need to read them*, she writes. *I wrote them.*

I scoot closer to her and put the notebook in my lap, then

circle a few lines of her chorus. I point to them again. *Read these as if you weren't the one who wrote them.*

She reluctantly looks down at the notebook and reads the chorus.

> *You don't know me like you think you do*
> *I pour me one, when I really want two*
> *Oh, you're living a lie*
> *Living a lie*
>
> *You think we're good, but we're really not*
> *You coulda fixed things, but you missed your shot*
> *You're living a lie*
> *Living a lie*

When I'm certain she's had time to read them, I pick up the pen and write: *These words came from somewhere inside you, Sydney. You can tell yourself you were better off with him, but read the lyrics you wrote. Go back to what you were feeling when you wrote them.* I circle several lines, then read her words along with her.

> *With a right turn, the tires start to burn*
> *I see your smile, it's been hiding for a while*
> *For a while*
>
> *Your foot pushes down against the ground*
> *The world starts to blur, can't remember who you were*
> *Who you were*

I look at her, and she's still staring at the paper. A single tear trickles down her cheek, and she quickly wipes it away.

She picks up the pen and begins writing. *They're just words, Ridge.*

I reply, *They're* your *words, Sydney. Words that came from you. You say you feel lost without him, but you felt lost even when you were* with *him. Read the rest.*

She inhales a deep breath, then looks down at the paper again.

> *I yell, slow down, we're almost out of town*
> *The road gets rough, have you had enough*
> *Enough*
>
> *You look at me, start heading for a tree*
> *I open up the door, can't take any more*
> *Any more*
>
> *Then I say,*
>
> *You don't know me like you think you do*
> *I pour me one, when I really want two*
> *Oh, you're living a lie*
> *Living a lie*
>
> *You think we're good, but we're really not*
> *You coulda fixed things, but you missed your shot*
> *You're living a lie*
> *Living a lie*

Sydney

I continue to stare at the words in the notebook.

Is he right? Did I write them because that's how I really feel?

I never give it much thought when I write lyrics, because I've always felt no one would read them, so it doesn't matter what the meaning is behind the words. But now that I think about it, maybe the fact that I don't give them much thought proves that they really are a reflection of how I feel. To me, lyrics are harder to write when you have to invent the feelings behind them. That's when lyrics take a lot of thought, when they aren't genuine.

Oh, wow. Ridge is absolutely right. I wrote these lyrics weeks ago, long before I knew about Hunter and Tori.

I lean back against the headboard and open my laptop again.

Me: Okay, you win.

Ridge: It's not a competition. Just trying to help you see that maybe this breakup is exactly what you needed. I don't know you very well, but based on the lyrics you wrote, I'm guessing you've been craving the chance to be on your own for a while now.

Me: Well you claim not to know me very well, but you seem to know me better than I know myself.

Ridge: I only know what you told me in those lyrics. Speaking of which, you feel like running through them? I was about to compile them with the music to send to Brennan and could use your ears. Pun intended.

I laugh and elbow him.

Me: Sure. What do I do?

He stands and picks up his guitar, then nods his head toward the balcony. I don't want to go out on that balcony. I don't care if I was ready to leave Hunter, I sure wasn't ready to leave Tori. And being out there will be too much of a distraction.

I crinkle my nose and shake my head. He glances across the courtyard at my apartment, then pulls his lips into a tight, thin line and slowly nods his head in understanding. He walks over to the bed and sits on the mattress next to me.

Ridge: I want you to sing the lyrics while I play. I'll watch you so I can make sure we're on the same page with where they need to be placed on the sheet music.

Me: No. I'm not singing in front of you.

He huffs and rolls his eyes.

Ridge: Are you afraid I'll laugh at how awful you sound? I can't HEAR YOU, SYDNEY!

He's smiling his irritating smile at me.

Me: Shut up. Fine.

He sets the phone down and begins playing the song. When the lyrics are supposed to come in, he looks up, and I freeze. Not because I'm nervous, though. I freeze because I'm doing that thing again where I'm holding my breath because seeing him play is just . . . he's incredible.

He doesn't miss a beat when I skip my intro. He just starts over from the beginning and plays the opening again. I shake myself out of my pathetic awe and begin singing the words. I would probably never be singing lyrics in front of anyone one-on-one like this, but it helps that he can't hear me. He does stare pretty hard, though, which is a little unnerving.

He pauses after every stanza and makes notes on a page. I lean over and look at what he's writing. He's putting musical notes on blank sheet-music paper, along with the lyrics.

He points to one of the lines, then grabs his phone.

Ridge: What key do you sing this line in?

Me: B.

Ridge: Do you think it would sound better if you took it a little higher?

Me: I don't know. I guess we could try.

He plays the second part of the song again, and I take his advice and sing in a higher key. Surprisingly, he's right. It does sound better.

"How did you know that?" I ask.

He shrugs.

Ridge: I just do.

Me: But how? If you can't hear, how do you know what sounds good and what doesn't?

Ridge: I don't need to hear it. I feel it.

I shake my head, not understanding. I can maybe understand how he's taught himself to play a guitar. With enough
practice and a good teacher and maybe a ton of studying, it's
possible for him to play as he does. But that doesn't explain
how he can know which key a voice should be in and especially
which key *sounds* better.

Ridge: What's wrong? You look confused.

Me: I AM confused. I don't understand how you can
differentiate between vibrations or however you say you feel it.
I'm beginning to think you and Warren are trying to pull off the
ultimate prank and you're only pretending to be deaf.

Ridge laughs, then scoots back on the bed until his back
meets the headboard. He sits up straight and holds his guitar to
his side. He spreads his legs, then pats the empty spot between
them.

What the hell? I hope my eyes aren't open as wide as I
think they are. There's no way I'm sitting that close to him. I
shake my head.

He rolls his eyes and picks up his phone.

Ridge: Come here. I want to show you how I feel it. Get over
yourself, and stop thinking I'm trying to seduce you.

I hesitate a few more seconds, but the agitation on his face
makes me think I'm being a little immature. I crawl forward,
then turn around and carefully sit in front of him with my back
to his chest but with several inches between us. He pulls the
guitar in front of me and wraps his other arm around me until
he's holding it in position. He pulls it closer, which pushes me
flush against him. Ridge reaches down to his side and picks up
his phone.

Ridge: I'm going to play a chord, and I want you to tell me where you feel it.

I nod, and he brings his hand back to the guitar. He plays a chord and repeats it a few times, then pauses. I grab my phone.

Me: I felt it in your guitar.

He shakes his head and picks up his phone again.

Ridge: I know you felt it in the guitar, dummy. But where in your body did you feel it?

Me: Play it again.

I close my eyes this time and try to take this seriously. I've asked him how he feels it, and he's trying to show me, so the least I can do is try to understand. He plays the chord a few times, and I'm really trying hard to concentrate, but I feel the vibration everywhere, especially in the guitar pressed against my chest.

Me: It's hard for me, Ridge. It just feels like it's everywhere.

He pushes me forward, and I scoot up. He sets the guitar down, stands up, and walks out of the bedroom. I wait for him, curious about what he's doing. When he comes back, he's holding something in his fist. He holds his fist out, so I hold up my palm.

Earplugs.

He slides in behind me, and I scoot back against his chest again, then put the earplugs in. I close my eyes and lean my head back against his shoulder. He wraps his arms around me and picks up his guitar, pulling it against my chest. I can feel his head rest lightly against mine, and the intimate way we're seated suddenly registers. I've never sat like this with someone I wasn't seriously dating.

It's odd, because it seems so natural with him. Not at all as if he's got anything other than music on his mind. I like that about him, because if I were pressed up against Warren like this, I'm positive his hands wouldn't be on the guitar.

I can feel his arms moving slightly, so I know he's playing, even though I can't hear it. I concentrate on the vibration and focus all my attention on the movement inside my chest. When I'm able to pinpoint exactly where I feel it, I bring my hand to my chest and pat it. I can feel him nod his head, and then he continues playing.

I can still feel it in my chest, but it's much lower this time. I move my hand down, and he nods again.

I pull away from him and turn around to face him.
"Wow."
He lifts his shoulders and smiles shyly. It's adorable.

Me: This is crazy. I still don't understand how you can play an instrument like this, but I know how you feel it now.

He shrugs off my compliment, and I love how modest he is, because he clearly has more talent than anyone I've ever met.
"Wow," I say again, shaking my head.

Ridge: Stop. I don't like compliments. It's awkward.

I set down my phone and we both move back to the laptops.

Me: Well, you shouldn't be so impressive, then. I don't think you realize what an incredible gift you have, Ridge. I know you say you work hard at it, but so do thousands of people who can hear, and they can't put together songs like you can. I mean, I can maybe understand the whole guitar thing now that you've explained it, but what about the voices? How in the heck can you know what a voice sounds like and what key it needs to be in?

Ridge: Actually, I can't differentiate the sounds of a voice. I've never felt a person sing the way I "listen" to a guitar. I can place vocals to a song and develop melodies because I've studied a lot of songs and have learned which keys match up to which notes, based on the written form of music. It doesn't just come naturally. I work hard at this. I love the idea of music, and even though I can't hear it, I've learned to understand and appreciate it in a different way. I've had to work harder at the melodies. There are times I'll write a song, and Brennan will tell me we can't use it because it either sounds too much like an existing song or it doesn't actually sound good to hearing ears like I assumed it would.

He can downplay this all he wants, but I'm convinced I'm sitting next to a musical genius. I hate that he thinks his ability comes from working so hard at it. I mean, I'm sure it helps, because all talents have to be nurtured in order to excel, even for the gifted. But his talent is mind-blowing. It makes me hurt for him, knowing what he could do with his gift if he could hear.

Me: Can you hear anything? At all?

He shakes his head.

Ridge: I've worn hearing aids before, but they were more inconvenient than helpful. I have profound hearing loss, so they didn't help at all when it came to hearing voices or my guitar. When I used them, I could tell there were noises, but I couldn't decipher them. In all honesty, hearing aids were a constant reminder that I couldn't hear. Without them, I don't even think about it.

Me: What made you want to learn guitar, knowing you would never be able to hear it?

Ridge: Brennan. He wanted to learn when we were kids, so we learned together.

Me: The guy who used to live here? How long have you known him?

Ridge: 21 years. He's my little brother.

Me: Is he in your band?

Ridge glances at me in confusion.

Ridge: Have I not told you about our band?

I shake my head.

Ridge: He's the singer. He also plays guitar.

Me: When do you play next? I want to watch.

He laughs.

Ridge: I don't play. It's kind of complicated. Brennan insists that I have as much stake in the ownership of the band as he does because I write the majority of the music, which is why I refer to myself as being part of the band sometimes. I think it's ridiculous, but he's convinced we wouldn't be where we are at this point without me, so I agree to it for now. But with the success I think he's about to have, I'll make him renegotiate eventually. I don't like feeling as though I'm taking advantage of him.

Me: If he doesn't feel that way, then you definitely shouldn't feel that way. And why don't you play with them?

Ridge: I have a few times. It's kind of difficult, not being able to hear everything else going on with the band during a song, so I feel like I throw them off when I play with them. Besides, they're on tour right now, and I can't travel, so I've just been sending him the stuff I write.

Me: Why can't you tour with them? Don't you work from home?

Ridge: Other obligations. But next time they're in Austin, I'll take you.

I'll take you. I think I like that part of his message a little too much.

Me: What's the name of the band?

Ridge: Sounds of Cedar.

I slam my laptop shut and swing my eyes to his. "Shut up!" He nods, then reaches down and opens my laptop again.

Ridge: You've heard of us?

Me: Yes. Everyone on campus has heard of your band, considering they played almost every single weekend last year. Hunter loves you guys.

Ridge: Ah. Well, this is the first time I've ever wished we had one less fan. So you've seen Brennan play?

Me: I only went with Hunter once, and it was one of the last shows, but yes. I think I may have most of the songs on my phone, actually.

Ridge: Wow. Small world. We are close to a record deal. That's why I've been stressing so much about these songs. And why you need to help me.

Me: OMG! I just realized I'm writing lyrics for SOUNDS OF CEDAR!!!

I slide my laptop over, then roll onto my stomach and squeal into the mattress while I kick my legs up and down.

Holy crap! This is too cool.

I compose myself, ignoring Ridge's laughter, then sit up straight again and grab my laptop.

Me: So you wrote most of those songs?

He nods.

Me: Did you write the lyrics to the song "Something"?

He nods again. I seriously can't believe this is happening right now. Knowing he wrote those lyrics and now I'm sitting here next to him is exciting me way too much.

Me: I'm about to listen to your song. Since you get to decipher my lyrics, it's my turn to decipher yours.

Ridge: I wrote that song two years ago.

Me: Still. It came from you. From somewhere inside you, Ridge. ;)

He picks up a pillow and throws it at my head. I laugh and scroll through the music folder on my phone until I find the song, and I hit play.

SOMETHING

I keep on wondering why
I can't say 'bye to you
And the only thing I can
think of is the truth

It's hard to start over
Keep checkin' that rearview, too
But something's coming
Something right for you
Just wait a bit longer

You'll find something you wanted
Something you needed
Something you want to have repeated
Oh, that feeling's all right

You'll find that if you listen
Between all the kissing
What made it work
Wound up missing
Oh, that seems about right

I guess I thought that we would
Always stay the same
And I can tell that you find
Somebody to blame

And I know in my heart,
In my mind, it's all a game
Our hopes and wishes

Won't relight the flame
Just wait a bit longer

You'll find something you wanted
Something you needed
Something you want to have repeated
Oh, that feeling's all right

You'll find that if you listen
Between all the kissing
What made it work
Wound up missing
Oh, that seems about right

You don't ever have to wonder
'Cause you will always know
That what we had was for sure
For sure
Now that thing is no more
No more

You'll find what you wanted
You'll find what you needed
You'll find what you wanted
You'll find what you needed
You'll find what you needed

When the song ends, I sit back up on the bed. I would ask him about the lyrics and the meaning behind them right now, but I'm not sure I want to. I want to listen to it again without him watching me, because it's really hard to concentrate when he's staring at me. He's resting his chin in his hands, casually watching me. I try to hide my grin, but it's hard. I see a smile spread across his lips before he looks down at his phone.

Ridge: Why do I feel like you're fangirling right now?

Probably because I am.

Me: I'm not fangirling. Don't flatter yourself. I've witnessed how evil you can be with your revenge schemes, and I've been exposed to your severe alcoholism, so I'm not as enamored with you as I could be.

Ridge: My father was a severe alcoholic. Your jokes are a little off-putting.

I look up at him apologetically and with a hint of embarrassment. "I'm sorry. I was kidding."

Ridge: I'm kidding, too.

I kick him in the knee and glare at him.

Ridge: Well, sort of kidding. My father really is a raging alcoholic, but I don't give a shit if you joke about it.

Me: I can't now. You ruined the fun.

He laughs, and it's followed by an awkward moment of silence. I grin and drop my eyes back to my phone.

Me: OMG. Can I have your autograph?

He rolls his eyes.

Me: Please? And can I have my picture taken with you? OMG, I'm in Ridge Lawson's bed!

I'm laughing, but Ridge isn't finding me amusing.

Me: Ridge Lawson, will you sign my boobs?

He puts his laptop down beside him, leans over to his nightstand and picks up a marker, then turns back to me.

I don't *really* want his autograph. Surely he knows I'm kidding.

He pulls the lid off the marker, swiftly lunges across the bed, and knocks me onto my back, bringing the marker to my forehead.

He's trying to sign my *face*?

I lift my legs and create a barrier with my knees as I try to force his hands away.

Dammit, he's strong.

He puts one of my hands under his knee and locks my arm to the bed. His other arm grabs my arm that's pushing his face away, and he pushes that hand to the bed, too. I'm screaming and laughing and trying to turn my face away from him, but every time I move, the marker moves over my face while he tries to sign his name.

I'm unable to overpower him, so I eventually sigh and hold my head still so he'll stop drawing all over my face.

He hops up, puts the lid back on the marker, and smirks at me. I reach over to my laptop.

Me: You are no longer my prank master. This has officially turned into a three-way war. Excuse me while I go Google my revenge.

I fold up my laptop and walk quietly out of the room while he laughs at me. As I head through the living room toward my bedroom, Warren glances at me. Twice.

"Should have stayed in here and watched porn with me," he says, taking in the marker all over my face.

I ignore his comment. "Ridge and I just finished discussing TV rules," I lie. "I get Thursdays."

"No, you don't," Warren says. "Tomorrow is Thursday. I watch Thursday-night porn on Thursday."

"Not anymore you don't. Guess you should have asked about my television habits when you were interviewing me."

He groans. "Fine. You can have Thursdays, but only if you wear that dress you had on earlier."

I laugh. "I'm burning that dress."

Ridge

"Why'd you give Sydney the TV tonight?" Warren signs. He drops onto the couch next to me. "You know I love Thursday night. I'm off work on Fridays."

"I never talked to Sydney about TV nights."

He glances toward Sydney's bedroom door with a scowl on his face. "What a little liar. How did you meet her, anyway?"

"Music-related. She's writing lyrics for the band."

Warren's eyes bulge, and he straightens up on the couch, turning to look at me as if I've just betrayed him.

"Don't you think this is something your manager should know about?"

I laugh and sign back to him. "Good point. Hey, Warren, Sydney is officially writing lyrics for us."

He frowns. "And don't you think your manager should have discussed a financial arrangement with her? What percentage are we giving her?"

"We're not. She feels guilty taking a percentage while she's not paying rent, so we're good for now."

He's standing now, glaring down at me. "How do you know you can trust her? And what if something happens with a song she helped write? What if it makes the cut on the album and she suddenly decides she wants a percentage? And why the hell aren't *you* writing the lyrics anymore?"

I sigh. We've been over this so many times it's making my head hurt. "I can't. You know I can't. It's just for a little while, until I get over my block. And calm down, she's agreed to sign over anything she helps with."

He drops back onto the couch, frustrated. "Just don't add

any more people to our band without consulting me first, okay? I feel like I'm being shut out when you don't include me." He folds his arms across his chest and pouts.

"Is sweet little Warren pouting?" I lean forward and wrap my arms around him, and he tries to shove me off. I climb on top of him and kiss his cheek, and he starts hitting me in the arm, trying to pull away from my grasp. I laugh and let go of his face, then look up at Sydney, who just walked into the room. She's staring at us. Warren slides his hand up my thigh and lays his head on my shoulder. I reach up and pat his cheek while we both stare up at her, straight-faced. She shakes her head slowly and walks back into her bedroom.

As soon as her bedroom door closes, we separate.

"I wish I hated Bridgette a little more than I do at night, because Sydney definitely needs me," Warren signs.

I laugh, knowing Sydney is more than likely swearing off guys based on the week she's had. "That girl doesn't need anything other than the opportunity to be alone for a while."

Warren shakes his head. "No, that girl definitely needs me. I wonder how I can pull off an elaborate prank that involves her agreeing to have sex with me."

"Bridgette," I remind him. I don't know why I remind him. I never remind him about Bridgette when he talks about other girls.

"You're a dream crusher," he signs, falling back against the couch at the same moment I receive a text.

Sydney: Can I ask you a question?

Me: As long as you promise never again to start a question off with whether or not you can propose a question.

Sydney: Okay, asshole. I know I shouldn't be thinking about him at all, but I'm curious. What did he write on that paper when we went to get my purse? And what did you write back that made him hit you?

Me: I agree that you shouldn't be thinking about him at all, but I'm honestly shocked it's taken you this long to ask me about it.

Sydney: Well?

Ugh. I hate writing it verbatim, but she wants to know, so . . .

Me: He wrote, "Are you fucking her?"

Sydney: OMG! What a prick!

Me: Yep.

Sydney: So what did you say back to him that made him punch you?

Me: I wrote, "Why do you think I'm here for her purse? I gave her a hundred for tonight, and now she owes me change."

I reread the text, and I'm not so sure it sounds as funny as I thought it did.

My eyes dart up to her bedroom door, which is now swinging open. She runs into the living room, directly toward the couch. I don't know if it's the look on her face or the hands that are coming at me, but I immediately cover my head and duck behind Warren. He doesn't really like being used as a human shield, though, so he jumps off the couch. She continues slapping at my arms until I'm curled up in a fetal position on the couch. I'm trying not to laugh, but she hits like a girl. This is nothing compared to what I saw her do to Tori.

She backs away, and I reluctantly uncover my head. She marches back to her room, and I watch as she slams her door.

Warren is now standing next to the couch with his hands on his hips. He looks at me, then looks back at Sydney's door. He puts his palms up and shakes his head, then retreats into his bedroom.

I should probably apologize to her. It was just a joke, but I guess I can see how it would piss her off. I knock on her door a couple of times. She doesn't open it, so I text her.

Me: Can I come in?

Sydney: That depends. Do you have any bills smaller than a hundred this time?

Me: It seemed funny at the time. I'm sorry.

A few seconds pass, and then her door opens and she steps aside. I raise my eyebrows and smile, attempting to look innocent. She shoots me a dirty look and walks back to her bed.

Sydney: It wasn't what I would have wanted you to say, but I can see why you said it. He's a jerk, and I probably would have wanted to piss him off in that moment, too.

Me: He is a jerk, but I probably should have responded differently. I'm sorry.

Sydney: Yes, you should have. Maybe instead of insinuating that I was a whore, you could have gone with "If I could only be so lucky."

I laugh at her comment, then offer up another alternative answer.

Me: I could have gone with "Only when you're being faithful to her. Which is never."

Sydney: Or you could have said, "No, I'm not. I'm madly in love with Warren."

At least she's making jokes about it. I really do feel sort of bad for saying that to him, but it felt oddly appropriate at the time.

Me: We didn't really get any work done last night. Are you in the mood to make beautiful music together?

Sydney

Ridge puts down his guitar for the first time in more than an hour. We haven't texted at all, because we've been on a roll. It's pretty cool how well we seem to work together. He plays a song over and over while I lie across his bed with a notebook in front of me. I write down the lyrics as they come to me, most of the time crumpling up the paper, chucking it across the room, and starting over. But I've finished lyrics for almost an entire song tonight, and he's only crossed out two lines he didn't like. I'd say that's progress.

There's something about these moments when we're writing music that I absolutely love. All my worries and thoughts about everything wrong in my life seem to go away for the short times we write together. It's nice.

> Ridge: Let's do the whole song now. Sit up so I can watch you sing it. I want to make sure we have it perfect before I send it to Brennan.

He starts playing the song, so I begin singing. He's watching me closely, and the way his eyes seem to read my every movement makes me uneasy. Maybe it's because he can't express words through speaking, but everything else about him seems to make up for that.

As easy as he is to read, it's only that way when he *wants* to be read. Most of the time, he's able to hold back his expressions, and I don't know what the hell he's thinking. He holds the crown in the nonverbal department. I'm pretty sure that with the looks he gives, if he *could* speak, he'd never even have to.

I feel uncomfortable watching him watch me sing, so I close my eyes and try to recall the lyrics as he continues to play the song. It's awkward singing them with him only a few feet away. When I wrote the lyrics the first time, he was playing his guitar but was a good two hundred yards away on his balcony. Still, though, as much as I tried to pretend I was writing them about Hunter at the time, I knew I was imagining Ridge singing them all along.

A LITTLE BIT MORE

Why don't you let me
Take you away
We can live like you wanted
From place to place

I'll be your home
We can make our own
'Cause together makes it pretty hard
to be alone

We can have everything we ever wanted
And just a little bit more
Just a little bit more

His guitar stops, so naturally, *I* stop. I open my eyes, and he's watching me with one of his expressionless expressions.

I take that back. This expression isn't expressionless at all. He's thinking. I can tell by the squint in his eyes that he's coming up with an idea.

He glances away in order to pick up his phone.

Ridge: Do you mind if I try something?

Me: As long as you promise never again to propose a question by asking if I mind if you can try something.

Ridge: Nice try, but that made no sense.

I laugh, then look up at him. I nod softly, scared of what he's about to "try." He sits up on his knees and leans forward, placing both hands on my shoulders. I attempt to hold in my gasp, but it's a failed attempt. I don't know what he's doing or why he's getting so close to me, but holy crap.

Holy crap.

Why is my heart spazzing out right now?

He pushes me until I'm flat on his mattress. He reaches behind him and picks up his guitar, then lays it on the other side of me. He lies down next to me.

Calm down, heart. Please. Ridge has supersonic senses, and he'll feel you beating through the vibrations of the mattress.

Ridge scoots closer to me and by the way he's hesitating, it makes me think he's unsure if I'll allow him any closer.

I will. I absolutely will.

He's staring at me now, contemplating his next move. I can tell he's not about to make a pass at me. Whatever he's about to do is making him way more apprehensive than if he were just planning to kiss me. He's eyeing my neck and chest as if he's searching for a particular part of me. His eyes stop on my abdomen, pause, then fall back to his phone.

Oh, Lord. What is he about to do? Put his hands on me? Does he want to feel me sing this song? Feeling requires touching, and touching requires hands. *His* hands. Feeling *me*.

Ridge: Do you trust me?

Me: I don't trust anyone anymore. My trust has been completely depleted this week.

Ridge: Can you replenish your trust for about five minutes? I want to feel your voice.

I inhale, then look at him—lying next to me—and I nod. He sets down his phone without breaking my gaze. He's watching me as if he's warning me to stay calm, but it's having the exact opposite effect. I'm sort of panicked right now.

He scoots closer and slides his arm under the back of my neck.

Oh.

Now he's even closer.

Now his face is hovering over mine. He reaches across my body and pulls the guitar flush against my side, bringing it closer to us. He's still eyeing me with a look that seems intended to produce a calming effect.

It doesn't. It doesn't calm me down at *all*.

He lowers his head to my chest, then presses his cheek against my shirt.

Oh, this is great. Now he definitely feels how spastic my heart is beating right now. I close my eyes and want to die of embarrassment, but I don't have time for that, because he begins strumming the strings of the guitar next to me. I realize he's playing with both hands, one from underneath my head and one over me. His head is against my chest, and I can feel his hair brush my neck. He's pretty much sprawled across me in order to reach his guitar with both arms.

Oh, my dear sweet baby Jesus in a wicker basket.

How does he expect me to *sing*?

I try to calm down by regulating my breathing, but it's hard when we're positioned like this. As usual when I miss an intro, he seamlessly starts the song over again from the beginning. When he reaches the point where I come in, I begin singing. Sort of. It's really quiet, because I'm still waiting for air to find its way back into my lungs.

After the first few lines, I find a steadiness to my voice. I close my eyes and do my best to imagine I'm simply sitting up on his bed right now the way I have been for the last hour.

I'll bring my suitcase
You bring that old map
We can live by the book
Or we can never go back

Feeling the breeze
Never felt so right
We'll watch the stars
Until they fade into light

We can have everything we ever wanted
And just a little bit more
Just a little bit more

He finishes the last chord but doesn't move. His hands remain stilled on his guitar. His ear remains firmly pressed against my chest. My breaths are heavier now that I've just sung an entire song, and his head rises with each intake of air.

He sighs a deep sigh, then lifts his head and rolls onto his back without making eye contact with me. We lie in silence for a few minutes. I'm not sure why he's being so unresponsive, but I'm too nervous to make any sudden movements. His arm is still underneath me, and he's making no effort to remove it, so I'm not even sure if he's finished with this little experiment yet.

I'm also not sure I'd even be able to move.

Sydney, Sydney, Sydney. What are you doing?

I absolutely, positively, do *not* want to be having this reaction right now. It's been a week since I broke up with Hunter. The very last thing I want—or even need—is to develop a crush on this guy.

However, I'm thinking that may have happened *before* this week.

Crap.

I tilt my head and look at him. He's watching me, but I can't tell what his face is trying to convey. If I had to guess, I'd say he's thinking, *Oh, hey, Sydney. Our mouths sure are close together. Let's do them a favor and close this gap.*

His eyes drop to my mouth, and I'm incredibly impressed with my telepathic abilities. His full lips are slightly parted as he quietly takes in several slow, deep breaths.

I can actually hear him breathing, which surprises me, because that's another of his sounds that he keeps complete and total control over. I like that he can't seem to control it right now. As much as I claim to want to be unattached from guys and independent and strong, the only thing I'm thinking is how much I wish he would take complete and total control over me. I want him to dominate this situation by rolling on top of me and forcing that incredible mouth onto mine, rendering me completely dependent on him for breath.

My phone receives a text, interrupting my clearly overactive imagination. Ridge closes his eyes and turns to face the opposite direction. I sigh, knowing he didn't even hear the text, so turning away was of his own accord. Which means I'm feeling pretty awkward right now for just having that rich internal dialogue sweep through my mind. I reach behind my head and feel around until I find my phone.

Hunter: Are you ready to talk yet?

I roll my eyes. *Way to ruin the moment, Hunter.* I was hoping that after days of avoiding his texts and phone calls, he would finally get a clue. I shake my head and text him back.

Me: Your behavior is bordering on harassment. Stop contacting me. We're done.

Ridge

Stop with the guilt trip, Ridge. You didn't do anything wrong. You aren't doing anything wrong. Your heart is beating like this simply because you've never felt anyone sing before. It was overwhelming. You had a normal reaction to an overwhelming event. That's all.

My eyes are still closed, and my arm is still underneath her. I should move it, but I'm still trying to recover.

And I *really* want to hear another song.

This might be making her uncomfortable, but I have to get her to push through her discomfort, because I can't think of any other situation where I'll be able to do this.

Me: Can I play another one?

She's holding her phone, texting someone who's not me. I wonder if she's texting Hunter, but I don't peek at her phone, as much as I want to.

Sydney: Okay. The first one didn't do anything for you?

I laugh. I think it did a little too much, in more ways than I'd like to admit. I'm almost positive it was also obvious to her by the end of the song, with the way I was pressed against her. But feeling her voice and what it was doing to all the other parts of me was way more important than what *she* was doing to me.

Me: I've never "listened" to anyone like that before. It was incredible. I don't even know how to describe it. I mean, you were here, and you were the one singing, so I guess you don't really need me to describe it. But I don't know. I wish you could have felt that.

Sydney: You're welcome, I guess. I'm not really doing anything profound here.

Me: I've always wanted to feel someone sing one of my songs, but it would be a little awkward doing this with one of the guys in the band. Know what I mean?

She laughs, then nods.

Me: I'll play the one we practiced last night, and then I want to play this last one again. Are you okay? If you're tired of singing, just tell me.

Sydney: I'm good.

She lays down her phone, and I reposition myself against her chest. My entire body is battling itself. My left brain is telling me this is somehow wrong, my right brain is wanting to hear her sing again, my stomach is nowhere to be found, and my heart is punching itself in the face with one arm and hugging itself with the other.

I might never have this opportunity again, so I wrap my arm over her and begin playing. I close my eyes and search for the beat of her heart, which has slowed down some since the first song. The vibration of her voice meets my cheek, and I swear my heart flinches. She feels the way I imagined a voice would feel during a song but multiplied by a thousand. I focus on how her voice blends with the vibration of the guitar, and I'm in complete awe.

I want to feel the range of her voice, but it's hard without using my hands to feel it. I pull my hand away from the guitar and stop playing. Just like that, she stops singing. I shake my head no and motion a circle in the air with my finger, wanting her to keep singing even though I'm no longer playing the chords.

Her voice picks back up, and I keep my ear pressed firmly to her chest while I lay my palm flat against her stomach. Her muscles clench beneath my hand, but she doesn't stop singing. I can feel her voice everywhere. I can feel it in my head, in my chest, against my hand.

I relax against her and listen to the sound of a voice for the very first time.

• • •

I wrap my arm around Maggie's waist and pull her in closer. I can feel her struggling beneath me, so I pull her even tighter. I'm not ready for her to go home yet. Her hand smacks my forehead, and she's lifting me off her chest as she attempts to wiggle out from beneath me.

I roll onto my back to let her off the bed, but instead, she's slapping my cheeks. I open my eyes and look up to see Sydney hovering over me. Her mouth is moving, but my vision is too fogged over to see what she's trying to say. Not to mention that the strobe light isn't helping.

Wait. I don't have a strobe light.

I sit straight up on the bed. Sydney hands me my phone and begins to text me, but my phone is dead. Did we fall asleep?

The lights. The lights are going on and off.

I grab Sydney's phone out of her hand and check the time: 8:15 A.M. I also read the text she just tried to send me.

Sydney: Someone's at your bedroom door.

Warren wouldn't be up this early on a Friday. It's his day off.

Friday.

Maggie.

SHIT!

I hurriedly jump off the bed and grab Sydney's wrists, then swing her to her feet. She looks shocked that I'm panicking, but she needs to get the hell back to her room. I open the bathroom door and motion for her to take that route. She walks into the bathroom, then turns and heads back into my bedroom. I grab her by the shoulders and force her back into the bathroom. She slaps my hands away and points into my bedroom.

"I want my phone!" she says, pointing toward my bed. I retrieve her phone, but before I hand it to her, I type a text on it.

Me: I'm sorry, but I think that's Maggie. You can't be in here, or she'll get the wrong idea.

I hand her the phone, and she reads the text, then looks back up at me. "Who's Maggie?"

Who's Maggie? How the hell can she not remember . . .

Oh.

Is it possible I've never mentioned Maggie to her before?

I grab her phone again.

Me: My girlfriend.

She looks at the text, and her jaw tightens. She slowly brings her eyes back to mine, and she snatches the phone out of my hand, grabs the doorknob, and steps back into the bathroom. The door closes in my face.

So was not expecting that reaction.

But I don't have time to respond, because my light is still flickering. I head straight to the bedroom door and unlock it, then open it.

Warren is standing in the doorway with his arm pressed against the frame. There's no sign of Maggie.

My panic instantly subsides as I walk backward and fall onto my bed. That could have been ugly. I glance up at Warren, because he's obviously here for something.

"Why aren't you answering my texts?" he signs from the doorway.

"My phone died." I reach over to my phone and place it on the charging base on the nightstand.

"But you never let your phone die."

"First time for everything," I sign.

He nods his head, but it's an annoying, suspicious, *You're hiding something* kind of nod.

Or maybe I'm just being paranoid.

"You're hiding something," he signs.

Or maybe I'm *not* being paranoid.

"And I just checked Sydney's room." He arches a suspicious brow. "She wasn't in there."

I glance to the bathroom, then look back at Warren, wondering if I should even lie about it. All we did was fall asleep. "I know. She was in here."

He holds his stern expression. "All night?"

I nod casually. "We were working on lyrics. I guess we fell asleep."

He's acting strange. If I didn't know him better, I'd think he was jealous. Wait. I *do* know him better. He *is* jealous.

"Does this bother you, Warren?"

He shrugs and signs back. "Yeah. A little."

"Why? You spend almost every night in Bridgette's bed."

He shakes his head. "It's not that."

"What is it, then?"

He breaks his gaze, and I can see the discomfort cross his face before he exhales. He makes the sign that indicates Maggie's name. He brings his eyes back to mine. "You can't do this,

Ridge. You made this choice for yourself years ago, and I tried to tell you then what I thought about it. But you're in it now, and if I have to be the annoying friend to remind you of that, so be it."

I wince, because it kind of pisses me off how he's referring to my and Maggie's relationship. "Don't refer to my relationship with Maggie as being 'in it' ever again."

His expression grows apologetic. "You know what I mean, Ridge."

I stand and walk toward him. "How long have we been best friends?"

He shrugs. "That's all I am to you? A best friend? Ridge, I thought we were so much more than that." He smirks as if he's trying to be funny, but I don't laugh. When he sees how much his remarks have bothered me, his expression quickly sobers. "Ten years."

"Ten. Ten years. You know me better than that, Warren."

He nods, but his face is still full of doubt.

"Good-bye," I sign. "Shut the door on your way out." I turn and walk back to my bed, and when I face the door again, he's gone.

8.

Sydney

Why am I so pissed? We didn't do anything.

Did we?

I can't even tell what the hell happened last night before we fell asleep. Technically, it wasn't anything, but then again, it was, which is probably why I'm so pissed, because I'm so freaking confused.

First he doesn't tell me about Hunter for two solid weeks. Then he fails to mention that he's deaf, although I really have no right to be upset about that. That's not something I should feel obligated to have been told.

But Maggie?

Girlfriend?

How could he fail to mention in the three weeks I've been talking to him that he has a girlfriend?

He's just like Hunter. He has a dick and two balls and no heart, and that makes him Hunter's twin. I should probably just start calling him Hunter. I should just call them *all* Hunter. From here on out, all men shall be referred to as Hunter.

My father should be thanking the high heavens that I'm not in law school, because I am by far the absolute worst judge of character who has ever walked the planet.

Ridge: False alarm. It was just Warren. Sorry about that.

Me: SCREW. YOU.

Ridge: ???

Me: Don't even.

A few seconds pass with me staring at my silent phone, and then a knock comes from the bathroom. Ridge swings the door open and enters my room, holding his hands with his palms up in the air as if he has no idea why I'm upset. I laugh, but it isn't a happy laugh at all.

Me: This conversation will require a laptop. I have a lot to say.

I open my computer as he makes his way back to his room. I give him a minute to log on, then I open our chat.

Ridge: Can you please explain why you're so pissed?

Me: Hmm. Let me count the ways. (1) You have a girlfriend. (2) You have a girlfriend. (3) Why, if you have a girlfriend, was I even in your BEDROOM? (4) You have a girlfriend!

Ridge: I have a girlfriend. Yes. And you were in my room because we agreed to work on lyrics together. I don't recall anything happening between us last night to warrant this reaction from you. Or am I mistaken?

Me: Ridge, it's been three weeks! I've known you for three weeks now, and you've never ONCE mentioned that you have a girlfriend. And speaking of Maggie, does she even know I moved in?

Ridge: Yes. I tell her everything. Look, it wasn't an intentional omission, I swear. You and I have just never had a conversation where she came up.

Me: Okay, I'll let it go that you failed to mention her, but I'm not about to let everything else slide.

Ridge: And this is where I'm confused, because I'm not clear on what you think we did.

Me: You're such a guy.

Ridge: Ouch? I guess.

Me: Can you honestly say that your reaction to the possibility of her being at your door earlier was a normal, innocent reaction? You were freaking out that she would see me with you, which means you were doing something you wouldn't want her to see. I know all we did was fall asleep, but what about the WAY we fell asleep? Do you think she would have been okay with the fact that you had your arms around me all night and your face was practically glued to my chest? And not only that, but what about the fact that I sat between your legs the other night? Would she have smiled and kissed you hello if she had walked in right then? I doubt it. I'm fairly certain that would have ended with me being punched.

Ugh! Why is this upsetting me so much? I bang my head lightly against the headboard out of frustration.

Moments later, Ridge appears in the doorway between our bathroom and my bedroom. He's chewing on the corner of his bottom lip. His features are a lot calmer than when he was in here just a few minutes ago. He walks slowly into my room, then sits on the edge of my bed with his laptop on his knees.

Ridge: I'm sorry.

Me: Yeah. Good. Whatever. Go away.

Ridge: Really, Sydney. I haven't been looking at it like that at all. The last thing I want is for things to be weird between us. I like you. I have fun with you. But if for one second I led you to believe that something was going to happen between us, I am so, so sorry.

I sigh and attempt to blink the tears away.

Me: I'm not upset because I thought something was going to happen between us, Ridge. I don't WANT anything to happen between us. I haven't even been single for a whole week yet. I'm upset because I feel like there was a moment, or maybe two, when—as much as neither of us wants to cross that line— we almost did. And you can deal with your actions on your own, but the fact that I was unaware that you had a girlfriend was really unfair to me. I feel like—

I lean my head back against the headboard and squeeze my eyes shut, long enough to force back the tears once more.

Ridge: You feel like what?

Me: I feel like you almost made me a Tori. I absolutely would have kissed you last night, and the fact that I didn't know you were involved with someone would have made me a Tori. I don't want to be a Tori, Ridge. I can't tell you how much their betrayal hurts me, and I will never, ever do that to another girl. So that's why I'm upset. I don't even know Maggie, yet you made me feel like I've already betrayed her. And as innocent as you may be, I'm blaming you for that one.

Ridge finishes reading my message, then calmly lies back on the bed. He brings his palms to his forehead and inhales a deep breath. We both remain still as we think about the situation. After several quiet minutes, he sits back up.

Ridge: I don't even know what to say right now other than I'm sorry. You're right. Even though I thought you knew about Maggie, I can absolutely see what you're saying. But I also need you to know that I would never do something like that to her. Granted, what happened between us last night is not something I would ever want Maggie to see, but that's mostly because Maggie doesn't understand the process of writing music. It's a very intimate thing, and because I can't hear, I do have to use my hands or my ears to understand things that come naturally to others. That's all it was. I wasn't trying to cause anything to happen between us. I was just curious. I was intrigued. And I was wrong.

Me: I understand. I never thought for a second that your intentions weren't genuine when you asked me to sing for you. Everything just happened so fast earlier, and I was still trying to recover from the fact that I woke up in your bed and the lights were flickering. Then you go and flash the word "girlfriend" in my face. It's a lot to process. And I believe you when you say you thought I knew about her.

Ridge: Thank you.

Me: Just promise me one thing. Promise me you will never be a Hunter, and I will never, ever be a Tori.

Ridge: I promise. And that's impossible, because we're so much more talented than they are.

He glances up and smiles his smiley smile at me, which makes me automatically smile in return.

Me: Now, get out of here. I'm going back to sleep, because someone spent the whole night drooling on my boobs and snoring way too loud.

Ridge laughs, but before he leaves, he messages me one last time.

Ridge: I'm excited for you to meet her. I really think you'll like her.

He closes his laptop, stands, and walks back to his room.
I close my laptop and pull the covers over my head.
I hate that my heart is wishing so bad that he didn't have a girlfriend.

• • •

"No, she already moved in," Bridgette says. Her cell phone is propped up on her shoulder, and from the sound of it, she just broke the news to her sister that I've taken the empty bedroom. Bridgette completely ignores that I'm even in the same room with her and continues talking about me.

I know the fact that I haven't clarified that I'm not deaf is a little mean, but who is she to assume I can't read lips?

"I don't know; she's a friend of Ridge's. I should have ignored him when he asked if I would go—in the *rain*, mind you—and bring her up to the apartment. Apparently, her boyfriend dumped her, and she had nowhere else to go."

She pulls a seat out at the bar and sits with her back facing me. She laughs at something the person on the other end of the line says. "Tell me about it. He seems to enjoy taking in strays, doesn't he?"

I grip the remote in my hand and hold it tightly in an attempt to keep from hurling it at the back of her head.

"I told you not to ask about Warren," she says with a sigh. "You know he irritates the hell out of me, but I just . . . *dammit*, I just can't stay away."

Wait. Did I just hear that correctly? Might Bridgette have . . . *feelings*?

She's lucky I like Warren, or the remote would be greeting her pretty little head right now. She's also lucky someone is knocking at the door loudly enough to distract me from hurting her.

Bridgette stands up and turns to face me, pointing at the front door. "SOMEONE'S . . . AT . . . THE . . . DOOR!" Rather than answer it, she walks to her bedroom and closes her door.

So hospitable, that one.

I stand and make my way to the front door, knowing it's more than likely Maggie. I place my hand on the doorknob and inhale a steady breath.

Here we go.

I open the door, and standing in front of me is one of the most beautiful women I've ever laid eyes on. Her hair is straight and jet-black, and it falls around two naturally tanned shoulders. Her face is smiling. Her whole, entire face is beaming. She's nothing but a face full of beautiful white teeth, and they're smiling at me, and it's making me smile back, even though I really don't want to.

I was really hoping she was ugly. I don't know why.

"Sydney?" she says. It's just one word, but I can tell by her voice that she's deaf, like Ridge. But, unlike Ridge, she speaks. And she enunciates really well.

"You must be the girlfriend!" I say with feigned excitement. *Is* it feigned? Maybe not. Her entire demeanor is making me feel sunny and happy, and maybe I am a tiny bit excited to meet her?

Weird.

She steps forward and gives me a hug. I close the door behind us, and she slips off her shoes and heads to the refrigerator.

"Ridge has told me a lot about you," she says as she pops open a soda, then walks to the cabinet for a glass. "I think it's great that you're helping him through his writer's block. Poor guy has been stressing for months now." She fills her cup with ice and soda. "So how are you fitting in? I see you've survived Bridgette. And Warren has to be a pain in the ass." She looks at me expectantly, but I'm still loving the fact that she's so . . . Pleasant? Likable? Cheerful?

I smile back at her and lean against the counter. I'm trying to figure out exactly how to respond to her. She's speaking to me as if she can hear me, so I reply the same way.

"I like it," I say. "I've never lived with this many people before, so it's taking some getting used to."

She smiles and tucks a lock of her hair behind her ear.

Ugh. Even her ears are pretty.

"Good," she says. "Ridge told me about your shitty birthday last weekend and how he took you out for cake, but it didn't make up for you never having the chance to celebrate."

I have to be honest. It bothers me that he told her he took me out for cake. It bothers me, because maybe he's right and he does tell her everything. And it also bothers me because he seems to tell me nothing. Not that I've earned that right from him.

God, I hate feelings. Or I hate my conscience. The two are constantly at war, and I'm not sure which one I'd rather turn off.

"So," she says, "we're going out tonight to celebrate."

I pause. "We?"

She nods. "Yeah. Me, you, Ridge, Warren, if he's not busy. We can invite Bridgette, but that's laughable." She walks past me toward Ridge's bedroom, then turns to face me again. "Can you be ready in an hour?"

"Um." I shrug. "Okay."

She opens Ridge's bedroom door and slips inside. I stand frozen, listening. Why am I listening?

I hear Maggie giggling behind the closed door, and it makes me wince.

Oh, *yay*. This should be *fun*.

Ridge

"Are you sure you don't want to stay in tonight?"

Maggie shakes her head. "That poor girl needs to have some fun, with the week she's had. And I've been so overwhelmed with my internship and the T word. I need a night out." She leans forward and kisses me on the chin. "Do you want to get a cab so you can drink, or do you want to drive?"

She knows I won't drink around her. I don't know why she always tries her reverse psychology on me. "Nice try," I sign. "I'll drive."

She laughs. "I have to change and get ready. We're leaving in an hour." She tries to slide off me, but I grip her waist and roll her onto her back. I know for a fact that it never takes her more than half an hour to get ready. That leaves a good thirty minutes.

"Allow me to help you out of your clothes, then." I pull her shirt off over her head, and my eyes drop to the very thin, intricately laced bra she has on. I grin. "Is this new?"

She nods and smiles her sexy smile. "I bought it for you. Front clasp, just how you like it."

I pinch the clasp and undo it. "Thank you. I can't wait to try it on."

She laughs and slaps my arm. I take off her bra, then lower myself on top of her and drop my mouth to hers.

I spend the next half hour reminding myself how much I've missed her. I remind myself how much I love her. I remind myself how good it feels when we're together. I keep reminding myself over and over, because for the past week, it felt as if I was starting to forget.

•   •   •

Me: Be ready in thirty minutes. We're going out.

Warren: I don't want to go, have an early shift tomorrow.

No. He has to go. I can't go out with Maggie and Sydney by myself.

Me: No, you're going. Be ready in thirty minutes.

Warren: No, I'm not. Have fun.

Me: You're going. 30.

Warren: Not going.

Me: Going.

Warren: Not.

Me: Yes.

Warren: No.

Me: Please? You owe me.

Warren: What the hell do I owe you for?

Me: Let's see, about a year's worth of rent, for one.

Warren: Low blow, man. Fine.

Thank God. I don't know what Sydney gets like when she drinks, but if she's a lightweight like Maggie is, I don't think I can handle the two of them on my own.

I walk to the kitchen, and Maggie is at the sink, pulling out the bottle of Pine-Sol. She holds it up to ask if I want any, and I shake my head.

"Figured I'd save money if I downed a couple of shots here first. You think Sydney wants any?"

I shrug but pull out my phone to ask her.

Me: You want a shot before we go?

Sydney: No, thank you. Not sure I feel like drinking tonight, but you go right ahead.

"She doesn't want any," I sign to Maggie. Warren walks out of his bedroom and sees Maggie pouring a shot from the Pine-Sol container.

Shit. There goes the hiding spot.

He doesn't even blink when he sees her filling her shot glass. "Make it two," he says to her. "If Ridge is forcing me to go out tonight, I'm getting so wasted he'll regret it."

I cock my head. "How long have you known that wasn't cleaning solution?"

He shrugs. "You're deaf, Ridge. You would be surprised how many times I'm behind you and you don't even know it." He picks up the shot Maggie poured, and they both turn their attention to something behind me. Their shocked expressions force me to turn around and see what they're looking at.

Oh, wow.

I shouldn't have turned around.

Sydney is walking out of her bedroom, but I'm not sure if it's really Sydney. This girl isn't wearing baggy shirts or walking around with her hair pulled up and a naked face. This girl is wearing a strapless black dress that's anything but simple. Her blond hair is down and thick, and I'm thinking it probably smells as incredible as it looks. She smiles past me and says

"Thanks" to either Maggie or Warren, one of whom more than likely just told her how great she looks. She's smiling at them, but then she holds her hands up and yells, "No!" just as a mist of liquid rains down on me from behind.

I spin around, and Warren and Maggie are both coughing and spitting into the sink. Warren is sipping straight from the faucet, making a face that says he didn't enjoy whatever just went down his throat.

"What the hell?" Maggie says, scrunching up her face and wiping her mouth.

Sydney runs into the kitchen with her hand over her mouth. She's shaking her head, trying not to laugh, but she looks apologetic at the same time. "I'm sorry," she keeps saying over and over.

What the hell just happened?

Warren composes himself, then turns to Sydney. He speaks and signs at the same time, which I appreciate. He can't know how isolating it feels when you're in a group of people who hear, but no matter what, he always signs when I'm in the room with him. "Did we actually just almost drink an entire shot of Pine-Sol?"

He's eyeing Sydney hard. She answers him, and he signs her response for my benefit. She says, "You two weren't supposed to drink it. It was supposed to be Ridge. And no, I didn't actually put Pine-Sol in there, idiot. I'm not trying to kill the guy. It was apple juice and vinegar."

She tried to prank me.

And she failed.

I start laughing and text her.

Me: Nice try. That was a valiant effort, although it backfired.

She flips me off.

I look at Maggie; luckily, she's laughing about it. "There is no way I could live here," she says. She walks to the refrigerator and pulls out the milk, then makes herself and Warren a quick drink to wash away the aftertaste.

"Let's go," Warren says after he downs the milk and tosses his cup into the sink. "Ridge is driving cuz I won't be able to walk in three hours."

9.

Sydney

I have no idea where we're going, but I'm doing my best to appear engaged. I'm in the backseat with Warren, and he's talking to me about the band, explaining his involvement in it. I ask the appropriate questions and nod at the appropriate moments, but my mind isn't here at all.

I know I can't expect the hurt and heartache to go away this quickly, but today has been the worst day so far since my actual birthday. I realize that all the pain I've been feeling hasn't been quite as bad because I've had Ridge this week. I don't know if it's the way he brings comedic relief when he's around or if it's because I really was developing a crush on him, but the times I've spent with him were the only times I felt remotely happy. They were the only times I wasn't thinking about what Hunter and Tori did to me.

But now, watching him in the front seat with his hand clasping Maggie's . . . I don't like it. I don't like how his thumb occasionally sweeps back and forth. I don't like the way she looks at him. I especially don't like the way he looks at her. I didn't like how he slipped his fingers through hers when we reached the bottom of the apartment stairs. I didn't like how he opened her door, then placed his hand on her lower back while she climbed inside the car. I didn't like how they had a silent conversation while he was putting the car in reverse. I didn't like how he laughed at whatever she said and then pulled her to him so he could kiss her forehead. I don't like how all of these things make me feel as though the only good moments I've had since last week are now over.

Nothing has changed. Nothing significant happened between the two of us, and I know we'll continue with the way things have been. We'll still write lyrics together. He might still listen to me sing. We'll still continue to interact the way we've done since I met him, so this situation shouldn't be bothering me.

I know in my heart that I didn't want anything to happen with him, especially at this point in my life. I know I need to be on my own. I *want* to be on my own. But I also know that the reason I'm feeling so conflicted by this entire situation is that I did have a little hope. Although I wasn't ready for anything right now, I thought the possibility would be there. I assumed that maybe someday, when I was ready, things could have developed between us.

However, now that Maggie is in the picture, I realize there can't be a *maybe someday* between us. There will never be a *maybe someday*. He loves her, and she obviously loves him, and I can't blame them, because whatever they have is beautiful. The way they look at each other and interact and obviously care about each other is something I didn't realize was missing between Hunter and me.

Maybe someday I'll have that, but it won't be with Ridge, and knowing that diminishes whatever ray of hope shone through the storm of my week.

Jesus, I'm so depressed.

I hate Hunter.

I really hate Tori.

And right now, I'm so pathetically miserable, I even hate myself.

"Are you crying?" Warren asks.

"No."

He nods. "Yes, you are. You're crying."

I shake my head. "I am not."

"You were about to," he says, looking at me sympathetically. He puts his arm around my shoulder and pulls me against him. "Chin up, little girl. Maybe tonight we can find someone who will screw the thought of that jerkoff ex right out of that pretty little head of yours."

I laugh and slap him in the chest.

"I would volunteer to do it, but Bridgette doesn't like to share," he says. "She's kind of a bitch like that, if you haven't noticed."

I laugh again, but when my eyes meet Ridge's in the rearview mirror, my smile fades. His jaw is firm, and his eyes lock with mine for a few seconds before he refocuses on the road in front of him.

He's unreadable most of the time, but I could swear I saw a small flash of jealousy behind those eyes. And I don't like how seeing him jealous that I'm leaning against Warren actually feels good.

Turning twenty-two has rotted my soul. Who am I, and why am I having these awful reactions?

We pull into the parking lot of a club. I've been here a few times with Tori, so I'm relieved that it won't be completely unfamiliar. Warren takes my hand and helps me out of the car, then puts an arm around my shoulders and walks with me toward the entrance.

"I'll make you a deal," he says. "I'll keep my hands off you tonight so guys won't assume you're madly in love with me. I hate cock blockers, and I refuse to be one. But if anyone makes you uncomfortable, just look at me and give me a signal so I can swoop in and pull you out of the situation."

I nod. "Sounds like a plan. What kind of signal do I give you?"

"I don't know. You can lick your lips seductively. Maybe squeeze your breasts together."

I elbow him in the side. "Or maybe I can just scratch my nose?"

He shrugs. "That works, too, I guess." He opens the door, and we all make our way inside. The music is overwhelming, and the second the doors close behind us, Warren leans in to shout into my ear. "There are usually booths open on the balcony level. Let's go there!" He tightens his grip on my hand, then turns to Ridge and Maggie and motions for them to follow.

• • •

I haven't had to use the secret code Warren and I agreed on, and we've been here more than two hours now. I've danced with several people, but as soon as the song ends, I make it a point to smile politely and head back to the booth. Warren and Maggie seem to have made a nice dent in the liquor stock, but Ridge hasn't had a drop. Other than a shot Warren persuaded me to take when we first arrived, I haven't had anything to drink, either.

"My feet hurt," I say.

Maggie and Ridge have danced a couple of times but that was to slow songs, so I made it a point not to watch them.

"No!" Warren says, attempting to pull me back up. "I want to dance!"

I shake my head. He's drunk and loud, and every time I try to dance with him, he ends up butchering my feet almost as badly as he butchers the moves.

"I'll dance with you," Maggie says to him. She climbs over Ridge in the booth, and Warren takes her hand. They head down to the lower level to dance, and it's the first time Ridge and I have been alone in the booth.

I don't like it.

I like it.

I don't.

I do.

See? Rotten soul. Corrupted, rotten soul.

Ridge: Having fun?

I'm not really, but I nod, because I don't want to be that annoying, brokenhearted girl who wants everyone around her to feel how miserable she is.

Ridge: I need to say something, and I may be way off base here, but I'm attempting to improve on how I unintentionally omit things from you.

I look up at him and nod again.

Ridge: Warren is in love with Bridgette.

I read his text twice. Why would he need to say that to me? Unless he thinks I like Warren.

Ridge: He's always been a flirt, so I just wanted to clear that up. I don't want to see you get hurt again. That's all.

Me: Appreciate your concern, but it's unnecessary. Really. Have no interest there.

He smiles.

Me: You were right. I like Maggie.

Ridge: I knew you would. Everyone likes Maggie. She's very likable.

I lift my eyes and look around when a Sounds of Cedar song begins to play. I scoot to the back of the booth and look over the railing. Warren and Maggie are standing by the DJ's table, and Warren is interacting with the DJ while Maggie dances around next to him.

Me: They're playing one of your songs.

Ridge: Yeah? That always happens when Warren's around. Are they playing "Getaway"?

Me: Yeah. How'd you know?

Ridge presses a flat palm to his chest and smiles.

Me: Wow. You can differentiate your songs like that?

He nods.

Me: What's Maggie's story? She communicates really well. She seems to dance really well. Does she have a different level of hearing loss from yours?

Ridge: Yes, she has mild hearing loss. She hears most things with hearing aids, which is why she also speaks so well. And she does dance well. I stick to slow songs when she wants me to dance with her, since I can't hear them.

Me: Is that why Maggie speaks out loud and you don't? Because she can hear?

His eyes swing up to mine for a few seconds, and then he looks back at his phone.

Ridge: No. I could speak if I wanted to.

I should stop. I know he's probably annoyed by these questions, but I'm too curious.

Me: Why don't you, then?

He shrugs but doesn't text me back.

Me: No, I want to know. There has to be a reason. It seems like it would make things a lot easier for you.

Ridge: I just don't. I get along fine with how I do things now.

Me: Yes, especially when Maggie and Warren are around. Why would you need to talk when they can do it for you?

I hit send before I realize I probably shouldn't have said that. I have noticed Maggie and Warren do a lot of his talking for him, though. They've ordered for him every time the waitress has come by the booth, and I've noticed Warren do it several times this week in different situations.

Ridge reads my text, then looks back up at me. It seems I made him uncomfortable, and I immediately regret saying what I did.

Me: I'm sorry. I didn't mean for that to come out how it probably sounded. I just meant you seem to let them do things for you that they wouldn't necessarily have to do if you would speak for yourself.

My explanation seems to bother him even more than the initial text. I feel as if I'm digging myself a hole.

Me: Sorry. I'll stop. It's not my place to judge your situation, because I obviously can't put myself in your shoes. I was just trying to understand.

He looks at me and pulls the corner of his bottom lip into his mouth. I've noticed he does this when he's thinking hard about something. The way he continues to stare at me makes my throat go dry. I break his gaze, pull the straw into my mouth, and take a sip of my soda. When I look back at him, he's texting again.

Ridge: I was nine when I stopped verbalizing.

His text does more to my stomach than his stare did. I don't know why.

Me: You used to talk? Why did you stop?

Ridge: It might take me a while to text the explanation.

Me: It's fine. You can tell me about it at home when we have our laptops.

He scoots to the edge of the booth and peers over the balcony. I follow his gaze down to Maggie and Warren, who are still both hovering around the DJ booth. When he sees that they're still occupied, he moves away from the railing and leans forward across the table, resting his elbows in front of him as he begins to text.

Ridge: They don't look like they're ready to leave, so I guess we have time now. Brennan and I didn't luck out in the parent department. They both had issues with addiction. They might still have them, but we wouldn't know, because we haven't spoken to either of them in years. My mother spent most of our childhood in bed, doped up on pain pills. Our father spent most of our childhood in bars. When I was five, I was enrolled in a school for the deaf. That's where I learned sign language. I would come home and teach Brennan, because neither of my parents knew ASL. I taught him because I was five years old and had never had a conversation with anyone before. I was so desperate to communicate I was forcing my two-year-old brother to learn signs like "cookie" and "window" just so I would have someone to talk to.

My heart sinks to my stomach. I look up at him, but he's still texting.

Ridge: Imagine walking into your first day of school to the realization that there is actually a way to communicate. When I saw kids having conversations with their hands, I was amazed. I lived the first five years of my life never knowing what it was like to communicate. The school began teaching me how to form words using my voice, how to read, how to sign. I spent the next few years practicing everything I learned on Brennan. He became just as fluent in ASL as I was. I wanted him to know it, but I also didn't want to use him as my way to communicate with my parents. So when I would talk to them, I would always speak my words. I couldn't hear my own voice, of course, and I know it sounds different when deaf people speak, but I wanted a way to communicate with them since they didn't know ASL. One day, when I was talking to my father, he told Brennan to tell me to shut up, then had Brennan speak for me. I didn't understand why, but he was angry. Every time I would try to talk to my father after that, the same thing would happen, and he would tell Brennan to tell me to stop voicing my words. Brennan would translate what my father wanted him to say back to me. I finally realized my father didn't want me to talk because he didn't like the way my voice sounded. It embarrassed him that I couldn't hear. He didn't like for me to speak when we were in public, because people would know I was deaf, so he would tell me to shut up every time I did it. One day at home, he became so angry that I was still doing it that he started yelling at Brennan. He assumed that since I continued speaking my words, Brennan wasn't relaying the fact that he didn't want me to speak. He was really drunk that day and took his anger too far, which wasn't uncommon. But he hit Brennan so hard upside the head it knocked him out.

Tears begin to well in my eyes, and I have to inhale a calming breath.

Ridge: He was only six years old, Sydney. Six. I never wanted to give my father another reason to hit him, so that was the last day I ever spoke out loud. I guess it just became habit after that.

He lays his phone on the table and folds his arms in front of him. He doesn't seem to be waiting for a response from me. He may not even want one. He watches me, and I know he sees the tears falling down my cheeks, but he doesn't react to them. I take a deep breath, then reach over and pick up a napkin and wipe my eyes. I wish he wouldn't see me responding like this but I can't hold it back. He smiles softly and begins to reach across the table for my hand, and then Warren and Maggie reappear at the booth.

Ridge pulls his hand back and looks up at them. Maggie's arms are draped across Warren's shoulders, and she's laughing at nothing in particular. Warren keeps trying to grab the back of the booth—it looks as if he's about to need support, too, but he can't seem to grasp anything. Ridge and I both stand up and assist them. Ridge pulls Maggie off Warren, and I wrap Warren's arm around my shoulders. He presses his forehead to mine.

"Syd, I'm so happy you got cheated on. I'm so happy you moved in."

I laugh and push his face away from mine. Ridge nods his

head toward the exit, and I nod in agreement. Another drink, and we would probably have to carry these two out.

"I like that dress you wear, Syd. That blue one? But please don't wear it again." Warren is leaning his head against mine as we make our way toward the stairs. "I don't like your ass in it, because I think I might love Bridgette, and your dress makes me love your ass."

Wow. He's really drunk if he's admitting that he might love Bridgette.

"I already told you I was burning that dress," I say, laughing.

"Good," he says with a sigh.

We reach the exit, and I notice Ridge is carrying Maggie now. Her arms are draped around his neck, and her eyes are closed. Once we reach the car, she opens her eyes as Ridge tries to stand her up. She attempts to take a step but ends up stumbling. Ridge opens the back door, and she practically falls inside. He scoots her to the other side of the seat, and she falls against the door, closing her eyes again. Ridge steps out of the way and motions for Warren to climb in. Warren steps forward and reaches up to Ridge's face. He pats Ridge's cheek and says, "I feel bad for you, buddy. I bet it's really hard not to kiss Sydney, cuz it's hard for me, and I don't even like her like you do."

Warren climbs inside the car and falls against Maggie. I'm thankful that he was too drunk to sign any of that, because I know that Ridge didn't understand what he said. I can tell by the confused look Ridge is giving me. He laughs and bends down, lifting Warren's leg, which is still hanging out of the car. He pushes it inside the car and closes the door, and my mind is still stuck on Warren's words.

Ridge reaches in front of me and pulls on the handle of the front passenger door, then opens it. I step forward, but the second Ridge's hand rests against my lower back, I pause.

I glance up at him, and he's looking straight down at me. His hand remains on my lower back as I force myself to slowly close the gap between myself and the car. The second I begin to lower myself into the seat, his hand slips away, and he waits until I'm all the way inside the car, then closes the door.

I lean my head back into the seat and close my eyes, terrified of what that simple gesture just did to me.

I hear him take his position behind the wheel, and the car cranks, but I continue to keep my eyes closed. I don't want to look at him. I don't want to feel what I feel when I look at him. I don't like how every minute I spend with him, I feel more and more like a Tori.

My phone receives a text, so I'm forced to open my eyes. Ridge is holding his phone, watching me.

> Ridge: She doesn't do this a lot. Probably not even three times a year. She's been under a lot of stress lately, and she likes to go out. It helps.

> Me: I wasn't judging her.

> Ridge: I know. I just wanted you to know she's not a raging alcoholic like I am.

He winks at me, and I laugh. I glance into the backseat, where Warren is draped across Maggie. They're both out cold. I turn back around in my seat and text him again.

> Me: Thank you for telling me all that earlier. You didn't have to, and I know you probably didn't want to, but thank you.

He gives me a sideways glance, then returns his attention to his phone.

Ridge: I've never told anyone that story. Not even Brennan. He was probably too young to even remember it.

He sets his phone down and puts the car in reverse, then begins to back out.

Why is it that the only question I wish I could ask him right now is the most inappropriate one? I want to ask him if he's ever told Maggie, but his answer shouldn't matter to me. It shouldn't matter at all, but it does.

He begins to drive, and he reaches down and turns on the radio, which confuses me. He can't hear it, so I don't understand why he would care if it was on or off.

But then I realize he didn't do it for himself.

He turned it on for me.

Ridge

After stopping at a drive-thru for food, we pull up to the apartment complex. I put the car in park.

Me: Take the food up and unlock the door while I wake them up.

She picks up our two drinks and the bag of food. She heads up to the apartment, and I walk to the back door and open it. I shake Warren awake and help him out of the car. Then I wake Maggie up and help her out. She's still too out of it to walk, so I pick her up and shut the door behind me. I make sure Warren walks ahead of me up the stairs, because I'm not positive he won't fall down them.

When we make it inside, Warren stumbles to his bedroom, and I walk Maggie into my room. I lay her on the bed and take off her shoes, then her clothes. I pull the covers over her, then head back into the dining room, where Sydney has laid out our food. It's almost midnight, and we haven't eaten since lunch. I take a seat in front of her.

Me: So now that you know one of my deep, dark secrets, I want to know one of yours.

We both have our phones out on the table while we eat. She smiles and begins to text me back.

Sydney: You have more than one deep, dark secret?

Me: We're talking about you right now. If we're going to be working together, I need to know what I'm getting myself into. Tell me about your family. Any raging alcoholics?

Sydney: No, just raging assholes. My father is a lawyer, and he hates that I'm not going to law school. My mother stays home. She's never worked a day in her life. She's a great mom, but she's also one of those perfect moms, you know? Think *Leave It to Beaver* meets *Stepford Wives*.

Me: Siblings?

Sydney: Nope. Only child.

Me: I wouldn't have pegged you as an only child. Nor would I have guessed you were a lawyer's daughter.

Sydney: Why? Because I'm not pretentious and spoiled?

I smile at her and nod.

Sydney: Well, thanks. I try.

Me: I don't mean for this to come off as insensitive, but if your father is a lawyer and you still have a relationship with your parents, why did you not call them last week? When you had nowhere to go?

Sydney: The primary thing my mother instilled in me was the fact that she didn't want me to be her. She had no education and has always been completely dependent on my father. She raised me to be very independent and financially responsible, so I've always taken pride in not asking for their help. It's hard sometimes, especially when I really need their help, but I always get by. I also don't ask for their help because my father would point out in a not-so-nice way that if I were in law school, he'd be paying for it.

Me: Wait. You're paying for school on your own? But if you changed your major to prelaw, your father would pay for it?

She nods.

Me: That's not really fair.

Sydney: Like I said, my father is an asshole. But I don't go around blaming my parents for everything. I have a lot to be thankful for. I've grown up in a relatively normal household, both of my parents are alive and well, and they support me to an extent. They're better than most, just worse than some. I hate it when people spend their entire lives blaming their parents for every bad thing that happens to them.

Me: Yeah. I completely agree, which is why I was emancipated at sixteen. Decided to take my life into my own hands.

Sydney: Really? What about Brennan?

Me: I took him with me. The courts thought he stayed with my parents, but he moved in with me. Well, with Warren. We've been friends since we were fourteen. Both of his parents are deaf, which is how he knows ASL. Once I became emancipated, they allowed me and Brennan to stay with them. My parents still had guardianship over Brennan, but as far as they were concerned, I did them a huge favor by taking him off their hands.

Sydney: Well, that was incredibly considerate of Warren's parents.

Me: Yes, they're great people. Not sure why Warren turned out the way he did, though.

She laughs.

Sydney: Did they continue to raise Brennan after you left for college?

Me: No, we actually only stayed with them for seven months. When I turned seventeen, I moved us into an apartment. I dropped out of school and got a GED so I could start college sooner.

Sydney: Wow. So you raised your brother?

Me: Hardly. Brennan lived with me, but he was never the type who could be raised. He was fourteen when we got our own place. I was only seventeen. As much as I'd like to say I was the responsible, mature adult, I was quite the opposite. Our apartment became the hangout for everyone who knew us, and Brennan partied just as hard as I did.

Sydney: That shocks me. You seem so responsible.

Me: I wasn't as wild as I probably could have been, being on my own at that young an age. Luckily, all our money went to bills and rent, so I never got into any bad habits. We just liked to have fun. Our band was formed when Brennan was sixteen and I was nineteen, so that took up a lot of our time. That's also the year I started dating Maggie, and I calmed down a lot after that.

Sydney: You've been with Maggie since you were nineteen?

I nod but don't text her back. My food has hardly been touched from all the texting, so I pick up my burger. She does the same, and we eat until both of us are finished. We stand up and clear off the table. Then she gives me a wave and heads off to her room. I sit on the couch and turn on the TV. After about fifteen minutes of channel surfing, I finally stop on a movie channel. The captioning has been turned off on the TV, but I don't bother turning it back on. I'm too tired to read and follow along with the movie, anyway.

The door to Sydney's bedroom opens, and she walks out, looking slightly startled when she sees I'm still awake. She's in one of her baggy shirts again, and her hair is wet. She walks back to her room, then comes out with her phone and sits on the couch with me.

Sydney: I'm not tired. What are you watching?

Me: I don't know, but it just started.

She pulls her feet up and rests her head on the arm of the couch. Her eyes are on the TV, but my eyes are on her. I have to admit, the Sydney who went out tonight is a completely different Sydney from the one lying here. Her makeup is gone, her hair is no longer perfect, her clothes even have holes in them, and I can't help but laugh just looking at her. If I were Hunter, I'd be punching myself in the face right now.

She's beginning to lean forward for her phone when she cuts her eyes in my direction. I want to look back at the TV and pretend she didn't just catch me staring at her, but that would make this even more awkward. Luckily, she doesn't seem to care that I was looking at her, because she gives her attention to her phone.

Sydney: How are you watching this without captions?

Me: Too tired to read along right now. Sometimes I just like to watch movies without captions and try to guess what they're saying.

Sydney: I want to try it. Put it on mute, and we'll deaf-watch it together.

I laugh. Deaf-watch? That's a new one. I point the remote to the TV and press the mute button. She turns her attention back to the TV, but once again, I fail to look away from her.

I don't understand my sudden obsession with staring at her, but I can't seem to stop. She's several feet away. We aren't touching. We aren't speaking. She isn't even looking at me. Yet the simple fact that I'm staring at her makes me feel incredibly guilty, as if I'm doing something wrong. Staring is harmless, so why do I feel so guilty?

I attempt to talk myself out of the feelings of guilt, but deep down, I know exactly what's happening.

I don't feel guilty simply because I'm staring at her. I feel guilty for how it's making me feel.

•   •   •

This makes twice in a row I've been woken up like this. I push away the hand that's slapping me and open my eyes. Warren is standing over me. He slaps a piece of paper on my chest, then whacks his hand against the side of my head. He walks to the front door and grabs his keys, then leaves for work.

Why is he going to work this early?

I pick up my phone, and it says 6:00 A.M. I guess he's *not* leaving early.

I sit up on the couch and see Sydney still curled up at the

other end, sound asleep. I pull the paper from Warren off my chest and look down at it.

How about you go to your room and sleep in the bed with your girlfriend!

I wad up the note and stand, then take it to the trash can and bury it. I go back to the couch, put my hand on Sydney's shoulder, and shake her awake. She rolls onto her back and rubs her eyes, then looks up at me.

She smiles when she sees me. That's it. All she did just now was smile, but all of a sudden, my chest is on fire, and it feels as if a wave of heat just rolled down the entire length of my body. I recognize this feeling, and it's not good. It's not good at all. I haven't felt this way since I was nineteen.

Since I first began developing feelings for Maggie.

I point to Sydney's room to let her know she should go to bed, then quickly turn around and head into my bedroom. I pull off my jeans and T-shirt and softly slide into bed next to Maggie. I wrap my arms around her, pull her against my chest, and spend the next half hour falling asleep to a broken record of reminders.

You're in love with Maggie.
Maggie's perfect for you.
You're perfect for her.
She needs you.
You're happy when you're with her.
You're with the one and only girl you're meant to be with.

10.

Sydney

It's been two weeks since Ridge and I have worked on lyrics together. A few days after Maggie went home, Ridge ended up leaving for six days because of a family emergency. He was vague about what the emergency was, but it reminded me of when I still lived with Tori and he was absent from his balcony for several days. A family emergency was his excuse then, too.

Based on conversations I've heard Warren have on the phone with Brennan, I know it didn't have anything to do with Brennan. But he's never mentioned having family other than Brennan. When Ridge returned a few days ago, I asked him if everything was okay and he said things were fine. He didn't seem to want to share any details, and I'm trying to remind myself that his personal life is none of my concern.

I've immersed myself in school, and every now and then, I'll attempt to write lyrics on my own, but it isn't the same when I don't have the music to go along with it. Ridge has been home for a few days now, but he's spent most of his time in his room catching up on work, and I can't help but wonder if he's kept his distance for other reasons.

I've been hanging out with Warren a lot and have learned more about his relationship with Bridgette. I haven't had any more interactions with her, so as far as I know, she still assumes I'm deaf.

Based on what Warren has told me, their relationship is

anything but typical. Warren never met Bridgette before she moved in six months ago, but she's a longtime friend of Brennan's. Warren says that he and Bridgette don't get along at all, and during the day, they live separate lives. But at night, it's a completely different story. He has tried to go into more detail than I care to hear, so I force him to shut up when he begins to overshare.

I'm really wishing he would shut up right now, because he's in the midst of one of his oversharing moments. I have to leave for class in half an hour, and I'm trying to finish reading a last-minute chapter, but he's intent on telling me all about last night and how he wouldn't let her take her Hooters uniform off because he likes to role-play, and oh, my God, why does he think I care to hear this?

Luckily, Bridgette walks out of her room, and it's more than likely the first time I've ever been happy to see her.

"Good morning, Bridgette," Warren says, his eyes following her across the living room. "Sleep well?"

"Screw you, Warren," she says in return.

I'm beginning to understand that this is their typical morning greeting. She walks into the kitchen and glances at me, then at Warren seated next to me on the couch. She narrows her eyes at him and turns toward the refrigerator. Ridge is at the dining-room table, concentrating on his laptop.

"I don't like how she's up your ass all the time," Bridgette says with her back to me.

Warren looks at me and laughs. Apparently, Bridgette still assumes I can't hear her, but I'm not finding much humor in the fact that she's talking shit about me.

She spins around and eyes Warren. "You think that's funny?" she says to him. "The girl obviously has it bad for you, and you can't even respect me enough to distance yourself from her until I'm out of the house?" She turns her back to us again. "First she gives Ridge some sob story so he'll let her move in, and now she's taking advantage of the fact that you know sign language so she can flirt with you."

"Bridgette, stop." Warren isn't laughing anymore, because he can see how white my knuckles are, clasped around my book. I think he's afraid Bridgette's about to get hit upside the head with a hardback. He's right to be afraid.

"*You* stop, Warren," she says, turning back around to face him. "Either stop crawling into bed with me at night or stop shacking up on the couch with *her* during the day."

I drop my book onto my lap with a loud slap, then kick my feet up and down against the floor out of frustration, anger, and flat-out annoyance. I can't put up with this girl for another second.

"Bridgette, please!" I yell. "Shut up! Shut up, shut up, shut *up*! Christ! I don't know why you think I'm deaf, and I'm definitely *not* a whore, and I'm not using sign language to flirt with Warren. I don't even *know* sign language. And from now on, please stop yelling when you speak to me!"

Bridgette cocks her pretty little head, and her mouth hangs open in shock. She silently stares at me for several seconds. No one in the room makes a move. She turns her attention to Warren, and the anger in her eyes is replaced with hurt. She immediately looks away once the hurt takes over, and she heads straight back to her room.

I glance over to see Ridge staring at me, more than likely wondering what the hell just happened. I lean my head back against the couch and sigh.

I was hoping that would feel good, but it didn't feel good at all.

"Well," Warren says, "there goes my chance to act out all the role-playing scenes I've been imagining. Thanks a lot, Sydney."

"Screw you, Warren," I say, understanding a little bit where Bridgette's attitude comes from.

I slide my book off my lap and stand up, then walk to

Bridgette's door. I knock, but she doesn't open it. I knock again, turn the knob, and push the door slightly open to peek inside.

"Bridgette?"

A pillow meets the back of the door with a thud. "Get the hell out of my room!"

I ignore her and open the door a little further until I can see her. She's sitting on her bed, with her knees pulled up to her chest. When she sees me coming into her room, she quickly wipes her eyes, then turns the other way.

She's crying, and now I really feel shitty. I walk to her bed and sit on the edge of it, as far out of her reach as possible. I may feel bad, but I'm still scared to death of her.

"I'm sorry," I say.

She rolls her eyes and falls back onto the bed in a huff. "You are not," she says. "I don't blame you. I deserved it."

I tilt my head. Did she really just admit that she deserved it? "I'm not gonna lie, Bridgette. You are kind of a bitch."

She laughs softly, then folds her arm over her eyes. "God, I know. I just get so annoyed with people, but I can't help it. It's not like it's my goal in life to be a bitch."

I lie back on the bed with her. "So don't be one, then. It takes way more effort to be a bitch than it does to not be one."

She shakes her head. "You can say that because you're not a bitch."

I sigh. She may not think I'm a bitch, but I sure have been feeling like one lately. "For what it's worth, I'm more evil than you might think. I may not express my feelings in quite the same fashion as you, but I definitely have evil thoughts. And lately, evil intentions. I'm beginning to think I'm not as nice as I always thought I was."

Bridgette doesn't respond to my admission for a few quiet moments. She finally sighs heavily and sits up on the bed. "Can I ask you something? Now that I know you can actually answer me?"

I sit up, too, and nod.

"Are you and Warren . . ." She pauses. "You guys seem to get along really well, and I was curious if . . ."

I smile, because I know where she's going with this, and I interrupt her string of thought. "Warren and I are friends, and we could never be more than friends. He's sort of oddly infatuated with this bitchy Hooters waitress he knows."

Bridgette smiles, but then she quickly stops smiling and looks straight at me. "How long has Warren known that I thought you were deaf?"

I think back on the past few weeks. "Since the morning after I moved in?" I wince, knowing Warren's about to experience the side of Bridgette we all know too well. "But please go easy on him, Bridgette. As strangely as you two show it, he really does like you. He might even love you, but he was drunk when he said that, so I don't know for sure."

If it's possible to hear a heart stop, I just heard hers come to a screeching halt. "He said that?"

I nod. "A couple of weeks ago. We were leaving the club, and he was wasted, but he said something about how he's pretty sure he might love you. I probably shouldn't be telling you this, though."

She drops her eyes to the floor and is quiet for several seconds, then looks back up at me. "You know, most things people say when they're drunk are more accurate and honest than the things they say when they're sober."

I nod, unsure if that's a true fact or just a Bridgette fact. She stands up and walks swiftly to the door, then swings it open.

Oh, no.

She's about to kill Warren, and it's partly my fault. I stand up and rush to the door, prepared to catch the blame for telling her what Warren said. However, once I reach the living room, she's swinging her leg over his, sliding onto his lap. Warren's eyes are wide, and he's looking at her in fear, which tells me this isn't one of her usual moves.

Bridgette takes Warren's face in her hands, and he hesitantly brings his hands to her lower back. She sighs, staring him hard in the eyes. "I can't believe I'm falling in love with such a stupid, stupid asshole," she says to him.

He stares at her for several seconds while her comment registers, and then his hands fly up to the back of her head and he crashes their lips together. He scoots forward and stands with Bridgette wrapped around him. Then, without breaking for air, he takes her directly to his bedroom, where the door shuts behind them.

I'm smiling, because Bridgette is more than likely the only girl in existence who could pull off calling someone an asshole and in the same breath confess her love. And oddly enough, Warren is probably one of the few guys who would find that appealing.

They're perfect for each other.

Ridge: How in the hell did you pull that one off? I was waiting for her to come out here and strangle him. You spend two minutes with her, and she's all over him.

Me: She's actually not as bad as she seems.

Ridge: Really?

Me: Well, maybe she is. But I guess I admire that about her. She's true to herself.

Ridge smiles, sets his phone down, and drops his eyes back to his laptop. There's something different about him now. I can't pinpoint exactly what it is, but I can see it in his eyes. He looks distraught. Or sad. Or maybe just tired?

He actually looks like a little bit of all three, and it makes me hurt for him. When I first met him, he seemed to have everything together. Now that I've gotten to know him better, I'm beginning to think that's not the case. The guy standing in front of me right now looks as if his life is a mess, and I haven't even begun to scratch the surface.

Ridge: I'm still a little behind on work, but I should be caught up by tonight. If you feel like running through a new song, you know where to find me.

Me: Sounds good. I have an afternoon study group, but I'll be back by seven.

He smiles halfheartedly and heads to his room. I know I'm beginning to understand most of his expressions. The one he just shot me was definitely a look of nervousness.

Ridge

I assumed she didn't feel like writing tonight when she didn't show, and I told myself I was okay with that.

However, it's a few minutes past eight, and my light just flickered. I can't ignore the rush of adrenaline pumping through me. I tell myself my body is having the reaction it's having because I'm passionate about writing music, but if that were the case, why don't I get this excited when I write alone? Or with Brennan?

I close my eyes and gently lay my guitar next to me while inhaling a steady breath. It's been weeks since we've done this. Since the night she let me hear her sing and it completely changed the dynamic of our working relationship.

That's not her fault, though. I'm not even sure if it's my fault. It's nature's fault, because attraction is an ugly beast, and I'll be damned if I don't conquer it.

I can do this.

I open the door to my bedroom and step aside while she comes in with her notebook and her laptop. She walks confidently toward the bed and drops down onto it, then opens her laptop. I sit back down and open mine.

Sydney: I couldn't pay attention in class today, because all I wanted to do was write lyrics. I wouldn't let myself write any, though, because it comes so much better when you play. I've missed this. I didn't think I would like it at first, and it made me nervous, but I love writing lyrics. Love, love, love it. Let's go, I'm ready.

She's smiling at me and giddily patting her palms against the mattress.

I smile back as I lean against the headboard and begin playing the opening to a new song I've been working on. I haven't finished it yet, but I'm hoping that with her help, we'll make some headway tonight.

I play the song several times, and she watches me some of the time, then writes some of the time. She uses her hands to tell me to pause or back up or move on to the next chorus or to restart the song altogether. I keep a close eye on her while I play, and we continue this dance for more than an hour. She does a lot of scratching out and makes a heck of a lot of faces that I'm not sure convey that she's having any fun.

She eventually sits up and tears the paper out of the notebook, then wads it up and tosses it into the trash can. She slaps her notebook shut and shakes her head.

Sydney: I'm sorry, Ridge. Maybe I'm just exhausted, but it's not clicking right now. Can we try this again tomorrow night?

I nod, doing my best to hide my disappointment. I don't like seeing her frustrated. She takes her laptop and notebook and starts to walk back toward her bedroom. She turns back around and mouths, "Good night."

As soon as she disappears, I'm off the bed and digging through the trash can. I pull out her wadded-up sheet of paper and take it back to my bed and unfold it.

> *Watching him from here*
> *So far away*
> *Want him closer than my heart can take*
> *I want him here I want*
> *Maybe one of these days Someday*

There are random sentences, some marked out, some not. I read all of them, attempting to work my way around them.

> *I'd run for ~~him~~ you, if I could stand*
> *But I can't make that demand*
> *I can't be his right now*
> ~~*Why can't he take me away*~~

Reading her words feels like an invasion of her privacy. But is it? Technically, we're in this together, so I should be able to read what she's writing as she writes it.

But there's something different about this song. It's different because this song doesn't sound like it's about Hunter.

This song sounds a little like it could be about me.

I shouldn't be doing this. I should not be picking up my phone right now, and I should definitely not be contemplating how to persuade her to help me finish this song tonight.

Me: Don't be mad, but I'm reading your lyrics. I think I know where your frustration is coming from.

Sydney: Could it be coming from the fact that I suck at writing lyrics and a few songs is all I had in me?

I pick up my guitar and head to her bedroom. I knock and open her door, assuming she's still decent since she just left my room two minutes ago. I walk to her bed and sit, then grab her notebook and pen and place her lyrics on top of the notebook. I write a note and hand it to her.

You have to remember the band you're writing lyrics for is all guys. I know it's hard to write from a male point of view, since you're obviously not male. If you stop writing this song from your own point of view and try to feel it from a different point of view, the lyrics might come. Maybe it's been hard because you know a guy will be singing it, but the feelings are coming from you. Just flip it around and see what happens.

She reads my note, then picks up the pen and shifts back on her bed. She looks at me and nods her head toward my guitar, indicating that she'll give it a try. I scoot off the bed and onto the floor, then stand my guitar upright and pull it against my chest. When I'm working out chords to a new song, it helps to play this way sometimes so I can feel the vibrations more clearly.

I close my eyes, lean my head against the guitar, and begin playing.

11.

Sydney

Oh, God. He's doing that thing again. The mesmerizing thing.

When I've seen him play his guitar like this in the past, it was before I knew he couldn't hear himself play. I thought maybe he just played this way to get a different angle on the strings, but now I know he does it so he can feel the music better. I don't know why, but knowing this makes me love watching him even more.

I should probably be working on the lyrics, but I watch him play the entire song without once opening his eyes. When he finishes, I quickly glance down to my notebook, because I know he's about to open his eyes and look up at me. I pretend I'm writing, and he flips his guitar around the correct way, then leans back against my dresser and begins playing the song again.

I focus on the lyrics and think about what he said. Ridge was right. I wasn't thinking about the fact that a guy would be singing them. I was focused on pouring my feelings onto paper. I close my eyes and try to picture Ridge singing the song.

I try to imagine what it would be like to be honest about what I'm feeling for him and use that to take the lyrics a little further. I open my eyes and cross out the first line of the song, then begin rewriting the first verse.

> ~~Watching him from here~~
> *Seeing something from so far away*

Get a little closer every day
Thinking that I want to make it mine

I think the real reason I'm not able to write tonight is that every line that ends up on paper is about Ridge, and I know Ridge will be able to see through it. He pulled the lyrics out of the trash and already read through them, so he has to have an idea. Still . . . he's here, wanting me to finish the song. I focus on the second verse and try to keep his advice in mind.

I'd run for ~~him~~ you if I could stand
~~But I can't make that demand~~
What I want I can't demand
'Cause what I want is you

I continue to go through the lyrics on the page, crossing out the old lines and changing them up as Ridge plays the song several times.

~~If I could be his, I would wait~~
And if I can't be yours now
I'll wait here on this ground
Till you come, till you take me away
Maybe someday
Maybe someday

The page becomes messy and hard to read, so I set it aside and open my notebook to rewrite everything. Ridge stops playing for a few minutes while I transfer everything onto the new page. When I look up at him, he points to the page, wanting to read what I've written. I nod.

He walks to the bed and sits next to me, leaning in toward me to read what I've got so far.

I'm extremely aware that he might see right through the lyrics and know they have more to do with him than with Hunter, which causes panic to course through my veins. He pulls the notebook closer to him, but it's still on my lap. His shoulder is pressed to mine, and his face is so close he could probably feel my breath against his cheek . . . if I were breathing. I force my eyes to fall where his have, onto the lyrics rewritten across the page on my lap.

> *I try to ignore what you say*
> *You turn to me*
> *I turn away*

Ridge picks up the pen and marks through the last line, then tilts his head to face me. He points the pen at himself and makes a writing motion in the air, indicating that he wants to change something.

I nod, full of nerves and fear that he doesn't like it. He presses his pen to the paper, next to the lyrics he crossed out. He pauses for a few seconds before writing and slowly turns to face me again. His expression is full of trepidation, and I'm curious about what's causing it. His eyes fall from mine, slowly grazing over me until his attention is back on the page. He inhales and carefully exhales, then begins writing the new lyrics. I watch him write out the lyrics to the entire song as I follow closely along, deciphering the new lyrics he adds in himself.

> MAYBE SOMEDAY
> *Seeing something from so far away*
> *Get a little closer every day*
> *Thinking that I want to make it mine*
>
> *I'd run for you if I could stand*
> *But what I want I can't demand*
> *'Cause what I want is you*

Chorus:
And if I can't be yours now
I'll wait here on this ground
Till you come
Till you take me away
Maybe Someday
Maybe Someday

I try to ignore what you say
You turn to me, I turn away
But Cupid must have shot me twice

I smell your perfume on my bed
Thoughts of you invade my head
Truths are written, never said

Repeat Chorus

You say it's wrong, but it feels right
You cut me loose, then hold on tight
Words unfinished, like our song

Nothing good can come this way
Lines are drawn, but then they fade
For her I bend, for you I break

Repeat Chorus

When he's finished writing, he sets the pen down across the paper. His eyes turn to mine again, and I don't know if he's expecting me to respond to what he just wrote, but I can't. I'm trying not to allow myself to feel as if there's any truth behind his lyrics, but his words from the first night we wrote together flash through my head.

"They're your words, Sydney. Words that came from you."

He was telling me then that lyrics have truth behind them, because they come from somewhere inside the person who wrote them. I look back down at the page.

For her I bend, for you I break

Oh, my God, I can't. I didn't ask for this. I don't *want* this.

But it feels so good. His words feel good, his closeness feels good, his eyes searching mine make my heart go haywire, and for the life of me, I can't figure out how something that feels like this can be so wrong.

I'm not a bad person.

Ridge isn't a bad person.

How can two good people who both have such good intentions end up with feelings, derived from all the goodness, that are so incredibly bad?

Ridge's expression grows more concerned, and he pulls his gaze away from mine and picks up his phone.

Ridge: Are you okay?

IIa. Am I okay? Yeah. That's why my palms are sweating and my chest is heaving and I'm clenching the sheet beside me on the bed so I don't do something to him with these hands that I'll never forgive myself for.

I nod, then gently push him aside as I stand up and walk to the bathroom. I shut the door behind me and lean against it, closing my eyes and silently repeating the mantra in my head that I've been repeating for weeks now.

Maggie, Maggie, Maggie, Maggie, Maggie.

Ridge

After several minutes, she finally walks back into her bedroom. She smiles at me, walks to the bed, and picks up her phone.

Sydney: Sorry. I felt sick.

Me: You okay?

Sydney: Yeah. Just needed water, I guess. I love the lyrics, Ridge. They're perfect. Do we need to run through them again, or can we call it a night?

I really would like to run through them again, but she looks tired. I'd also give anything to feel her sing them again, but I'm not sure that's a good idea. I already beat up my conscience enough while I was writing the rest of the lyrics down. However, the fact that I was more than likely writing about her didn't seem to stop me, because the only thing on my mind was the simple fact that I was actually *writing*. I haven't been able to write lyrics in months, and in just a matter of minutes, it was as if a fog lifted and the words began to flow effortlessly. I would have kept going if I didn't feel I'd already gone way too far.

Me: We'll call it a night. I'm really happy with this one, Syd.

She smiles, and I pick up my guitar and head to my room.

I spend the next several minutes transferring her lyrics into the music program on my laptop, and filling in the guitar chords. Once it's all entered, I hit send, close it out, and text Brennan.

> Me: Just sent you a very rough draft with lyrics. I really want Sydney to hear this one, so if you have time this week to work up a rough acoustic, send it over. I think it'll be good for her to finally be able to hear something she created come to life.

> Brennan: Looking at it now. I hate to admit this, but I think you were right about her. She really was sent to earth just for us.

> Me: Starting to seem that way.

> Brennan: Give me an hour. Not busy, so I'll see what we can work up.

An hour? He's sending it tonight? I immediately text Sydney.

> Me: Try not to fall asleep. I might have a little surprise for you after a while.

> Sydney: Um, . . . okay?

• • •

Forty-five minutes later, I get an e-mail with an attachment from Brennan that says, *Rough cut, Maybe Someday.* I open it on my phone, find a set of earbuds in the kitchen drawer, and head to Sydney's room. She opens the door after I knock and lets me into her room. I walk over to sit on her bed and motion to the spot on the mattress beside me. She looks at me questioningly but walks to the bed. I hand her the earbuds and pat her pillow, so she lies down and places them in her ears. She continues to watch me warily, as if I'm about to pull an elaborate prank on her.

I scoot down next to her and prop myself up on my elbow, then hit play. I set the phone down between us and watch her.

A few seconds pass, and her head swings in my direction. An "Oh, my God" passes her lips, and she's looking at me as if I've just given her the world.

And it feels pretty damn good.

She smiles and puts her hand over her mouth as her eyes fill with tears. She tilts her face back up to the ceiling, more than likely because she's embarrassed by her emotional reaction. She shouldn't be. It's exactly what I was hoping to see.

I continue to watch her as she listens, and her face conveys a mixture of emotions. She smiles, then exhales, then closes her eyes. When the song ends, she looks at me and mouths, "Again."

I smile and hit play on my phone again. I continue to watch her, but the second her lips begin moving and I realize she's singing along to the song, my smile is washed away by a sudden emotion I didn't expect to feel at all.

Jealousy.

Never in all my life and in all my years of living in a world of silence have I wanted to hear something as much as I want to hear her sing right now. I want to hear her so bad it physically hurts. The walls of my chest feel as if they're closing in on my heart, and I don't even realize that my hand has moved to her chest until she turns to me, startled. I shake my head, not wanting her to stop. She nods slightly, but the beat of her heart against my hand is increasing by the second. I can feel the vibration of her voice against my palm, but the material between my hand and her skin hinders my ability to feel her the way I want to. I move my hand upward, until it's at the base of her throat, and then I slide it up even farther, until my fingers and palm are flush against her neck. I scoot closer to her so that my chest is pressed against her side, because the overwhelming need to hear her has completely taken over, and

I don't allow myself to think about where the invisible lines are drawn.

The vibration of her voice stops, and I feel her swallow as she looks up at me with the exact emotions that inspired most of the lines in this song.

Say it's wrong, but it feels right.

There's no other way to describe how I feel. I know that the way I think about her and feel about her is wrong, but I struggle so much with how *right* it feels when I'm with her.

She's no longer singing. My hand is still wrapped around her throat, and her face is tilted toward mine. I slide my hand a little higher until it's grazing her jaw. I run my finger around the cord to the earbuds and pull them away from her. I return my fingers to her jaw, slowly slipping my hand behind her neck. My palm conforms so perfectly to the back of her head it's as if my hands were made to hold her like this. I gently pull her toward me, and she turns her body slightly toward mine. Our chests meet, and it creates a force so powerful that every other part of me is demanding to be pressed against every other part of her.

She reaches her hands up to my neck and lightly places her palms against my skin, then slowly eases her fingers up and into my hair. Having her so close feels as though we've created our own personal space, and nothing from outside our world can make its way in, and nothing from inside our world can make its way out.

Her breaths fall in waves against my lips, and although I can't hear them, I imagine they sound like how a heartbeat feels. I let my forehead fall against hers, and I feel a rumble from deep within my chest rise up my throat. The sound I feel pass my lips causes her mouth to open in a gasp, and the way her lips are slightly parted causes my mouth to immediately connect with hers in search of the relief I desperately need.

Relief is exactly what I find the second our lips meet. It's as if every pent-up, denied feeling I've held toward her is suddenly uncaged, and I'm able to breathe for the first time since I met her.

Her fingers continue to sift through my hair, and my grip tightens against the back of her head, pulling her closer. She allows my tongue to slip inside and find hers. She's warm and soft, and the vibrations from her moans begin to leave her mouth and flow straight into mine.

My lips softly close over hers, and then I part them, and we do it all over again, but with less hesitation and more desperation. Her hands are now running down my back, and my hand is slipping to her waist, and my tongue is exploring the incredible way hers dances against mine to a song only our mouths can hear. The desperation and speed at which we're escalating this kiss make it apparent that we're both attempting to get as much out of each other as we can before the moment ends.

Because we both know it has to end.

I grip her waist tightly as my heart begins to tear in two, half of it remaining where it's always been, with Maggie, and the other half being pulled to the girl beneath me.

Nothing in my life has ever felt so good yet hurt so achingly *bad*.

I tear my mouth away from hers, and we both gasp for breath as the desperate grip she has on me keeps me locked against her. I refuse to allow our mouths to reconnect as I struggle to figure out which half of my heart I want to save.

I press my forehead to hers and keep my eyes closed, inhaling and exhaling in rapid succession. She doesn't attempt to kiss me again, but I can feel her chest as her movements change from begging for breath to fighting back tears. I pull back and open my eyes, looking down on her.

Her eyes are shut tightly, but the tears are beginning to fall. She turns her face and covers her mouth with her hand as she tries to roll onto her side, away from me. I lift up onto my hands and look down at what I've done to her.

I've done the one thing I promised her I would never do.

I just made her a Tori.

I wince and drop my forehead to the side of her head and press my lips against her ear. I find her hand and reach for the pen beside us on the nightstand. I turn her hand over and press the tip of the pen to her palm.

I'm so sorry.

I kiss her palm, then crawl off the bed and back away. She opens her eyes long enough to look at her hand. She makes a tight fist and pulls her hand to her chest, then begins to sob into her pillow. I take my guitar, my phone, and my shame . . . and I leave her completely alone.

12.

Sydney

I don't want to get out of bed. I don't want to go to class. I definitely don't want to go job hunting again. I don't want to do anything but keep this pillow pulled over my eyes, because it's creating a nice barrier between myself and every mirror in this apartment.

I don't want to look in the mirror, because I'm scared I'll see myself for who I really am this time. A girl with no morals or respect for other people's relationships.

I can't believe I kissed him last night.

I can't believe he kissed *me*.

I can't believe I broke into tears the second he pulled away from me and I saw the look on his face. I didn't think it was possible to cram so much regret and sorrow into one expression. Seeing how much he regretted being in that moment with me was one of the biggest blows my heart has ever taken. It hurt worse than what Hunter did to me. It hurt worse than what Tori did to me.

But as much as it hurt seeing the regret on his face, it was nothing compared to the guilt and shame I felt when I thought of what I had done to Maggie. What *he* had done to Maggie.

I knew the moment he put his hand on my chest and moved closer to me that I should have flown off the bed and made him leave the room.

But I didn't. I *couldn't*.

The closer he moved and the longer we stared at each other, the more my body was consumed by need. It wasn't a basic need, like a need for water when I'm thirsty or a need for food when I'm hungry. It was an insatiable need for relief. Relief from the want and desire that had been pent up for so long.

I never realized how powerful desire could be. It consumes every part of you, enhancing your senses by a million. When you're in the moment, it enhances your sense of sight, and all you can do is focus on the person in front of you. It enhances your sense of smell, and suddenly, you're aware of the fact that his hair has just been washed and his shirt is fresh out of the dryer. It enhances your sense of touch and makes your skin prickle and your fingertips tingle, and it leaves you craving to *be* touched. It enhances your sense of taste, and your mouth becomes hungry and wanting, and the only thing that can satisfy it is the relief of another mouth in search of the same.

But the sense my desire enhanced the most?

Hearing.

As soon as Ridge placed the headphones in my ears and the music began to play, the hair on my arms rose, chills erupted from my skin, and it felt as if my heart rate slowly conformed to the beat of the song.

As much as Ridge craved that sense, too, he couldn't experience it. In that moment, all of his other senses combined failed to make up for the one sense he desired the most. He wanted to hear me just as much as I wanted him to hear me.

What happened between us didn't happen because we were weak. Ridge didn't run his hand up my jaw and around to the back of my head simply because I was in front of him and he was in the mood to make out. He didn't press his body against mine because he thinks I'm attractive and knew it would feel good. He didn't part my lips with his because he enjoys kissing and knew he wouldn't get caught.

Despite how hard we tried to fight it, all of those things happened between us because our feelings for each other are becoming so much stronger than our desire. Desire is easy to fight. Especially when the only weapon desire possesses is attraction.

It's not so easy when you're trying to win a war against the heart.

• • •

The house has been quiet since I woke up more than an hour ago. The more I lie here and allow myself to think about what happened, the less I want to face him. I know if we don't get it over with, the confrontation will only be harder the longer we wait.

I reluctantly get dressed and head to the bathroom to brush my teeth. His bedroom is quiet, and he usually has late nights that result in late mornings, so I decide to let him sleep. I'll wait it out in the living room. I hope Warren and Bridgette are either occupied with each other in a bed somewhere or still asleep, because I don't know if I can take either of them this morning.

I open the door and walk into the living room.

I pause.

Turn around, Sydney. Turn around and go back to your room.

Ridge is standing at the bar. However, it isn't the sight of Ridge that's rendered me completely immobile. It's the girl he has his arms around. It's the girl he's pressed against. It's the girl he's looking directly at, as if she's the only thing that has, does, and will ever matter to him. It's the girl who planted herself between me and my *maybe someday.*

Warren exits his bedroom and sees them standing together in the kitchen. "Hey, Maggie. I thought you weren't coming for a couple more weeks."

Maggie spins around at the sound of Warren's voice. Ridge's eyes move from Maggie over to me. His body tenses, and he stands up straighter, putting a slight distance between the two of them.

I'm still immobile, or I'd be putting distance between myself and all three of them.

"I'm about to leave," Maggie says, and signs simultaneously, facing Warren. Ridge steps away from her, then quickly breaks his gaze from mine and refocuses his attention on Maggie. "My grandfather was admitted to the hospital yesterday. I got here last night." She turns and gives Ridge a light peck on the lips, then heads for the front door. "It's nothing serious, but I'm staying with him until they release him tomorrow."

"Oh, man. Sorry about that," Warren says. "But you'll be here the weekend of my party, right?"

Party?

Maggie nods and takes a step back toward Ridge. She circles her arms around his neck, and he wraps his arms around her waist—two simple movements that completely shatter entire sections of my heart.

He rests his mouth against hers and closes his eyes. He brings his hands to her face, then pulls back and leans in again to kiss her on the tip of her nose.

Ouch.

Maggie exits the apartment without ever having noticed that I was standing here. Ridge closes the door behind her, turns around, and brings his eyes back to mine with an unreadable expression.

"What are we doing today?" Warren asks, moving his head back and forth between Ridge and me. Neither of us breaks our stare to respond to him. After several seconds, Ridge makes the slightest movement with his eyes, motioning toward his bedroom. He turns to Warren and signs something, and I walk back to my room.

It's amazing how many reminders I've had to give my organs in the last three minutes that should be basic, common knowledge.

Breathe in, breathe out.

Contract, expand.

Beat, beat, pause. Beat, beat, pause.

Inhale, exhale.

I walk to the bathroom and head for Ridge's bedroom. It was obvious he wants to talk, and I still think confronting it now is better than waiting. It's definitely better than not confronting it at all.

The journey across the bathroom is only a few feet and should take no longer than a few seconds, but I somehow stretch it out for five whole minutes. I place a nervous hand on his doorknob, then open it and walk into his room.

He's walking in at the same time as I'm closing the door to the bathroom. We pause and stare at each other. These stare-downs are going to have to end, because my heart can't take much more.

We both walk to his bed, but I pause before sitting down. I assume we're about to do some serious talking, so I hold up my finger and turn to get my laptop out of my room.

He's sitting on his bed with his laptop when I return, so I sit, lean against the headboard, and open mine. He hasn't messaged me yet, so I type something to him first.

Me: Are you okay?

I hit send, and after he reads my question, he turns his face toward mine and appears slightly puzzled. He turns back to his computer and begins typing.

Ridge: In what sense?

Me: All of them, I guess. I know it was probably difficult seeing Maggie after what happened between us, so I just wanted to know if you were okay.

Ridge: I think I'm a little confused right now. Are you not pissed at me?

Me: Should I be?

Ridge: Considering what happened last night, I would say so.

Me: I have no more of a right to be mad at you than you do to be mad at me. I'm not saying I'm not upset, but how will being mad at you help us work through this?

He reads my message and expels a huge breath, leaning his head back against the headboard. He closes his eyes for a moment before lifting his head and responding to me.

Ridge: Maggie showed up last night an hour after I got back to my room. I was convinced you were going to barge in and tell her what a jerk I am for kissing you. Then, in the kitchen earlier, when I saw you standing outside your door, I was bracing myself.

Me: I would never tell her, Ridge.

Ridge: Thank you for that. So what now?

Me: I don't know.

Ridge: Can we not do the thing where we brush it under the rug and act like it never happened, because I don't think that's going to work with us. I have a lot I need to say, and I'm scared if I don't say it right now, I'll never say it.

Me: I have a lot to say, too.

Ridge: You first.

Me: No, you first.

Ridge: How about we go at the same time? When we're both finished typing, we'll hit send together.

Me: Deal.

I have no idea what he's about to say to me, but I don't let it influence what I need to say to him. I tell him exactly what I want him to know, then I pause and wait for him to finish typing. When he finally stops, we look at each other, and he nods, and we both hit enter.

Me: I think what happened between us happened for a lot of reasons. We're obviously attracted to each other, we have a lot in common, and under any other circumstance, I honestly believe we'd be good for each other. I could see myself with you, Ridge. You're smart, talented, funny, compassionate, sincere, and a little bit evil, which I like. ;) And last night—I can't even describe it. It is by far the most I've ever felt while kissing someone. Although the feelings aren't all good. There's a lot of guilt mixed in there, too.

So as much as the thought of us being together makes sense, it also makes no sense whatsoever. I can't leave a relationship with as much hurt as I did and expect to find happiness within a few short weeks. It's too fast, and I still want to be on my own, no matter how right something might feel.

I don't know where your head is, and honestly, I'm scared to hit enter on this message, because I want us to be on the same page. I want us to work together to try to push past whatever it is we're feeling so we can continue to make music and be friends and pull ridiculous pranks on Warren. I'm not ready for that to end, but if my being here is too hard or makes you feel guilty when you're with Maggie, I'll leave. Just say the word, and I'll go. Well, I guess you can't really SAY the word. You could TYPE the word, and I'll go. (Sorry for the lame joke at your expense, but there's just too much seriousness going on right now.)

Ridge: First and foremost, I'm sorry. I'm sorry I put you in that position. I'm sorry I couldn't be stronger in that moment. I'm sorry I broke my promise to you about never becoming a Hunter. But I'm mostly sorry for leaving you crying on your bed last night. Walking out and leaving that whole situation unresolved was the worst move I could have made.

I wanted to come back and talk to you, but when I finally worked up the courage, Maggie showed up. If I knew she was coming, I would have warned you. After what I did to you last night and then seeing the look on your face when you saw us together this morning, I knew it was one of the most hurtful things I could have done.

I have no idea what's going through your head, but I have to say this, Sydney. No matter how I feel about you or how much I think we could work, I will never, ever leave her. I love her. I've loved her since the moment I met her, and I'll love her until the moment I die.

But please don't let that take away from how I feel about you. I never thought it was possible to have honest feelings for more than one person, but you've convinced me of how incredibly wrong I was. I'm not going to lie to myself and say I don't care about you, and I'm definitely not going to lie to you. I just hope you understand where I'm coming from and that you will give us a chance to navigate through this, because I believe we can. If there are two people in this world capable of figuring out how to be friends, it's us.

We read through each other's messages. I read his more than once. I didn't expect him to be so forthcoming and honest, especially about the fact that he cares about me. I never for one second expected him to contemplate leaving Maggie for me. That would be the worst outcome of all of this. If he left her and we attempted to build a relationship from that, it would never work. The entire relationship would be built on betrayal and deceit, and those two things have never made and will never make for a good foundation.

Ridge: Wow. I'm impressed with us. We're both so mature.

His comment makes me laugh.

Me: Yes, we are.

Ridge: Sydney, I can't tell you what your message just did for me. Seriously. I feel like the weight of all nine planets (because yes, Pluto will always be a planet to me) has been crushing my chest since the moment I walked away from you last night. But knowing that you don't hate me and that you're not mad and that you aren't concocting an evil revenge scheme feels so damn good right now. Thank you for that.

Me: Hold on. I never said I wasn't concocting an evil revenge scheme. ;) Also, while we're being so blunt, can I ask you a question?

Ridge: What did I tell you about initiating a question with whether or not you can propose a question?

Me: Oh, my God, I can't believe I ever kissed you. You're so ANNOYING!

Ridge. LOL. What's your question?

Me: I'm concerned. We obviously have an issue with the fact that we're attracted to each other. How do we get past that? I want to write music with you, but I also know that the few moments we've had that wouldn't make Maggie very happy have all been while we're writing music. I think I'm just too desirable when I'm being creative, and I want to know what I need to do to lessen my attractiveness. If that's even possible.

Ridge: Keep up the egotism. It's very unattractive, and if it continues, I won't even be able to look at you in a week's time.

Me: Deal. But what do I do about my attraction to YOU? Tell me some personal flaws that I can engrave into my memory.

He laughs.

Ridge: I sleep so late on Sundays I don't even brush my teeth until Monday.

Me: That's a start. I need a few more.

Ridge: Let's see. Once, when Warren and I were fifteen, I had a crush on a girl. Warren didn't know I liked her, and he asked me if I would ask her out for him. I did, and she agreed, because apparently, she had a crush on Warren in return. I told him she said no.

Me: Ridge! That's terrible!

Ridge: I know. I need a flaw from you now.

Me: When I was eight, we went to Coney Island. I wanted an ice cream, and my parents wouldn't buy me one because I was wearing a new shirt that "June Cleaver" didn't want me to get dirty. We were walking by a trash can, and there was a melted ice cream cone in it, so when my parents turned around, I picked it up and started eating it.

Ridge: Yeah, that's pretty gross. But you were only eight, so it really doesn't count. I need something more recent. High school? College?

Me: Oh! One time in high school, I spent the night at a girl's house who I didn't know very well. We made out. I wasn't into it, and it was really gross, but I was seventeen and curious.

Ridge: No. That does NOT count as a flaw, Sydney. Jesus Christ, work with me here.

Me: I like the smell of puppy breath.

Ridge: Better. I can't hear my own farts, so sometimes I'll forget that other people can hear them.

Me: Oh, my God. Yes, this is the type of thing that definitely sheds a different light on you. I think I'll be good for a while.

Ridge: One more from you, and then I think we'll be equally repulsed.

Me: A few days ago, when I was getting off the campus bus, I noticed Tori's car was gone. I used my extra key to let myself into her apartment, because I needed a few things I had forgotten. Before I left, I opened all her bottles of liquor and spit in them.

Ridge: For real?

I nod, because I'm too ashamed to type the word *yes.*
He laughs.

Ridge: Okay. I think we're good. Meet me here at eight tonight,
and we'll see if we can navigate through a song. If we need
to take breaks from the music every now and then in order to
replenish our repulsiveness with a few more flaws, just let me
know.

Me: Deal.

I close my laptop and begin to slide off the bed, but he
grabs my wrist. I turn around, and he's looking at me with a
serious expression. He leans over and grabs a pen, then picks up
my hand and writes: *Thank you.*

I press my lips together and nod. He releases my hand, and
I walk back to my room, attempting to ignore the fact that all
the repulsive details in the world couldn't stop my heart from
reacting to that simple gesture. I look down at my chest.

Hey, heart. Are you listening? You and I are officially at war.

Ridge

As soon as she's out of my bedroom and the door shuts behind her, I close my eyes and exhale.

I'm thankful that she isn't angry. I'm thankful that she isn't vindictive. I'm thankful that she's reasonable.

I'm also thankful that she appears to have more willpower than I do, because whenever I'm around her, I've never felt so weak.

13.

Sydney

Not much has changed in the way we practice together, other than the fact that we now practice five feet apart from each other. We've completed a couple of songs since "the kiss," and although the first night was a little awkward, we seem to have found our groove. We haven't talked about the kiss, and we haven't talked about Maggie, and we haven't discussed why he plays on the floor and why I write alone on the bed. There's no reason to discuss it, because we're both very aware of all of it.

The fact that we've admitted our attraction to each other doesn't seem to have eliminated it the way we'd hoped. For me, it's like a huge elephant in the room. It feels as if it takes up so much space when I'm with him that it presses me against the wall, squeezing the last traces of breath out of me. I keep telling myself it'll get better, but it's been almost two weeks since the kiss, and it hasn't gotten easier at all.

Luckily, I have two interviews next week, and if I get hired, at least it'll get me out of the house more. Warren and Bridgette both work and go to school, so they're not here a whole lot. Ridge works from home, so the fact that we're both here alone the majority of the day is always at the front of my mind.

Out of all the hours in the day, though, the hour I hate the most is when Ridge is in the shower. Which means I really hate this hour, since that's where he is right now. I hate where my thoughts go when I know he's one wall away from me, completely unclothed.

Jesus, Sydney.

I hear the water turn off and the shower curtain slide open, and I squeeze my eyes shut, trying once again not to picture him. This would probably be a good time of day to turn on some music to drown out my thoughts.

As soon as the door closes between the bathroom and his bedroom, there's a knock at the front door. I gladly jump off the bed and head toward the living room to get my mind off the fact that I know Ridge is in his room getting dressed right now.

I don't even bother looking through the peephole, which is a very bad oversight on my part. I swing open the door to find Hunter standing sheepishly at the top of the stairs. He eyes me, his expression apologetic and nervous. My heart drops to my stomach at the mere sight of him. It's been weeks since I last laid eyes on him. I was beginning to forget what he looked like.

His dark hair is longer since I last saw him, and it reminds me that I'm always the one to schedule his hair appointments. The fact that he hasn't even bothered to make his own appointment makes him that much more pathetic to me.

"Should I give Tori the number for your barber? Your hair looks awful."

The mention of Tori's name makes him grimace. Or maybe it's the fact that I'm not jumping back into his arms that's causing that regretful expression on his face.

"You look good," he says, capping his words off with a smile.

"I *am* good," I say, not sure if I'm lying to him or not.

He runs a free hand over his jaw and turns away from me, appearing to regret the fact that he's here.

How *is* he here? How does he even know where I live?

"How did you know where to find me?" I ask, tilting my head in curiosity.

I see the split-second shift of his eyes as they glance across the courtyard toward Tori's apartment. It's obvious he doesn't want me to notice what's going on in his mind, because it would only shed light on the fact that he's still visiting Tori on a regular basis.

"Can we talk?" he asks, his voice void of the confidence I've always known him to have.

"If I let you in and convince you it's over, will you promise to stop texting me?"

He barely nods his head, so I step aside, and he walks into the living room. I walk to the dining-room table and pull out a chair, making it obvious that he's not making himself comfortable by sitting on the couch. He walks toward the table as his eyes work their way around the room, more than likely in search of information on who lives here with me.

He grips the back of the chair and pulls it out slowly while his eyes focus on a pair of Ridge's shoes tucked beside the couch. I like that he noticed them.

"Are you living here now?" he asks, his voice tight and controlled.

"For now," I say, my voice even more controlled. I'm proud of myself for keeping calm, because I'm not going to lie and say it doesn't hurt to see him. I gave him two years of my life, and all the things I felt for him can't just be cut off at once. Feelings take time to disappear, so they're still here. They're just mixed and swirled together with a hell of a lot of hatred now. It's confusing to feel this way when I see him, because I never thought I could dislike the man in front of me. I never thought he would betray me the way he did.

"Do you think that's safe? Just moving in with some strange guy you barely know?" He's eyeing me disapprovingly as he takes his seat, as if he has the right to judge any part of my life.

"You and Tori didn't leave me much choice, did you? I found myself screwed over and homeless on my birthday. If anything,

I would think you should be congratulating me for handling it all so well. You sure as hell can't sit here and judge me."

He huffs, then leans forward over the table and closes his eyes, pressing the palms of his hands against his forehead. "Sydney, please. I didn't come here to fight or make excuses. I came here to tell you how sorry I am."

If there's one thing I'd like to hear from him, it's an apology. If there are *two* things I'd like to hear, it's an apology followed by a good-bye.

"Well, you're here now," I say quietly. "Have at it. Tell me how sorry you are." My voice isn't confident anymore. In fact, I want to punch myself, because it sounds really sad and heartbroken, and that's the last thing I want him to think I feel.

"I'm sorry, Sydney," he says, spitting the words out fast and desperately. "I'm so, so sorry. I know it won't make it better, but things have always been different between Tori and me. We've known each other for years, and I know it's not an excuse, but our relationship was sexual before you even met us. But that's all it was. It was just sex, and once you were in the picture, neither of us could figure out how to just put a stop to something that had been going on between us for years. I know this doesn't make sense, but what I had with her was completely separate from what I had with you. I love you. If you'll just give me one more chance to prove myself, I'll never speak to Tori again."

My heart is pounding as hard as it was the moment I found out they were sleeping together. I'm inhaling controlled breaths in an effort not to climb across the table and beat the shit out of him. I'm also clenching my fists in an effort not to climb across the table and kiss him. I would never take him back, but my head is so damned confused right now, because I miss what we had so much. It was simple and good, and my heart never ached the way it's been aching these past few weeks.

What's confusing me the most is the fact that my heart

hasn't been aching like this because I can't be with Hunter. It's aching because I can't be with Ridge.

I realize as I'm sitting here that I'm more upset that Ridge came into my life than I am that Hunter left it. How screwed up is that?

Before I can respond, Ridge's bedroom door opens, and he walks out. He's in jeans and nothing else, and I tense from the way my body responds to his presence. However, I love the fact that Hunter is about to turn around and witness Ridge looking like this.

Ridge pauses just feet from the table when he sees Hunter sitting across from me. He glances from Hunter to me, just as Hunter turns to see who I'm looking at. I can see the concern wash over Ridge's face, along with a flash of anger. He eyes me hard, and I know exactly what's going through his head right now. He's wondering what the hell Hunter is doing here, just as I am. I nod in reassurance, letting Ridge know I'm fine. I shift my eyes to his bedroom and silently tell him that Hunter and I need privacy.

Ridge doesn't move. He doesn't like that I just told him to go back to his bedroom. From the looks of it, he doesn't really trust Hunter alone with me. Maybe it's the fact that he wouldn't be able to hear me if I needed him to return for any reason. Whatever it is, I just made him completely uncomfortable with my request. Regardless, he nods and turns back toward his room, but not before eyeing Hunter with a warning shot.

Hunter faces me again, but his expression is no longer apologetic.

"What the hell was that?" he asks, his voice dripping in jealousy.

"That was Ridge," I reply firmly. "I believe the two of you have already met."

"Are the two of you . . . like . . . ?"

Before I answer him, Ridge walks back into the room with his laptop and heads straight to the couch. He drops down onto the sofa, eyeing Hunter the entire time while he opens his laptop and props his feet up on the coffee table in front of him.

The fact that Ridge refuses to leave me alone with Hunter pleases me way too much.

"Not that it's any of your business," I say, "but no, we aren't dating. He has a girlfriend."

Hunter returns his attention to me and laughs under his breath. I have no idea what he just found funny, but it pisses me off. I fold my arms while I glare at him and lean back against my seat.

Hunter leans forward and looks straight into my eyes. "Please tell me you see the irony in this, Sydney."

I shake my head, absolutely not seeing any irony in this situation.

My lack of comprehension makes him laugh again. "I'm trying to explain to you that what happened between Tori and me was strictly physical. It meant nothing to either of us, but you won't even try to understand my side of it. Yet you're practically eye-fucking your roommate who happens to be in love with another woman, and you don't see the hypocrisy in your actions? You can't tell me you haven't slept with him in the two months you've been here. How can you not see that what the two of you are doing isn't any different from what Tori and I did? You can't justify your own actions without forgiving mine."

I'm trying to keep my jaw off the floor. I'm trying to keep my anger subdued. I'm trying to keep myself from reaching across this table and punching him square between his accusing eyes, but I've learned the hard way that punching isn't all it's cracked up to be.

I allow myself several moments to calm down before I respond. I glance at Ridge, who is still eyeing me. He knows by the look on my face that Hunter just crossed the line. Ridge's hands are gripping the screen of his laptop, prepared to shove it aside if I need him.

I don't need him. I've got this.

I square up with Hunter, pulling my gaze off Ridge and focusing on the eyes I so desperately want to rip out of Hunter's head.

"Ridge has an amazing girlfriend who doesn't deserve to be cheated on, and luckily for her, he's the type of guy who realizes her worth. With that said, you're wrong about the fact that I'm sleeping with him, because I'm not. We both know how unfair it would be to his girlfriend, so we don't act on our attraction. You should take note that simply because a girl makes your dick hard, that doesn't mean you have to go *shove it inside her!*"

I push myself away from the table at the same time as Ridge sets his laptop aside and stands.

"Go, Hunter. Just go," I say, unable to look at him for another second. The simple fact that he thought he had Ridge pegged as being anything like him pisses me off, and he'd be smart to leave.

He stands up and walks straight to the door. He opens it and leaves without even looking back. I'm not sure if his exit was so simple because he finally understands that I'm not willing to take him back or if it's because Ridge looked as if he was about to kick his ass.

I have a good feeling I won't be hearing from Hunter anymore.

I'm still staring at the door when my phone sounds off. I take it out of my pocket and turn to Ridge. He's holding his phone, looking at me with concern.

Ridge: Why was he here?

Me: He wanted to talk.

Ridge: Did you know he was coming over?

I look up at Ridge after reading his text, and for the first time, I notice his jaw is tense and he doesn't look very happy. I'd almost label his reaction as slightly jealous, but I don't want to admit that.

Me: No.

Ridge: Why did you let him in?

Me: I wanted to hear him apologize.

Ridge: Did he?

Me: Yes.

Ridge: Don't let him in here again.

Me: I wasn't planning on it. BTW, you're kind of being a jerk right now.

He glances up at me and shrugs.

Ridge: It's my apartment, and I don't want him here. Don't let him in again.

I don't like his attitude right now, and to be honest, the fact that he just referred to this as his apartment doesn't sit right with me. It feels like a low blow to remind me that I'm at his mercy. I don't bother responding. In fact, I toss the phone onto the couch so he can't text me, and I head toward my room.

When I reach my bedroom door, my emotions catch up with me. I'm not sure if it's seeing Hunter again and having all of those hurtful feelings resurface or if it's the fact that Ridge is being an asshole. Whatever it is, the tears begin to well in my eyes, and I hate that I'm letting either of them get to me in the first place.

Ridge grabs my shoulder and turns me around to face him, but I keep my eyes trained on the wall behind him. I don't even want to look him in the eye. He puts my phone back in my hand, wanting me to read whatever he just texted, but I still don't want to. I throw the phone toward the couch again, but he intercepts it, then tries to force it back into my hand. I take it this time, but I press the power button down until the phone shuts off, and then I toss it onto the couch again. I look him in the eye now, and his expression is angry. He takes two steps toward the coffee table, grabs a pen out of the drawer, and walks back to me. He takes my hand, but I pull it from him, still not wanting to know what he has to say to me. I've had enough apologies for tonight. I try to turn away from him, but he grabs my arm and presses it against the door, holding it forcefully while he writes on it. When he's finished writing, I pull my arm away and watch as he tosses his pen onto the couch, then walks back to his bedroom. I look down at my arm.

Let him in next time if he's really what you want.

My barrier completely breaks. Reading his angry words depletes me of whatever strength I had left to hold back my tears. I rush through my bedroom door and straight into the bathroom. I turn on the faucet and squirt soap into my hands, then begin scrubbing his words off my arm while I cry. I don't even look up when the door to his bedroom opens, but I see him out of my peripheral vision as he closes the door behind him and slowly walks toward me. I'm still scrubbing the ink off my arm and sniffling back the tears when he reaches across me for the soap.

He dispenses some onto the palm of his hand, then wraps his fingers around my wrist. The tenderness in his touch lashes out and scars my heart. He runs the soap up my wrist where the words begin and lathers my skin as I drop my other hand away and grip the edge of the sink, allowing him to wash his words away.

He's apologizing.

He massages his thumbs into the words, rubbing them away with the water.

I'm still staring down at my arm, but I can feel his gaze directly on me. I'm aware of the exaggerated breaths I have to take in now that he's next to me, so I attempt to slow them down until there are no longer traces of ink on my skin.

He grabs a hand towel and dries my arm, then releases me. I bring my arm to my chest and hold it with my other hand, not knowing what move to make now. I finally bring my eyes to meet his, and I instantaneously forget why I'm even upset with him in the first place.

His expression is reassuring and apologetic and maybe even a little longing. He turns and walks out of the bathroom, then returns seconds later with my phone. He powers it on and hands it to me while he leans against the counter, still looking at me regretfully.

Ridge: I'm sorry. I didn't mean what I said. I thought maybe you were entertaining the thought of accepting his apology, and it upset me. You deserve better than him.

Me: He showed up unannounced. I would never take him back, Ridge. I was just hoping an apology from him would help me move on from the betrayal a little quicker.

Ridge: Did it help at all?

Me: Not really. I feel even more pissed than before he showed up.

As Ridge reads my text, I notice the tension ease in his expression. His reaction to my situation with Hunter borders on jealousy, and I hate that this makes me feel good. I hate that every time something Ridge-related makes me feel good, it's immediately followed up with guilt. Why do things between the two of us have to be so complicated?

I wish we could keep things simple, but I have no idea how to do that.

Ridge: Let's go write an angry song about him. That might help.

He looks at me with a sly grin, and it makes my insides swirl and melt. Then I freeze just as fast from the guilt of those feelings.

For once, it would be nice not to be consumed with shame. I nod and follow him to his room.

Ridge

I'm sitting on the floor again. It's not the most comfortable place to play, but it's much better than being on the bed next to her. I can never seem to focus on the actual music when I'm in her personal space and she's in mine.

She requested that I play one of the songs I used to play when I sat out on my balcony to practice, so we've been working through it. She's lying on her stomach, writing on her notepad. Erasing and writing, erasing and writing. I'm sitting here on the floor, not even playing. I've played the song enough for her to know the melody by now, so I'm just waiting while I watch her.

I love how she focuses so intently on the lyrics, as if she's in her own world and I'm just a lucky observer. Every now and then, she'll tuck behind her ear the hair that keeps spilling in front of her face. My favorite thing to watch her do is erase her words. Every time the eraser meets the paper, she pulls her top lip in with her bottom teeth and chews on it.

I hate that it's my favorite thing to watch her do, because it shouldn't be. It triggers all these *what-ifs* in my head, and my mind begins imagining things it shouldn't be imagining. I begin to picture myself lying next to her on the bed while she writes. I imagine her lip being tucked in while I'm just inches from her, looking down on the words she's written. I imagine her glancing up at me, noticing what she's doing to me with her small, innocent gestures. I imagine her rolling onto her back, welcoming me to create secrets with her that'll never leave this room.

I close my eyes, wanting to do whatever I can to stop the thoughts. They make me feel just as guilty as if I were to act on them. Sort of similar to how I felt a couple of hours ago when I thought there was a chance she was getting back together with Hunter.

I was pissed.

I was jealous.

I was having thoughts and feelings I knew I shouldn't be having, and it was scaring the shit out of me. I've never had an issue with jealousy until now, and I don't like the person it's turning me into. Especially when the jealousy I'm feeling has nothing to do with the girl I'm in an actual relationship with.

I flinch when something hits me on the forehead. I immediately open my eyes and look at Sydney. She's on the bed, laughing, pointing at my phone. I pick it up and read her text.

Sydney: Are you falling asleep? We aren't finished.

Me: No. Just thinking.

She moves over on the bed to make more room and pats the spot next to her.

Sydney: Come think right here so you can read these. I have most of the lyrics down, but I'm hung up on the chorus. I'm not sure what you want.

We haven't openly discussed the fact that we don't write on the bed together anymore. She's focused on the lyrics, though, so I need to pull my shit together and focus on them, too. I set my guitar down and pull myself up, then walk to the bed and lie beside her. I take the notebook out of her hands and pull it in front of me to read what she's written so far.

She smells good.

Damn.

I try to block off my senses somehow, but I know it's a wasted effort. Instead, I focus on the words she's written, quickly impressed at how effortlessly they come to her.

Why don't we keep
Keep it simple
You talk to your friends
And I'll be here to mingle

But you know that I
I want to be
Right by your side
Where I ought to be

And you know that I
That I can see
The way that your eyes
Seem to follow me

After reading what she's written, I hand her back the notebook and pick up my phone. I'm confused about the lyrics, because they aren't at all what I was expecting. I'm not sure I like them.

Me: I thought we were writing an angry song about Hunter.

She shrugs, then begins texting me back.

Sydney: I tried. The subject of Hunter doesn't really inspire me anymore. You don't have to use them if you don't like them. I can try something different.

I stare at her text, not sure how to respond. I don't like the lyrics, but not because they aren't good. It's because the words she's written down make me think she's somehow able to read my mind.

Me: I love them.

She smiles and says, "Thank you." She flips onto her back, and I catch myself appreciating this moment and this night and her low-cut dress way more than I probably should. When my eyes make their way back to hers, she's watching me, plainly aware of what's going through my head. Eyes don't lie, unfortunately.

When neither of us breaks our gaze, I'm forced to swallow the huge lump in my throat.

Don't get yourself in trouble, Ridge.

Thank God she sits up when she does.

Sydney: I'm not sure where you want the chorus to come in. This song is a little more upbeat than the ones I'm used to. I've written three different ones, but I don't like how any of them sound. I'm stuck.

Me: Let me watch you sing it one more time.

I roll off the bed and grab the guitar, then take it back to the bed but sit on the edge this time. We turn to face each other, and I play while she sings. When we make it to the chorus, she stops singing and shrugs, letting me know this is where she's stuck. I take her notebook and read the lyrics over a few times. I glance up at her without being too obvious about it and write the first thing that comes to mind.

> *And I must confess*
> *My interest*
> *The way that you move*
> *When you're in that dress*
>
> *It's making me feel*
> *Like I want to be*
> *The only man*
> *That you ever see*

I pause from writing and look up at her again, feeling every bit of the words in this chorus. I think we both know the words we write have to do with each other, but that doesn't seem to stop us at all. If we keep having moments like these with words that are way too honest, we'll *both* end up in trouble. I quickly look back down at the paper as more lyrics begin to enter my head.

> *Whoa, oh, oh, oh*
> *I'm in trouble, trouble*
> *Whoa, oh, oh, oh*
> *I'm in trouble now*

I refuse to look up at her again while I write. I keep my mind focused on the words that somehow seem to flow from my fingertips every time we're together. I don't question what's inspiring me or what they mean.

I don't question it . . . because it's obvious.

But it's art. Art is just an expression. An expression isn't the same as an act, as much as it sometimes feels that way. Writing lyrics isn't the same as directly informing someone of your feelings.

Is it?

I keep my eyes on the paper and continue to write the words I honestly wish I didn't feel.

The second I'm finished writing, I'm so worked up I don't allow myself to witness her reaction to the words. I quickly hand her back the notebook and pull my guitar around and begin playing so she can work through the chorus.

14.

Sydney

He's not looking at me. He doesn't even know I'm not singing the lyrics. I *can't* sing them. I've listened to him play this song dozens of times from his balcony, yet it never held emotion or meaning until this moment.

The fact that he can't even look at me makes the song feel way too personal. It feels as if this song somehow just became his song to me. I turn the notebook over, not wanting to read the words anymore. This song is just one more thing that never should have happened, even though I'm positive it's my new favorite.

> Me: Do you think Brennan can make a rough cut of this one? I want to hear it.

I nudge him with my foot after I send the text, then nod toward his phone when he looks at me. He picks it up to read the text and nods. He doesn't reply or make eye contact with me, though. I glance back down to my phone as the room grows quiet in the absence of the sound of his guitar. I don't like how awkward things just got between us, so I attempt to make small talk to fill the void. I roll onto my back and type out a question that's been on my mind for a while to break up the stillness around us.

> Me: Why don't you ever practice on your balcony like you used to?

This question gets me immediate eye contact from him, but it doesn't last. His eyes flicker across my face, down my body, and finally back to his phone.

Ridge: Why would I? You're not out there anymore.

And just like that, my defenses are down, and my willpower is shot to hell with his honest reply. I nervously pull my bottom lip in and chew on it, then slowly raise my eyes back to his. He's looking at me as if he wishes he were a guy like Hunter who cared only about himself.

He's not the only one wishing that.

I want to be Tori right now so much it hurts. I want to be just like her and not give a shit about my self-respect or about Maggie for just a few minutes. Long enough to allow him to do everything his lyrics make clear he wants to do.

His eyes fall to my lips, and my mouth runs dry.

His eyes fall to my chest, and it begins to heave deeper than it already was.

His eyes fall to my legs, and I have to cross them, because the way his gaze penetrates my body makes it seem as though he can see right through this dress I'm wearing.

His eyes close tightly, and knowing the effect I'm having on him makes me feel as if there might be a lot more truth to his lyrics than he'd like there to be.

It's making me feel like I want to be the only man that you ever see.

Ridge suddenly stands and drops his phone onto the bed, then walks straight into the bathroom and slams the door. I listen as the shower curtain slides open and the water kicks on.

I roll onto my back and release all my pent-up breaths. I'm flustered and confused and angry. I don't like the situation we've put ourselves in, and I know for a fact that even though we haven't acted on it again, nothing about this is innocent.

I sit up on the bed, then quickly stand. I need to get out of his room before it completely closes in on me. Just as I'm walking away from the bed, Ridge's phone vibrates on the mattress. I look down at it.

Maggie: I'm missing you extra hard today. When you're finished writing with Sydney, can we video chat? I need to see you. ;)

I stare at her text.
I hate her text.
I hate that she knows we were just writing together.
I hate that he tells her everything.
I want these moments to belong to me and Ridge and no one else.

•   •   •

It's been two hours since he got out of the shower, and I can't bring myself to leave my bedroom. I'm starving, though, and really want to go to the kitchen. I just don't want to see him, because I hate how we left things. I don't like that we both know we almost crossed a line tonight.

Actually, I don't like that we *did* cross a line tonight. Although we aren't verbalizing what we're thinking and feeling, writing it in lyrics isn't any less harmful.

There's a knock on my door, and knowing that it's more than likely Ridge causes my heart to betray me by dancing rapidly in my chest. I don't bother getting up to open the door, because he nudges it open right after knocking. He holds up a set of headphones and his cell phone, indicating that he has something he wants me to hear. I nod, and he walks over to the bed and hands them to me. He hits play but takes a seat on the floor while I scoot back onto the bed. The song begins to play, and I spend the next three minutes barely breathing. Ridge and I never once break our stare throughout the duration of the song.

I'M IN TROUBLE

Why don't we keep
Keep it simple
You talk to your friends
And I'll be here to mingle

But you know that I
I want to be
Right by your side
Where I ought to be

And you know that I
That I can see
The way that your eyes
Seem to follow me

And I must confess
My interest
The way that you move
When you're in that dress

It's making me feel
Like I want to be
The only man
That you ever see

Whoa oh, oh, oh
I'm in trouble, trouble
Whoa oh, oh, oh
I'm in trouble, trouble
Whoa oh, oh, oh
I'm in trouble now

I see you some places
from time to time
You keep to your business
and I keep to mine

But you know that I
I want to be
Right by your side
Where I ought to be

And you know that I
That I can see
The way that your eyes
Seem to follow me

And I must confess
My interest
The way that you move
When you're in that dress

It's making me feel
Like I want to be
The only man
That you ever see

Whoa oh, oh, oh
I'm in trouble, trouble
Whoa oh, oh, oh
I'm in trouble, trouble
Whoa oh, oh, oh
I'm in trouble now

Ridge

Maggie: Guess who gets to see me tomorrow?

Me: Kurt Vonnegut?

Maggie: Guess again.

Me: Anderson Cooper?

Maggie: No, but close.

Me: Amanda Bynes?

Maggie: You're so random. YOU get to see me tomorrow, and you get to spend a whole two days with me, and I know I'm trying to save money, but I bought you two new bras.

Me: How did I ever get so lucky to find the one and only girl who supports and encourages my transvestite tendencies?

Maggie: I ask myself that same question every day.

Me: What time do I get to see you?

Maggie: Well, it all depends on the dreaded T word again.

Me: Ah. Yes. Well, we shall discuss it no further. Try to be here by six, at least. Warren's birthday party is tomorrow night, and

I want to spend time with you before all his crazy friends get here.

Maggie: Thank you for reminding me! What should I get him?

Me: Nothing. Sydney and I are pulling the ultimate prank. We told everyone to donate to charity in lieu of gifts. He'll be pissed when people start handing him all the donation cards in his honor.

Maggie: You two are evil. Should I bring something? A cake, maybe?

Me: Nope, we got it. We felt bad for the "no gifts" prank, so we're about to bake him five different flavored cakes to make up for it.

Maggie: Make sure one of them is German chocolate.

Me: Already got you covered, babe. I love you.

Maggie: Love you, too.

I close out our texts and open up the unread one I have from Sydney.

Sydney: You forgot vanilla extract, dumbass. It was on the list. Item 5. Now you have to go back to the store.

Me: Maybe next time you should write more legibly and return my texts when I'm at the grocery store, attempting to decipher item 5. I'll be back in 20. Preheat the oven, and text me if you think of anything else.

I laugh, put my phone into my pocket, grab my keys, and head to the store. Again.

• • •

We're on cake number three. I'm beginning to believe that those who are musically gifted seriously lack talent in the kitchen-skills department. Sydney and I work really well together when it comes to writing music, but our lack of finesse and knowledge when it comes to mixing a few ingredients together is a little pathetic.

She insisted that we bake the cakes from scratch, whereas I would have grabbed the boxed mixes. But it's been kind of fun, so I'm not complaining.

She places the third cake in the oven and sets the timer. She turns around and mouths "thirty minutes," then pushes herself up onto the counter.

Sydney: Is your little brother coming tomorrow?

Me: They're gonna try. They open for a band in San Antonio at seven tomorrow night, so as long as they get loaded up on time, they should be here by ten.

Sydney: The whole band? I get to meet the whole band?

Me: Yep. And I bet they'll even sign your boobs.

Sydney: SQUEEEE!

Me: If those letters really make up a sound, I am so, so glad I can't hear it.

She laughs.

Sydney: How did y'all come up with the band name Sounds of Cedar?

Any time anyone's asked how I came up with the name of the band, I just say I thought it sounded cool. But I can't lie to Sydney. There's something about her that pulls stories about my childhood out of me that I've never told anyone. Not even Maggie.

Maggie has asked in the past why I never speak out loud and where I came up with the name of the band, but I don't like to bring up anything negative that might cause her even the smallest amount of concern. She's got enough to deal with in her own life. She doesn't need to add my childhood issues to that. They're in the past and there's no need to bring them up.

However, Sydney's a different story. She seems so curious about me, about life, about people in general. It's easy to tell her things.

Sydney: Uh-oh. Looks like I need to prepare myself for a good story, because you look like you don't want to answer that.

I turn around until my back is pressed against the countertop she's sitting on, and I lean against it.

Me: You just love the heart-wrenching stuff, huh?

Sydney: Yep. Give it to me.

Maggie, Maggie, Maggie.
I often find myself repeating Maggie's name when I'm with Sydney. Especially when Sydney says things like "Give it to me."

The last couple of weeks have been okay since our talk. We've definitely had our moments, but one of us is usually quick to begin pointing out flaws and repulsive personality traits to get us back on track.

Aside from a couple of weeks ago, when our writing session ended with me having to take a cold shower, two nights ago was probably the hardest time of all for me. I don't know what it is about the way she sings. I can simply be watching her, and I get the same feeling I get when I press my ear to her chest or rest my hand against her throat. She closes her eyes and starts singing the words, and the passion and feelings that pour from her are so powerful I sometimes forget I can't even hear her.

This particular night, we were writing a song from scratch, and we couldn't communicate well enough to understand it. I needed to hear her, and although we were both reluctant, it ended with my head pressed to her chest and my hand resting against her throat. While she was singing, she casually brought her hand to my hair and was twirling her fingers around.

I could have stayed in that position with her all night.

I would have, if every touch of her hand didn't make me crave a little bit more. I finally had to tear myself away from her, but just being on the floor wasn't enough separation. I wanted her so bad; it was all I could think about. I ended up asking her to tell me one of her flaws, and instead of giving me one, she stood up and left my bedroom.

The way she had been touching my hair was a very natural thing for her to do, considering the way we were positioned. It's what a guy would do to his girlfriend if he were holding her against his chest, and it's what a girl would do to her boyfriend if he were wrapped around her. But we aren't those things.

The relationship we have is different from anything I've experienced. Mostly because we do have a lot of physical closeness based on the nature of writing music together and the fact that I have to use my sense of touch to replace my sense of hearing in some situations. So while we're in those situations, the lines become muddy, and reactions become unintentional.

As much as I wish I could admit we've moved past our attraction for each other, I can't deny that I feel mine growing with each day that passes. Being around her isn't necessarily hard all the time, though. Just most of the time.

Whatever is going on between us, I know Maggie wouldn't approve, and I try to do right by my relationship with her. However, since I can't really define where the line is drawn between inappropriate and appropriate, it makes it hard to stay on the right side sometimes.

Like right now.

I'm staring down at my phone, about to text her, and she's leaning behind me, both of her hands kneading the tension out of my shoulders. With as much writing as we've been doing and the fact that I sit on the floor now instead of the bed, I've had a few issues with my back. It's become natural for her to rub it when she knows it's hurting.

Would I let her do this when Maggie was in the room? Hell, no. Do I stop her? No. Should I? Absolutely.

I know without a doubt that I don't want to cheat on Maggie. I've never been that type of guy, and I don't ever want to be that type of guy. The problem is, I'm not thinking about Maggie when I'm with Sydney. The times I spend with Sydney are spent with Sydney, and nothing else crosses my mind. But the times I spend with Maggie are spent with Maggie. I don't think about Sydney.

It's as though times with Maggie and times with Sydney occur on two different planets. Planets that don't intersect and in time zones that don't overlap.

Until tomorrow, anyway.

We've all spent time together in the past, but not since I've been honest with myself about how I feel for Sydney. And although I would never want Maggie to know I've developed feelings for someone else, I'm worried she'll be able to tell.

I tell myself that with enough effort, I can learn to control my feelings. But then Sydney will do or say something or give me a look, and I can literally feel the part of my heart that belongs to her getting fuller. As much as I want it to empty. I'm worried that feelings are the one thing in our lives that we have absolutely no control over.

15.

Sydney

Me: What's taking you so long? Are you writing a damn book?

I don't know if my rubbing his shoulders is putting him to sleep, but he's been staring at his phone for five solid minutes.

Ridge: Sorry. Lost in thought.

Me: I can see that. So, Sounds of Cedar?

Ridge: It's kind of a long story. Let me grab my laptop.

I open up our Facebook messages on my phone. When he returns, he leans against a counter several feet away from me. I'm aware of the fact that he's put space between us, and it makes me feel somewhat uncomfortable, because I know I shouldn't have been rubbing his shoulders. It's too much, considering what's happened between us in the past, but I feel as if it's my fault his shoulders hurt in the first place.

He doesn't really complain about what playing on the floor is doing to him, but I can tell it hurts sometimes. Especially after nights like last night, when we wrote for three hours straight. I asked him to start playing on the floor to help with the fact that things seem to be more difficult when he's on the bed. If I didn't still have such a huge crush on his guitar playing, it might not be as big a problem.

But I do still have a definite crush on his guitar playing. And I would say I have a definite crush on *him*, but crush doesn't even begin to define it. I'm not even going to try to define how I feel about him, because I refuse to let my thoughts go there. Not now and not ever.

Ridge: We had all been playing together for fun for about six months before we got our first real gig at a local restaurant. They needed us to give them the name of our band so they could put us on the schedule. We had never really considered ourselves an actual band before that, since it was all in fun, but that night, we agreed that maybe for local things like the restaurant, it would be good to have a name. We all took turns throwing out suggestions, but we couldn't seem to agree on anything. At one point, Brennan suggested we call ourselves Freak Frogs. I laughed. I told him it sounded like a punk band, that we needed a title with more of an acoustic sound. He got upset and said I shouldn't really be allowed to comment on how music or titles sound, since, well, yay for lame deaf jokes from sixteen-year-old little brothers.

Anyway, Warren didn't like how cocky Brennan was back then, so he said I should choose the name and everyone had to agree on it. Brennan got pissed and walked off, said he didn't want to be in the band anyway. I knew he was just having a Brennan tantrum. He didn't have them often, but when he did have them, I understood. I mean, the kid had virtually no parents, and he was raising himself, so I thought he was pretty damn mature despite the sporadic tantrums. I told the guys I wanted to think on it for a while. I tried to come up with names that I thought would mean something to everyone, but mostly to Brennan. I thought back on what got me into listening to music in the first place.

Brennan was around two years old, and I was five. I've already shared to you all the qualities my parents possessed, so I won't go back into that. But in addition to all their addictions, they also liked to party. They would send us to our rooms at night once all their friends began to arrive. I noticed that Brennan was always wearing the same diapers when he woke up that he wore to bed. They never checked on him. Never fed him at night or changed him or even checked to see if he was breathing. This is probably something that had been occurring since he was an infant, but I didn't really notice until I started school, because I think I was just too young. We weren't allowed to leave our rooms at night. I don't remember why I was too scared to leave my room, but I'm sure I'd been punished for it before, or it wouldn't have bothered me. I would wait until the parties were over and my parents went to bed before I could leave my room and go check on Brennan. The problem with this was that I couldn't hear, so I never knew when the music would stop, and I never knew if they had gone to their bedroom, because I wasn't allowed to open my door. Instead of risking being caught, I would just press my ear to the floor and feel the vibrations of the music. Every night, I would lie there for no telling how long, just waiting for the music to stop. I began to recognize the songs based on how they felt through the floor, and I learned how to predict which songs were coming next, since they played the same albums night after night. I even began to learn how to tap along with the rhythm. After the music would finally stop, I would keep my ear pressed to the floor and wait for my parents' footsteps to indicate that they had gone to their bedroom. Once I knew the coast was clear, I would go to Brennan's room and bring him back to bed with me. That way, when he woke up crying, I could help him.

Which brings me back to the point of this story, how I came up with the band name. I learned how to differentiate chords and sounds through all the nights my body and my ears were pressed against the cedar floor. Hence Sounds of Cedar.

Inhale, exhale.
Beat, beat, pause.
Contract, expand.

I don't even realize how on edge I am until I see the white in my knuckles as I grip my phone. We both remain still for several moments while I attempt to get the image of the five-year-old Ridge out of my head.

It's gut-wrenching.

Me: I guess that explains how you can differentiate vibrations so well. And I guess Brennan agreed once you told him the name, because how could he not appreciate that?

Ridge: Brennan doesn't know that story. Once again, you're the first person I've ever shared it with.

I lift my eyes back to his and inhale, but for the life of me, I can't remember how to exhale. He's a good three feet away, but I feel as if every single part of me that his eyes fall on is being directly touched by him. For the first time in a while, the fear etches its way back into my heart. Fear that one of these moments will be one neither of us can resist.

He sets his laptop on the counter and folds his arms across his chest. Before his eyes meet mine, his gaze falls on my legs, and then he slowly works his eyes up the entire length of my body. His eyes are narrow and focused. The way he's looking at me makes me want to lunge for the freezer and crawl inside.

His eyes are fixed on my mouth, and he quietly swallows, then reaches beside him and picks up his phone.

Ridge: Hurry, Syd. I need a serious flaw, and I need it now.

I force a smile, although my insides are screaming for me not to text him back a flaw. It's as if my fingers are fighting with themselves as they fly over the screen in front of me.

Me: Sometimes when I'm frustrated with you, I wait until you look away, and then I yell mean things at you.

He laughs, then looks back up at me. "Thank you," he silently mouths.

It's the first time he's ever mouthed words, and if he weren't walking away from me right now, I'd be begging for him to do it again.

Heart 1.

Sydney 0.

. . .

It's after midnight, but we finally finish adding icing to the fifth and final cake. He cleans the last of the ingredients off the counter while I secure the Saran wrap around the cake pan and slide it next to the other four pans.

Ridge: Do I finally get to meet the raging alcoholic side of you tomorrow night?

Me: I'm thinking you just might.

He grins and flips off the kitchen light. I walk to the living room to power off the TV. Warren and Bridgette should come home sometime in the next hour, so I leave the lamp on in the living room.

Ridge: Will it be weird for you?

Me: Being drunk? Nope. I'm pretty good at it.

Ridge: No. I mean Maggie.

I look up at him where he's standing in front of his bedroom door, watching his phone, not making eye contact with me. He looks nervous that he even asked the question.

Me: Don't worry about me, Ridge.

Ridge: Can't help it. I feel like I've put you in an awkward situation.

Me: You haven't. I mean, don't get me wrong, it would help if you weren't so attractive, but I'm hoping Brennan looks a lot like you. That way, when you're shacking up with Maggie tomorrow night, I can have drunk, wild fun with your little brother.

I hit send, then immediately gasp. What the hell was I thinking? That wasn't funny. It was *supposed* to be funny, but it's after midnight, and I'm never funny after midnight.

Shit.

Ridge is still looking down at the screen on his phone. His jaw twitches, and he shakes his head slightly, then looks up at me as if I've just shot him through the heart. He drops his arm and runs his free hand through his hair, then turns to walk to his room.

I. Suck.

I rush to him and put my hand on his shoulder, urging him to turn back around. He rolls his shoulder to brush my hand off but pauses, only partially turning to face me with a guarded expression. I step around to his front so he's forced to look at me.

"I was kidding," I say, slowly and very seriously. "I'm sorry."

His face is still tense and hard and even a little disappointed, but he lifts his phone and begins texting again.

Ridge: And therein lies the problem, Sydney. You should be able to screw whoever you want to screw, and I shouldn't give a shit.

I suck in a breath. At first, it pisses me off, but then I focus in on the one word that reveals the entire truth behind his statement.

Shouldn't.

He didn't say, "I don't give a shit." He said, "I shouldn't give a shit."

I look up at him, and his face is so full of pain it's heartbreaking.

He doesn't want to feel like this. *I* don't want him to feel like this.

What the hell am I doing to him?

He runs both of his hands through his hair, looks up at the ceiling, and squeezes his eyes shut. He stands like this for a while, then exhales and drops his hands to his hips, lowering his eyes to the floor.

He feels so guilty he can't even look at me.

Without making eye contact, he lifts an arm and grabs my wrist, then pulls me toward him. He crushes me to his chest, wraps one arm around my back, and curves his other hand against the back of my head. My arms are folded up and tucked between us while his cheek rests against the top of my head. He sighs heavily.

I don't pull away from him in order to text him a flaw, because I don't think he's in need of one right now. The way he's holding me is different, unlike all the times in the past few weeks when we've had to separate ourselves in order to breathe.

He's holding me now as if I'm a part of him—a wounded

extension of his heart—and he's realizing just how much that extension needs to be severed.

We stand like this for several minutes, and I begin to get lost in the way he's wrapped himself around me. The way he's holding me gives me a glimpse of what things could be like between us. I try to push those two little words into the back of my head, the two words that always inch their way forward when we're together.

Maybe someday.

The sound of keys hitting a counter behind me jerks me to attention. I pull back, and Ridge does the same as soon as he feels my body flinch against his. He looks over my shoulder and toward the kitchen, so I spin around. Warren has just walked through the front door. His back is toward us, and he's slipping off his shoes.

"I'm only going to say this once, and I need you to listen," Warren says. He still isn't facing us, but I'm the only one in the apartment who can hear him, so I know he's directing his comment to me. "He will never leave her, Sydney."

He walks to his bedroom without once looking over his shoulder, leaving Ridge to believe he never even saw us. The door to Warren's bedroom closes, and I turn back to face Ridge. His eyes are still on Warren's door. When they flick back to mine, they're full of so many things I know he wishes he could say.

But he doesn't. He just turns and walks into his room, closing the door behind him.

I remain completely motionless as two huge tears spill from my eyes, scarring their way down my cheeks in a trail of shame.

Ridge

Brennan: Gotta love rain. Looks like I'll be there early. I'm coming alone, though. The guys can't make it.

Me: See you when you get here. Oh, and before you leave tomorrow, make sure you get all your shit out of Sydney's room.

Brennan: Will she be there? Do I finally get to meet the girl who was brought to this earth for us?

Me: Yeah, she'll be here.

Brennan: I can't believe I've never asked this, but is she hot?

Oh, no.

Me: Don't even think about it. She's been through too much shit to be added to your list of concubines.

Brennan: Territorial, are we?

I toss my phone onto the bed and don't even bother with a reply. If I make her too off-limits to him, it'll just make him try that much harder with her.

When she made the joke last night about screwing him, she was just trying to add humor to the seriousness of the situation, but the way her text made me feel terrified me.

It wasn't the fact that she texted about hooking up with someone. What terrified me was my knee-jerk reaction. I wanted to throw my phone against the wall and smash it into a million pieces, then throw *her* against the wall and show her all the ways I could ensure that she never thinks about another man again.

I didn't like feeling that way. I probably should encourage Brennan. Maybe it would be better for my relationship with Maggie if Sydney actually started dating someone else.

Whoa.

The wave of jealousy that just rolled over me felt more like a tsunami.

I walk out of my bedroom and head to the kitchen to help Sydney get things together for dinner before everyone gets here. I pause when I see her bent over, rummaging through the contents of the refrigerator. She's wearing the blue dress again.

I hate it when Warren is right. My eyes slowly scroll from the dress, down her tanned legs, and back up again. I exhale and contemplate asking her to go change. I'm not sure I can deal with this tonight. Especially when Maggie gets here.

Sydney straightens up, pulls away from the refrigerator, and turns toward the counter. I notice she's talking, but she isn't talking to me. She pulls a bowl out of the refrigerator, and her mouth is still moving, so naturally, my eyes scan the rest of the apartment to see who it is she's talking to.

And that's when both halves of my heart—which were somehow still connected by a small, invisible fiber—snap apart and separate completely.

Maggie is standing in front of the bathroom door, eyeing me hard. I can't read her expression, because it's not one I've ever been exposed to before. The half of my heart that belongs to her immediately begins to panic.

Look innocent, Ridge. Look innocent. All you did was look at her.

I smile. "There's my girl," I sign as I walk to her. The fact that I'm somehow able to hide my guilt seems to ease her concern. She smiles back and wraps her arms around my neck when

I reach her. I slip my arms around her waist and kiss her for the first time in two weeks.

God, I've missed her. She feels so good. So familiar.

She smells good, she tastes good, she *is* good. I've missed her so damn much. I kiss her cheek and her chin and her forehead, and I love that I'm so relieved to have her here. For the past few days, I began to fear that I wouldn't have this reaction the next time I saw her.

"I have to go really bad. Long drive." She winces and points to the door behind her, and I give her another quick kiss. Once she's inside the bathroom, I slowly turn back around to gauge Sydney's reaction.

I've been as upfront and honest with Sydney as I can possibly be about my feelings for Maggie, but I know it's not easy for her to see me with Maggie. There's just no way around it. Do I compromise my relationship with Maggie to spare Sydney's feelings? Or do I compromise Sydney's feelings to spare my relationship with Maggie? Unfortunately, there's no middle ground. No right choice. My actions are becoming split directly down the middle, just like my heart.

I face her, and our eyes meet briefly. She refocuses her attention down to the cake in front of her and inserts candles. When she finishes, she smiles and looks back up at me. She sees the concern in my expression, so she pats her chest and makes the "*okay*" sign with her hand.

She's reassuring me that she's fine. I practically have to pry myself away from her every night, and then I maul my girlfriend right in front of her—and she's reassuring *me*?

Her patience and understanding with this whole screwed-up situation should make me happy, but they have the opposite effect. They disappoint me, because they make me like her that much more.

I can't win for losing.

• • •

Oddly enough, Maggie and Sydney seem to be having fun together in the kitchen, prepping ingredients for a pot of chili. I couldn't hang, so I retreated to my room and claimed I had a lot of work to catch up on. As good as Sydney is with this, I'm not as skilled. It was awkward for me every time Maggie would kiss me or sit on my lap or trail her fingers seductively up my chest. Which, come to think of it, was a bit odd. She's never really all that touchy-feely when we're hanging out, so she's either feeling a tad bit territorial, or she and Sydney have already been hitting the Pine-Sol.

Maggie comes into the bedroom just as I'm shutting the laptop. She kneels down on the edge of the bed, leans forward, and inches her way toward me. She's looking up at me with a flirtatious smile, so I set the laptop aside and smile back at her.

She crawls her way up my body until she's face-to-face with me, and then she sits back on her heels, straddling me. She cocks an eyebrow and tilts her head. "You were checking out her ass."

Shit.

I was hoping that moment had come and gone.

I laugh and cup my hands around Maggie's backside and scoot her a little closer. I let go and bring my hands back around in front of her and answer her. "I walked out of my room to a rear end pointed toward my bedroom door. I'm a guy. Guys notice things like that, unfortunately." I kiss her mouth, then pull back.

She's not smiling. "She's really nice," Maggie signs. "And pretty. And funny. And talented. And . . ."

The insecurity in her words makes me feel like a jerk, so I grab her hands and still them. "She's not you," I tell her. "No one can ever be you, Maggie. Ever."

She smiles halfheartedly and places her palms on the sides of my face and slowly runs them down to my neck. She leans forward and presses her mouth to mine with so much force I can feel the fear rolling off of her.

Fear that I put there.

I grab her face and kiss her with everything I have, doing all I can to erase her worries. The last thing this girl needs is something else to stress her out.

When she breaks apart from me, her features are still full of every single negative emotion I've spent the past five years helping her drown out.

"Ridge?" She pauses, then drops her eyes while she blows out a long, controlled breath. The nervousness in her demeanor twists around my heart and squeezes it. She brings her eyes carefully back to mine. "Did you tell her about me? Does she know?" Her eyes search mine for an answer to the question she should never even feel the need to ask.

Does she not know me by now?

"No. *God*, no, Maggie. Why would I do that? That's always been your story to tell, not mine. I would never do that."

Her eyes fill with tears, and she tries to blink them away. I let my head fall back against the headboard. This girl still has no idea how far I'll go for her.

I lift my head away from the headboard and look her hard in the eyes. "To the ends of the earth, Maggie," I sign, repeating our phrase to her.

She forces a sad smile. "And back."

16.

Sydney

Someone is removing my clothes. Who in the hell is removing my clothes?

I begin slapping away the hand that's pulling my shorts down past my knees. I try to remember where I am, why I'm here, and how I got here.

Party.

Cake.

Pine-Sol.

Spilling Pine-Sol on my dress.

Changing.

Drinking more Pine-Sol.

Lots of Pine-Sol.

Watching Ridge love Maggie.

God, he loves her so much. I saw it in the way he watches her from across the room. I saw it in the way he touches her. In the way he communicates with her.

I can still smell the alcohol. I can still taste it as I slide my tongue over my lips.

I danced . . .

I drank more Pine-Sol . . .

Oh! The drinking game. I invented my own solitary drinking game, where every time I saw how much Ridge loved Maggie, I downed a shot. Unfortunately, that made for a hell of a lot of shots.

Who in the hell is pulling off my shorts?

I try to open my eyes, but I can't tell if it's working. They feel open, but it's still dark inside my head.

Oh, my God. I'm drunk, and someone is undressing me.

I'm about to be raped!

I start kicking at the hands that are yanking the shorts from my feet.

"Sydney!" a girl yells. "Stop!" She's laughing. I focus for a few seconds and can tell the voice belongs to Maggie.

"Maggie?"

She comes closer, and a soft hand brushes back my hair as the bed dips down next to me. I squeeze my eyes shut, then force them wide open several times, until I finally begin to adjust to the dark. She puts her hands on my shirt and attempts to unbutton it.

Why in the hell is she still taking off my clothes?

Oh, my God! Maggie wants to rape me!

I slap at her hand, and she grips my wrist. "Sydney!" She laughs. "You're covered in puke. I'm trying to help you."

Puke? *Covered* in it?

That explains the massive headache. But . . . it doesn't explain why I'm laughing. Why am I laughing? Am I still drunk? "What time is it?" I ask her.

"I don't know. Tonight, I think. Like, midnight?"

"That's it?"

She nods, then starts laughing with me. "You threw up on Brennan."

Brennan? I met Brennan?

It looks as if her eyes are trying hard to focus on my face. "Can I tell you a secret?" she says.

I nod. "Okay, but I probably won't remember it, because I think I'm still drunk."

She smiles and leans forward. She's so pretty. Maggie is really, really pretty. "I can't stand Bridgette," she says quietly.

I laugh.

Maggie starts laughing again, too, and tries to pull my shirt off, but she's laughing too hard and keeps having to pause for deep breaths.

"Are you drunk, too?" I ask her.

She inhales again, attempting to pause her laughter, and then she exhales. "*So* drunk. I thought I took your shirt off already, but your shirt keeps coming back on, and I don't know how many shirts you have, but"—she lifts the edge of my shirt sleeve, which is still on my arm, and looks at it in confusion— "oh, my God, I really thought I took it off already, and here it is *again*."

I lift myself up on the bed, then help her pull my shirt off. "Why am I already in bed if it's only midnight?"

She shrugs. "I have no idea what you just said."

She's funny. I reach to the nightstand and turn on the lamp. Maggie scoots off the bed and lowers herself to the floor. She lies flat on her stomach with a sigh and begins moving her arms, making snow angels against the carpet.

"I don't want to go to bed yet," I tell her.

She flips over onto her back and looks up at me. "Then don't. I told Ridge to let you stay up and play because we were having so much fun, but you threw up in Brennan's lap, so he made you go to bed." She sits up. "Let's go play some more. I want more cake." She pushes up on her hands and stands, then reaches for my hands and pulls me off the bed.

I look down at myself. "But you took off my clothes," I say, pouting.

She looks at my bra and underwear. "Where'd you get that bra? It's so cute."

"JCPenney."

"Oh. Ridge likes the kind that clasp in the front, but yours is really cute. I want one."

"You should get one," I say, smiling. "We could be bra twins."

She pulls me toward the door. "Let's go see if Ridge likes it. I want him to buy me one."

I smile. I hope he likes it. "Okay."

Maggie opens the door to my room and pulls me behind her into the living room. "Ridge!" she yells. I laugh, because I don't know why she's yelling for him. He can't hear her.

"Hey, Warren," I say, grinning when I see him on the couch. "Happy Birthday." Bridgette is seated next to him, glaring at me. She's looking me up and down, probably jealous because my bra really is cute.

Warren shakes his head and laughs. "That's only the fiftieth time you've said that tonight, although it's a little more fitting now that you're practically in your birthday suit."

Ridge is sitting on the other side of Bridgette. He's shaking his head like Warren. "Maggie wants to know if you like my bra," I say to Ridge. I pull on Maggie's hand so she'll turn around and sign to him.

"It's a very nice bra," Ridge says, staring at it with a cocked eyebrow.

I smile. Then I frown.

Did he just . . .? I yank my hand out of Maggie's and turn back toward Ridge. "Did you just *speak?*"

He laughs. "Did you not just ask me a question?"

I glare at him hard, especially when Warren bursts out into a fit of laughter.

Oh.

My.

God.

He's not deaf?

This whole time, he's been lying to me? It's been a prank?

I instantly want to strangle him. *Both* of them. Tears sting at my eyes, and the second I lunge forward, a strong hand grips my wrist and yanks my arm back. I turn and look up at . . .
Ridge?

I turn back to the couch and look at . . . *Ridge?*

Warren is doubled over Bridgette's lap now, he's laughing so hard. Ridge Number 1 is laughing now, too. His whole face doesn't laugh when he laughs, like Ridge Number 2's face does.

And his hair is shorter than Ridge Number 2's hair. And darker.

Ridge Number 2 has his arm wrapped around my waist, and he's picking me up.

Now I'm upside down.

Not good for my stomach.

My face is toward his back, and my stomach is slumped over his shoulder as he carries me back toward my bedroom. I look at Warren and the guy I now realize is Brennan, and then I squeeze my eyes shut, because I think I'm about to throw up all over Ridge Number 2.

I'm being seated on something cold. A floor.

As soon as my mind comprehends where he's put me, my hands reach forward until I grasp the toilet, and then it suddenly feels as if I've eaten Italian food all over again. He holds my hair back while the toilet fills with Pine-Sol.

I wish it really *were* Pine-Sol. I wouldn't have to clean it.

"Don't you love her bra?" Maggie says from behind me, giggling. "I know it's a back clasp, but look at how cute the straps are!"

I feel a hand on one of my bra straps. I can feel Ridge pull her hand away. His arm moves, and I know he's signing something.

Maggie huffs. "I don't want to go to bed yet."

He signs something else, and then she sighs and walks into his bedroom.

When I'm finished, Ridge wipes my face with a rag. I allow my back to fall against the wall of the tub, and I look up at him.

He doesn't look very happy. In fact, he looks a little angry.

"It's a *party*, Ridge," I mumble, and close my eyes again.

His hands are under my arms, and I'm being carried again. He makes his way into . . . *his* room? He lowers me onto his bed, and I roll over and open my eyes. Maggie is grinning at me from the pillow next to me.

"Yay. A sleepover," she says with a groggy smile. She grabs my hand and holds it.

"Yay," I say, smiling.

Covers are pulled over both of us, and I close my eyes.

Ridge

"How did you get yourself into this mess?"

Warren and I are both standing at the edge of my bed, staring down at Maggie and Sydney. They're asleep. Sydney is spooning Maggie on the left side of the bed, because the right side of the bed is now covered in Maggie's puke.

I sigh. "This has been the longest twelve hours of my life."

Warren nods, then pats me heavily on the back. "Well," he signs, "I wish I could stay and help you nurse them back to health, but I'd rather pretend I have something better to do and leave." He turns and walks out of my room as Brennan makes his way in.

"I'm headed out," he signs. "Got my stuff out of Sydney's room."

I nod and watch as his eyes fall on Sydney and Maggie.

"I wish I could say it was fun getting to know Sydney, but I have a feeling I didn't even meet the real Sydney."

I laugh. "Believe me, you didn't. Maybe next time."

He waves and walks out of my bedroom.

I turn and look at them, at both halves of my heart, cuddled tightly together in a bed of irony.

• • •

I spent the entire morning assisting them as they alternated between the trash can and the bathroom. By lunch, Sydney's vomiting had subsided, and she made her way back to her own room. It's late afternoon now, and I'm spoon-feeding Maggie liquids and forcing her to down medicine.

"I just need sleep," she signs. "I'll be fine." She rolls over and pulls the covers up to her chin.

I tuck a lock of hair behind her ear, then run my hand down to her shoulder, where I trace circles with my thumb. Her eyes are now closed, and she's curled up in a fetal position. She looks so fragile right now, and I wish I could wrap myself around her like a cocoon and shield her from every single thing this world has left to throw at her.

I look over at the nightstand when the screen on my phone lights up. I tuck the covers more securely around Maggie and bend forward and kiss her cheek, then reach for my phone.

> Sydney: Not that you haven't done enough, but could you please tell Warren to turn the volume down on the porn?

I laugh and text Warren.

> Me: Turn the porn down. It's so loud even *I* can hear it.

I stand and walk into Sydney's room to check on her. She's flat on her back, staring up at the ceiling. I sit on the edge of her bed, reach to her face, and brush back a strand of hair from her forehead.

She tilts her face toward me and smiles, then picks up her phone. Her body is so weak she makes it look as if the phone weighs fifty pounds when she tries to text me.

I take the phone from her and shake my head, letting her know she just needs to rest. I set the phone on her nightstand and bring my attention back to her. Her head is relaxed against the pillow. Her hair is in waves, trailing down her shoulders. I run my fingers over a section of her sun-kissed hair, admiring how soft it is. She tilts her face toward my hand until her cheek is resting flush against it. I brush across her cheekbone with my thumb and watch as her eyes fall closed. The lyrics I wrote about her flash through my mind: *Lines are drawn, but then they fade. For her I bend, for you I break.*

What kind of man does that make me? If I can't prevent myself from falling for another girl, do I even deserve Maggie? I refuse to answer that, because I know that if I don't deserve Maggie, I also don't deserve Sydney. The thought of losing either of them, much less both of them, is something I can't bring myself to entertain. I lift my hand and trace the edge of Sydney's face with my fingertips, running them across her hairline, down her jaw, and up her chin, until my fingers reach her lips. I slowly trace the shape of her mouth, feeling the warm waves of breath pass her lips each time I circle around them. She opens her eyes, and the familiar pool of pain floats behind them.

She lifts a hand to my fingers. She pulls them firmly to her mouth and kisses them, then pulls our hands away, bringing them to rest on her stomach.

I'm looking at our hands now. She opens a flat palm, and I do the same, and we press them together.

I don't know a lot about the human body, but I would be willing to bet there's a nerve that runs directly from the palm of the hand, straight to the heart.

Our fingers are outstretched until she laces them together, squeezing gently when our hands connect completely, weaving together.

It's the first time I've ever held her hand.

We stare at our hands for what feels like an eternity. Every feeling and every nerve are centered in our palms, in our fingers, in our thumbs, occasionally brushing back and forth over one another.

Our hands mold together perfectly, just like the two of us. Sydney and me.

I'm convinced that people come across others in life whose souls are completely compatible with their own. Some refer to them as soul mates. Some refer to it as true love. Some people believe their souls are compatible with more than one person, and I'm beginning to understand how true that might be. I've known since the moment I met Maggie years ago that our souls were compatible, and they are. That's not even a question.

However, I also know that my soul is compatible with Sydney's, but it's also so much more than that. Our souls aren't just compatible—they're perfectly attuned. I feel everything she feels. I understand things she never even has to say. I know that what she needs is exactly what I could give her, and what she's wishing she could give me is something I never even knew I needed.

She understands me. She respects me. She astounds me. She predicts me. She's never once, since the second I met her, made me feel as if my inability to hear is even an inability at all.

I can also tell just by looking at her that she's falling in love with me. It serves as further proof that I need to do what should have been done a long time ago.

I very reluctantly lean forward, reach over to her nightstand, and grab a pen. I pull my fingers from hers and open her palm to write on it: *I need you to move out.*

I close her fingers over her palm so she doesn't read it while I'm watching her, and I walk away, leaving behind an entire half of my heart as I go.

17.

Sydney

I watch as he closes the door behind him. I'm clutching my hand to my chest, terrified to read what he wrote.

I saw the look in his eyes.

I saw the heartache, the regret, the fear . . . the *love*.

I keep my hand clutched tightly to my chest without reading it. I refuse to accept that whatever words are written on my palm will obliterate what little hope I had for our *maybe someday*.

· · ·

My body flinches, and my eyes flick open.

I don't know what just woke me up, but I was in the middle of a dead sleep. It's dark. I sit up on the bed and press my hand to my forehead, wincing from the pain. I don't feel nauseated anymore, but I've never in my life been this thirsty. I need water.

I stand up and stretch my arms above my head, then glance down to the alarm clock: 2:45 A.M.

Thank God. I could still use about three more days of sleep to recover from this hangover.

I'm walking toward Ridge's bathroom when an unfamiliar feeling washes over me. I pause before reaching the door. I'm not sure why I pause, but I suddenly feel out of place.

It feels strange, walking toward this bathroom right now.

It doesn't feel as if I'm walking toward *my* bathroom. It doesn't feel as if it belongs to me at all, unlike how my bathroom felt in my last apartment. That bathroom felt like *my* bathroom. As if it belonged partly to me. That apartment felt like *my* apartment. All the furniture in it felt like *my* furniture.

Nothing about this place feels like me. Other than the belongings that were contained in the two suitcases I brought with me that first night, nothing else here feels even remotely like mine.

The dresser? Borrowed.

The bed? Borrowed.

Thursday-night TV? Borrowed.

The kitchen, the living room, my entire bedroom. They all belong to other people. I feel as if I'm just borrowing this life until I find a better one of my own. I've felt as if I've been borrowing everything since the day I moved in here.

Hell, I'm even borrowing boyfriends. Ridge isn't mine. He'll never be mine. As much as that hurts to accept, I'm so sick of this constant, ongoing battle with my heart. I can't take this anymore. I don't deserve this kind of self-torture.

In fact, I think I need to move out.

I do.

Moving out is the only thing that can start the healing, because I can't be around Ridge anymore. Not with what his presence does to me.

You hear that, heart? We're even now.

I smile at the realization that I'm finally about to experience life on my own. I'm consumed with a sense of accomplishment. I open the bathroom door and flip on the light . . . then immediately fall to my knees.

Oh, God.

Oh, no.

No, no, no, no, no!

I grab her by the shoulders and turn her over, but her whole body is limp. Her eyes are rolled back in her head, and her face is pale.

Oh, my God! "Ridge!" I crawl over her and reach for the door to his bedroom. I'm screaming his name so loudly my throat feels as if it's ripping apart. I attempt to turn the doorknob several times, but my hand keeps slipping.

She begins to convulse, so I lunge over her and lift her head, then drop my ear to her mouth to make sure she's breathing. I'm sobbing, screaming his name over and over. I know he can't hear me, but I'm scared to let go of her head.

"Maggie!" I cry.

What am I doing? I don't know what to do.

Do something, Sydney.

I lower her head carefully back to the floor and spin around. I grip the doorknob more firmly and pull myself to my feet. I swing his bedroom door open and rush toward the bed, then jump on it and climb over to where he's lying.

"Ridge!" I scream, shaking his shoulder. He lifts an elbow in defense as he rolls over, then lowers it when he sees me hovering over him.

"Maggie!" I yell hysterically, pointing to the bathroom. His eyes flash to the empty spot on his bed, and his focus shoots up to the open bathroom door. He's off the bed and on the bathroom floor on his knees in seconds. Before I even make it back to the bathroom, he's got her head cradled in his arms, and he's pulling her onto his lap.

He turns his head to look at me and signs something. I shake my head as the tears continue to flow down my cheeks. I have no idea what he's trying to say to me. He signs again and points toward his bed. I look at the bed, then look back at him helplessly. His expression is growing more frustrated by the second.

"Ridge, I don't know what you're asking me!"

He slams his fist against the bathroom cabinet out of frustration, then holds his hand up to his ear as if he's holding a phone.

He needs his phone.

I rush to the bed and search for it, my hands flying frantically over the bed, the covers, the nightstand. I finally find it under his pillow and run it back to him. He enters his password to unlock it, then hands it back to me. I dial 911, put the phone to my ear, and wait for it to ring while I drop to my knees next to them.

His eyes are full of fear as he continues to hold her head against his chest. He's watching me, nervously waiting for the call to connect. He intermittently presses his lips into her hair as he continues to try to get her to open her eyes.

As soon as the operator answers, I'm bombarded with a list of questions that I don't know the answers to. I give her the address, because it's the only thing I know, and she begins firing more questions I don't know how to communicate to him.

"Is she allergic to anything?" I say to Ridge, repeating what the operator is asking.

He shrugs and shakes his head, not understanding me.

"Does she have any preexisting conditions?"

He shakes his head again to tell me he has no idea what I'm asking him.

"Is she diabetic?"

I ask Ridge the questions over and over, but he can't understand me. The operator is firing questions at me, and I'm firing them at Ridge, and we're both too frantic for him even to read my lips. I'm crying. We're both terrified. We're both frustrated with the fact that we can't communicate.

"Is she wearing a medical bracelet?" the operator asks.

I lift both of her wrists. "No, she doesn't have anything on her."

I look up to the ceiling and close my eyes, knowing that I'm not helping a damn bit.

"Warren!" I yell.

I'm off my feet and out of the bathroom, making my way to Warren's bedroom. I swing open his door. "Warren!" I run to his bed and shake him while I hold the phone in my hand. "Warren! We need your help! It's Maggie!"

His eyes open wide, and he throws off his covers, springing into action. I push the phone toward him. "It's 911, and I can't understand anything Ridge is trying to tell me!"

He grabs the phone and puts it to his ear. "She has CFRD," he yells hastily into the phone. "Stage two CF."

CFRD?

I follow him to the bathroom and watch as he signs to Ridge while holding the phone in the palm of his hand, away from his ear. Ridge signs something back, and Warren runs into the kitchen. He opens the refrigerator, reaches toward the back of the second shelf, and pulls out a bag. He runs with it to the bathroom and drops to his knees next to Ridge. He lets the phone fall to the floor and shoves it aside with his knee.

"Warren, she has questions!" I yell, confused about why he tossed the phone aside.

"We know what to do until they get here, Syd," he says. He pulls a syringe from the bag and hands it to Ridge. Ridge pulls the lid off of it and injects Maggie in the stomach.

"Is she diabetic?" I ask, watching helplessly as Warren and Ridge silently converse. I'm ignored, but I don't expect anything different. They're in what looks like familiar territory for both of them, and I'm too confused to keep watching. I turn around and lean against the wall, then squeeze my eyes shut in an attempt to calm myself. A few silent moments pass, and then there's banging at the door.

Warren is running toward the door before I can even react. He lets the paramedics inside, and I step out of the way, watching as everyone in the room around me seems to know what the hell is going on.

I continue to back out of everyone's way until my calves meet the couch, and I fall down onto it.

They lift Maggie onto the gurney and begin pushing her toward the front door. Ridge walks swiftly behind them. Warren comes from Ridge's bedroom and tosses him a pair of shoes. Ridge puts them on, then signs something else to Warren and slips out the door behind the gurney.

I watch as Warren rushes to his room. He reemerges with a shirt and shoes on and his baseball cap in hand. He grabs his keys off the bar and heads back into Ridge's bedroom. He comes back out with a bag of Ridge's things and heads for the front door.

"Wait!" I yell. Warren turns to look at me. "His phone. He'll need his phone." I rush to the bathroom, grab Ridge's phone from the floor, and take it back to Warren.

"I'm coming with you," I say, slipping my foot into a shoe by the front door.

"No, you're not."

I look up at him, somewhat in shock at the harshness of his voice as I slip my other shoe on. He begins to pull the door shut on me, and I slap a palm against it.

"I'm coming with you!" I say again, more determined this time.

He turns and looks at me with hardened eyes. "He doesn't need you there, Sydney."

I have no idea what he means by that, but his tone pisses me off. I push against his chest and step outside with him. "I'm *coming*," I say with finality.

I walk down the stairs just as the ambulance begins to pull away. Ridge is standing with his hands clasped behind his head, watching as it leaves. Warren makes it to the bottom of the stairs, and as soon as Ridge sees him, they both rush toward Ridge's car. I follow them.

Warren climbs into the driver's seat, Ridge into the passenger seat. I open the door to the backseat and pull it shut behind me.

Warren pulls out of the parking lot and speeds until we're caught up to the ambulance.

Ridge is terrified. I can see it in the way his arms are wrapped around himself and he's shaking his knee, fidgeting with the sleeve of his shirt, chewing on the corner of his bottom lip.

I still have no idea what's wrong with Maggie, and I'm scared that she might not be okay. It still doesn't feel like my business, and I'm definitely not about to ask Warren what's going on.

The nervousness seeping from Ridge is making my heart ache for him. I move to the edge of the backseat and reach forward, placing a comforting hand on his shoulder. He lifts his hand to mine and grabs it, then squeezes it tightly.

I want to help him, but I can't. I don't know how. All I can think about is how completely helpless I feel, how much he's hurting, and how scared I am that he might lose Maggie, because it's so painfully obvious how that would kill him.

He brings his other hand up to mine, which is still gripping his shoulder. He squeezes both of his hands around mine desperately, then tilts his face toward his shoulder. He kisses the top of my hand, and I feel a tear fall against my skin.

I close my eyes and press my forehead against the back of his seat, and I cry.

• • •

We're in the waiting room.

Well, Warren and I are in the waiting room. Ridge has been with Maggie since we arrived an hour ago, and Warren hasn't spoken a single word to me.

Which is why I'm not speaking to *him*. He obviously has an issue, and I'm not really in the mood to defend myself, because I've done absolutely nothing to Warren that should even require defending.

I slouch back in my chair and pull up the search browser on my phone, curious to know about what Warren said to the 911 operator.

I type *CFRD* into the search box and hit enter. My eyes are pulled to the very first result: *Managing cystic fibrosis–related diabetes.*

I click on the link, and it explains the different types of diabetes but doesn't explain much more. I've heard of cystic fibrosis but don't know enough about it to know how it affects Maggie. I click a link on the left of the page that says, *What is cystic fibrosis?* My heart begins to pound and my tears are flowing as I take in the same words that stick out on every single page, no matter how many pages I click.

Genetic disorder of the lungs.

Life-threatening.

Shortened life expectancy.

No known cure.

Survival rates into mid- and upper thirties.

I can't read any more through all the tears I'm crying for Maggie. For Ridge.

I close the browser on my phone, and my eyes are pulled to my hand. I take in the unread words in Ridge's handwriting across my palm.

I need you to move out.

Ridge

Both Warren and Sydney spring to their feet when I round the corner to the waiting room.

"How is she?" Warren signs.

"Better. She's awake now."

Warren nods, and Sydney is looking back and forth between us.

"The doctor says the alcohol and dehydration probably caused her . . ." I stop signing, because Warren's lips are pressed into a firm line as he watches my explanation.

"Verbalize for her," I sign, nodding my head toward Sydney.

Warren turns and looks at Sydney, then refocuses his attention on me. "This doesn't concern her," he signs silently.

What the hell is his problem?

"She's worried about Maggie, Warren. It does concern her. Now, verbalize what I'm saying for her."

Warren shakes his head. "She's not here for Maggie, Ridge. She doesn't care how Maggie's doing. She's only worried about you."

I bury my anger, then slowly step forward and stand directly in front of him. "Verbalize for her. *Now*."

Warren sighs but doesn't turn toward Sydney. He stares straight at me as he both signs and verbalizes for us. "Ridge says Maggie's okay. She's awake."

Sydney's entire body relaxes as her hands go to the back of her head and relief washes over her. She says something to him, and he closes his eyes, takes a quick breath, then opens them.

"Sydney wants to know if either of you need anything. From the apartment."

I look at Sydney and shake my head. "They're keeping her overnight to monitor her blood sugar. I'll come by tomorrow if we need anything. I'm staying a few days at her house."

Warren verbalizes again, and Sydney nods.

"You two head back and get some rest."

Warren nods. Sydney steps forward and gives me a tight hug, then backs away.

Warren begins to turn toward the exit, but I grab his arm and make him look at me again. "I don't know why you're upset with her, Warren, but please don't be a jerk to her. I've done that enough already."

He nods, and they turn to leave. Sydney looks back over her shoulder and smiles a painful smile. I turn and walk back to Maggie's room.

The head of her bed is slightly raised now, and she looks up at me. There's an IV drip in her arm, replenishing her fluids. Her head slowly rolls across her pillow as her eyes follow me across the room.

"I'm sorry," she signs.

I shake my head, not even remotely wanting or needing any type of apology from her. "Stop. Don't feel bad. Like you always say, you're young. Young people do crazy things like get drunk and have hangovers and puke for twelve hours straight."

She laughs. "Yes, but like *you* always say, probably not young people with life-threatening conditions."

I smile as I reach her bed, then scoot a chair close to it and take a seat. "I'm going back to San Antonio with you. I'll stay a few days until I feel better about leaving you alone."

She sighs and turns her head, looking straight up to the ceiling. "I'm *fine*. It was just an insulin issue." She turns back to face me. "You can't baby me every time this happens, Ridge."

My jaw clenches at "baby me." "I'm not *babying* you, Maggie. I'm *loving* you. I'm *taking care* of you. There's a difference."

She closes her eyes and shakes her head. "I'm so tired of having this same conversation over and over."

Yeah. So am I.

I lean back in my chair and fold my arms over my chest while I stare at her. Her refusal of help has been understandable up to this point, but she's not a teenager anymore, and I can't understand why she won't allow things to progress with us.

I lean forward, touching her arm so she'll look at me and listen. "You need to stop being so hell-bent and determined to have your independence. If you don't take better care of yourself, these brief one-night hospital stays will be a thing of the past, Maggie. Let me take care of you. Let me be there for you. I constantly worry myself sick. Your internship is causing you so much stress, not to mention the thesis. I understand why you want to live a normal life and do all the things other people our age do, like go to college and have a career." I pause to run my hands through my hair and focus on the point I want to make. "If we lived together, I could do so much more for you. Things would be easier for both of us. And when things like this happen, I'll be there to help you so you don't convulse alone on the bathroom floor until you die!"

Breathe, Ridge.

Okay, that was harsh. Way too harsh.

I roll my neck and look down at the floor, because I'm not ready for her to respond yet. I close my eyes and try to hold back my frustration. "Maggie," I sign, looking at her tear-soaked eyes. "I . . . love . . . you. And I am so scared that one of these days, I won't be able to walk out of the hospital with you still in my arms. And it'll be my own fault for allowing you to continue to refuse my help."

Her bottom lip is quivering, so she tucks it into her mouth and bites it. "Sometime in the next ten or fifteen years, Ridge, that *will* be your reality. You *are* going to walk out of the hospital without me, because no matter how much you want to be my hero, I can't be saved. You can't save me from this. We both know you're one of the few people I have in this world, so until the day comes when I can absolutely no longer take care of myself, I refuse to become your burden. Do you know what that does to me? To know that I've put that much pressure on you? I'm not living alone simply because I crave independence, Ridge. I want to live alone because . . ."

Tears are streaming down her cheeks, and she pauses to wipe them away. "I want to live alone because I just want to be the girl you're in love with . . . for as long as we can draw that out. I don't want to be your burden or your responsibility or your obligation. The only thing I want is to be the love of your life. That's *all*. Please, just let that be enough for now. Let it be enough until the time comes when you really do have to go to the ends of the earth for me."

A sob breaks free from my chest, and I reach forward and press my lips to hers. I grip her face desperately between my hands and lift my leg onto the bed. She wraps her arms around me as I pull the rest of my body on top of hers and do whatever I can to shield her from the unfairness of this evil, goddamned world.

18.

Sydney

I close the door to Ridge's car and follow Warren up the stairs toward the apartment. Neither of us said a word to each other on the drive home from the hospital. The rigidness in his jaw said all he needed to say, which was, more or less, *Don't speak to me*. I spent the drive with my focus out the window and my questions lodged in my throat.

We walk into the apartment, and he tosses his keys onto the bar as I shut the door behind me. He doesn't even turn around to look at me as he stalks off toward his bedroom.

"Good *night*," I say. I might have said it with a little bit of sarcastic bite, but at least I'm not screaming, "Screw you, Warren!" which is kind of what I feel like saying.

He pauses, then turns around to face me. I watch him nervously, because whatever he's about to say to me isn't "good night." His eyes narrow as he tilts his head, shaking it slowly. "Can I ask you a question?" he finally says, eyeing me with curiosity.

"As long as you promise never again to begin a question by asking whether or not you can propose a question."

I want to laugh at my use of Ridge's comment, but Warren doesn't even crack a smile. It only makes things much more awkward. I shift on my feet. "What's your question, Warren?" I say with a sigh.

He folds his arms over his chest and walks toward me. I

swallow my nervousness as he leans forward to speak to me, barely a foot away. "Do you just need someone to fuck you?"

Breathe in, breathe out.

Expand, contract.

Beat beat, pause. Beat beat, pause.

"What?" I say, dumbfounded. I'm positive I didn't hear him right.

He lowers his head a few inches until he's at eye level with me. "Do you just need someone to *fuck* you?" he says, with more precise enunciation this time. "Because if that's all it is, I'll bend you over the couch right now and fuck you so hard you'll never think about Ridge again." He continues to stare at me, cold and heartless.

Think before you react, Sydney.

For several seconds, all I can do is shake my head in disbelief. Why would he say that? Why would he say something so disrespectful to me? This isn't Warren. I don't know who this asshole is standing in front of me, but it definitely isn't Warren.

Before I allow myself time to think, I react. I pull my arm back, then make four punches my lifetime average as my fist meets his cheek.

Shit.

That hurt.

I look up at him, and his hand is covering his cheek. His eyes are wide, and he's looking at me with more surprise than pain. He takes a step back, and I keep my eyes focused hard on his.

I grab my fist and pull it up to my chest, pissed that I'm going to have another hurt hand. I wait before going to the kitchen to get ice for it, though. I might need to hit him again.

I'm confused by his obvious anger toward me for the past twenty-four hours. My mind rushes through anything I could have said or done to him that would make him feel this much hatred toward me.

He sighs and tilts his head back, pulling his hands through his hair. He gives no explanation for his hateful words, and I try to understand them, but I can't. I've done nothing to him to warrant something that harsh.

Maybe that's his problem, though. Perhaps the fact that I've done nothing to him—or *with* him—is what's pissing him off like this.

"Is this jealousy?" I ask. "Is that what's making you this evil, wretched excuse for a human being? Because I never *slept* with you?"

He takes a step forward, and I immediately back up until I fall down onto the couch. He bends down, bringing himself to my eye level.

"I don't want to *screw* you, Sydney. And I am definitely not jealous." He pushes himself away from the couch. Away from me.

He's scaring the living shit out of me, and I want to pack my suitcases and leave tonight and never, ever see any of these people again.

I begin crying into my hands. I hear him sigh heavily, and he drops down onto the couch beside me. I pull my feet up and turn my knees away from him, curling into the far corner of the couch. We sit like this for several minutes, and I want to stand up and run to my room, but I don't. I feel as if I'd have to ask permission, because I don't even know if I have a room here anymore.

"I'm sorry," he finally says, breaking the silence with something other than my crying. "God, I'm sorry. I just . . . I'm trying to understand what the hell you're doing."

I wipe my face with my shirt and glance at him. His face is a jumbled mixture of sadness and sorrow, and I don't understand anything he's feeling.

"What is your problem with me, Warren? I've never been anything but nice to you. I've even been nice to your bitch of a girlfriend, and believe me, that takes effort."

He nods in agreement. "I know," he says, exasperated. "I know, I know, I know. You *are* a nice person." He laces his fingers together and stretches his arms out, then brings them back down with a heavy sigh. "And I know you have good intentions. You have a good heart. *And* a pretty good right swing," he says, grinning slyly. "I guess that's why I'm so mad, though. I know you have a good heart, so why in the hell haven't you moved out yet?" His words hurt me more now than the vulgar ones he spit at me five minutes ago.

"If you and Ridge wanted me gone this bad, why did you both wait until this weekend to tell me?"

My question seems to catch Warren off-guard, because his eyes cut to mine briefly before he looks away again. He doesn't answer that question, though. Instead, he begins to prepare one of his own. "Has Ridge ever told you the story of how he met Maggie?" he asks.

I shake my head, completely confused by the direction this conversation has taken.

"I was seventeen, and Ridge had just turned eighteen," he says. He leans back against the couch and stares down at his hands.

I recall Ridge saying he began dating Maggie when he was nineteen, but I keep silent and let him continue.

"We had been dating for about six weeks, and . . ."

Scratch that thought. Can no longer keep silent. "We?" I ask hesitantly. "As in you and *Ridge*?"

"No, dumbass. As in me and *Maggie*."

I try to hide my shock, but he doesn't look at me long enough to even see my reaction.

"Maggie was my girlfriend first. I met her at a fund-raising event for children who were deaf. I was there with my parents, who were both on the committee." He pulls his hands behind his head and leans against the couch.

"Ridge was with me the first time I saw her. We both

thought she was the most beautiful thing we had ever laid eyes on, but, fortunately for me, my eyes landed on her about five seconds before his did, so I called dibs. Of course, neither one of us expected to actually have a chance with her. I mean, you've seen her. She's incredible." He pauses for a moment, then props a leg on the table in front of us.

"Anyway, I spent the whole day flirting with her. Charming her with my good looks and my killer body."

I laugh, but only out of courtesy.

"She agreed to go on a date with me, so I told her I'd pick her up that Friday night. I took her out, made her laugh, took her back home, and kissed her. It was great, so I asked her out again, and she agreed. I took her out for a second date, then a third date. I liked her. We got along well; she laughed at my jokes. She also got along with Ridge, which scored major points in my book. The girl and the best friend have to get along, or one of the two will suffer. Luckily, we all got along great. On our fourth date, I asked her if she wanted to make it official, and she agreed. I was stoked, because I knew she was by far the hottest girl I'd ever dated or ever *would* date. I couldn't let her slip away, especially before I was able to go all the way with her."

He laughs. "I remember saying that to Ridge the same night. Told him if there was one girl on this earth I needed to devirginize, it was Maggie. Told him I'd go on a hundred dates with her if that's what it took. He turned his head to me and signed, 'What about a hundred and *one*?' I laughed, because I didn't understand what the hell Ridge meant. I didn't understand at the time that he liked her the way he did, and I never really understood all the little gems he would spout. Still don't. Looking back on the whole situation and the way he would sit there and have to listen to the punk-ass things I said about her, I'm surprised he didn't punch me sooner than he did."

"He punched you?" I ask. "Why? Because you talked about screwing her?"

He shakes his head, and a look of guilt washes over him. "No," he says quietly. "Because I *did* screw her."

He sighs but continues. "We were staying the night at Ridge and Brennan's. Maggie spent a lot of time over there with me, and we had been dating for about six weeks. I know that's not long in virgin weeks, but it's a damn eternity in guy weeks. We were lying in bed together, and she told me she was ready to go all the way, but before she would have sex with me, there was something she needed to tell me. She said I had a right to know, and she wouldn't feel right continuing a relationship until I was fully informed. I remember panicking, thinking she was about to tell me she was a dude or some shit like that."

He glances at me and raises an eyebrow. "Because let's be honest, Syd. There are some really hot transvestite-looking dudes out there."

He laughs and looks straight ahead again. "That's when she told me about her illness. Told me about the statistics . . . the fact that she didn't want children . . . the reality of how much time she had left. She said she wanted to lay the truth out for me because it wouldn't be fair to anyone who saw something long-term with her. She said the likelihood of her making it to the age of forty or even thirty-five was small. She said she needed to be with someone who understood that. Someone who accepted that."

"You didn't want that responsibility?" I ask him.

He shakes his head slowly. "Sydney, I didn't care about the responsibility. I was a seventeen-year-old guy, in bed with the most beautiful girl I had ever seen, and all she was asking me to do was agree to love her. When she mentioned the words 'future' and 'husband' and not wanting kids, it took all I had not to roll my eyes, because in my head, those were a lifetime away. I would be with a million girls before then. I didn't know how to think that far ahead, so I just did what I thought any guy would do in that situation. I reassured her and told her that her illness didn't matter to me and that I loved her. Then I kissed her, took off her clothes, and took her virginity."

He hangs his head in what looks like shame. "After she left the next morning, I was bragging to Ridge about finally getting to bang a virgin. Probably went into way too much detail. I also mentioned the conversation we had beforehand and told him all about her illness. I was brutally honest with him to a fault sometimes. I told him that her whole situation kind of freaked me out and that I was going to give it two weeks before I broke up with her so I wouldn't look like such a douche. That's when he beat the living shit out of me."

My eyes widen. "Good for Ridge," I say.

Warren nods. "Yeah. Apparently, he liked her a whole lot more than he let on, but he just kept his mouth shut and allowed me to make an ass of myself for the whole six weeks I dated her. I should have caught on about how he felt, but Ridge is a lot more selfless than I am. He would have never done anything to betray what we had, but after that night, he lost a whole lot of respect for me. And that hurt, Sydney. He's like my brother. I felt like I had disappointed the one person I looked up to the most."

"So you broke up with Maggie, and Ridge started dating her?"

"Yes and no. We had a long conversation about it that afternoon, because Ridge is big on sharing his thoughts and shit. We agreed we had to honor the bro code, and it wouldn't really be good for us if he picked up and started dating a girl I had just screwed. But he liked her. He liked her a lot, and even though I knew it was hard for him, he waited until the term ended before he asked her out."

"The term?"

Warren nods. "Yeah. Don't ask where we came up with it, but we agreed twelve months was a decent length of time before the bro code became null. We figured enough time would have passed, and if he wanted to ask her out after a year, it wouldn't be so weird. By that time, she might have dated other people and wouldn't be going straight from my bed into Ridge's. As much as I could have tried to be cool about it, it would have been too weird. Even for us."

"Did Maggie know how he felt about her? During the twelve months?"

Warren shakes his head. "No. Maggie never even knew he liked her like he did. He liked her so much he didn't go on a single date for the entire twelve months I made him wait. He had the date circled on a calendar. I saw it once in his room. He never mentioned her, never asked about her. But I'll be damned if the day that year was up, he wasn't knocking on her front door. And it took her a while to come around, especially knowing she would have to interact with me. But things eventually worked themselves out. She ended up with the right guy in the end, thanks to Ridge's persistence."

I exhale. "Wow," I say. "Talk about devotion."

He turns his head toward mine, and our eyes meet. "Exactly," he says firmly, as if I just summed up his whole point. "I have never in my life met another human being with more devotion than that man. He's the best damn thing that's ever happened to me. The best thing that's ever happened to Maggie."

He pulls his feet up onto the couch and faces me full-on. "He's gone through hell and back for that girl, Sydney. All the hospital stays, driving back and forth to take care of her, promising her the world, and giving up so much of himself in return. And she deserves it. She's one of the purest, most selfless people I've ever met, and if there are two people who deserve each other in this world, it's the two of them.

"So when I see how he looks at you, it pains me. I saw the way the two of you watched each other at the party the other night. I saw the jealousy in his eyes every time you spoke to Brennan. I've never seen him struggle with his choice or the sacrifices he's made for Maggie until you showed up. He's falling in love with you, Sydney, and I know you know that. However, I also know his heart, and he'll never leave Maggie. He loves her. He would never do that to her. So seeing him torn apart because of the way he feels about you and knowing his life is with Maggie, I just don't understand why you're still here. I don't understand why you're putting him through that much pain. Each day you're still here and I see him looking at you the same way he used to look at Maggie, it makes me want to shove you out the damn door and tell you to never come back. And I know that's not your fault. I *know* that. Hell, you didn't even know the half of what he's going through until tonight. But now you do. And as much as I love you and think you're one of the coolest damn chicks I've ever met, I also never want to see your face again. Especially now that you know the truth about Maggie. And forgive me if this is harsh, but I don't want you getting it into your head that the love you have for Ridge will be enough to hold you over until the day Maggie dies. Because Maggie isn't dying, Sydney. Maggie's *living*. She'll be around a lot longer than Ridge's heart could ever survive you."

My head rolls forward into my hands as the sobs erupt from my chest. Warren's arm folds over my back, and he pulls me against him. I don't know who I'm crying for right now, but my heart hurts so much I just want to rip it from my fucking chest and throw it over Ridge's balcony, because that's where this whole mess began.

Ridge

Maggie has been asleep for a couple of hours now, but I've yet to sleep. That's usually how it is when I'm with her in the hospital. After five years of sporadic stays, I've learned it's much easier not to sleep at all than it is to get a half-ass couple of hours.

I open my laptop and pull up my messages to Sydney, then send her a quick hello to see if she's online. We haven't had a chance to discuss the fact that I asked her to move out, and I hate not knowing if she's okay. I know it's wrong to be messaging her at this point, but it seems even more wrong to leave things unsaid.

She returns my message almost immediately, and the tone of it already relieves some of my worry. I don't know why I always expect she'll respond unreasonably, because she's never once shown a lack of maturity or regard for my situation.

Sydney: Yeah, I'm here. How's Maggie?

Me: She's good. She'll be discharged this afternoon.

Sydney: That's good. I've been worried.

Me: Thank you, by the way. For your help last night.

Sydney: I wasn't much help. I felt like I was in the way more than anything.

Me: You weren't. There's no telling what could have happened if you hadn't found her.

I wait a moment for her to respond, but she doesn't. I guess we've reached the point in this conversation where one of us needs to bring up what we both know must be discussed. I feel responsible for this entire situation with her, so I bite the bullet and lay it out there.

Me: Do you have a minute? I really have some things I'd like to say to you.

Sydney: Yes, and likewise.

I glance up at Maggie again, and she's still asleep in the same position. Having this conversation with Sydney in her presence, as innocent as it is, makes me uneasy. I take my laptop and walk out of the hospital room and into the empty hallway. I sit on the floor beside the door to Maggie's room and reopen my laptop.

Me: The main thing I've appreciated about our time together over the last couple of months is the fact that we've been upfront and consistent with each other. With that being said, I don't want you to leave with the wrong idea about why I need you to move out. I don't want you to think you did anything wrong.

Sydney: I don't need an explanation. I've more than worn out my welcome, and you have enough to stress about without adding me into the mix. Warren found an apartment for me this morning, but it isn't available for a few days. Is it okay if I stay here until then?

Me: Of course. When I said I needed you to move, I didn't literally mean today. I just meant soon. Before things become too hard for me to continue to walk away.

Sydney: I'm sorry, Ridge. I didn't mean for any of this to happen.

I know she's referring to the way we feel about each other. I know exactly what she means, because I didn't mean for it to happen, either. In fact, I've done everything I could to stop it from happening, but somehow my heart never got the message. If I know it wasn't intentional on my part, I know it wasn't intentional on her part, so she has nothing to apologize for.

Me: Why are you apologizing? Don't apologize. It's not your fault, Sydney. Hell, I'm not even sure it's MY fault.

Sydney: Well, usually when something goes wrong, someone is at fault.

Me: Things didn't go wrong with us. That's our problem. Things are way too right between us. We make sense. Everything about you feels so right, but—

I pause for a few moments to gather my thoughts, because I don't want to say anything I'll regret. I inhale, then type out the best way to describe how I feel about our entire situation.

Me: There isn't a doubt in my mind that we could be perfect for each other's life, Sydney. It's our lives that aren't perfect for us.

Several minutes pass without a response. I don't know if I crossed the line with my comments, but however she's reacting to them, I needed to say what I had to say before I could let her go. I'm beginning to close my laptop when another message pops up from her.

Sydney: If there's one thing I've learned from this whole experience, it's that my ability to trust wasn't completely broken by Hunter and Tori like I initially thought. You've always been upfront with me about how you feel. We've never skirted around the truth. If anything, we've worked together to find a way to change our course. I want to thank you for that. Thank you so much for showing me that guys like you actually exist, and not everyone is a Hunter.

She somehow has a way of making me sound so much more innocent than I actually am. I'm not nearly as strong as she thinks I am.

Me: Don't thank me, Sydney. You shouldn't thank me, because I failed miserably at trying not to fall in love with you.

I swallow the lump forming in my throat and hit send. Saying what I've just said to her fills me with more guilt than the night I kissed her. Words can sometimes have a far greater effect on a heart than a kiss.

Sydney: I failed first.

I read her last message, and the finality of our imminent good-bye hits me full-force. I feel it in every single part of me, and I'm shocked at the reaction I'm having to it. I lean my head against the wall behind me and try to imagine my world before Sydney entered it. It was a good world. A consistent world. But then she came along and shook my world upside down as if it were a fragile, breakable snow globe. Now that she's leaving, it feels as if the snow is about to settle, and my whole world will be upright and still and consistent again. As much as that should make me feel at ease, it actually terrifies me. I'm scared to death that I'll never again feel any of the things I felt during the little time she's been in my world.

Anyone who has made this much of an impact deserves a proper good-bye.

I stand and walk back into Maggie's hospital room. She's still asleep, so I walk over to her bed, give her a light kiss on the forehead, and leave her a note explaining that I'm heading to the apartment to pack a few things before she's released.

Then I leave to go and give the other half of my heart a proper good-bye.

•   •   •

I'm outside Sydney's bedroom door, preparing to knock. We've said everything that needs to be said and even a lot that probably shouldn't have been said, but I can't not see her one last time before I go. She'll be gone by the time I get back from San Antonio. I have no plans to contact her after today, so the fact that I know this is definitely good-bye is pressing on the walls of my chest, and it fucking hurts like hell.

If I were to look at my situation from an outsider's point of view, I would be telling myself to forget about Sydney's feelings, that my loyalty should lie solely with Maggie. I would be telling myself to leave and that Sydney doesn't deserve a good-bye, even after all we've been through.

Is life really that black-and-white, though? Can a simple right or wrong define my situation? Do Sydney's feelings not count in this mix somewhere despite my loyalty to Maggie? It doesn't seem right just to let her go. But it's unfair to Maggie *not* to just let her go.

I don't know how I ever got myself into this mess to begin with, but I know the only way to end it is to break off all contact with Sydney. I knew the moment I held her hand last night that there wasn't a flaw in the world that could have stopped my heart from feeling what it was feeling.

I'm not proud of the fact that Maggie doesn't make up all of my heart anymore. I fought it. I fought it hard, because I didn't want it to happen. Now that the fight is finally coming to an end, I'm not even sure if I'm winning or losing. I'm not even sure which side I'm rooting for, much less which side I was on.

I knock lightly on Sydney's door, then place my palms flat against the doorframe and look down, half of me hoping she refuses to open it and half of me restraining myself from breaking down the damn door to get to her.

Within seconds, we're face-to-face for what I know is the last time. Her blue eyes are wide with fear and surprise and maybe even a small amount of relief when she sees me standing in front of her. She doesn't know how to feel about seeing me here, but her confusion is comforting. It's good to know I'm not alone in this, that we're both sharing the same mixture of emotions. We're in this together.

Sydney and me.

We're just two completely confused souls, scared of a much unwanted yet crucial good-bye.

19.

Sydney

Be still, heart. Please, be still.

I don't want him to be standing here in front of me. I don't want him to be looking at me, wearing the expression that mirrors my own feelings. I don't want him to hurt like I'm hurting. I don't want him to miss me like I'll miss him. I don't want him to be falling for me like I've been falling for him.

I want him to be with Maggie right now. I want him to *want* to be with Maggie right now, because it would make this so much easier knowing our feelings were less a reflection of each other's and more like a one-way mirror. If this weren't so hard for him, it would make it easier for me to forget him, easier to accept his choice. Instead, it makes my heart hurt twice as much knowing that our good-bye is hurting him just as much as it's hurting me.

It's *killing* me, because nothing and no one could ever fit my life the way I know he could. I feel as though I'm willingly forking over my one chance for an exceptional life, and in return, I'm accepting a mediocre version without Ridge in it. My father's words ring in my head, and I'm beginning to wonder if he had a point after all. *A life of mediocrity is a waste of a life.*

Our eyes remain in their silent embrace for several moments, until we both break our gaze, allowing ourselves to take in every last thing about each other.

His eyes scroll carefully over my face as if he's committing me to memory. His memory is the last place I want to be.

I would give anything to always be in his present.

I lean my head against my open bedroom door and stare at his hands still gripping the doorframe. The same hands I'll never see play a guitar again. The same hands that will never hold mine again. The same hands that will never again touch me and hold me in order to listen to me sing.

The same hands that are suddenly reaching for me, wrapping themselves around me, gripping my back in an embrace so tight I don't know if I could break away even if I tried. But I'm not trying to break away. I'm reciprocating. I'm hugging him with just as much desperation. I find solace against his chest while his cheek presses against the top of my head. With each heavy, uncontrolled breath that passes through his lungs, my own breaths try to keep pace. However, mine are coming in much shorter gasps, thanks to the tears that are working their way out of me.

My sadness is consuming me, and I don't even try to hold it in as I cry huge tears of grief. I'm crying tears over the death of something that never even had the chance to live.

The death of *us*.

Ridge and I remain clasped together for several minutes. So many minutes that I'm trying not to count, for fear that we've been standing here way too long for it to be an appropriate embrace. Apparently, he notices this, too, because he slides his hands up my back and to my shoulders, then pulls away from me. I lift my face from his shirt and wipe at my eyes before looking back up at him.

Once we make eye contact again, he removes his hands from my shoulders and tentatively places them on either side of my face. His eyes study mine for several moments, and the way he's looking at me makes me hate myself, because I love it so much.

I love the way he's looking at me as if I'm the only thing that matters right now. I'm the only one he sees. He's the only one *I* see. My thoughts once again lead back to some of the lyrics he wrote.

It's making me feel like I want to be the only man that you ever see.

His gaze flickers between my mouth and my eyes, almost as if he can't decide if he wants to kiss me, stare at me, or talk to me.

"Sydney," he whispers.

I gasp and clutch a hand to my chest. My heart just disintegrated at the sound of his voice.

"I don't . . . speak . . . well," he says with a quiet and unsure voice.

Oh, my heart. Hearing him speak is almost too much to take in. Each word that meets my ears is enough to bring me to my knees, and it's not even the sound of his voice or the quality of his speech. It's the fact that he's choosing this moment to speak for the first time in fifteen years.

He pauses before finishing what he needs to say and it gives my heart and my lungs a moment to catch up with the rest of me. He sounds exactly as I imagined he would sound after hearing his laughter so many times. His voice is slightly deeper than his laughter, but somewhat out of focus. His voice reminds me of a photograph in a way. I can understand his words, but they're out of focus. It's as if I'm looking at a picture and the subject is recognizable, but not in focus . . . similar to his words.

I just fell in love with his voice. With the out-of-focus picture he's painting with his words.

With . . . *him.*

He inhales softly, then nervously exhales before continuing. "I need you . . . to hear this," he says, cradling my head in his hands. "I . . . will *never* . . . regret you."

Beat, beat, pause.

Contract, expand.

Inhale, exhale.

I just officially lost the war on my heart. I don't even bother verbalizing a response to him. My reaction can be seen in my tears. He leans forward and presses his lips to my forehead; then he drops his hands and slowly backs away from me. With each move he makes to pull apart from me, I feel my heart crumbling. I can almost hear us being ripped apart. I can almost hear his heart tearing in two, crashing to the floor right next to mine.

As much as I know he should leave, I'm a breath away from begging him to stay. I want to fall to my knees, right next to our shattered hearts, and beg him to choose me. The pathetic part of me wants to beg him just to kiss me, even if he doesn't choose me.

But the part of me that ultimately wins is the part that keeps her mouth shut, because I know Maggie deserves him more than I do.

I keep my hands to my sides as he backs away another step, preparing to turn through my bedroom door. Our eyes are still locked, but when my phone sounds off in my pocket, I jump, quickly tearing my gaze from his. I hear his phone vibrate in his pocket. The sudden interruption of both of our phones is only obvious to me until he sees me opening my cell phone at the same time as he pulls his out of his pocket. Our eyes meet briefly, but the interruption of the outside world seems to have brought us both back to the reality of our situation. Back to the fact that his heart belongs with someone else, and this is still good-bye.

I watch as he reads his text first. I'm unable to take my eyes off of him in order to read mine. His expression quickly becomes tortured by whatever words he's reading, and he slowly shakes his head.

He winces.

Until this very moment, I'd never seen a heart break right before my eyes. Whatever he just read has completely shattered him.

He doesn't look at me again. In one swift movement, he grips his phone tightly in his hand as if it's become an extension of him, and he heads straight for the front door and swings it open. I step out into the living room, watching him in fear as I walk toward the front door. He doesn't even shut the door behind him as he takes the stairs two at a time, jumping over the edge of the railing to shave off another half a second in his frantic race to get to wherever it is he desperately needs to be.

I look down at my phone and unlock the screen. Maggie's number shows as the last incoming text message. I open it and see that Ridge and I were the only recipients. I read it carefully, immediately recognizing the familiar string of words she's typed out to both of us.

> Maggie: "Maggie showed up last night an hour after I got back to my room. I was convinced you were going to barge in and tell her what a jerk I am for kissing you."

I immediately walk to the couch and sit, no longer able to support my body weight. Her words knocked the breath out of me, sucked the strength from my limbs, and robbed me of any sense of dignity I thought I had left.

I try to recall the medium through which Ridge's words were initially typed.

His laptop.

Oh, no. Our messages.

Maggie is reading our messages. No, no, no.

She won't understand. She'll only see the words that'll hurt. She won't be able to see how much Ridge has been fighting this for her.

Another text shows up from Maggie, and I don't want to read it. I don't want to see our conversation through Maggie's eyes.

Maggie: "I never thought it was possible to have honest feelings for more than one person, but you've convinced me of how incredibly wrong I was."

I turn my phone on silent and toss it onto the couch beside me, then start crying into my hands.

How could I do this to her?

How could I do to her what was done to me, knowing it's the worst feeling in the world?

I've never in my life known this kind of shame.

Several minutes pass, full of regrets, before I realize the front door is still wide open. I leave my phone on the couch and walk to the door to shut it, but my eyes are drawn to the cab pulled up directly in front of our complex. Maggie is stepping out, looking up at me as she closes the door. I'm not at all prepared to see her, so I quickly step back out of her sight to regain my bearings. I don't know if I should go hide in my room or stay out here and try to explain Ridge's innocence in all of this.

But how would I do that? She obviously read the conversations herself. She knows we kissed. She knows he admitted having feelings for me. As much as I can try to convince her that he did everything he could not to feel that way, it doesn't excuse the fact that the guy she's in love with has openly admitted his feelings for someone else. Nothing can excuse that, and I feel like complete shit for being a part of it.

I'm still standing with the door open when she makes it to the top of the stairs. She's looking at me with a stern expression. I know she's more than likely here for anything other than me, so I take a step back and open the door wider. She looks down at her feet when she passes me, unable to continue the eye contact.

I don't blame her. I wouldn't be able to look at me, either. In fact, if I were her, I'd be punching me right now.

She heads to the kitchen counter, and she drops Ridge's laptop onto it without delicacy. Then she heads straight to Ridge's room. I hear her rummaging through stuff, and she eventually comes out with a bag in one hand and her car keys in the other. I'm still standing motionless with my hands on the door. She continues to keep her eyes focused on the floor as she passes me again, but this time, she makes a quick movement with her hand and wipes away a tear.

She walks out the door, down the stairs, and straight to her car, never speaking a word.

I wanted her to tell me she hated me. I wanted her to punch me and scream at me and call me a bitch. I wanted her to give me a reason to be angry, because right now, my heart is breaking for her, and I know there isn't a damn thing I could say to make her better. I know this for a fact, because I've recently been in the same situation that Ridge and I have just put her in.

We just made her a Sydney.

Ridge

The third and final text comes through when I pull up to the hospital. I know it's the final text, because it's pulled from the conversation I had with Sydney less than two hours ago. It's the very last thing I messaged her.

> Maggie: "Don't thank me, Sydney. You shouldn't thank me, because I failed miserably at trying not to fall in love with you."

I can't take any more. I throw the phone into the passenger seat and exit the vehicle, then sprint into the hospital and straight up to her room. I push open the door and rush inside, preparing to do whatever I can to persuade her to hear me out.

When I'm inside her room, I'm instantly gutted.

She's gone.

I press my palms against my forehead and pace the empty room, trying to figure out how I can take it all back. She read *everything*. Every single conversation I've ever had with Sydney on my laptop. Every single honest feeling I've shared, every joke we've made, every flaw we've listed.

Why was I so damn *careless*?

Twenty-four years I've lived without ever experiencing this type of hatred. It's the type of hatred that completely overwhelms the conscience. It's the type of hatred that excuses otherwise inexcusable actions. It's the type of hatred that can be felt in every facet of the body and in every inch of the soul. I've never known it until this moment. I've never hated anything or anyone with as much intensity as I hate myself right now.

20.

Sydney

"Are you crying?" Bridgette asks without compassion as she comes through the front door. Warren follows closely behind her, but he pauses the second his eyes meet mine.

I don't know how long I've been sitting motionless on the couch, but it still isn't long enough for reality to have been absorbed just yet. I'm still hoping this is a dream. Or a nightmare. This isn't how things were supposed to turn out.

"Sydney?" Warren says hesitantly. He knows something is wrong, because I'm sure my swollen, bloodshot eyes clearly give me away.

I attempt to form an answer, but I fail to come up with one. As much a part of this as I am, I still feel that Ridge and Maggie's situation isn't mine to be sharing.

Luckily, Warren doesn't have to ask me what's wrong, because I'm spared by Ridge's presence. He's barging through the front door, taking both Bridgette's and Warren's attention off of me.

He pushes between the two of them and heads straight for his room. He swings open the door, then comes out through the bathroom seconds later. He looks at Warren and signs something. Warren shrugs and signs back, but I can't follow their conversation at all.

When Ridge responds again, Warren looks directly at me. "What does he mean?" Warren asks me.

I shrug. "I failed to learn sign language between now and the last time we spoke, Warren. How the hell should I know?"

I don't know where my unwarranted sarcasm is coming from, but I feel Warren should have anticipated that one.

He shakes his head. "Where's Maggie, Sydney?" Warren points at the counter toward Ridge's computer. "He says she had his computer, so she had to come by here after she left the hospital."

I look at Ridge to answer but can't deny the fact that jealousy is coursing through me at watching his reaction when it comes to Maggie. "I don't know where she went. All she did was walk in, set your computer down, and grab her things. She's been gone for half an hour."

Warren is signing everything I'm saying to Ridge. When he finishes, Ridge runs a frustrated hand through his hair, then takes a step toward me. His eyes are angry and hurt, and he begins signing with forceful movements of his hands. His obvious anger makes me wince, but his disappointment in me fills me with my own share of anger.

"He wants to know how you could just let her leave," Warren says.

I immediately stand up and look Ridge directly in the eye. "What did you expect me to do, Ridge? Lock her in the damn closet? You can't be mad at me for this! I'm not the one who failed to delete messages I wouldn't want someone else to read!"

I don't wait for Warren to finish signing for Ridge. I walk to my bedroom and slam the door behind me, then drop down onto my bed. Moments later, I hear the door to Ridge's bedroom slam shut, too. The sounds don't stop there, though. I hear things crashing against his bedroom walls, one by one, as he takes his frustration out on any inanimate object in his path.

I don't hear the knock through the sounds coming from Ridge's bedroom. My door opens, and Warren slips inside. He shuts my bedroom door, then leans his back against it. "What happened?" he asks.

I turn my head to face the other direction. I don't want to answer him, and I don't want to look at him, because I know anything I say to him will only cause him to be disappointed in Ridge and me. I don't want him to be disappointed in Ridge.

"Are you okay?" His voice is closer now. He sits down on the bed beside me and places a comforting hand on my back. The reassuring contact from him causes me to break down again as I bury my face in my arms. I feel as though I'm drowning, but I have no fight left to even bother coming up for air.

"You said something about messages to Ridge. Did Maggie read something that upset her?"

I turn my head back over and look up at him. "Go ask Ridge, Warren. It's not my place to tell you Maggie's business."

Warren purses his lips in a tight line, nodding slowly while he thinks. "I kind of think it is your place, though. Isn't it? Does it not have everything to do with you? And I can't ask Ridge. I've never seen him like this before, and frankly, I'm a little terrified of him right now. But I'm worried about Maggie, and I need you to tell me what happened so I can figure out if there's anything I can do to help."

I close my eyes, wondering how I can answer Warren's question with a simplified response. I open my eyes and look at him again. "Don't be angry with him, Warren. The only thing Ridge has done wrong is fail to delete a few messages."

Warren tilts his head and narrows his doubtful eyes. "If that's the only thing Ridge did wrong, then why is Maggie avoiding him? Are you saying that the messages she read weren't wrong? Whatever has been going on between the two of you isn't wrong?"

I don't like the condescending undertone in his voice. I sit up on the bed and scoot back, putting space between the two of us as I respond. "The fact that Ridge has been honest in his conversations with me is not something he did wrong. The fact that he has feelings for me also isn't wrong, when you know exactly how much he's fought those feelings. People can't control matters of the heart, Warren. They can only control their actions, which is exactly what Ridge did. He lost control once for ten seconds, but after that, every single time temptation reared its ugly head, he walked in the other direction. The only thing Ridge has done wrong is fail to delete his messages, because by doing so, he failed to protect Maggie. He failed to protect her from the harsh truth that people don't get to choose who they fall in love with. They only get to choose who they *stay* in love with." I look up at the ceiling and blink back tears. "He was choosing to stay in love with *her*, Warren. Why can't she see that? This will kill him so much more than it's killing her."

I fall back onto the bed, and Warren remains beside me, quiet and still. Several long moments pass, and then he stands and slowly makes his way to my bedroom door. "I owe you an apology," he says.

"An apology for what?"

He drops his eyes to the floor and shifts his feet. "I didn't think you were good enough for him, Sydney." He slowly brings his gaze back to mine. "You are. You and Maggie both are. This is the first moment since meeting Ridge that I don't envy him."

He leaves the room, somehow having made me feel the tiniest bit better and a whole hell of a lot worse.

I continue to lie still on my bed, listening for the sound of Ridge's anger to return, but it doesn't. It's completely quiet throughout the apartment. The only thing any of us can hear is the lingering shattering of Maggie's heart.

I pick up my phone for the first time since I put it on silent and see that I have a missed text from Ridge, sent just a few minutes ago.

Ridge: I changed my mind. I need you to leave today.

Ridge

I pile a few things into a bag, hoping I'll actually need it once I get to her house. I have no idea if Maggie will even allow me to step through her front door, but the only thing I can do right now is be optimistic, because the alternative is unacceptable. It just is. I refuse to accept that this is it.

I know she's hurt, and I know she hates me right now, but she has to understand how much she means to me and how my feelings for Sydney were never intentional.

I clench my fists again, wondering why in the hell I ever had those conversations with Sydney in the first place. Or why I failed to delete them. I never thought Maggie would be in a position to read them. I guess in a way, I just didn't feel guilty. The way I've felt toward Sydney wasn't something I wanted to happen, but the feelings are there, and refusing to act on them since our initial kiss has taken a hell of a lot of effort. In an oddly sadistic way, I've actually been proud of myself for being able to fight it the way I have.

But Maggie won't see that side of it, and I completely understand. I know Maggie, and if she read all the messages, she's more upset about the connection I've made with Sydney than she is over the fact that I kissed her. The feelings I have for Sydney aren't something I'm sure I can talk my way out of.

I grab my bag and my phone and head into the kitchen to pack the laptop. When I reach the counter, I notice a piece of paper peeking out from the computer. I find a sticky note stuck to the screen.

Ridge,

It was never my intention to read your personal stuff, but when I opened your laptop, it was all right there in front of me. I read all of it, and I wish I never saw it. Please give me time to process everything before you show up. I'll contact you when I'm ready to talk in a few days.

Maggie

A few days?

God, please don't let her be serious. There's no way my heart will survive this for a few days. I'll be lucky if I make it through the end of today knowing how I've made her feel.

I toss my bag back toward my bedroom door since I won't need it for a while. I lean forward in defeat and rest my elbows on the bar, crumpling the note up in my fist. I stare down at the laptop before me.

Piece of shit computer.

Why the hell didn't I have a password on it? Why the hell didn't I take it with me when I left the hospital? Why the hell didn't I delete everything? Why the hell did I even write anything to Sydney in the first place?

I've never hated an inanimate object as much as I hate this computer. I slam the screen shut and bring my fist down on top of it with all my strength. I wish I could hear it crack. I wish I could hear the sound my fist makes each time I bring it down forcefully. I want to hear it crushed beneath my fist the same way my heart feels crushed inside my chest.

I stand up straight and pick the laptop up, then slam it down on the bar. I see Warren exit his bedroom out of the corner of my eye, but I'm too pissed to care if I'm making too much noise. I continue to pick the laptop up and slam it against the bar over and over, but it doesn't diminish the hatred I feel for it in the least, and it also doesn't do enough damage to the casing. Warren walks toward the kitchen and heads to a cabinet. He reaches inside and grabs something, then walks over to me. I pause my attack on the computer and look up to see him holding out a hammer. I gladly take it, then step back and bring the hammer down against the laptop with all my might. This time, I can actually see the cracks appear with each hit.

Much better.

I hit it over and over and watch as pieces fly in all directions. I'm also leaving a hefty amount of damage on the bar beneath my mangled computer, but I don't give a shit. Countertops are replaceable. What this computer destroyed of Maggie isn't.

When there isn't much left of the computer to destroy, I finally drop the hammer on the bar. I'm out of breath. I turn and slide down to the floor with my back against the cabinets.

Warren walks around me and sits on the floor in front of me, resting his back against the wall behind him. "Feel better?" he signs.

I shake my head. I don't feel better, I just feel worse. Now I know for a fact that it's not the laptop I'm mad at. It's me. I'm mad at myself.

"Anything I can do to help?"

I ponder his question. The only thing that could help me get Maggie back is to prove to her that there's nothing going on between me and Sydney. In order to prove that to her, I need to not have any interaction with Sydney whatsoever. That's kind of hard with her in the very next room.

"Can you help Sydney move?" I sign. "Today?"

Warren lowers his chin at my request, eyeing me with disappointment. "Today? Her apartment won't be ready for three more days. Besides, she needs furniture, and what we ordered this morning isn't even being delivered until the day she moves in."

I pull my wallet out of my pocket and remove my credit card. "Take her to a hotel, then. I'll pay for her room until her apartment is ready. I need her out in case Maggie comes back. She can't be here."

Warren takes my card and stares at it for several seconds before bringing his eyes back to mine. "This is kind of a shitty move considering this is your fault. Don't expect me to be the one to ask her to leave today. You owe her that much."

I have to admit, Warren's reaction surprises me. Yesterday he seemed to hate Sydney. Today he's acting as if he's protecting her. "I already told her I need her to leave today. Do me a favor, and make sure she gets moved in okay this week. Get her anything she needs. Groceries, extra furniture, whatever."

I'm beginning to stand up when the door to Sydney's room opens. She's walking out backward, pulling both of her suitcases. Warren scrambles to his feet next to me, and as soon as she turns around and her eyes lock with mine, she freezes.

The guilt over what I'm having her do hits me when I see the tears in her eyes. She doesn't deserve this. She hasn't done anything to deserve all that I've put her through. The way it makes me feel to know I've hurt her is exactly why I need her to leave, because I shouldn't care this much.

But I do. God, I care about her so much.

I break eye contact with her and look back to Warren. "Thank you for helping her," I sign. I head back to my room, not wanting to watch Sydney walk out the front door. I can't imagine losing both her and Maggie in the course of a few hours, but it's actually happening.

Warren grabs my arm as I pass him, forcing me to turn and look at him. "You aren't even going to tell her good-bye?" he signs.

"I can't tell her good-bye when I don't really want her to leave." I continue toward my room, thankful that I can't hear the sound of the front door closing behind her when she leaves. I don't know if I could take it.

I pick up my phone and lie down on my bed. I pull up Maggie's number and send her a text.

> Me: I'll give you however much time you need. I love you more than you even realize. I'm not going to deny anything I said to Sydney, because it was all true, especially the parts about you and how much I love you. I know you're hurt, and I know I betrayed you, but please. You have to know how much I've fought for you. Please don't end us like this.

I hit the send button and pull the phone to my chest. Then I fucking cry.

21.

Sydney

"Let me get those," Warren says as he bends to pick up my suit-cases. He carries them down the steps, and I follow him. Once we make it to his car, I realize I don't even know where I'm going. I haven't thought this far ahead. As soon as Ridge told me he needed me to leave today, I just packed my things and walked out without even a plan for what I'm going to do for the next three days. My new apartment isn't ready, but I'm wishing I could be in it. I want to be as far away as I can get right now from Ridge and Maggie and Warren and Bridgette and Hunter and Tori and everything and everyone.

"Ridge wants me to take you to a hotel until your apart-ment is ready, but is there anywhere else you'd rather go?"

Warren is now sitting in the driver's seat, and I'm in the front passenger's seat. I don't even remember our getting into his car. I turn and look at him, and he's just staring at me. The car hasn't even been cranked yet.

God, I feel so pathetic. I feel like a burden.

"It's laughable, isn't it?" I say.

"What?"

I gesture to myself. "This." I lean my head against the headrest and close my eyes. "I should just go back home to my parents. I'm obviously not cut out for this."

Warren sighs. "Not cut out for what? College? Real life?"

I shake my head. "Independence in general, really. Hunter

was right when he told me I'd be better off living with him than on my own. He was right about that, at least. I've been in Ridge's life less than three months, and I've successfully ruined his entire relationship with Maggie." I look out the window, up to his empty balcony. "I've also ruined his entire friendship with me."

Warren cranks the car, then reaches over and squeezes my hand. "Today is a really bad day, Syd. A really, really bad day. Sometimes in life, we need a few bad days in order to keep the good ones in perspective." He lets go of my hand and backs out of the parking spot. "And you've made it this long without having to go back to your parents. You can make it three more days."

"I can't afford a hotel, Warren. I spent my savings on furniture and the deposit for the new apartment. Just take me to the bus station. I'll go stay with my parents for a few days." I pick up my phone in order to bite the bullet and call them, but Warren pulls it out of my hands.

"First of all, you need to stop blaming yourself for what's happening with Ridge and Maggie. Ridge is his own person, and he knows right from wrong. He was the one in the relationship, not you. Second, you need to allow Ridge to pay for this hotel, because he's the one making you leave without a notice. As much as I love the guy, he sort of owes you big-time."

I watch the empty balcony as we drive away. "Why do I feel like I've been taking Ridge's handouts since the day I met him?" I look away from the balcony, feeling the anger building in my chest, but I don't even know who I'm mad at. Love, maybe? I think I'm mad at love.

"I don't know why you feel the way you do," Warren says, "but you need to stop. You've never asked any of us for a single thing."

I nod, trying to agree with him.

Maybe Warren is right. Ridge is just as guilty in this as I

am. He's the one in the relationship. He should have asked me to leave as soon as he knew he was developing feelings for me. He also should have given me more than five minutes to move out. He made me feel like more of a liability than someone he's supposed to care about.

"You're right, Warren. And you know what? If Ridge is paying, I want you to take me to a really nice hotel. One with room service and a minibar full of tiny bottles of Pine-Sol."

Warren laughs. "That's my girl."

Ridge

It's been seventy-two hours.

Three days.

Enough time for me to come up with even more things I need to say to Maggie. Enough time for Warren to let me know that Sydney is finally in her own apartment. He wouldn't tell me which one, but that's probably for the best.

Seventy-two hours has also been enough time for me to realize that I miss having Sydney in my life almost as much as I miss Maggie. And it's enough time to know that I'm not going another day without talking to Maggie. I need to know that she's okay. I've done nothing but pace this apartment since the moment I lost her.

Since the moment I lost both of them.

I pick up my phone and palm it for several minutes, too scared to text her. I'm afraid of what her response will be. When I finally do type out a text, I close my eyes and hit send.

Me: Are you ready to talk about it?

I stare at my phone, waiting for her to respond. I want to know if she's okay. I want to be able to tell her my side. The fact that she's more than likely thinking the worst is killing me, and it feels as if I haven't been able to breathe since she found out about Sydney and me.

Maggie: I'll never be ready, but it needs to be done. I'm home all night.

As ready as I am to see her, I'm also scared to death. I don't want to see her heartbroken.

Me: I'll be there in an hour.

I grab my things and head straight out the door—straight back to the half of my heart that needs the most mending.

•   •   •

I have a key to her place. I've had a key to her place for three years, but I haven't had to ring her doorbell in all that time.

I'm ringing her doorbell right now, and it doesn't feel right. It feels as though I'm asking permission to break through an invisible barrier that shouldn't even be here in the first place. I take a step away from the door and wait.

After several painfully long seconds, she opens the door and makes brief eye contact with me as she steps aside to let me in. I pictured her on the drive over with her hair a mess, makeup smudged underneath her eyes from all the crying, and sporting three-day-old pajamas. The typical heartbroken attire for a girl who just lost all trust in the man she loves.

I think I would rather she looked the way I pictured her than how she actually looks. She's dressed in her typical jeans, and her hair is neatly pulled back. There isn't a smudge of makeup on her face or a tear in her eyes. She gives me a faint smile as she closes the front door.

I watch her closely, because I'm not sure what to do. Of course, my first instinct is to pull her to me and kiss her, but my first instinct probably isn't the best. Instead, I wait until she goes into her living room. I follow her, wishing more than anything that she would turn toward me and throw her arms around me.

She does turn to face me before she takes a seat, but she doesn't throw her arms around me.

"Well?" she signs. "How do we do this?" Her expression is hesitant and pained, but at least she's confronting it. I know this is hard for her.

"How about we quit acting like we're not allowed to be ourselves?" I sign. "This has been the hardest three days of my life, and I can't go another second without touching you."

I don't give her a chance to respond before my arms are wrapped around her and I'm pulling her against me. She doesn't resist. Her arms wrap tightly around me, and as soon as my cheek is pressed against the top of her head, I feel her begin to cry.

This is the Maggie I need. The vulnerable Maggie. The Maggie who still loves me, despite what I've put her through.

I hug her and pull her to the couch, keeping her secured against me as I sit with her now on my lap. We continue to hold each other, neither of us knowing how to begin the conversation. I press a long kiss into her hair.

What I wouldn't give to just be able to whisper all my apologies into her ear. I want her as close to me as possible while I tell her how sorry I am, but I can't do that and sign everything I need to say at the same time. I hate these moments in life where I'd give anything to be able to communicate the same way so many others take for granted.

She slowly lifts her face, and I reluctantly let her pull back. She keeps her palms pressed against my chest and looks me directly in the eyes.

"Are you in love with her?" she asks.

She doesn't sign her question; she only speaks it. The fact that she doesn't sign it makes me think it was too hard for her even to ask. So hard that maybe she doesn't really want to know the answer, so she didn't really want me to understand her question.

I did understand it.

I grab both of her hands pressed against my chest, and I lift them, kissing each of her palms before releasing her hands to answer her.

"I'm in love with *you*, Maggie."

Her expression is tight and controlled. "That's not what I asked."

I look away from her, not wanting her to see the struggle in my eyes. I close them and remind myself that lying won't get us back to where we need to be. Maggie's smart. She also deserves honesty, which isn't at all what I've been giving her. I open my eyes and look at her. I don't answer her with a yes or a no. I shrug, because I honestly don't know if I'm in love with Sydney. How could I be when I'm in love with Maggie? It shouldn't be possible for the heart to love more than one person at once.

She diverts her eyes away and scoots off my lap. She stands and slowly walks the length of the living room and back. She's thinking, so I give her a moment. I know my answer has hurt her, but I know a lie would have hurt her even more. She finally turns to me.

"I can spend all night asking you really brutal questions, Ridge. I don't want to do that. I've had a lot of time to think this through, and I have a lot I need to say to you."

"If brutal questions will help you, then ask me brutal questions. Please. We've been together five years, and I can't let this tear us apart."

She shakes her head, then takes a seat on the couch opposite me. "I don't need to ask the questions, because I already know all the answers. I just need to talk to you now about where we go from here."

I lean forward, not liking where this is going. I don't like it at all. "At least, allow me to explain myself. You can't come to a decision about what happens to us without hearing me out first."

She shakes her head again, and my heart clenches. "I already know, Ridge. I know you. I know your heart. I've read your conversations with Sydney. I already know what you're going to tell me. You're going to tell me how much you love me. How you would do anything for me. You're going to apologize for developing feelings for another girl, despite how hard you tried to prevent that from happening. You're going to tell me you love me so much more than I know and how your relationship with me is so much more important to you than your feelings for Sydney. You're going to tell me you'll do anything to make it up to me and that I just need to give you a chance. You're probably going to be brutally honest with me, also, and tell me that you do have feelings for Sydney but they don't compare to how you feel about me."

She stands and moves to sit next to me on the couch. There are traces of tears in her eyes, but she isn't crying anymore. She faces me and begins signing again.

"And you know what, Ridge? I believe you. And I understand all of it. I do. I've read your conversations. It's as if I was right there, sifting through it all while the two of you were attempting to fight whatever was developing between you. I keep telling myself to quit logging back into your account, but I can't stop. I've read those conversations a million times. I deciphered every word, every sentence, every punctuation mark. I wanted to find the spot in your conversations that proved your disloyalty to me. I wanted to find the moment in your conversations where you became this despicable excuse for a man by admitting that what you felt for her was purely sexual. God, Ridge. I wanted to find that moment so bad, but I couldn't. I know you kissed her, but even the kiss seemed excusable after the two of you had that open discussion about it. I'm your girlfriend, and even *I* began to excuse it.

"I'm not saying what you did is readily forgivable, by any means. You should have asked her to move out the second you felt compelled to kiss her. Hell, you shouldn't have ever asked her to move in if there was even the slightest possibility that you were attracted to her. What you did was wrong in every sense of the word, but what's so messed up is that I feel like I understand it. Maybe it's because I know you too well, but the fact that you're falling in love with Sydney is obvious, and I can't just sit back and share your heart with her, Ridge. I can't do it."

No, no, no, no, no. I quickly pull her to me, wanting the comfort of her to subdue the panic building within me.

She can be heartbroken. She can even be pissed or terrified, but the one thing I won't let her be is okay. She can't just be okay with this.

Tears begin to sting my eyes as I hold her as if my embrace is somehow supposed to convince her of how I feel. I'm shaking my head no, trying to get her not to take this conversation where I'm afraid it's headed.

I press my lips against hers in an attempt to make it all go away. I hold her face in the palms of my hands and try desperately to show her how I feel without having to pull apart from her again.

Her lips part, and I kiss her, something I've done on a regular basis for more than five years but never with so much conviction or fear.

Her mouth tastes of tears, and I'm not sure whose they are, because we're both crying now. She pushes against my chest, wanting to speak to me, but I don't want her to. I don't want to watch her tell me how okay my feelings for Sydney are.

They're not okay. They shouldn't be okay at *all*.

She sits up and pushes me away from her, then wipes her tears. I lean my elbow into the couch and cover my mouth with my trembling hand.

"There's more. There's so much more I need to tell you, and I need you to give me the opportunity to get it out, okay?"

I simply nod, when all I want to do is tell her how hearing her out is the last thing my heart can take right now. She adjusts herself and pulls her legs onto the couch. She wraps her arms around them and rests her cheek on her knee, looking away from me. She's still and quiet and contemplating.

I'm a complete wreck as I sit here and wait.

She unwraps her hands from around her legs and slowly lifts her head to look me in the eyes. "Remember the day we met?" she asks.

There's a faint smile in her eyes, and my panic eases slightly at the pleasantness in her memory. I nod.

"I noticed you first, before I noticed Warren. When Warren approached me, I was hoping he was approaching me for you. I remember making eye contact with you over his shoulder, because I wanted to smile at you so you would know that you caught my eye the same way I caught yours. But when I realized Warren wasn't approaching me for you, I was disappointed. There was something about you that tugged at me in a way that Warren didn't, but you didn't seem to have that same reaction to me. Warren was cute, so I agreed to go out with him, especially since I thought you weren't into me that day."

I close my eyes and soak in her words for a moment. I never knew this. I'm not sure at this point that I *want* to know this. After several quiet moments, I reluctantly open my eyes again and let her finish.

"For the short time I dated Warren, you and I would have these brief conversations and moments of eye contact that always seemed to make you uncomfortable, and I knew it made you uncomfortable because you were developing feelings for me. But your loyalty to Warren was so strong that you wouldn't allow yourself to go there. I always admired that about you, because I knew the two of us would have worked so well. To be honest, I was secretly hoping you would betray his friendship and just kiss me or something, because you were all I thought about. I'm not even sure I was with Warren for Warren. I think I was with him for you all along.

"Then, a few weeks after Warren and I broke up, I began to think I'd never see you again, because you never came for me like I hoped you would. The thought of that terrified me, so I showed up at your apartment one day. You weren't there, but Brennan was. I think he knew why I was there, so he told me not to worry, that I just needed to give you time. He told me about the deal you and Warren made and that you really did have feelings for me but didn't feel right pursuing them yet. He even showed me the date you had circled on the calendar. I'll never forget how that made me feel, and from that point on, I counted down the days until you showed up at my front door."

She wipes away a tear. I briefly close my eyes and try to show her respect by not allowing myself to pull her to me again, but it's so hard. I never knew she came for me. Brennan never told me, and right now, I'm struggling with wanting to let him know how pissed I am that he kept quiet and how much I love him for informing Maggie of how I felt.

"I fell in love with you during that year of waiting for you. I fell in love with your loyalty to Warren. I fell in love with your loyalty to me. I fell in love with your patience and your will-power. I fell in love with the fact that you didn't want to start things out wrong with us. You wanted everything to be as right as it could be, so you waited an entire year. Believe me, Ridge. I know how hard it was, because I was waiting right along with you."

I lift my hand and wipe a tear from her cheek, then let her finish.

"I swore I wouldn't allow my illness to interfere with us. I wouldn't let it prevent me from completely falling in love with you. I wouldn't let it be my crutch to push you away. You were so adamant that it didn't matter to you, and I was so desperate to believe you. We were both lying to ourselves. I think my illness is the thing you love the most about me."

My breath catches in my throat. Those words hurt me more

than any words ever have. "Why would you say something like that, Maggie?"

"I know it sounds absurd to you because you don't see it that way. It's who you are. You're loyal. You love people to a fault. You want to take care of everyone around you, including me, Brennan, Warren . . . Sydney. It's just who you are, and seeing how Warren treated me back then made you want to jump in and become my hero. I'm not saying you don't love me for me, because I know you do. I just think you love me the wrong way."

I run my palm over my forehead and try to squeeze the pain away. My head can't take another second of listening to how incredibly wrong she is. "Maggie, stop. If you're about to use your illness as an excuse to leave me, I won't listen to it. I can't. You're talking like you're about to just give up on us, and it's scaring the living hell out of me. I didn't come here for you to give up. I need you to fight with me. I need you to fight for *us*."

She tilts her head to the side, slowly shaking it in disagreement. "I shouldn't have to fight for us, Ridge. I fight every goddamned day of my life just to survive. I should be able to *revel* in us, but I can't. I'm constantly living in fear that I'm going to upset you or make you angry because you want so badly to form a protective bubble around me. You don't want me taking risks or doing anything that causes me one iota of stress. You don't see the point in my going to college, since we both know my fate. You don't see the point in me having a career, because you think it's better if I just let you take care of me while I take it easy. You don't understand my yearning to experience the things that give people that rush of adrenaline. You get mad when I bring up the idea of traveling, because you don't think it's safe for my health. You refuse to go on tour with your brother, because you want to be the one to take care of me when I get sick. You give up so much of your life to make sure

I'm not having to give up any of mine, and sometimes it's so suffocating."

Suffocating?

I'm *suffocating*?

I stand up and pace the room for several moments, attempting to breathe the air back into my lungs that she's repeatedly knocking out. After I'm calm enough to respond, I return to the couch and face her again.

"I'm not trying to suffocate you, Maggie. I just want to protect you. We don't have the luxury of time like every other couple. Is it wrong that I want to prolong what we have for as long as we possibly can?"

"No, Ridge. It's not wrong. I love that about you so much, but I don't love it for *me*. It always feels as though you're trying to be my lifeguard. I don't need a lifeguard, Ridge. I need someone who is willing to watch me brave the ocean and then dare me not to drown. But you wouldn't be able to let me *near* the ocean. It's not your fault that you can't give me that."

I know it's just an analogy, but she's only using it to make excuses.

"You think that's what you want," I sign. "It's not. You can't tell me you'd rather be with someone who would allow you to risk the time you have left than have someone who would do whatever he could to prolong his life with you."

She exhales. I can't tell if she's admitting I'm right or if she's frustrated because I'm wrong. She looks me square in the eyes and leans forward, then briefly presses her lips to mine. As soon as I lift my hands to her face, she pulls back again.

"I've known all my life that I could die at any moment. You don't know what that's like, Ridge, but I want you to try to put yourself in my shoes. If you knew all your life that you were going to die at any moment, would you be okay with just barely living? Or would you live as hard as you could? Because you're needing me to barely live, Ridge. I can't do that. When I die, I need to know that I did everything I've ever wanted to do, and I've seen everything I've ever wanted to see, and I've loved everyone I've ever wanted to love. I can't just barely live anymore, and it's not in your nature to stick by my side and watch me do all the things I still have left to do in my life.

"You've spent five years of your life loving me like no one's ever loved me. My love has matched yours minute for minute. I don't want you to ever doubt that. People take so much for granted, and I never want you to feel that I took you for granted. Everything you do for me is so much more than I deserve, and you need to know how much that means to me. But there are times when I feel like our devotion to each other is tying us down. Keeping us both from really living. The past few days have helped me realize that I'm still with you because I'm scared to break your heart. But if I don't find the courage to do it, I'm scared I'll just keep holding you back. Holding *myself* back. I feel like I can't live the life I want to live for fear of hurting you, and you can't live the life you want to live because your heart is too loyal for your own good. As much as it hurts me to admit this, I think I might be better off without you. I also think that maybe someday you'll realize you're better off without *me*."

My elbows meet my knees as I lean forward and turn away from her. I can't watch her say another word to me. Every single thing she's saying is not only breaking my heart, but it feels as if it's also breaking the heart *within* my heart.

It hurts so much, and I'm so damn scared, because for a moment, I begin to think there's a possibility that she's right.

Maybe she *doesn't* need me.

Maybe I *do* hold her back.

Maybe I'm *not* the hero to her I've always tried so hard to be, because right now, I feel as if she doesn't even need a hero. Why would she? She has someone so much stronger than I'll ever be for her. She has herself.

The realization that I may not be what she needs in her life consumes me, and my regret and guilt and shame fold in on themselves, completely devouring the strength I have left.

I feel her arms wrap around me, and I pull her to me, needing to feel her against me. I love her so damn much, and all I want right now is for her to know that, even if it doesn't change anything. I pull her to me and press my forehead to hers as we both cry, holding on to each other with all we have left. Tears are streaming down her cheeks as she slides onto my lap.

She mouths, "I love you," then presses her lips to mine. I pull her against my chest as close as I possibly can without crawling inside of her, which is exactly what my heart is trying to do. It wants to embed itself within the walls of her chest, and it never wants to let go.

22.

Sydney

My cable won't be connected until next week. My eyes hurt from reading too much, and maybe also from crying. I finally put a down payment on a car with my leftover student loans, but until I get a job, I can't really afford the gas. I'd better find a job soon, because I'm pretty sure I've fictionalized how great living alone is. I'm tempted to try to get my job back at the library, even if I have to beg. I just need something to keep me busy.

I'm. Freaking. Bored.

So bored that I'm looking at my hands, counting random things that make absolutely no sense to even be counting.

One: the number of people constantly on my mind. (Ridge.)

Two: the number of people I wish would contract a sexually transmitted disease. (Hunter and Tori.)

Three: the number of months since I broke up with my lying, cheating bastard of a boyfriend.

Four: the number of times Warren has checked up on me since I moved out of the apartment.

Five: the number of times Warren has knocked on my door in the last thirty seconds.

Six: the number of days since I last saw Ridge.

Seven: the number of feet from my couch to the front door.

I open the door, and Warren doesn't even wait for me to invite him in. He smiles and slips past me, holding two white bags in his hands.

"I brought tacos," he says. "I was driving by on my way home from work and thought you might want some." He sets the bags on my kitchen counter, then walks to the sofa and plops down.

I close the door and face him. "Thanks for the tacos, but how do I know you aren't pranking me? What'd you do, switch the beef out with tobacco?"

Warren looks up at me and grins, impressed. "Now, that's a genius prank idea, Sydney. I think you might finally be getting the hang of it."

I laugh and take a seat next to him. "Figures, now that I have no roommates to prank."

He laughs and pats my knee. "Bridgette doesn't get off work until midnight. Want to go catch a movie?"

My head sinks into the back of the couch almost as quickly as my heart sinks into my stomach. I hate feeling as if he's only here because he feels sorry for me. The last thing I want to be is someone's worry.

"Warren, you don't have to keep coming by here to check on me every day. I know you're trying to be nice, but I'm fine."

He shifts his weight on the couch so that he's facing me. "I'm not coming by here because I feel sorry for you, Sydney. You're my friend. I miss having you around the apartment. *And* I might be coming by here because I feel a tad bit remorseful for treating you like complete shit the night Maggie was admitted to the hospital."

I nod. "Yeah. You were quite the asshole that night."

"I know." He laughs. "Don't worry, Ridge hasn't let me forget it."

Ridge.

God, even hearing his name hurts.

Warren realizes his slip-up when he sees the change in my expression. "Shit. Sorry."

I press my palms into the couch and stand up, wanting to

escape the awkwardness of our conversation. It's really not a subject I need to be talking about, anyway.

"Well, are you hungry?" I ask as I head to the kitchen. "I just spent hours slaving over the stove to make these tacos, so you'd better eat one."

Warren laughs, walks into the kitchen with me, and takes one of the tacos. I unwrap one and lean against the bar, but before I even bring it to my mouth, I become too nauseated to eat. In all honesty, I haven't slept or eaten very much in the six days since I moved out. I hate knowing that I had a part in causing so much hurt in another person. Maggie didn't do anything to deserve how we made her feel. It's also hard as hell not knowing how things have turned out between the two of them. I haven't asked Warren about it for obvious reasons, because whatever the outcome, it wouldn't change things. But now it feels as if I have this huge, gaping hole in my chest from the constant curiosity. As much as I've wished for the last three months that Ridge didn't have a girlfriend, it's nothing compared to how much I've hoped she could forgive him.

"Penny for your thoughts?"

I glance up at Warren, who's leaning against the counter, watching me think. I shrug my shoulders and set my uneaten food aside, then hug myself and stare down at my feet, afraid that if I look directly at him, he'll know what I'm thinking.

"Look," he says, dipping his head to try to get me to look him in the eye. "I know you haven't asked about him because you know as well as I do how much you need to move on. But if you have questions, I'll answer them, Sydney. I'll answer them because you're my friend, and that's what friends do."

My chest rises with my deep intake of breath, and before I can fully release it, the question spills from my mouth. "How is he?"

Warren clenches his jaw, which makes me think he wishes

he hadn't given me the opening to ask about Ridge. "He's okay. He'll *be* okay."

I nod but instantly have a million follow-up questions to ask.

Did she take him back?

Has he asked about me?

Does he seem happy?

Do you think he regrets me now?

I decide to take it one question at a time, because I'm not even sure his answers will be good for me at this point. I swallow nervously, then look up at him. "Did she forgive him?"

Warren is the one who can't hold the eye contact now. He straightens up, turns around with his back to me, and places his palms flat on the counter. His head hangs between his shoulders as he sighs uncomfortably.

"I'm not sure if I should be telling you this." He pauses for a moment, then turns back around to face me. "She did forgive him. From what he told me, she understood the situation between you and Ridge. I'm not saying she wasn't upset about it at all, but she did forgive him."

His answer completely slays me. I slap my hand over my mouth to muffle my cry, and then I turn away from Warren. I'm confused by my reaction and confused by my heart. I'm immediately consumed with relief to know that she forgave him, but the relief washes away with grief at the realization that she forgave him. I don't even know how to feel. I'm relieved for Ridge and grieving for myself.

Warren sighs heavily, and I feel awful for allowing him to see me react this way. I shouldn't have asked. Dammit, why did I ask?

"I wasn't finished, Sydney," he says quietly.

I shake my head and keep facing the opposite direction while he gets out the rest of what he wants to say.

"She forgave him for what happened with you, but what happened with you was also an eye opener about why they were even together in the first place. It turns out she couldn't find a good enough reason to take him back. Ridge said she's got a lot of life left to live, but she can't live it to the fullest when he's constantly trying to hold her back."

I bring both hands to my face, completely perplexed by my heart now. Just seconds ago, I was grieving because she forgave him, and now I'm grieving because she didn't.

Just three months ago, I was sitting outside on my suitcases in the rain, believing I was experiencing what it felt like to be heartbroken.

God, I was wrong. So damn wrong.

This is heartbroken.

This.

Right now.

Warren's arms wrap around me, and he pulls me to him. I know he doesn't want to see me upset, and I'm really trying my best not to appear that way. Crying about it won't help, anyway. It hasn't helped for the past six days I've been doing it.

I pull away from Warren and walk to the counter, where I tear off a paper towel. I wad it up and wipe my eyes with it. "I hate feelings," I say as I sniffle back more tears.

Warren laughs and nods in agreement. "Why do you think I chose to be with a girl who has none?"

The Bridgette diss makes me laugh. I do my best to suck it up and wipe away the rest of my tears, because, as I told myself before, the outcome of Ridge and Maggie doesn't matter to my situation. No matter how things turn out between them, it still doesn't mean anything for Ridge and me. Things are entirely too complicated between us, and nothing but space and time can change that.

"I'll go watch a movie with you," I say to Warren. "But it better not be a porn."

Ridge

"Give me my damn keys, Ridge," Warren signs.

I calmly shake my head for the third time in five minutes. "I'll give you the keys when you tell me where she lives."

He glares at me hard, still refusing to budge. I've had his keys for most of the day now, and I'll be damned if I'll give them back before he gives me the information I need. I know it's only been three weeks since Maggie broke up with me, but I haven't been able to stop thinking about how everything I've done to Sydney has affected her. I need to know if she's okay. I've gone this long without contacting her simply because I'm not sure what I'll say when I eventually do see her. All I know is that I need to see her, or I'll more than likely never sleep again. It's been more than three weeks since the last time I had a full night's sleep, and my mind just needs reassurance.

Warren sits across from me at the table, and I return my attention to the computer in front of me. Despite the fact that I want to blame my entire past few weeks on computers, I know it was all my fault, so I sucked it up and bought a new one. I still have to rely on a computer for income, unfortunately.

Warren reaches across the table and slams my laptop shut, forcing me to look up at him.

"Nothing good will come of it," he signs. "It's only been three weeks since you and Maggie ended things. I'm not giving you Sydney's address, because you don't need to see her. Now, give me my keys, or I'm taking your car."

I grin smugly. "Good luck finding my keys. They're in the same spot I hid yours."

He shakes his head in frustration. "Why are you being

such a dick, Ridge? She's finally on her own and making a life for herself and doing well, and you want to barge in and confuse her all over again?"

"How do you know she's doing well? Do you talk to her?" The desperation in my question surprises me, because I didn't know until this second just how much I need her to be okay.

"Yeah, I've seen her a few times. Bridgette and I had lunch with her yesterday."

I fall back against my chair, slightly annoyed that he didn't tell me this but relieved to know she's not holed up in her apartment, devastated.

"Has she asked about me? Does she know about Maggie and me?"

He nods. "She knows. She asked how things went with the two of you, so I told her the truth. She hasn't brought it up since then."

Jesus Christ. Knowing that she knows the truth should relieve my worry, but it only intensifies it. I can't imagine what she must think about my lack of communication with her now that she knows about Maggie. The fact that I haven't contacted her at all probably has her believing I blame her. I lean forward and look pleadingly to Warren.

"Please, Warren. Tell me where she lives."

He shakes his head. "Give me my keys."

I shake my head.

He rolls his eyes at our matched stubbornness and pushes himself away from the table, then storms off to his room.

I open my texts to Sydney, and begin scrolling through them as I do every single day, wishing I had the courage to text her. I'm afraid it will be easier for her to shut me out through a text than it would be if I were to show up at her front door, which is why I haven't texted her. Despite the fact that I don't want to agree with Warren, I know that nothing good will come from my contacting her. I know we're not in a place to start a relationship, and seeing her in person would only exacerbate how much I miss her. However, knowing what I should do and abiding by what I should do are two completely different things.

• • •

My light flicks on. Seconds later, my shoulders are being violently shaken. I smile through the grogginess, knowing by Warren's presence alone that I've got him right where I want him. I turn over and look up at him.

"Something wrong?" I sign.

"Where are they?"

"Where are what?"

"My condoms, Ridge. Where the hell did you hide my condoms?"

I knew that if stealing his keys didn't work, then stealing his condoms would. I'm just glad he thought to put on shorts before leaving Bridgette in his bed and storming into my room.

"You want your condoms?" I sign. "Tell me where she lives."

Warren runs his palms over his face, and from the looks of it, I think he's groaning. "Forget it. I'll go to the store and buy new ones."

Before he turns to walk out of my room, I sit up on the bed. "How do you plan on driving to the store? I have your keys, remember?"

He pauses for a second, and then his face relaxes when he's hit with a new epiphany. "I'll take Bridgette's car."

"Good luck finding *her* keys."

Warren stares at me hard for several seconds, then finally slumps his shoulders and turns toward my dresser. He grabs a pen and paper and writes something down, wads it up, and throws it at me. "Here's her address, asshole. Now, give me my keys."

I unfold the paper and double-check to make sure he actually wrote an address down. I reach behind my nightstand, and grab his box of condoms, and toss it to him.

"That should do you for now. I'll tell you where your keys are after I confirm that this is really her address."

Warren pulls one of the condoms out of the box and tosses it at me.

"Take this with you when you go, because that's definitely her address." He turns and leaves the room, and no sooner is he gone than I'm up and dressed and heading out the front door.

I don't even know what time it is.

I don't even care.

23.

Sydney

Sound triggers.

They happen a lot, but mostly when I hear certain songs. Especially songs Hunter and I both loved. If I listen to a song during a particularly depressing period, then hear it later on down the road, it brings back all the old feelings associated with that song. There are songs I used to love that now I absolutely refuse to listen to. They trigger memories and feelings I don't want to experience again.

My text tone has become one of those sound triggers.

Namely, Ridge's text tone. It's very distinct, a snippet from the demo of our song "Maybe Someday." I assigned it to him after I heard the song for the first time. I'd like to say that sound trigger is a negative one, but I'm not so sure it is. The kiss I experienced with him during the song certainly led to negative feelings of guilt, but the kiss itself still turns my heart into a hot mess just thinking about it. And I think about it a lot. Way more than I should.

In fact, I'm thinking about it right now as the snippet of our song pours from the speakers of my cell phone, indicating that I'm receiving a text.

From Ridge.

I honestly never expected to hear this sound again.

I roll over on my bed and stretch my arm to the nightstand, my now-trembling fingers grasping at my phone. Knowing that I've received a text from him has once again wreaked havoc with my organs, and they've forgotten how to function properly. I pull the phone to my chest and close my eyes, too nervous to read his words.

Beat, beat, pause.

Contract, expand.

Inhale, exhale.

I slowly open my eyes and hold up the phone, then unlock the screen.

Ridge: Are you home?

Am I home?

Why would he care if I were home? He doesn't even know where I live. Besides, he made it pretty clear where his heart's loyalty resided when he told me to move out three weeks ago.

But I *am* home, and despite my better judgment, I want him to know I'm home. I'm tempted to respond with my address and tell him to come find out for himself whether or not I'm home.

Instead, I go with something safer. Something less telling.

Me: Yes.

I pull the covers off and sit up on the edge of the bed, watching my phone, too afraid even to blink.

Ridge: You're not answering the door. Am I at the wrong apartment?

Oh, God.

I *hope* he's at the wrong apartment. Or maybe I hope he's at the *right* apartment. I can't really tell, because I'm happy he's here, but I'm pissed off that he's here.

These conflicting feelings are exhausting.

I stand and run out of my bedroom, straight to my front door. I peer through the peephole, and sure enough, he's at my front door.

Me: You're outside my door, so yeah. Right apartment.

I look out the peephole again after hitting send, and he's standing with his palm flat against the door, staring at his phone. Seeing the pained expression on his face and knowing it derives from the battle his heart is going through makes me want to swing open the door and throw my arms around him. I close my eyes and press my forehead to the door in order to give myself time to think before making any rash decisions. My heart is being pulled toward him, and I can't think of anything I want more right now than to open this door.

However, I also know that opening the door won't do either of us any good. He just broke up with Maggie a matter of weeks ago, so if he's here for me, he can turn right around and leave. There's no way anything could work between us when I know he's still heartbroken over someone else. I deserve more than what he can give me right now. I've been through too much this year to let someone screw with my heart like this.

He shouldn't be here.

Ridge: Can I come in?

I turn until my back is pressed against the door. I clutch the phone to my chest and squeeze my eyes shut. I don't want to read his words. I don't want to see his face. Everything about him makes me lose sight of what's important, what's best for me. He isn't what's best for my life right now, especially considering what he's gone through in his own life, and I should walk away from this door and not let him in.

But everything in me wants to let him in.

"Please, Sydney."

The words are almost an inaudible whisper through the other side of the door, but I definitely heard them. Every single part of me heard them. The desperation in his voice, combined with the simple fact that he spoke, completely slays me. I allow my heart to make my decision for me this time as I slowly face the door. I turn the lock and slide the latch loose, then open the door.

I can't describe what it feels like to see him standing in front of me again without using the term *terrifying*.

Everything about the way he makes me feel is absolutely terrifying. The way my heart wants to be held by him is terrifying. The way my knees seem to forget how to hold me up is terrifying. The way my mouth wants to be claimed by his is terrifying.

I do my best to hide what his presence does to me by turning away from him and walking toward the living room.

I don't know why I'm trying to hide my reaction from him, but isn't that what people do? We try so hard to hide everything we're really feeling from those who probably need to know our true feelings the most. People try to bottle up their emotions, as if it's somehow wrong to have natural reactions to life.

My natural reaction in this moment is to turn and hug him, regardless of the reason he's here. My arms want to be around him, my face wants to be pressed against his chest, my back wants to be cradled by him—yet I'm standing here trying to pretend that's the last thing I need from him.

Why?

I inhale a calming breath, then turn around when I hear him close the front door behind him. I lift my eyes to meet his, and he's standing several feet in front of me, watching me. I can tell by the tightness in his expression that he's doing exactly what I'm doing. He's holding back everything he's feeling for the sake of . . . what?

Pride?

Fear?

The one thing I've always admired about my relationship with Ridge is that we're so honest and real with each other. I've always been able to say exactly what I was thinking, and so has he. I don't like this shift we've made.

I try to smile at him, but I'm not sure if my smile is working right now. I speak to him and enunciate clearly so he can read my lips. "Are you here because you need a flaw?"

He laughs and exhales at the same time, relieved that I'm not angry.

I'm *not* angry. I've never been mad at him. The decisions he's made during the time he's known me aren't decisions I can hold against him. The only thing I hold against him is the night he kissed me and ruined me for every other kiss I'll ever experience.

I take a seat on the couch and look up at him. "Are you okay?" I ask.

He sighs, and I quickly look away. It's hard enough being in the same room as him right now, but even harder to make eye contact with him. He completes the walk into the living room and sits on the couch next to me.

I debated buying more furniture, but one couch was all I could afford. A love seat at that. I'm not so sure I'm sad about my lack of furniture, though, because his leg is touching my thigh, and the simple contact causes heat to roll through me like a riptide. I look down at our knees when they brush together and realize I'm still wearing the T-shirt I threw on right before I went to bed. I guess I was so shocked by the fact that he said he was at my apartment door that I didn't concern myself with how I looked. I'm in nothing but an oversized cotton T-shirt that falls to my knees, and my hair is more than likely a wreck.

He's in jeans and a gray Sounds of Cedar T-shirt. I would say I feel underdressed, but I'm actually dressed appropriately for what I was doing before he showed up, which was going to bed.

Ridge: I don't know if I'm okay. Are you okay?

I forgot I even asked him a question for a second.

I shrug. I'm sure I will be fine, but I'm not going to lie and tell him I am. I think it's obvious that neither one of us can really be okay with how everything has turned out. I'm not okay with losing Ridge, and Ridge isn't okay with losing Maggie.

Me: I'm sorry about Maggie. I feel awful. She'll come around, though. Five years is a lot to give up for a misunderstanding.

I hit send and finally look up at him. He reads the text, then eyes me. The concentration in his expression makes the breath catch in my lungs.

Ridge: It wasn't a misunderstanding, Sydney. She understood a little too well.

I read his text several times, wishing he would expand on it. *What* wasn't a misunderstanding? The reason they broke up? His feelings for me? Rather than ask him what he means, I cut to the question I want the answer to the most.

Me: Why are you here?

He works his jaw back and forth before responding.

Ridge: Do you want me to leave?

I look at him and slowly shake my head no. Then I pause and shake my head yes. Then I pause again and just shrug. He smiles endearingly, completely understanding my confusion.

Me: I guess whether or not I want you here depends on why you're here. Are you here because you need me to try to help you win back Maggie? Are you here because you miss me? Are you here because you want to try to work out some sort of friendship?

Ridge: Would I be wrong if I answered none of the above? I don't know why I'm here. Part of me misses you so much it hurts, while part of me wishes I never even met you to begin with. I guess today is one of the days I was hurting, so I stole Warren's keys and forced him to give me your address. I didn't think this through or come up with any kind of speech. I just did what my heart needed me to do, which was to see you.

His brutally honest reply melts my heart and pisses me off all at the same time.

Me: What about tomorrow? What if tomorrow is one of the days you wished you never met me? What am I supposed to do then?

The intensity in his stare is unnerving. Maybe he's trying to gauge if that was an angry response. I'm not sure if it was or not. I'm not sure how I feel about the fact that he doesn't even know why he's here.

He doesn't respond to my text, and it proves one thing: he's having the same internal conflict with himself that I've been having.

He wants to be with me, but he doesn't.

He wants to love me, but he doesn't know if he should.

He wants to see me, but he knows he shouldn't.

He wants to kiss me, but it would hurt just as much as it did the first time he kissed me and had to walk away. I suddenly feel uncomfortable staring at him. We're way too close together on this couch, yet my body is making it very clear to me that it doesn't think we're close enough at all. What it's wishing would happen right now are all the things that aren't.

Ridge looks away and slowly scans my apartment for a few moments, then returns his attention to his phone.

Ridge: I like your place. Good neighborhood. Seems safe.

I almost laugh at his text and the casual conversation he's trying to make, because I know we're no longer in a place for casual conversation. We can't be friends at this point. We also can't be together with so much against us. Casual conversation has no place between us right now, yet I can't bring myself to reply any differently.

Me: I like it here. Thank you for helping me out with the hotel until I could move in.

Ridge: It was the least I could do. Absolutely the least I could do.

Me: I'll pay you back as soon as I get my first paycheck. I got my job back at the campus library, so it should only be another week.

Ridge: Sydney, stop. I don't even want you to offer.

I have no idea what to say in response. This whole situation is awkward and uncomfortable, because we're both dancing around all the things we wish we had the courage to do and say.

I set my phone facedown on the couch. I want him to know that I need a break. I don't like that we aren't being us.

He takes the hint and lays his phone down on the armrest

beside him, then sighs heavily as he drops his head against the back of the couch. The silence makes me wish I could experience the world from his perspective for once. I find it almost impossible to put myself in his shoes, though. People with the advantage of hearing take so much for granted, and I've never understood that to the extent that I understand it now. There's nothing being spoken between us, yet I understand by his heavy sigh that he's frustrated with himself. I understand how much he's holding back by the way his breaths are being sharply pulled in.

I suppose his expertise in a silent world gives him an ability to read people, just in different ways. Instead of focusing on the sounds of my breaths, he focuses on the rise and fall of my chest. Rather than listening to quiet sighs, he more than likely watches my eyes, my hands, my posture. Maybe that's why his face is tilted toward mine now, because he wants to see me and get a feel for what's going through my head.

I feel as if he reads me too well. The way he's watching me forces me to try to control every facial expression and every breath. I close my eyes and lean my head back, knowing he's staring, trying to get a sense of where I am.

I also wish I could just turn to him and tell him. I want to tell him how much I've missed him. I want to tell him how much he means to me. I want to tell him how horrible I feel, because before I showed up in his life, everything seemed perfect for him. I want to tell him that even though we both regretted it, that minute we spent kissing was the one minute out of my entire life that I wouldn't trade for the world.

At moments like these, I'm thankful he *can't* hear me, or there would have been so many things spoken that I would regret.

Instead, there are so many things left unsaid that I wish I had the courage to say.

Ridge's weight shifts on the couch, and my eyes naturally

open out of curiosity. He's leaning across the arm of the couch, reaching for something. When he turns back around, he's holding a pen in his hand. He smiles softly, then picks up my arm. He turns his body toward mine and presses the pen to my open palm.

I swallow hard and slowly look up at his face, but he's looking down at my hand as he writes. I could swear I almost see a faint smile flash across his lips. When he's finished, he brings my palm to his mouth and blows softly to dry the ink. His lips are moist and puckered into a pout, and holy hell, it just got really warm in this apartment. He lowers my hand, and I look down at it.

Just wanted to touch your hand.

I laugh softly. Mostly because his words are so innocent and sweet compared to the things he's written on me in the past. I've been sitting here on this couch with him for ten minutes, wishing he would touch me, and then he goes and admits he was thinking the exact same thing. It's so juvenile, as if we're teenagers. I'm almost embarrassed that it pleases me this much that he's touching me, but I can't recall a time I've ever wanted anything more.

He hasn't released my hand yet, and I'm still looking down at his writing, smiling. I brush my thumb across the back of his hand, and he gasps quietly. The permission I just gave him with that tiny movement seems to have broken some invisible barrier, because he immediately slides his hand over mine and presses our palms together, then intertwines our fingers. The warmth of his hand doesn't come close to the warmth that just shot through my entire body.

God, if just holding hands with him feels this intense, I can't imagine what everything else with him would feel like.

We're both watching our hands now, feeling every bit of the connection pulsating through our palms. He brushes over my thumb and flips our hands over, then takes the pen and presses it to my wrist. He moves the pen slowly up my wrist, drawing in a straight line all the way up my forearm. I don't stop him. I simply watch him. When he reaches the crease in my elbow, he begins to write again. I read each word as he writes it.

Just an excuse to touch you here, too.

Without releasing my hand, he lifts my arm and keeps his eyes focused on mine as he bends forward and blows softly up and down my arm. He presses his lips lightly against his words and kisses them without once breaking eye contact. When his lips meet my arm, I feel a soft flick of his tongue tease my arm for a split second before his mouth closes over my skin.

That might have just made me whimper.

Yep. Pretty sure I just whimpered.

God, I'm so glad he couldn't hear that.

He pulls his lips away from my arm and continues to watch me, gauging my reaction. His eyes are dark and piercing, and they're focused all over me. On my lips, on my eyes, on my neck, on my hair, on my chest. He can't seem to take me in fast enough.

He presses the pen against my skin again, starting where he left off. He rolls the pen slowly up my arm, watching it intently the whole time. When he reaches the sleeve of my T-shirt, he pushes it up carefully until my shoulder is exposed. He makes a small mark with the pen, then slowly leans over me. My head falls back against the couch when I feel his lips meet my skin. His breath is close and warm against my shoulder. I'm not even thinking about the fact that he's drawing all over me. That can be washed off later. Right now, I just want his pen to keep going and going until it's completely out of ink.

He pulls away and releases my hand, switching the pen to his other hand. He pulls my sleeve back down over my shoulder, then slips his fingers inside the collar of my T-shirt, tugging it to expose more of my collarbone. He puts the tip of the pen on my shoulder and glances up at me while he proceeds with caution, making his way to my neck. His expression is heated, and I can tell he's proceeding with caution despite the fact that I know exactly what he wishes were happening right now and where he plans to go with this pen. He doesn't have to verbalize it when his eyes clearly state it for him.

He moves the pen slowly up my neck. I naturally tilt my head to the side, and as soon as I do, I hear a rush of air hiss quietly through his teeth. He comes to a stop just below my ear. I squeeze my eyes shut and hope my heart doesn't explode when he leans in, because it definitely feels as if it could. His lips press gently against my skin, and I swear the room flips upside down.

Or maybe that was just my heart.

One of my hands slides up his arm and grasps the back of his head, not wanting him to pull away from this spot. His tongue makes another quick appearance against my neck, but he doesn't let my desperation stall him. He lifts away and looks back down at me. His eyes are smiling, knowing how crazy he's driving me.

He rolls the pen from the spot below my ear, back down my neck, and around to the dip in the base of my throat. Before kissing the spot he just marked, he grabs me by the waist and lifts me up, sliding me onto his lap.

I grasp his arms and suck in a rush of air the second he pulls me against him. My T-shirt slides up my thighs, and the fact that I'm not wearing anything under it except underwear pretty much guarantees that I've gotten myself into something that's going to be damn hard to pull away from.

His eyes drop to the base of my throat as he slides a hand up my thigh, over my hip, and all the way up and into my hair. He grasps the back of my head, then pulls my neck against his mouth. This kiss is harder and not at all cautious like the rest of them. I slide my hands into his hair and keep his mouth pressed against my neck.

He works his kisses all the way up my neck until his mouth meets my chin. Our bodies are meshed firmly together, and one of his hands has found my lower back and is keeping me flush against him.

I can't move. I'm literally panting for breath, wondering where in the hell the strong Sydney went. Where's the Sydney who knows this shouldn't be happening?

I'll look for her later. After he finishes with his pen.

He pulls away when his lips come close to my mouth. Our bodies are as close as they can get without his mouth being on mine. He removes his hand from my lower back and brings the pen back around to my throat. When he touches the tip of it to my skin, I gulp, anticipating which direction he's about to go with it.

North or south, north or south. I don't really care.

He begins to scroll upward, but then he stops. He pulls the pen away from my neck and shakes it, then touches it to my neck again. He makes another movement upward with the pen but stops again. He pulls back slightly and frowns at the pen, which I'm assuming has just run out of ink. He looks back at me and tosses the pen over my shoulder. I hear it land on the floor behind me.

His eyes drop to my lips, which I'm assuming would have been the pen's final destination. We're both breathing heavily, knowing exactly what's about to come next. What we're about to experience again for the second time, knowing how much our first kiss affected us.

I think he's as terrified as I am right now.

I'm leaning all my weight into him, because I've never been this weak. I can't think, I can't move, I can't breathe. I just . . . *need*.

He brings both hands to my cheeks and looks directly into my eyes.

"Your call," he whispers.

Jesus Christ, that voice.

I stare at him, not sure if I like that he just put the control in my hands. He wants this to be my decision.

It's so much easier having someone else to blame when things go where they shouldn't. I know we shouldn't be putting ourselves into a situation we're only going to regret once it's over. I could put a stop to it right here. I could make it easier by asking him to leave now, rather than when things get even more complicated between us. I could slide off his lap and tell him he shouldn't be here because he hasn't even had time to forgive himself for what happened with Maggie. I could tell him to go away and not come back until his heart isn't confused anymore about who it wants.

If that day ever comes.

There are so many things I could and should and need to do, but none of them is what I *want* to do.

The pressure picks the worst possible time to break me. The *worst* possible time.

I squeeze my eyes shut when I feel a tear begin to work its way out. It trickles down my cheek, falling slowly toward my jaw. It's the absolutely slowest descent a tear has ever made. I open my eyes, and Ridge is watching it. He's following the wet trail with his eyes, and I can see his jaw growing more tense with every second that passes. I want to reach up and wipe it away, but the last thing I want to do is hide it from him. My tears say a whole lot more about how I'm feeling right now than I'm willing to say in a text.

Maybe I need him to know that this is hurting me.

Maybe I want it to hurt him, too.

When the tear finally curves and disappears under my jaw, he brings his eyes back to mine. I'm surprised by what I see in them.

His own tears.

Knowing that he's hurting because I'm hurting shouldn't make me want to kiss him, but it absolutely does. He's here because he cares about me. He's here because he misses me. He's here because he needs to feel what we felt in our first kiss again, just as I do. I've wanted that feeling back since the second his mouth left mine and he walked away.

I remove my hands from his shoulders and grab the back of his head, then lean into him, bringing my mouth so close to his that our lips brush.

He grins. "Good call," he whispers.

He closes the space between our mouths, and everything else falls away. The guilt, the worries, the concern over what happens after this kiss ends. It all melts away the second his mouth claims mine. He gently coaxes my lips apart with his tongue, and all the chaos running through my heart and head is eliminated when I feel his warmth inside my mouth.

Kisses like his should come with a warning label. They can't be good for the heart. He runs a hand around to my upper thigh, then slips it beneath the hem of my T-shirt. His hand glides across my back, and he grips me tightly, then lifts his hips at the same time as he pulls me harder against him.

Oh.

My.

Goodness.

I become weaker and weaker with every rhythmic movement he creates with our bodies. I find whatever parts of him I can hold on to, because I feel as if I'm falling. I grab his shirt and his hair while I moan softly into his mouth. When he feels the sound escape my throat, he quickly pulls away from my mouth and squeezes his eyes shut, breathing heavily. When he opens his eyes again, he's staring at my throat.

He pulls his hand from beneath my shirt, then slowly brings it up to my neck.

Oh, my dear, sweet God.

He wraps his fingers around my neck, gently pressing his palm into the base of my throat while he stares at my mouth.

The thought of him wanting to feel what he's doing to me makes my head swarm and the entire room spin. I'm somehow able to glance into his eyes long enough to see them transform from a calm desire to an almost carnal need.

With his other hand still curved around the back of my head, he pulls me to him with more urgency, covering my mouth with his. The second his tongue finds mine again, I give him more moans than he can possibly keep up with.

This is exactly what I've wanted from him. I've wanted him to show up and tell me how much he's missed me. I've needed to know that he cares about me, that he wants me. I've needed to feel his mouth on mine again so I could know that the way his first kiss made me feel wasn't just in my head this whole time.

Now that I have it, I'm not sure I'm strong enough for it. I know that the second this ends and he walks out the front door, my heart will die all over again. The more I open up to him, the more I need him. The more I admit to myself that I need him, the more it hurts to know that I still don't exactly have him.

I'm still not convinced that he's here for the right reasons. Even if he *is* here for the right reasons, it's still wrong timing. Not to mention all the questions still running through my head. I try to push them away, and for brief moments, it works. When his hands graze my cheek or his lips close over mine, I forget all about those questions that I can't seem to run away from. But then he'll pause to catch his breath, and he'll look me in the eye, and all those questions just cram right back into the front of my head, until they're so heavy that they're forcing more tears to want to escape.

I clench his arms when the uncertainty begins to take over. I shake my head and try to push against him. He pulls away from my mouth and sees my doubt building, and he shakes his head to get me to stop analyzing this moment between us. His eyes are pleading as he strokes my cheek, pulls me flush against him, and tries to kiss me again, but I struggle out of his arms.

"Ridge, no," I say. "I can't."

I'm still shaking my head when his hand grips my wrist. I slide off his lap and keep walking until his fingers fall away from me.

I walk straight to the kitchen sink and dispense soap into my hands, then begin scrubbing the ink off my arm. I reach into a drawer and pull out a rag, then wet it and press it to my neck. Tears are streaming down my cheeks as I try to wash away the reminders of what just happened between us. The reminders are going to make him that much harder to overcome.

Ridge comes up behind me and places his hands on my shoulders. He turns me around to face him. When he sees that I'm crying, his eyes fill with apology, and he pulls the rag from my hand. He brushes the hair off my shoulder and gently rubs my skin, washing away the ink. He looks incredibly guilty for making me cry, but it's not his fault. It's never his fault. It's no one's fault. It's both our faults.

When he's finished rubbing away the ink, he tosses the rag behind me onto the counter, then pulls me against his chest. The comfort that surrounds me makes this even harder. I want this all the time. I want *him* all the time. I want these tiny snippets of perfection between us to be our constant reality, but that can't happen right now. I completely understand his earlier comment, when he said that there are times he misses me and times he wishes he never met me, because right now, I'm wishing I never set foot out onto my balcony the first time I heard his guitar.

If I never experienced how he could make me feel, then I wouldn't miss it after he's gone.

I wipe my eyes and pull away from him. There's so much we need to discuss, so I walk to the couch, retrieve our phones, and bring his to him. I move away from him to lean against the other counter while I type, but he grabs my arm and pulls me back. He leans against the bar and pulls my back against his chest, then wraps his arms around me from behind. He kisses the side of my head, then moves his lips to my ear.

"Stay here," he says, wanting me to remain pressed against him.

It's crazy how being held by someone for just a few minutes can forever change how it feels *not* to be held by him. The second he releases his hold on you, it suddenly feels as if a part of you is missing. I guess he feels it, too, which is why he wants me near him.

Does he feel this way about Maggie, too?

Questions like this refuse to leave my mind. Questions like this keep me from believing he could ever be happy with the outcome of his situation, because he lost her in the end. I don't want to be someone's second choice.

I lean my head against his shoulder and squeeze my eyes shut, trying my best not to let my mind go there again. However, I know I have to go there if I ever want to find a sense of closure.

Ridge: I wish I could read your mind.

Me: Believe me, I wish you could, too.

He laughs quietly and squeezes me tightly in his arms. He keeps his cheek pressed against my head as he types out another text.

Ridge: We've always been able to say whatever is on our minds. You still have that with me, you know. You can say whatever you need to say, Sydney. That's what I've always loved about us the most.

Why do all the words he says and writes and texts have to pierce my heart?

I inhale a deep breath, then exhale carefully. I open my eyes and look down at my phone, terrified to ask the one question I don't really want the answer to. I ask it anyway, because as much as I don't *want* to know the answer, I *need* to know the answer.

Me: If she texted you right now and said she made the wrong choice, would you go? Would you walk out my front door without thinking twice?

My head stills when the rapid rise and fall of his chest comes to a sudden halt.

I can no longer hear his breaths.

His grip around me loosens slightly.

My heart crumbles.

I don't need to read an answer from him. I don't even need to *hear* it. I can feel it in every part of him.

It's not as if I were expecting his answer to be any different. He spent five years with her. It's obvious that he loves her. He's never said otherwise.

I was just hoping he was wrong.

I immediately break away from him and walk swiftly toward my bedroom. I want to lock myself inside until he leaves. I don't want him to see what this does to me. I don't want him to see that I love him the same way he loves Maggie.

I reach my bedroom and swing open the door. I rush inside and begin to shut the door behind me, but he pushes the door open. He steps into my bedroom and turns me around to face him.

His eyes are searching mine, desperately trying to get across whatever it is he wishes he could say. He opens his mouth as if he's going to speak, but then he closes it again. He releases my arms, then turns around and runs his hands through his hair. He grips the back of his neck, then kicks my bedroom door shut with a frustrated groan. He leans his forearm into the door and presses his forehead against it. I do nothing but stand still and watch him try to fight the war within himself. The same war I've been fighting.

He remains in the same position while he lifts his phone and responds to my text.

Ridge: That's not a fair question.

Me: Yeah, well, you didn't really put me in a fair situation by showing up here tonight.

He turns until his back is flat against my bedroom door. He brings two frustrated hands to his forehead, then lifts his leg at the knee and kicks the door behind him. Seeing him struggle with who he really wants is more pain than I'm willing to endure. I deserve more than he can give me right now, and his conflict is screwing with my heart. Screwing with my head. Everything with him is just too much.

Me: I want you to leave. I can't be around you anymore. It terrifies me that you're wishing I were her.

He hangs his head and stares at the floor for several moments while I continue to stare at him. He isn't denying that he'd rather be with Maggie right now. He isn't making excuses or telling me he could love me more than he loves her.

He's completely quiet . . . because he knows I'm right.

Me: I need you to leave. Please. And if you really care about me, you won't come back.

He slowly turns and faces me. His eyes lock with mine, and I've never seen more emotions flash through them than in this moment.

"No," he says firmly.

He begins walking toward me, and I begin backing away from him. He's shaking his head pleadingly. He reaches me just as my legs meet my bed, and then he grabs my face between his hands and presses his lips to mine.

I shake my head and push against his chest. He steps away from me and winces, looking even more frustrated with his inability to communicate with me. His eyes search the room for whatever will help him convince me I'm wrong, but I know nothing can help our situation. He just needs to realize this, too.

He looks down at my bed, then back at me. He grabs my hand and pulls me around to the side of the bed. He places his hands on my shoulders and pushes me down until I'm seated. I have no idea what he's doing, so I don't resist.

Yet.

He continues to lower me until I'm lying with my back flat on the bed. He stands straight up and removes his T-shirt. Before he even has it completely over his head, I'm already attempting to roll off the bed. If he thinks sex will fix our situation, he's not as smart as I thought he was.

"No," he says again when he sees me trying to escape.

The sheer conviction in his voice causes me to freeze, and I fall back against my mattress again. He kneels down on the bed, grabs a pillow, and lays it beside my head. He lies down next to me, and my whole body tenses from his close proximity. He picks up his phone.

Ridge: Listen to me, Sydney.

I stare at the text in anticipation of what he'll type next. When I notice that he's not even texting me a follow-up, I look at him. He shakes his head and pulls my phone from my hands, then tosses it beside him. He takes my hand and places it over his heart.

"Here," he says, patting my hand. "Listen to me here."

My chest tightens when I realize what he wants me to do. He pulls me to him, and I willingly allow it. He gently lowers my head to his heart as he adjusts himself beneath me and helps me get comfortable.

I relax against his chest, finding the rhythm of his heartbeat.

Beat, beat, pause.

Beat, beat, pause.

Beat, beat, pause.

It's absolutely beautiful.

The way it sounds is beautiful.

The way it cares is beautiful.

The way it loves is beautiful.

He presses his lips to the top of my head.

I close my eyes . . . and I cry.

Ridge

I hold her against me for so long I'm not even sure if she's awake. I still have so much I want to say to her, but I don't want to move. I love the way she feels when we're wrapped together like this. I'm afraid if I move, she'll come to her senses again and ask me to leave.

It's barely been three weeks since Maggie and I broke up. When Sydney asked if I'd take Maggie back, I didn't answer, but only because I know she wouldn't believe my answer.

I love Maggie, but I honestly don't think Maggie and I are best for each other anymore. I know exactly where we went wrong. The beginning of our relationship was romantic to the point where it was almost fictionalized. We were nineteen years old. We barely knew each other. The way we waited for an entire year only built up feelings that weren't based on anything except false hopes and idealized love.

By the time Maggie and I were finally able to be together, I think we were more in love with the idea of us, rather than with the actual us. Of course, I loved her. I still love her. But until I met Sydney, I had no idea how much my love for Maggie was built up from my desire to swoop in and save her.

Maggie was right. I've done nothing for the past five years but try to be the hero who protects her. The problem? Heroines don't need protecting.

When Sydney put me on the spot earlier, I wanted to tell her no, that I wouldn't take Maggie back. When she said she was terrified that I was wishing she were Maggie, I wanted to grab hold of her and prove to her how I've never, not once, wished I were anywhere else when I'm with her. I wanted to tell her the only regret I have is not realizing sooner which one of them I was better for. Which girl I made more sense with. Which girl I grew to love in a realistic, natural way, not in an idealized sense.

I didn't say anything because I'm terrified she won't understand. I've chosen Maggie over her time and time again, and it's my own fault that I've put doubt into Sydney's head. And even though I know that the scenario she's painting could never happen because Maggie and I both accept that it's over, I'm not so sure I *wouldn't* take Maggie back. However, my decision wouldn't be because I want to be with Maggie more. It wouldn't even be because I love Maggie more. But how do I possibly convince Sydney of that when it's hard for *me* to comprehend?

I don't want Sydney ever to feel like my second choice, when I know in my heart that she's the *right* choice. The *only* choice.

I keep my arm around her, and I pick up my phone. She lifts her head and rests her chin on my chest, looking up at me. I hand her back her phone, and she takes it, then turns away from me and presses her ear against my heart again.

Me: Do you want to know why I needed you to listen to me?

She doesn't respond with a text. She just nods her head yes, remaining pressed against my chest. One of her hands is slowly tracing up and down from my waist to my arm. The feel of her hands against my skin is something I never want to become a memory. I lower my left hand to the back of her head and stroke her hair.

Me: It's kind of a long explanation. Do you have a notebook I can write in?

She nods and slides off me. She reaches into her nightstand and takes out a notebook and a pen. I readjust myself against her headboard. She hands me the notebook but doesn't move closer to me. I grab her wrist and part my legs, then motion for her to lie against me while I write. She crawls toward me and wraps her arms around my waist, pressing her ear to my heart again. I put my arms around her and prop the notebook on my knee, resting my cheek on top of her head.

I wish there was an easier way for us to communicate so all the things I have to say to her could be instant. I wish I could look into her eyes and tell her exactly how I feel and what's on my mind, but I can't, and I hate that for us. Instead, I lay my heart out on paper. She remains still against my chest while I take almost fifteen minutes to gather my thoughts and get them all down for her. When I'm finished, I hand her the notebook. She readjusts herself until her back is pressed against my chest. I keep my arms around her and hold her while she reads the letter.

Sydney

I have no idea what to expect from the words he's just written, but as soon as he hands me the paper I begin to soak every sentence up as quickly as my eyes can scan them. The fact that a barrier exists in the way we communicate makes every word I receive from him, in whatever form, something I feel the need to consume as quickly as possible.

I don't know if I'm actually more aware of my own heartbeat than other people are of theirs, but I tend to believe I am. The fact that I can't hear the world around me leaves me to focus more on the world inside me. Brennan told me the only time he's aware of his own heartbeat is when it's quiet and he's being still. That's not the case for me, because it's always quiet in my world. I'm always aware of my heartbeat. Always. I know its pattern. I know its rhythm. I know what makes it speed up and slow down, and I even know when to expect that. Sometimes I feel my heart react before my brain has the chance to. The reactions of my heart have always been something I was able to predict . . . until a few months ago.

The first night you walked out onto your balcony was the first night I noticed the change. It was subtle, but it was there. Just an extra little skip. I brushed it off because I didn't want to think it had anything to do with you. I liked how loyal my heart was to Maggie, and I didn't want my loyalty to her to change.

But then, the first time I saw you singing along to one of my songs, it happened again. Only that time, it was more obvious. It would speed up a little faster every time I saw your lips moving. It would start beating in places I never felt my heart beat before. That first night I saw you singing, I had to get up and go inside to finish playing, because I didn't like how you made my heart feel. For the first time, I felt as though I had absolutely no control over it, and that made me feel horrible.

The first time I walked out of my bedroom to find you standing in my apartment, soaking wet from the rain—my God, I didn't know hearts could beat like that. I knew my heart like the back of my hand, and nothing had ever made it react like you did. I put the blankets on the couch for you as quickly as I could, pointed you in the direction of the bathroom, and immediately went back to my bedroom. I'll spare you the details of what I had to do while you were in my shower in order to calm myself down after seeing you up close for the first time.

My physical reaction to you didn't worry me. Physical reactions are normal, and at that point, my heart still belonged to Maggie. My heartbeats were all for Maggie. They always had been, but the more time I spent with you, the more you started to unintentionally infiltrate and steal some of those heartbeats. I did everything I could to prevent it from happening. For a while, I convinced myself that I was stronger than my heart, which is why I allowed you to stay. I thought what I felt for you was nothing but attraction and that if I let myself have you in my fantasies enough, that would suffice in reality. However, I soon realized that the way I fantasized about you wasn't at all how guys normally fantasize about girls they're attracted to. I didn't imagine myself stealing kisses from you when no one was around. I didn't imagine myself sliding into your bed in the middle of the night and doing to you all the things we both wished I would do. Instead, I was imagining what it would feel like if you fell asleep in my arms. I was imagining what it would feel like to wake up next to you in the morning. I was imagining your smiles and your laughter and even how good it would feel to be able to comfort you when you cried.

The trouble I had gotten myself into became obvious the night I put those headphones in your ears and watched you sing the song we created together. Watching those words pass your lips and knowing I couldn't hear them and feeling how much my heart ached for us in that moment, I knew what was happening was so much more than I could control. My strength was overpowered by my weakness for you. The second my lips touched yours, my heart split completely in two. Half of it belonged to you from that point on. Every other beat of my heart was for you.

I knew I should have asked you to leave that night, but I couldn't bring myself to do it. The thought of saying good-bye to you hurt way too much. I had planned on asking you to move out the next day, but once we talked through everything, the ease with which we dealt with our situation gave me more excuses to ignore it. Knowing we were both fighting it gave me hope that I could give back to Maggie the part of my heart I had lost to you.

The weekend of Warren's party was when I realized it was too late. I spent the entire night of the party trying not to watch you. Trying not to be obvious. Trying to keep my attention focused on Maggie, where it should have been. However, all the effort and denial in the world couldn't have saved me from what happened the next day. When I walked into your room and sat down beside you on the bed, I felt it.

I felt you give me a piece of your heart.

And Sydney, I wanted it. I wanted your heart more than I've ever wanted anything. The second I reached down and held your hand in mine, it happened. My heart made its choice, and it chose you.

My relationship with Maggie was a great one, and I never want to disrespect what I had with her. When I told you I've loved her since the moment I met her and that I'd love her until the moment I die, I was being honest. I have always loved her, I do love her, and I always will love her. She's an incredible person who deserves so much more than what life has handed her, and it pisses me off to this day when I think about it. I would switch my fate with hers in a second if I had that option. Unfortunately, life doesn't work that way. Fate doesn't work that way. So even after I knew I had found in you what I would never find in my relationship with Maggie, it still wasn't enough. No matter how much I cared for you or how deep my feelings for you ran, it would have never been enough to get me to leave Maggie. If I couldn't change her fate, I was at least going to give her the best damn life I could give her. Even if it meant sacrificing aspects of my own, I would have done it without pause, and I never would have regretted it. Not even for a second.

However, until three weeks ago, I didn't realize that the best life I could give her was a life without me in it. She needed the opposite of what I could offer her, and I know that now. She knows that now. And we accept it.

So when you ask if I would choose her over you, you're presenting a situation that I can't give you a straight answer to. Because yes, at this point, I probably would walk away from you if she asked me to. The majority of my loyalty still lies with her. But if you're asking who I need more? Who I want to be with more? Who my heart craves more? My heart decided that for me a long time ago, Sydney.

When I've read the last word, I pull the notebook against my chest and cry. He slides me off of him until I'm on my back, and he hovers over me, guiding my eyes up to meet his.

"It's you," he says aloud. "My heart . . . wants you."

A sob breaks free from my chest when I hear his words. I immediately grab his shoulders and lift myself up, pressing my lips to the area directly over his heart. I kiss him over and over, silently thanking him for giving me reassurance that I haven't been in this alone.

When I lower my head back to the pillow, he lies beside me, then pulls me against him. He touches my cheek with his hand and slowly leans in to kiss me. His mouth caresses mine so carefully it feels as if he's holding my heart in his hand and is afraid he might drop it.

As much as I'm convinced he would do everything he could to protect my heart, I'm still too scared to hand it over. I don't want to give it to him until I know it's the only heart he's holding.

•   •   •

I don't open my eyes, because I don't want him to know I hear him leaving. I felt him kiss me. I felt him slide his arm out from beneath me. I heard him pull his shirt over his head. I heard him search for a pen. I heard him write me a letter, and I heard him place it on the pillow beside me.

I feel his hand as it presses into the mattress beside my head. His lips meet my forehead before he pulls away and walks out my bedroom door. When I hear the front door shut, I roll onto my side and pull the covers over my head to block out the sunlight. If I didn't have to work today, I'd stay right here in this position and cry myself dry.

I brush my hand across the mattress in search of his letter. When I find it, I pull it under the covers with me and read it.

Sydney,

A few months ago, we thought we had it all figured out. I was with the one girl I thought I would be with forever, and you were with a guy you thought deserved you way more than he did.

Look at us now.

Wanting more than anything to be free to love each other but cursed by bad timing and loyal hearts. We both know where we want to be; we just don't know how to get there. Or when we should get there. I wish things were as easy as they seemed when I was nineteen. We'd grab a calendar and pick a date, and we'd start a countdown until I could show up at your front door and start loving you.

However, I've learned that the heart can't be told when and who and how it should love. The heart does whatever the hell it wants to do. The only thing we can control is whether we give our lives and our minds the chance to catch up to our hearts.

I know that's what you want more than anything. Time to catch up.

As much as I want to stay here and allow this to begin between us, there's something I want from you even more than that. I want you to be with me in the end, and I know that can't happen if I keep trying to rush our beginning. I know exactly why you were hesitant to let me in last night: you aren't ready yet. Maybe I'm not, either. You've always said you wanted time to yourself, and the last thing I want is to start a relationship with you when I've barely given enough respect to the one that just ended with Maggie.

I don't know when you'll be ready for me. It might be next month or next year. Whenever it is, just know that I have absolutely no doubt that we can make this work. I know we can. If there are two people in this world capable of finding a way to love each other, it's us.

Ridge

P.S. I spent most of the night watching you sleep, so that's one fantasy I got to check off the list. I also wrote lyrics to an entire song, which was unfortunate for Brennan. I didn't have my guitar, so I forced him to make a rough cut of it at five o'clock this morning so I could leave it with you.

One of these days, I'll play it for you, along with all the other songs I plan to write for you while we're apart. Until then, I'll be waiting patiently.

Just say when.

I fold the letter and pull it against my chest. As much as it hurts to know he's walking away, I also know that I need to let him. I asked for this. We need this. *I* need this. I need to get myself to a point where I know that we can finally be together without all the doubt running through my head. He's right. My mind needs to catch up to my heart.

I run the back of my hand across my eyes, then open my texts.

Me: Can you come over? I need your help.

Warren: If this has to do with the fact that I gave Ridge your address last night, I'm sorry. He forced it out of me.

Me: This has nothing to do with that. I need to ask you for a huge favor.

Warren: Be there when I get off work tonight. Should I bring condoms?

Me: Funny guy.

I close out the text to Warren and open up the song Ridge just sent me. I reach into my drawer for my headphones, then fall back against my pillow and hit play.

IT'S YOU

Baby, everything you've ever done
Underneath this here sun
It doesn't even matter anymore
Oh, of this I'm sure

'Cause you've taken me
Places I want to be
And you show me
Everything that I could ever
Want to see
You, you know it's
You know it's you

I think about you every single day
Trying to think of something better to say
Maybe hi, how are you
Not just anything will do

'Cause you've taken me
Places I want to be
And you show me
Everything that I could ever
Want to see
You, you know it's
You know it's you

24.

Ridge

Me: I'm looking at your schedule for March. You're free on the 18th.

Brennan: Why do I feel like I'm about to be busy on the 18th?

Me: I'm planning a show, and I need your help. We'll do it locally.

Brennan: What kind of show? Full band?

Me: No, just you and me. Maybe Warren if he'll sign for us.

Brennan: Why do I feel like this has to do with Sydney?

Me: Why do I feel like I don't care what you feel like?

Brennan: The ball is in her court, Ridge. You really should just leave things alone until she's ready. I know how you feel about her, and I don't want you to screw it up.

Me: March 18 is still three months away. If she hasn't made up her mind by that date, then all I'm doing is giving her a little shove. And when did you start giving relationship advice? How long has it been since you were in one? Oh, wait. That would be never.

Brennan: If I agree to help you, will you STFU? What do you need me to do?

Me: Just carve out some time for me between now and then to run through some new songs.

Brennan: Is someone over his writer's block?

Me: Yeah, well, someone once told me heartache is good for lyrical inspiration. Unfortunately, he was right.

Brennan: Sounds like a smart guy.

I close out my texts to Brennan and open one up to Warren.

Me: March 18. I need a local venue. A small one. Then I need you to get Sydney to go there with you that night.

Warren: Is she supposed to know you orchestrated this?

Me: No. Lie to her.

Warren: Not a problem. I'm good at lying.

I set my phone down, pick up my guitar, and walk out onto my balcony. It's been almost a month since I last saw her. Neither of us has texted the other. I know Warren still keeps in contact with her, but he refuses to tell me anything, so I just stopped asking. As much as I miss her and as much as I want to beg her to just let this begin with us, I know time is better for both of us right now. There was still too much guilt rolled up in the thought of starting something too soon, despite how much we wanted to be together. Waiting until we're both in a good place is definitely what needs to happen.

However, I feel as if I'm already there. Maybe it's easier for me because I know where Maggie and I stand, and I know where my heart stands, but Sydney doesn't have that reassurance. If time will give her that reassurance, then I'll give her time. Just not too much. March 18 is only three months away. I hope to hell she's ready by then, because I'm not sure I can keep myself away from her for longer than that.

I scoot my chair to the edge of the balcony and fold my arms over the railing, then look over at her old balcony. Every time I come out here and see her empty chair, it makes all of this so much harder. But I can't seem to find anything inside my apartment that reminds me of her anymore. She left nothing when she moved, and she really never had anything while she was here. Being outside on this balcony is the closest I can come to feeling her since it seems we're so far apart.

I lean back in my chair, pick up a pen, and begin writing the lyrics to another song, with nothing but her on my mind.

> *The cool air running through my hair*
> *Nights like these, doesn't seem fair*
> *For you and I to be so far away*
> *The stars all shimmer like a melody*
> *Like they're playing for you and me*
> *But only I can hear their sounds.*

I pick up my guitar and work through the first few chords. I want these songs to be enough to convince her that we're ready, so every single thing has to be perfect. I'm just nervous that I'm relying too much on Warren to help make it happen. I hope he's more reliable in this situation with Sydney than he is with his rent checks.

25.

Sydney

"I'm not going."

"Yes, you are," Warren says, kicking my legs off the coffee table. "I'm bored out of my mind. Bridgette works all weekend, and Ridge is off doing God knows what with God knows who."

I immediately look up at him with my heart caught in my throat.

He laughs. "That got your attention." He reaches forward, grabs my hands, and pulls me off the couch. "I'm kidding. Ridge is at home working, being a mopey little shit, just like you're trying to be. Now, go get pretty and come out with me tonight, or I'll sit on the couch with you and force you to watch porn."

I pull my hands from his and walk to the kitchen. I open a cabinet, then grab a cup. "I don't want to go out tonight, Warren. I had class all day, and it's my only night off from the library. I'm sure you can find someone else to go with you." I grab a container of juice from the refrigerator and fill my glass. Leaning against the counter, I take a sip as I watch Warren pout in my living room. He's kind of adorable when he pouts, which is why I always give him such a hard time.

"Listen up, Syd," he says, walking toward the kitchen. He grabs a bar stool and pulls it out, then takes a seat. "I'm about to lay things out for you, okay?"

I roll my eyes. "I doubt I can stop you, so go ahead."

He lays his palms flat on the counter in front of him and leans forward. "You suck."

I laugh. "That's it? That's what you needed to lay out for me?"

He nods. "You suck. So does Ridge. Since the night I gave him your address, you've both sucked. All he does is work or write music. He doesn't even play pranks on me anymore. Every time I'm over here, you're just focused on studying. You never want to go out. You never want to hear my sex stories anymore."

"Correction," I say, interrupting him. "I've never wanted to hear your sex stories. That's nothing new."

"Whatever," he says, shaking his head. "My point is that the two of you are miserable. I know you need time and blah, blah, blah, but that doesn't mean you have to give up fun while you're figuring your life out. I want to go have fun. No one wants to have fun with me anymore, and that's all your fault, because you're the only one who can put a stop to the misery you and Ridge are going through. So, yes. You suck. You suck, you suck, you suck. And if you want to stop sucking so much, then go get dressed so we can go out and not suck together for just a few hours."

I don't know how to argue with that. I do suck. I suck, I suck, I suck. Only Warren could put it in such a simple, straightforward way that would actually make sense. I know I've been miserable the past few months, and it doesn't help to know that Ridge has been miserable, too. He's miserable because he's sitting around waiting for me to get over whatever it is that's keeping me from contacting him.

The last thing he said in his letter to me was *Just say when.*

I've been trying to say when since the moment I read that letter, but I'm just too scared. I've never felt about anyone or anything the way I feel about him, and the thought of our not working out is enough to keep me from saying that one little word. I feel as if the longer we wait and the more time we have to heal, the better chance we'll have at our *maybe someday*.

I keep waiting for the moment when I know for sure that he's moved on from Maggie. I keep waiting for the moment when I know for sure that he's ready to commit fully to me. I keep waiting for the moment when I know for sure that I'm not going to be consumed with guilt for allowing myself to trust someone with my heart again.

I don't know when I'll get to that point, and it hurts to know that my inability to move forward is holding Ridge back.

"Now," Warren says, shoving me out of the kitchen. "Get dressed."

. . .

I can't believe I've let him talk me into this. I check my makeup one last time and grab my purse. As soon as he sees me, he shakes his head. I huff and throw my hands in the air.

"What now?" I sigh. "I'm not dressed appropriately?"

"You look great, but I want you to wear the blue dress."

"I burned that dress, remember?" I say.

"The hell you did," he says, pushing me back toward my bedroom. "You were wearing it last week when I stopped by. Go put it on so we can leave."

I spin around to face him. "I know how much you like that dress, and wearing it tonight while I'm out with you is a little too creepy, Warren."

He narrows his eyes. "Listen, Syd. I don't mean to be rude, but all this moping around for the past few months has caused you to put on a little weight. Your ass looks huge in those jeans. The blue dress may be able to hide a little of that, so go put it on, or I might be too embarrassed to go out with you."

I suddenly feel like slapping him again, but I know he's just got a peculiar sense of humor. I also know he might have a completely different reason for why he wants me to wear this dress and I'm trying not to let myself think it has anything to do with Ridge, but pretty much every situation I'm in somehow makes me think about Ridge. It's nothing new. But Warren is a guy who seems to put his foot in his mouth a lot, and I'm a girl, so I still wonder if his sarcastic remark has any truth to it. I *have* been replacing the void Ridge left in my life with food. I look down at my stomach and pat it, then look back up at Warren. "You're an asshole."

He nods. "I know."

The innocent smile on his face makes me instantly forgive any crudeness behind his joke. I change into the blue dress, but I am *so* cock-blocking him tonight. Jerk.

•   •   •

"Wow. This is . . . different," I say, taking in my surroundings. It's nothing like the clubs Warren usually likes to go to. This one is a lot smaller, without even much of a dance floor. There's an empty stage along one wall, but there's no one performing tonight. The jukebox is playing, and several people are scattered around at tables, talking quietly among themselves. Warren chooses a table toward the middle of the room.

"You're a cheap date," I say. "You didn't even feed me."

He laughs. "I'll buy you a burger on the way home."

Warren pulls out his phone and begins texting someone, so I look around for a while. It's kind of cozy. It's also kind of weird that Warren brought me here. But I'm thinking he doesn't have any evil intentions, because he's not even paying attention to me.

His attention is on his phone, and he keeps glancing at the door. I don't understand why he wanted to come out tonight, and I especially don't understand why he chose this place.

"You're actually the one who sucks," I say. "Stop ignoring me."

He responds without even looking up at me. "You aren't talking, so technically, I'm not ignoring you."

I'm curious now. He's not being himself, the way he's so distracted. "What's up with you, Warren?"

As soon as I ask the question, he looks up from his phone and smiles over my shoulder, then stands. "You're late," he says to someone behind me. I look to see Bridgette walking toward us.

"Screw you, Warren," she says to him with a small smile. He wraps his arms around her, and they kiss for several uncomfortable seconds. I reach up and tap him on the arm when I'm convinced that neither of them can breathe. He pulls away from Bridgette, winks at her, and slides out his chair for her.

"I have to go to the bathroom," he says to Bridgette. He points at me. "Don't go anywhere."

He says it as if it's a command, and it irritates me even more because he's being really rude tonight. I turn and face Bridgette once he's left the table. "Warren said you were working all weekend," I say.

She shrugs. "Yeah, well, he probably told you that because of the elaborate scheme he has planned for tonight. He made me come so you wouldn't leave when you found out about it. Oh, and I'm not supposed to tell you any of that, so if he comes back, play dumb."

My heart rate escalates. "Please tell me you're kidding."

She shakes her head and raises her arm in the air, calling over a waiter. "I wish I was kidding. I had to switch shifts to be here, and now I have to work a double tomorrow."

I drop my head into my hands, regretting the fact that I let Warren talk me into anything. Just when I'm reaching for my purse to leave, he walks out onto the empty stage.

"Oh, God," I groan. "What the hell is he doing?" My stomach is in knots. I have no idea what he has planned, but whatever it is, it can't be good.

He taps on the microphone, then adjusts the height of it. "I'd like to thank everyone for coming tonight. Not that any of you are here for this particular event, since it's a surprise, but I feel the need to thank you anyway."

He adjusts the microphone once more, then finds our table in the crowd and waves. "I want to apologize to you, Syd, because I feel really bad for lying to you. You haven't gained weight, and your ass looked great in those jeans, but you really needed to wear that dress tonight. Also, you don't suck. I lied about that, too."

Several people in the crowd laugh, but I just groan and bury my face in my hands, peeking through my fingers at him up on the stage.

"All right, let's get on with it, shall we? We have a few new songs for you tonight. Unfortunately, the whole band couldn't be here, because"—he looks to his left at the small width of the stage, then to his right—"well, I don't think they all could have fit. So I'd like to present to you a small portion of the band Sounds of Cedar."

My heart falls to the floor. I close my eyes when the crowd begins to clap.

Please, let it be Ridge.

Please, don't let it be Ridge.

Jesus, when will this confusion go away?

I can hear commotion up on the stage, and I'm too scared to open my eyes. I want to see him sitting up there so much it hurts.

"Hey, Syd," Warren says into the microphone. I inhale a slow, calming breath, then open my eyes and hesitantly look up at him. "Remember a few months ago when I told you sometimes we have to have really bad days in order to keep the good ones in perspective?"

I think I nod. I can't really feel my body anymore.

"Well, this is one of the good days. This is one of the really good days." He raises his hand in the air and motions to my table. "Somebody get that girl a shot of whatever will help loosen her up."

He moves the microphone to the stool next to him, and my eyes are glued to the empty chairs. Someone lays a shot on the table in front of me, and I instantly grab it and down it. I drop the shot glass back onto the table and look up just in time to see them walk onto the stage. Brennan is first, and Ridge is right behind him, carrying a guitar.

Oh, my God. He looks incredible. It's the first time I've ever seen him on a stage. I've been wanting to watch him perform since the first moment I heard his guitar on my balcony and here I am, about to watch my fantasy become reality.

He looks the same as he did the last time I saw him, just . . . incredible. I guess he looked incredible back then, too. I just didn't feel right allowing myself to admit it when I knew he wasn't mine. I must feel okay about it now, because holy crap. He's beautiful. He carries himself with such confidence and I can definitely see why. His arms look as if they were built for the sole purpose of carrying a guitar. It molds to him so naturally, it's as if it's an extension of him. There isn't a shadow of guilt clouding his eyes like there always was in the past. He's smiling, like he's excited for what's about to happen. His enigmatic smile lights up his face and his face lights up the entire room. At least it seems that way to me. He glances over the audience several times as he makes his way toward his seat, but he doesn't immediately spot me.

He takes a seat on the center stool, and Brennan sits to the left of him, Warren to his right. He signs to Warren, and Warren points at me. Ridge looks out into the audience and finds me. My hands are clamped over my mouth, and my elbows are propped up on the table. He smiles and gives me a nod and my heart crashes to the floor. I can't smile or wave or nod back at him. I'm too nervous to move.

Brennan leans forward and speaks into the microphone. "We've got a few new songs—"

His voice is cut off when Ridge pulls the microphone away from him and leans in toward it. "Sydney," Ridge says into the microphone, "some of these songs I wrote with you. Some of these songs I wrote *for* you."

I can hear a small difference in the way he speaks now. I've never heard him say so much at once out loud. He also seems to enunciate a little more clearly than the few times he's spoken to me in the past, like the subject in the photograph is slightly more in focus. It's obvious he's been working on it, and knowing he's continued to talk out loud makes my eyes tear up without even having heard a song yet.

"If you aren't ready to say the word, that's fine," he says. "I'll wait as long as you need me to. I just hope you don't mind this interruption tonight." He pushes the microphone away, then looks down to his guitar. Brennan leans into the microphone and looks at me.

"He can't hear what I'm saying right now, so I'll take this opportunity to tell you Ridge is full of shit. He doesn't want to wait anymore. He wants you to say the word more than he wants air. So please, for the sake of all that is holy, say the word tonight."

I laugh as I wipe a tear from my eye.

Ridge plays the opening chords to "Trouble," and I finally realize why Warren made me wear this dress. Brennan leans forward and begins to sing, and I remain completely immobile as Warren signs every word to the song while Ridge keeps his focus on the fingers strumming his guitar. Watching the three of them together, seeing the beauty they can create from a few words and guitars, is mesmerizing.

Ridge

When the song ends, I look up at her.

She's crying, but those tears are accompanied by a smile, and that's exactly what I was hoping I would see when I looked up from my guitar. Seeing her for the first time since I kissed her good-bye has a far greater effect on me than I thought it would. I'm trying my damndest to remember what it is I'm here to do, but all I want to do is toss my guitar aside, rush to her, and kiss her crazy.

Instead, I keep my eyes trained on hers while I play another song she helped me write. I begin the opening chords to "Maybe Someday." She smiles and clutches a hand to her chest while she watches me play.

It's times like these I'm actually thankful I can't hear. Not being distracted by anything at all allows me to focus on nothing but her. I can feel the music vibrating in my chest as I watch her lips singing along to the lyrics until the very last line.

I planned on playing a few more songs we wrote together, but seeing her has changed my mind. I want to get to the new songs I wrote for her, because I absolutely need to see her reaction to them. I start one of them, knowing Warren and Brennan will have no problem falling into step with the change-up. Her eyes glisten when she realizes that this is a song she's never heard before, and she leans forward in her chair, focusing intently on the three of us.

Sydney

There are only twenty-six letters in the English alphabet. You would think there would only be so much you could do with twenty-six letters. You would think there were only so many ways those letters could make you feel when mixed up and shoved together to make words.

However, there are infinite ways those twenty-six letters can make a person feel, and this song is living proof. I'll never understand how a few simple words strung together can change a person, but this song, these words, are completely changing me. I feel like my *maybe someday* just became my *right now*.

HOLD ON TO YOU
The cool air running through my hair
Nights like these, doesn't seem fair
For you and I to be so far away

The stars all shimmer like a melody
Like they're playing for you and me
But only I can hear their sound

Maybe if I ask them they will play for you
I try wishing on one, maybe I'll try two
It doesn't look like there's much for me to do

I want to hold on to you
Just like these memories I can't undo
I want to hold on to you
Without you here that's kind of hard to do

I want to hold
I want to hold on to you

The front seat's empty, and I know
When it's just me I seem to go
To places I never wanted to

I need you here to be a light
Star in the sky brighten up my night
Sometimes I need the dark to see

So come on, come on, turn it on for me
Just a little light, and I'll be able to see
Promise like a comet you won't fly by me

I want to hold on to you
Just like these memories I can't undo
I want to hold on to you

Without you here that's kind of hard to do
I want to hold
I want to hold on to you

Ridge

I finish the song and don't give myself time to look up at her before I begin playing another one. I'm afraid if I look at her, I'll lose every bit of willpower still keeping me up on this stage. I want to go to her so bad, but I know how important it is for her to hear this next song. I also don't want to be the one to make the final choice. If she's ready to be with me, she knows what I need from her. If she's not ready, I'll respect her decision.

However, if she's not ready to begin the life I know we could have together by the end of this song, I don't know if she'll ever be ready.

I keep my eyes trained on my fingers as they work the strings of the guitar. I glance at Brennan, and he leans forward into the microphone, his voice starting on cue. I glance to Warren, and he begins signing the words.

I slowly scan the crowd and find her again.

Our eyes lock.

I don't look away.

Sydney

"Wow," Bridgette whispers. Her eyes are glued to the stage just like mine. Just like every other pair of eyes in the room. The three of them make one hell of a team, but knowing that these words are Ridge's words and he wrote them specifically for me leaves me feeling more than overwhelmed. I can't look away from him. For the entire length of the song, I barely move. I barely breathe.

LET IT BEGIN

Time went fast
Time went fast till it was gone
You think it's right
You think it's right until it's wrong

Even after all this time
I still want you
Even after all my mind
Put me through

So won't you
Won't you let it begin
So won't you
Won't you let it begin

You hold it out
You hold your heart out in your hand
I snatch it up
I snatch it up fast as I can

Even after all this time
I still want you
Even after all my mind
Put me through

I stand here at your door
Until you come and let me in
I want to be your end
But you gotta let it begin

So won't you
Won't you let it begin
So won't you
Won't you just say when

Ridge

Our gazes never deviate from each other. Throughout the song, her focus remains solely on mine and mine on hers. When the song ends, I don't move. I wait for her mind and her life to catch up to her heart, and I hope it happens soon. Tonight. Right now.

She wipes tears from her eyes, then lifts her hands. She holds up her left index finger, brings her right index finger close to the left and circles it around, and then the tips of her fingers touch.

I can't move.

She just signed for me.

She just said "when."

Seeing her sign is something I never expected. It's something I never would have even asked her to do. Learning how to communicate with me the whole time we've been apart is the most amazing thing anyone has ever done for me.

I'm shaking my head, unable to get it through my mind that this girl is willingly mine and she's perfect and beautiful and good and, holy shit, I love her so much.

She's smiling, but I'm still frozen in shock.

She laughs at my response and signs the word again, several times. "When, when, when."

Brennan shoves my shoulder, and I look over at him. He laughs. "Go," he signs, nodding his head in Sydney's direction. "Go get your girl."

I immediately drop my guitar to the floor and rush off the stage. She pushes away from her table as soon as she sees me making my way toward her. She's only a few feet away, but I can't get to her fast enough. I take in the dress she has on and make a mental note to thank Warren later. I have a feeling he had something to do with that.

I look into her tear-filled eyes when I finally reach her. She's smiling up at me, and for the first time since the moment I met her, we're looking at each other without a trace of guilt or worry or regret or shame.

She throws her arms around my neck, and I pull her to me and bury my face in her hair. I hold her head firmly against me and close my eyes. We hold on to each other as if we're afraid to let go.

I can feel her crying, so I put enough space between us so I can look into her eyes. She lifts her head, and I've never seen tears look more beautiful.

"You signed," I say out loud.

She smiles. "You spoke. A lot."

"I'm not very good at it," I admit. I know my words are hard to understand, and I still feel uncomfortable when I speak, but I love seeing her eyes when she hears my voice. It makes me want to speak every single word I possibly can right here and now.

"I'm not good, either," she says. She pulls away from me and lifts her hands to sign. "Warren has been helping me. I only know about two hundred words, but I'm learning."

It's been several months since I last saw her, and while I've been trying to believe she still wanted to be with me, I did have my doubts. I was starting to question our decision to wait before starting our relationship. What I never expected was for her to spend those months learning how to communicate with me in a way my own parents didn't even care enough to learn.

"I just fell completely in love with you," I say to her. I glance at Bridgette, who is still seated at the table. "Did you see it, Bridgette? Did you see me just fall in love with her?"

Bridgette rolls her eyes, and I feel Sydney laugh. I look back down at her. "I did. Like twenty seconds ago. I fell completely in love with you."

She smiles and mouths her next words slowly so I can understand her. "I fell first."

When the last word passes her lips, I catch it with my mouth. Since the second I walked away from these lips, I've done nothing but think about the moment I would get to taste them again. She pulls me tightly against her, and I kiss her hard, then delicately, then fast and slow and every way in between. I kiss her every way I can possibly kiss her, because I plan on loving her every way I can possibly love her. Every single time we refused to cave in to our feelings in the past makes this kiss completely worth the sacrifices. This kiss is worth all the tears, all the heartache, all the pain, all the struggles, all the waiting.

She's worth it all.

She's worth more.

Sydney

We make it to my apartment somehow between all the kissing. He releases me long enough to let me unlock the door, but he loses his patience as soon as it's unlocked. I laugh when he shoves the door open and pushes me inside. He closes the door, locks it, and turns around to face me again. We look at each other for several seconds.

"Hi," he says simply.

I laugh. "Hi."

He looks around the room nervously before his eyes fall back to mine. "Is that good enough?" he asks.

I cock my head, because I don't really understand his question. "Is what good enough?"

He grins. "I was hoping that was enough talk for tonight."

Oh.

I get his question now.

I nod slowly, and he smiles, then steps forward and kisses me. He bends slightly and lifts me by the waist, wrapping my legs around him. He secures his arms around my back and begins walking me toward my bedroom.

As many times as I've seen this happen in movies and read about it in books, I've never actually been picked up and carried by a man before. I think I'm in love with it. Being carried into a bedroom by Ridge is quite possibly my new favorite thing out of any and all things.

That is, until he kicks my bedroom door shut behind him. Maybe Ridge kicking doors shut is my new favorite thing.

He gently lowers me to the bed, and even though I'm sad that he's not carrying me anymore, I'm a little bit happier to find myself beneath him. Every single move he makes is better and sexier than the last one. He pauses for a moment as he hovers over me, and his eyes roam sensually over my entire body, until they come to a pause on the hem of my dress. He reaches down and pushes it up, and I lift myself up off the bed just enough for him to pull it over my head.

He sucks in a breath when he looks down at me and sees that the only thing coming between him and a completely naked me is a very thin layer of panty. He begins to lower himself on top of me, but I push on his chest and shake my head, tugging on his shirt to let him know it's his turn. He grins and quickly pulls his shirt over his head, then leans in toward me again. I push against him once more, and he reluctantly lifts himself up, shooting me a look of amused annoyance. I point to his jeans, and he backs away from the bed, and in two swift movements, the rest of his clothes are somewhere on my bedroom floor. I don't quite catch where he tossed them, because my eyes are sort of preoccupied.

He makes his way on top of me again, and I don't stop him this time. I welcome him by wrapping my legs around his waist and my arms around his back and guiding his mouth back to mine.

We mold and fit together so perfectly it's as if we were made for this sole purpose. His left hand fits perfectly into mine as he brings my arm above my head and presses it into the mattress. His tongue melds perfectly with mine as he continues to tease my entire mouth as if it were made for this very purpose. His right hand seamlessly conforms to my outer thigh as he digs his fingers into my skin and shifts his weight perfectly against me.

His mouth leaves mine long enough to taste my jaw . . . my neck . . . my shoulder.

I don't know how being consumed by him could lend clarity to my purpose in life, but it absolutely feels that way. Everything about me and him and life makes so much more sense when we're together like this. He makes me feel more beautiful. More important. More loved. More needed. I feel more *everything*, and with every second that passes, I become more and more greedy, wanting all of every single part of him.

I push against his chest, needing space between us so I can sign to him. He looks down at my hands when he realizes what I'm doing. I hope I get it right, because I've practiced signing this sentence no fewer than a thousand times since I last saw him.

"I have something I need to say before we do this."

He pulls back a few inches, watching my hands, waiting.

I sign the words "I love you."

His eyebrows draw apart, and relief floods his eyes. He lowers his mouth to my hands and kisses them, over and over, then quickly pulls farther away, unwrapping my legs from around his waist. Just when I begin to fear he's come to some absurd notion that we need to stop, he lowers himself to my side but leans over me and presses his ear against my chest.

"I want to feel you say it."

I press my lips into his hair, then lightly secure him against me. "I love you, Ridge," I whisper.

His grip tightens around my waist, so I continue repeating it several times.

I keep his head pressed against my chest with both hands. He releases his grip on my waist and trails his hand over my stomach, causing my muscles to clench beneath his touch. He continues stroking his hand in sensuous circles over my stomach. I stop repeating the words and focus on where his hand is traveling, but he stops abruptly.

"I don't feel you saying it," he says.

"I love you," I quickly repeat. When the words leave my lips, his fingers begin moving again. As soon as I'm quiet, his fingers stop.

It doesn't take me long to figure out what game he's playing. I grin and say it again.

"I love you."

His fingers slip inside the top edge of my panties, and my voice grows quiet again. It's really hard for me to speak when his hand is that close. It's really hard to do anything. His fingers come to a pause just inside my panties when he doesn't feel me talking. I want his hand to keep moving, so I somehow breathe the words.

"I love you."

His hand slides further inside and stops. I close my eyes and say it again. Slowly.

"I . . . love . . . you."

What he does next with his hand causes me to repeat the words again instantly.

And again.

And again.

And again.

And again and again and again, until my panties are somewhere on the floor, and I've said the words so many times and so fast that I'm almost screaming them now. He continues to prove with the expertise of his hand that he's quite possibly the absolute best listener I've ever encountered.

"I love you," I whisper one last time between faltered and shallow breaths. I'm too weak to utter the words again, and my hands fall away from his head and land against the mattress with a thud.

He lifts his head away from my chest and scoots upward until his face is so close to mine our noses brush. "I love you, too," he says with a smug grin.

I smile, but my smile fades when he rolls away from me, leaving me alone on the bed. I'm too exhausted and spent to reach out for him. However, he returns to the bed as quickly as he left it. He tears open a condom wrapper and keeps his eyes focused on mine, never once looking away.

The way he's looking at me, as if I'm the only thing that

matters in his world, makes the moment take on a whole new feel. I'm completely consumed, not by waves of pleasure but by waves of raw emotion. I didn't know I could *feel* someone this much. I didn't know I could *need* someone this much. I had no idea I was capable of sharing this kind of connection with someone.

Ridge lifts a hand and wipes away a tear from my temple, then dips his head and kisses me, gentle and soft, coaxing even more tears out of me. It's the perfect kiss for the perfect moment. I know he feels what I'm feeling, because my tears don't alarm him at all. He knows they're not tears of regret or sadness. They're simply tears. Emotional tears stemming from an emotional moment that I never imagined could be this incredible.

He's waiting patiently for my permission, so I nod softly, and it's all the confirmation he needs. He lowers his cheek to mine and slowly begins to ease himself against me. I squeeze my eyes shut and focus on trying to relax, but my entire body is way too tense.

I've only ever had sex with one guy, and he didn't mean half as much to me as Ridge does. The thought of sharing this experience with Ridge, as much as I want to, makes me so nervous I'm physically unable to hide my discomfort.

He can sense my apprehension, so he pauses and stills himself above me. I love how in tune he is with me already. He looks down at me, his dark brown eyes searching mine. He takes both of my hands and pulls them over my head, then laces our fingers together and presses them into the mattress. He leans into my ear. "Want me to stop?"

I quickly shake my head no.

He laughs softly. "Then you have to relax, Syd."

I bite my bottom lip and nod, completely loving the fact that he just said "Syd" out loud. He runs his nose down my jawline, then brings his lips close to mine. Every touch sends waves of heat coursing through me, but it doesn't ease my apprehension. Everything about this moment is so perfect I'm afraid I might do something to mess it up. It can't get any better, so that only leaves things with one direction to go.

"Are you nervous?" he asks. His voice brushes across my mouth, and I slide my tongue over my bottom lip, convinced that I could taste his words if I tried.

I nod, and his eyes soften with his smile.

"Me, too," he whispers. He squeezes my hands tighter and then lays his head across my bare chest. I can feel the rhythm of his body rise and fall against mine with every tense breath. His entire body sighs, and one by one, each muscle begins to relax. His hands are still, and he's not exploring my body or listening to me sing or having me tell him I love him.

He's still, because he's listening to *me*.

He's listening to the beat of my heart.

His head lifts off my chest in one swift motion as he locks eyes with mine. Whatever realization he's just had causes his gaze to pierce mine with excitement.

"Do you have earplugs?" he says.

Earplugs?

I know the confusion can be seen in my expression. I nod anyway and point to the nightstand. He leans over me, opens the drawer, and feels around inside. When he finds them, he lowers himself beside me again, then places them in the palm of my hand. He motions for me to put them in my ears.

"Why?"

He smiles and kisses me, then trails his lips to my ear. "I want you to hear me love you."

I look down at the earplugs, then back up at him questioningly. "How can I hear you if I'm wearing these?"

He shakes his head, then places his hands over my ears. "Not here," he says. He moves a hand to my chest. "I want you to hear me from right here."

That's all the explanation I need. I quickly put the earplugs in, then adjust my head on my pillow. All the noise around me slowly fades away. I wasn't aware of all the sounds I was taking in until they no longer run through my head. I don't hear the clock ticking anymore. I no longer hear the usual activity outside my window. I can't hear the sheets moving beneath us or the pillow under my head or the bed when he shifts his weight.

I hear nothing.

He grabs my hand and opens up my palm, then turns my hand around and places it over my heart. Once my palm is flush against my heart, he reaches to my face and brushes his hand over my eyes, closing them. He scoots himself away from me until he's no longer touching any part of me.

He becomes still, and I no longer feel him moving next to me.

It's quiet.

It's dark.

I hear absolutely nothing. I'm not sure this is working out the way he imagined.

I hear nothing but complete silence. I hear what Ridge hears every moment of his life. The only thing I'm aware of is my own heartbeat and nothing else. Nothing at all.

Wait.

My heartbeat.

I open my eyes and look at him. He's several inches away from me on the bed, smiling. He knows I hear it. He smiles softly, then pulls my hand away from my heart and places it against his chest. Tears begin to well in my eyes. I have no idea how or if I even deserve him, but there's one thing I know for sure. As long as he's a part of it, I'll never live a life of mediocrity. My life with Ridge will be nothing short of remarkable.

He rolls on top of me and lowers his cheek to mine, holding completely still for several long seconds.

I can't hear his breaths, but I feel them as they fall against my neck.

I can't hear his movements, but I feel him when he begins making the softest, most subtle shifts against me.

Our hands are still locked between us, so I focus on the beat of his heart, drumming against my palm.

Beat, beat, pause.

Beat, beat, pause.

Beat, beat, pause.

I can feel my entire body relaxing beneath him while he continues to make the subtlest of movements against me. He presses his hips into mine for two seconds, then relaxes and pulls back for a brief second before repeating the motion. He repeats this movement several times, and I can feel my need for him growing with each rhythmic movement against me.

The more my desire builds, the more impatient I become. I want to feel his mouth on mine. I want to feel his hands all over me. I want to feel him push inside me and make me his completely.

The more I think about what I want from him, the more responsive I become to the subtle shifts of his weight against me. The more responsive I become, the faster our hearts race against the palms of our hands.

Beat, beat, pause.

Beatbeat, pause.

Beatbeatpause.

Beatbeatpause.

The faster our hearts race, the quicker his rhythm becomes, matching each beat of my heart movement for movement.

I gasp.

He's moving to the sound of my heart.

I wrap my free arm around his neck and focus on his heartbeat, instantly aware that our hearts are perfectly in sync. I tighten my legs around his waist and lift myself against him, wanting him to make my heart beat even faster. He skims his lips across my cheek until they're flush against my mouth, but he doesn't kiss me. The silence around me makes me even more aware of the pattern of his breath falling against my skin. I focus on my palm against his chest and feel his quick intake of air, seconds before I taste the sweetness of his breath as he exhales, teasing my mouth.

Inhale, exhale.

Inhale, exhale.

Inhale, exhale.

His rhythmic breathing becomes quicker when his tongue slips inside my mouth, gently caressing the tip of mine.

If I could hear, I'm positive I would have just heard myself whimper. It's becoming a habit whenever he's around.

I move my hand to the back of his head, needing to taste more of him. I pull him to me with such sudden urgency he moans into my mouth. Feeling his moan without hearing it is probably the most sensual thing I've ever experienced. His voice as it passes through me does more than hearing it ever could.

Ridge slides his hand away from my heart and presses his forearms into the mattress on both sides of my head. He boxes me in with his arms, and I slide my hand away from his chest, needing to grab hold of him with all my strength. What little I have left, anyway.

I feel him pull farther back, and then, without hesitation, he pushes inside me, claiming me, filling me.

I . . .

Can't . . .

My heart.

Christ. He just silenced my heart, because I can no longer feel it at all. The only thing I feel is him moving against me . . . away from me . . . inside of me . . . into me. I'm completely consumed by him.

I keep my eyes closed and listen to him without hearing a thing, experiencing him silently, the same way he's experiencing me. I soak in every single beautiful thing about the smoothness of his skin and the feel of his breath and the taste of our moans, until it's impossible to tell us apart.

We continue to explore each other quietly, finding all the parts of ourselves we've only been able to imagine up to this point.

When my body begins to tense again, it's not at all because I'm nervous this time. I can sense his muscles clenching beneath my hands, and I grip his shoulders, ready to fall with him. He presses his cheek firmly to mine, and I feel him groan against my neck, making two final, long thrusts at the same second as I feel the moans escaping my throat.

He begins to tremble with his release but somehow pulls his hand between us again and presses it against my heart. He's shaking against me, and I'm doing my best to regain control of my own shudders while he begins to slow himself down, once again to the rhythm of my heart.

His movements grow so soft and subtle I can barely feel them through all the tears I'm crying. I don't even know why I'm crying, because this is by far the most indescribable feeling that has ever come over me.

Maybe that's why I'm crying.

Ridge relaxes on top of me and brings his mouth back to mine. He kisses me so softly and for so long my tears eventually subside and are replaced with complete silence, accompanied only by the rhythm of our hearts.

Ridge

I close the bathroom door and return to her on the bed. Her face is illuminated by the moonlight pouring through the windows. Her mouth is curled up into a soft smile as I lower myself down beside her. I slide my arm beneath her shoulders, then lay my head on her chest and close my eyes.

I love the sound of her.

I love *her.* Everything about her. I love that she's never judged me. I love that she understands me. I love that despite everything I've put her heart through, she's done nothing but support my decisions, no matter how much they destroyed her at the time. I love her honesty. I love her selflessness. Most of all, I love that I'm the one who gets to love all these things about her.

"I love you," I feel her say.

I close my eyes and listen as she continues to repeat the phrase again and again. I adjust my ear until it's directly over her heart, savoring every single thing about her. Her smell, her touch, her voice, her love.

I've never felt so much at once.

I've never needed to feel *more.*

I lift my head and look back down into her eyes.

She's a part of me now.

I'm a part of her.

I kiss her softly on the nose and mouth and chin, then press my ear against her heart again. For the first time in my life, I hear absolutely everything.

Acknowledgments

So many people to thank and so few words to do it in. First, not a single book I've started writing would ever reach the end if it weren't for those who encourage me and give me feedback along the way. In no particular order, these people deserve a huge thanks for always tagging along during the writing process.

Christina Collie, Gloria Green, Autumn Hull, Tammara Webber, Tracey-Garvis Graves, Karen Lawson, Jamie McGuire, Abbi Glines, Marion Archer, Mollie Harper, Vannoy Fite, Lin Reynolds, Kaci Blue-Buckley, Pamela Carrion, Jenny Aspinall, Sarah Hansen, Madison Seidler, Aestas, Natasha Tomic, Kay Miles, Sali-Benbow Powers, Vilma Gonzalez, Crystal Cobb, Dana Ferrell, the ever-supportive Kathryn Perez, and everyone else I've bugged along the way.

Thank you to my girls of FP. There are no words. Except these seventeen words, I guess.

Thank you, Joel and Julie Williams, for being amazingly supportive.

Tarryn Fisher, for being my confidence and also my reality check.

My husband and boys, for being the best four men on the planet.

Elizabeth Gunderson and Carol Keith McWilliams for your feedback, knowledge, and support. You are simply beautiful, and I couldn't have done it without either of you.

Jane Dystel and the entire Dystel & Goderich team for their continued support.

Judith Curr, publisher of Atria Books, and her team for going above and beyond their duties. Your support is unmatched.

To my editor, Johanna Castillo. To say I was nervous about delivering my first stand-alone to you is an understatement. I should have known better than to be nervous, because the two of us make a great team. I am so lucky to have you.

A HUGE thank-you to the *Maybe Someday* team: Chris Peterson, Murphy Fennell, and Stephanie Cohen. You guys rocked it.

And last, but definitely not least, Griffin Peterson. Thank you. A million times thank you. Your talent and work ethic can't go unmentioned, but your support and enthusiasm go above and beyond. There isn't even an emoji worthy enough.

Oh, and to Dave and Pooh Bear, just for the heck of it.

Dear Reader,

I had the pleasure of collaborating with musician Griffin Peterson in order to provide an original soundtrack to accompany this novel. Griffin and I worked closely together to bring these characters and their lyrics to life so that you will be provided with the ultimate reading experience.

It is recommended these songs be heard in the order they appear throughout the novel. To listen, please visit: https://www.colleenhoover.com/portfolio/maybe-someday/.

Thank you for being a part of our project. It has been so much fun for us to create, and we hope it will be equally as enjoyable as you read and listen.

Thank you,
Colleen Hoover and Griffin Peterson

About the Author

COLLEEN HOOVER is the #1 *New York Times* bestselling author of the Slammed series, the Hopeless series, the Maybe Someday series, *Ugly Love*, *Confess*, *November 9*, *It Ends with Us*, *Without Merit*, and *All Your Perfects*. She is also the founder of The Bookworm Box, a bookstore and monthly subscription service offering signed novels donated by authors that supports various charities each month. She lives in Texas with her husband and their three boys. Visit ColleenHoover.com.